MW00936192

Redemption

CURT SMITH

Phil,
Good friends
Good Stories !
Good wishes

Curt

ISBN: 9781700398130

DEDICATION

To all who have been forgiven and transformed by the power of love.

There will be a time
When the power of love
Finally gets a hold on us
It may be a time
When we are pulled away
From what's familiar
It may be a time
When our heart has been broken
By one we took for granted
It may be a time
When our courage is being
tested
By something unimagined
But indeed, there will be a time
When we finally know
How important love is
Somewhere within our soul
We may yearn so deeply
That our priorities change
Somewhere in our heart
We may know that without love
We are nothing at all
And in that moment
We may quietly admit
That love is all there is
And that will be the time
When the power of love
Tenderly holds us again

© Curt Smith, 2004

PROLOGUE

There were times when Marco Jackson looked back over the years and wondered how he'd managed to live so long. He could account for most of it from youthful memories, but there had also been a long period of darkness, followed by an experience of redemption, which helped him reclaim his life. As he raised his glass to acknowledge many good wishes for his 80th birthday, he remembered that undeserved reprieve. It was something that had happened over 40 years earlier, but it was a true lens through which he could account for what he had become. And now, eighty years after his inauspicious beginning, Marco Jackson wanted everyone to know what had happened.

ONE

"*H*appy birthday to you! Happy birthday to you! Happy birthday dear Marco and Ellie! Happy birthday to you!"

Marco Jackson held onto his glass of champagne and did his best to smile.

"Come on, Marco!" someone called. "Tell us what it's like to be eighty years old and married to a younger woman!"

He steadied himself by touching the edge of a table and noticed smiles and reassuring nods from his friends. They stood and raised their glasses, but there was something he wanted to say, so he motioned for them to sit down.

"Okay, okay, listen up," he commanded. "I have something I need to say."

"Keep it brief," Frank called from the back of the room. "We all have short attention spans."

Their soft laughter reminded him of the trust he enjoyed with all of them, but what he was about to say had been more than 40 years in the making, and it was time to let them know.

---

*L*oving parents raised Marco to be a free spirit. Hank and Aileen Jackson treasured their only child and were probably a little over protective of him and even a little too lenient when it came to discipline; however, they felt it was their responsibility to give him every opportunity possible, especially because they suspected he was intellectually gifted and needed to be challenged. Physically, their son was strong and normal in every way except for his vision, which required him to wear eyeglasses. He had an insatiable curiosity but was frustrated when he couldn't see the things he wanted to see. It wasn't until he started school that his teacher realized he was having trouble seeing words. He also failed to identify colors correctly, so a school nurse brought it to the attention of his parents and recommended he have his eyes examined.

"He has intense hyperopia and mild color-blindness," the doctor explained, "and he will need to wear corrective lenses."

His mother sighed and wrinkled her brow because she also wore glasses to overcome her farsightedness. "I suspected he wasn't seeing clearly," she said, "so I'm glad to hear glasses will help."

"He's been compensating for his visual impairment throughout his childhood," the doctor added, "and he seems to be doing quite well in his blurry world, but I'm glad we caught it. It's a condition, which increases his chances for glaucoma."

"I doubt he'll be willing to tolerate glasses," his dad suggested. "He's a ball of energy and loves to run and play with his dog."

"That's true for most all children, but Mrs. Jackson, you mentioned Marco is a gifted child, so once he discovers how glasses improve his reading, they'll be his friend forever."

The doctor's prediction proved true, and as Marco continued growing, his glasses were a normal part of his attire.

His mother, who was always his champion and advocate, told him his glasses added to his good looks.

Their rural Illinois farm, which had been in the family for over a hundred years, could have easily been limiting for a gifted child's intellectual development because of its isolation, but in fact, it had been a perfect place for Marco's growth and creativity. It was a place for building a moral foundation, a place for family values, and a place for learning right from wrong. Located in southern Illinois, their three-story farmhouse could have easily been a cover picture for *Country Living,* which had been Aileen's favorite magazine for years. They had promised Hank's parents they would preserve family traditions, which gave character to the homestead, and they would lovingly tend more than 100 acres of rich farmland surrounding the century-old two-story house. Marco was assigned chores and worked with his dad to take care of things. He thrived in the country setting and loved his house, which was weathered by harsh winters and humid summers but filled with love. Sometimes, when walking toward the house, the setting sun silhouetted its stately form with its tall windmill clattering in the evening breeze, and Marco felt as though nature had painted the scene just for him.

There were more rooms than a family of three needed, and Marco was privileged to have an upstairs room where he was allowed to build his creations and leave them standing for as long as he wanted. He'd found boxes of treasures, which had been stored from previous generations, some of which had belonged to his father and even one large box containing some of his grandfather's toys. His favorite was a 200-piece Erector Set, which he'd assembled into countless fanciful structures. Best of all, he could set his creations aside where they would remain untouched for weeks at a time. The only drawback was the summer heat. Although his father faithfully installed screens on all windows before the 4th of July, it was just too hot to be inside.

Marco's big dog "Jake" seemed to have the right idea. He followed the shade and usually made a couple trips each day to a pond, which was about a half-mile from the house. He'd splash around to cool down before lumbering back to find another shady spot near the porch. Marco sometimes followed Jake's example, although he'd been warned many times about the possibility of snakes in the mucky area around the pond. Totally out of sight from the house or the road, he'd strip down and jump feet first into the cool water. One time he stepped on something that wiggled away from his toes, but between him and Jake, they effectively scared off anything lurking along the shore. Of course, during the winter the upstairs rooms were warmer than the main house, so he managed quite well at any time of year, and even though some would say his childhood was socially isolated, Marco enjoyed solitude, and there were only a few times he'd experienced loneliness.

"How's school?" his father asked shortly after Marco had started the 8th grade.

"Fine!"

"Is that all you have to say?" his dad asked with a smile. "I know you've been looking forward to science class, so how's that going?"

"Fine!"

"Oh, come on Marco," his father demanded. "Tell me about it."

"Well, Mr. Atkins, our science teacher, said something pretty interesting today."

"And what was that?"

"He told us about computers."

"And what else?"

"He said everything in the future is going to depend on computers."

"Well, you're thirteen this year, so are you going to depend on computers?"

"Probably," Marco said with confidence. "It's very interesting to me, and I think Mr. Atkins is right."

Their limited conversation was characteristic of their communication, and Hank Jackson had more or less accepted the fact that Marco valued reading and learning more than having conversations. He'd also learned that Marco had the academic ability to skip grades, but he resisted the idea primarily because he wanted to be among his friends, so Hank encouraged his choice to stay connected. Marco was already anticipating high school, but for all the years between then and now, he'd been on the same school bus with his friends, who lived miles away from his home. Marco accepted the fact his abilities were beyond his age-grade level, but he felt his friendships were too valuable to leave behind. One of his counselors had suggested he might skip junior high altogether, but he definitely resisted *that* idea.

"I don't want to be a twelve-year-old high school student," he lamented. "Besides, my friends and I already know how we're going to handle high school when we get there; we're going to stick together."

Of course, his parents wanted only the best, so Marco continued with his friends at his own grade-level while living in his own unique world of accelerated learning.

~

There were always assigned chores on the farm. From his earliest years, Marco's parents had given him responsibilities, mostly outside work with his dad, and he never complained. When he was old enough to begin school, his world expanded to include time away from home with his classmates, all of whom came from similar situations, so there was a solid work ethic in his family and among his friends. He grew up with strong mid-western values and a sense of trusting others. He loved living in the country and took the changing seasons in stride, adapting easily to limited chores in winter and endless work in summer. Since his work on the farm was mostly physical, he grew to be tall and strong, with a lean muscular body and wavy dark hair, which he took for granted until he entered the ninth grade and began noticing girls. Up until that time he'd socialized only with his buddies, who rode with him on the school bus, and during those years, they naturally segregated themselves with boys toward the back of the bus and girls toward the front. Any interaction between the boys and girls usually took the form of teasing. He knew a lot about the facts of life because of breeding animals on the farm, but by the ninth grade he had a new perspective about girls. He became more concerned with his appearance and wanted his hair to be perfectly in place, and he also persuaded his parents to buy him a more modern looking pair of glasses, which made him look even more handsome. In fact, in his early teenage years, Marco experienced changes, which gave him strong reasons to positively anticipate manhood. He still loved privacy, but he was also feeling a need to spend more time in his expanding world of relationships. However, the rhythm of life on the farm never changed, and even though *he* was changing, his steady life at home would affect his life in ways he never anticipated.

It was during those growing-up years that Marco had become more aware of his love for family. He enjoyed doing things with his mother and father, and he especially enjoyed being with his aunts, and uncles and cousins. However, he knew he was physically different from all of them. When he looked at photographs taken at family gatherings, he noticed his darker complexion and his hair, which made him stand out.

Of course, during his teen years, he anticipated leaving home. It was bound to happen, but everything he cherished was present in his routines and in his family. He loved the aroma of home-cooked meals, especially when his mother baked bread. There was something inviting about their spacious old house, and he sensed it was filled with memories from other generations. He'd never felt rebellious as some of his friends described. Possibly it was because he actually enjoyed family rituals such as gathering around their oversized dining room table for every evening meal. His mother had taken to covering only one end of the table with a linen tablecloth, so they could sit closer together.

"It's our time to be together," his mother explained. "It's our time to be a family."

It didn't happen all the time, but their conversations would sometimes evolve into wonderful stories his father would tell about when he was a boy sitting around the same old table with his brothers and sisters. Marco sometimes imagined what it would have been like to have the whole house filled with brothers and sisters. However, he liked being an only child and imagined it would be harder if he had to compete for his parent's attention. His love for home was a love for simplicity. Routines were predictable and being together was a daily activity. In the evenings, they sat together in a big living room where they each had their own chair. He remembered when he was small, he loved to sit on his father's lap and listen to him tell stories about the things he did when he was a boy. Of course, those days were long ago, but even now, as a teenager, Marco still loved to sit quietly in the living room with his father, and even though they didn't talk much, he knew he'd miss their time together after leaving home.

"How old were you when you left home?" he asked his dad during one of those quiet times.

His father put aside his newspaper and removed his reading glasses as though trying to remember. However, he clearly knew the answer.

"Eighteen!" he said and then resumed his reading.

"And you went to college . . . right?" His father nodded as though Marco already knew the answer to his question. "Then I expect it'll be the same for me."

His comment caused his father to lay the newspaper aside and look at Marco over the rim of his glasses. "Yes, I suppose it will," he concurred. "Have you been thinking about leaving home?"

"A little," Marco confessed, "but not until after high school."

His father smiled at his obvious comment. "You could have already been in college," he said matter-of-factly. "You're just biding your time, so you can be with your buddies. I imagine you know that?"

Marco nodded. "I prefer it that way," he agreed. "However, now that we're talking about it, I should tell you I'm really interested in computers."

His father looked at him and wrinkled his brow. "Well, I don't know much about computers," he confessed. "I've read a little about them, but I can't see why we'd need them."

Marco pouted his lips when his dad raised the newspaper to signal the finality of his conclusion. *I can't see why he'd say that. Someday, everything will depend on computers. Oh, well, at least Dad knows that's what I'm thinking.*

His teacher, Mr. Atkins, had talked a lot about what to expect in the near future, and Marco was fascinated by his predictions. In fact, he'd already decided he'd be an entrepreneur in computer science. When he thought about building things in the upstairs room of their old house, he imagined it would to easy to build computers, so he and Mr. Atkins shared similar interests.

"That's good, Marco," Mr. Atkins would say. "Your ideas are very creative."

That was all the encouragement he needed. However, for the moment, everything was exactly as it should be. He had love and support from his parents, plenty of chores to do, and he loved simplicity. His complex and notable ideas would have to wait a while longer, but he could see what was coming. He knew there'd be a time and a place for his creativity, because the world was waking up to technology and he intended to help make it happen.

TWO

Marco and his friends' plan for successfully navigating the challenges of high school worked well. One of his buddies, Hollis Phillips, surprised everyone by acquiring a car on his sixteenth birthday, which would be just a few weeks before the start of their freshman year. He didn't have much money to buy gas, so they all chipped in a little from their allowances to enjoy the luxury of driving to and from school on Fridays. There were six of them, all big guys physically, so when they squeezed into Hollis's Plymouth, they sat shoulder-to-shoulder. However, none was happier than Marco, who loved the exhilaration of a car ride to school. Of course, Monday through Thursday it was business as usual, riding the school bus to their regional high school, so Fridays were the exception rather than the rule. The main obstacle they faced when starting their freshman year was harassment by upperclassmen, who did their best to make life miserable for beginning students, but Marco's group presented a formidable challenge because of their bond of friendship and their physical size. There were a few attempts at intimidation, but none succeeded, and about three weeks into the school year, the harassment ended as everyone knuckled downs to prepare for their first exams.

Marco enjoyed most of his classes, but found none of them challenging, so "homework," which usually caused moans and groans from others, was somewhat incidental for him. Most of the time he had his assignments completed before going home. Study hall, a period at the end of each school day, provided all the time he needed to complete his assignments. However, because schoolwork was so easy, he also used this free period to do extra reading on the emerging field of computer science.

"What are you reading, Marco?"

He had noticed Emma Downing a number of times, but she surprised him with her question.

"It's just stuff about computers," he said, as he turned to look at her sitting at the desk behind him. He knew she was also a freshman and that she rode a different school bus than his, but it hadn't occurred to him to talk to her.

Emma, on the other hand, had been watching Marco for days, and even though he was unaware, she'd made it a point to sit near him during every study hall period.

"What's a computer?" she whispered to avoid attracting attention to their interaction.

"It's kind of like a calculator that can solve problems and then remember all the information it needs to do it faster and faster."

"Wow!" Emma exclaimed. "I could use one of those."

Marco smiled and nodded knowingly. "I'm reading about the future," he whispered and smiled.

Emma resumed her homework, and Marco kept reading, but now he had something else to think about. He'd been smitten by her brown eyes and auburn hair, and even after turning toward the front of the room, he was having a hard time concentrating. In fact, he read the same paragraph three times when it suddenly dawned on him that Emma was quite attractive.

When the bell signaled the end of the period, he gathered his things and turned to see an empty desk behind him. He had hoped otherwise, but Emma had quickly left without him noticing. He felt a twinge of remorse, but then when he left the room, she was waiting for him just outside the door.

"Can I see your book?"

Her soft and cheerful voice endeared him so completely, he would have gladly shared anything with her, so he fumbled to find the book and opened it for her. She seemed genuinely interested as she looked through the table of contents.

"You must be very smart to understand this stuff," she observed.

Marco thought it was easy, but when he tried to explain some of the concepts, Emma looked baffled, so he changed the subject. "Where do you live?" he asked.

"Route 13," she replied as Marco did some quick mental calculations trying to imagine her location compared to his.

"Is that like a highway?"

"Sort of like a highway, but actually, it's just a country road that goes past our farm."

"I also live on a farm!" he beamed.

"Maybe we could visit each other someday," she suggested. "Do you have a car?"

"No, but my friend does!"

"Well, my parents let me use their car," she said proudly. "I don't get to use it very often, but maybe . . ."

"Maybe you could drive to my house, and we could go for a ride," he said playfully. "However, right now I have to catch my bus."

She smiled knowingly and walked with him toward the exit. "It would be really nice to have a car, don't you think?"

He nodded vigorously.

Her smile captured his heart, and then she was gone. It was definitely a moment. In fact, it seemed like a beginning.

~

The chill of fall weather preceded the bone-cold days of winter, and those, who rode the bus, usually waited until it was in sight before hurrying to their pickup point by the road. Hollis' parents demanded he leave his car in the garage during the winter months, so Marco and his friends were relegated back to their "big yellow box" five days a week. However, despite the shivering cold of a severe Illinois winter, Marco and Emma developed a warm relationship, which included having lunch together each school day and a few visits at each other's home, where they received compliments from their parents, who loved asking lots of questions. Emma lived in a relatively modern house located in a farming community where neighbors were clustered along a main road with less than a mile between their houses. Although her parents kept a watchful eye on them, Marco's first visit to her home included some private time in her room, as long as the door remained open. He quickly discovered her artistic interests when he saw her bookshelves filled with books on art history as well as large photo books featuring works by her favorite artists.

"Are you an artist?"

She smiled and nodded yes, and then she opened a closet to reveal stacks of sketchpads and a number of rolled-up watercolors, which she proudly displayed on her bed.

"They're all mine," she explained with a look of satisfaction. "These three were done when I first tried painting in grade school, so they're a little amateurish, but hopefully the others show my improvement over the years. Now I'm using oils. Would you like me to show you my latest ones?"

"Absolutely," Marco agreed, because he was already appreciating her talent. "Show me your favorites."

It would have been easy just to play along and compliment her work just to be nice, but he was literally blown away with the quality of her paintings, and he told her so. He didn't consider himself to be an art critic, but he was immediately drawn to her use of color and her ability to create scenic landscapes as well as abstractions.

"Seriously," he said with wide-eyed appreciation, "these are beautiful. I thought I was getting to know you, but this is like discovering who you *really* are. You're a professional artist."

Emma smiled, and since her parents were downstairs . . . and since the door was still wide-open, she turned to Marco and looked into his eyes, and when he kissed her, it seemed like the most natural thing he'd ever done. Emma initiated a second and a third kiss, but then coyly smiled and whispered they should continue talking to avoid raising suspicion. He nodded understandingly, but felt an uncontrollable need to keep touching her, and he couldn't stop smiling.

Emma's mom finally called them to come downstairs for a snack, and Emma responded immediately; however, Marco felt reluctant to relax his hold around her waist.

"I love having you hold me in your arms," she whispered, "but we need to play by the rules."

~

*T*wo weeks after that glorious day when he'd savored his first kiss, Emma came to visit the Jackson farm for the first time. He was a little hesitant to contrast their generations-old house with her modern one, but as soon as she stepped out of the car, she started shouting superlatives for what she saw through her artist eyes.

15

"Oh, Marco, I've dreamed of painting a place like this. It's absolutely beautiful."

Her enthusiasm caught him completely off-guard, but he knew she was being sincere.

"This farm's been in our family for generations," he boasted. "Come on inside, and I'll show you around"

He took hold of her hand and held the door open for her. His mother greeted them, and Emma reached out to touch Aileen's arm as a way of connecting with her.

"Ah, Emma," Aileen exclaimed. "Welcome to our home. You've become a topic of conversation when we sit around our table. It seems Marco has had a lot to share about you."

Emma smiled and looked down until Mrs. Jackson extended her arms in welcome. Marco stood to the side feeling impressed with his mother's hospitality, and then, when his father suddenly entered the room, he made Emma feel special as well.

"Marco has told us about your home," he said as though reporting an unknown fact. "Our place must seem like a museum piece."

Emma shook her head no and smiled broadly. "Absolutely not," she declared. "I do paintings, and the minute I saw this lovely house, I envisioned it on canvas. It's so charming, and it's been maintained so well. Its value must be impressive."

"You're very kind," Mrs. Jackson observed. "And you're right. This place is very special to us. Anyway, I know Marco wants to show you around, so while he does that, I'll fix us some tea and lemon cake."

Emma assumed it would be freshly baked lemon cake, because the minute she'd entered the house, the aroma added to her welcome.

The tour lasted only minutes, and last on the itinerary was his room, which appeared quite tidy since he'd anticipated her visit and had made his bed. They had no sooner entered his room than he took her in his arms and kissed her.

"Oh, my," she whispered. "I wasn't expecting that."

"I was!" he declared with a smile, and then kissed her again.

She sighed and rested her head against his chest. Marco's lean and muscular body combined with his rugged good looks and wavy dark hair were more than Emma had ever hoped, so she literally swooned in his arms. She'd also noticed the contrast of his physical appearance with that of his parents but only in passing. She thought he had a darker complexion, so she assumed it was from being outside in the sun. Regardless, more than anything else, she thought he was strikingly handsome, and she loved being kissed.

"Tea time," his mother called, and Marco shrugged.

"I'd rather be alone with you," he said with a nonchalant nod, "but I think my mom and dad want some *get-to-know-you* time."

She took hold of his hand and pulled him into the hallway. "I want to get to know them as well," she announced. "Maybe we'll have some time alone later."

~

*F*rom 1951 to 1953, Emma and Marco enjoyed enough alone time to fall in love, although they'd not used the word. They'd discovered many similarities in their lives. They were both without siblings and had been raised by loving and supportive parents. They both lived on farms, except Emma's home was modern and his quite old. They had each grown up with chores to do and actually enjoyed the isolation of country life. Emma had a room in her house, which she called her studio, complete with easels, framed and unframed canvases, and paint dubs on the floor. Marco's special room, which was on the third floor of their farmhouse, was his creative space, so there were similarities. They were both attractive young people, and all the way to their senior year, they assumed they would be together forever. However, like a lightening bolt out of a clear sky, one day in the second week of their senior year, Emma met Marco during their lunch period and broke down in tears. He put his arms around her and ignored the attention she was attracting.

"We're moving," she sobbed.

The weight of her announcement pressed down on him immediately. "Where? Why are you moving?" he demanded.

"To California," she explained, "and I don't even know where in California."

Marco could hardly talk. He couldn't believe what she was saying, and then tears welled up in his eyes. Normally, he was strong and stoic, but Emma's surprise announcement had thrown him completely off-balance. When he tried to speak, he couldn't, and even though other students were watching, he just held her in his arms and tried to soothe her emotion. They hadn't used the word *love,* but Marco thought that's what it was between them. He felt love for her even though he hadn't found the right time to say it.

"This can't be true," he finally said in a voice broken by emotion. "What about us?"

"What about everything?" she countered with a longing look in her eyes. "I'm devastated!"

Marco shook his head in denial. "Tell me why! Why are your parents suddenly moving to California? There has to be a reason!"

"It's embarrassing."

"It doesn't matter! Tell me!"

"We're being forced to move. The farm has failed to provide enough income, so my parents have failed to make the payments and the bank has repossessed the farm."

Marco looked at her with an incredulous expression. "I thought your parents are rich; I mean they had a nice house and a car."

"Things are not always what they seem, Marco. They've been in dire straights for the last two years and kept it from me, so I'm as shocked as you are."

"If the bank's repossessing the farm, then how can they afford to go to California?"

"My aunt, my dad's sister, is going to help us. She and her husband own a large farm and she wants my dad to work for her. It's a big commercial business, and since he's been farming and growing stuff all his life, it's a good fit for him, but this whole ordeal has just about torn the heart out of our family. When my aunt made the offer, dad felt he had to take it. They don't want to leave and neither do I, but dad says we don't have a choice. I've been crying since they told me. I couldn't even sleep last night because I knew I'd have to tell you today, and my heart is aching, Marco. My heart is aching."

"My heart is aching too! California is a long way from where I'm going," he declared. "I've just learned I've received a full scholarship to MIT in Massachusetts, so I'm going east and you're going west. We may never see each other again."

He felt her shudder, and her crying continued.

"I don't want to leave, Marco, but it's a done deal. We're leaving next week."

It was like someone had just sucked all the oxygen out of the room, and he had a hard time breathing. Emma's eyes were red from crying, and she kept looking at him with a pleading expression, but he didn't know what else to say. Other students watched them as they left the cafeteria without eating, surrounded in sadness and lost without options. Dropping out and going with her immediately crossed his mind, but he'd already committed to MIT. He clung to Emma as though his

19

physical restraint would prevent her from leaving, but when they arrived at her locker in the school's hallway, the finality of what she'd told him hit him full force.

"I'm supposed to clean out my locker and take my books to the office."

He watched helplessly. It had just dawned on him it was Friday, so "next week" was only two days away, and neither of them had a car, so they couldn't be together. There was such finality to it he bent forward in anguish and ignored the bell indicating it was time for class. Other students rushed past them hurrying to their classrooms and soon, they stood alone in an empty hallway.

"Emma," he pleaded, "there's no way I can say goodbye to you. I've not said this before, but you're a part of me." She managed a weak smile, and then he continued. "I get all kinds of recognition for my academic abilities, but right now I feel like an empty shell. I've never had such hopeless feelings. I want to physically stop you from leaving, but I feel powerless to do it. I want to come up with a wild idea that will make your parents leave you here, but you're telling me it's a done deal. I really like your mom and dad. They're really nice people, but why would they want to do this to you? I mean, you're just starting your senior year, so why do they want to jerk you away from your school and your friends?"

Emma took a deep breath and sighed while shaking her head in denial. "There's no meanness in what they're doing, Marco. It's painful to admit, but they're acting out of desperation, and we have to stick together as a family. My aunt has already contacted the high school where I'll be going, and she says they'll do their best to help me, but beyond that, I don't know what's going to happen. I wish it could be otherwise, but that's the way it is."

When she shut the locker door, it sounded like a cell door shutting behind a prisoner. Emma sat her backpack on the floor, and then they held onto each other in the silence of the abandoned hallway. He felt sick inside and totally lost as he kissed her and heard her whisper goodbye. He didn't want to let go, but in spite of his resistance, she picked up her backpack and walked toward the office. He watched and then sat on the floor and wiped tears from his eyes.

~

*M*arco felt he'd suddenly been the victim of a sinister plot, and he wondered if he'd ever get over it. The emptiness and sadness remained with him despite the consolation he received from his parents.

"If you're meant to be together, you'll find a way," his mother suggested. "I know you're very fond of Emma, but you're both young, and life has a way of offering second chances."

He tried to accept what had happened, but it was never resolved. In addition, since he was only seventeen during his final year of high school, he watched most of his friends register for the draft and knew his impaired vision would probably exempt him from military duty when he turned 18, so in addition to losing Emma, he had failed to measure up for service to his country. Anger and frustration consumed him, and worst of all, he felt impotent.

He wasn't sure he could do it, but Marco fought his way through months of sadness, finished his senior year and graduated *summa cum laude,* which was in recognition of his exceptional academic achievements; however, during the ceremony, when he received his diploma and his certificate, his mood was sullen and hopeless. There seemed to be so many things out of his control, and he was having a hard time coping. His childhood innocence had been shattered, and it changed his attitude about life. During his final summer at home, he stayed mostly to himself, which concerned his parents, but in spite of his moodiness, they continued loving him and did their best to help him stay focused on what's ahead. *I wonder how mom and dad have made a go of it? If Emma's parents lost it all, how do my parents manage?*

He didn't like thinking about leaving home, but now that he was older, the farm seemed like a dying enterprise surrounded by a world of change. *Dad sits on the porch looking wistfully over his land, and mom labors to take care of this old house. I don't know how they do it. They'll probably hang on until they die right out here in the middle of nowhere.*

During those hot summer days before leaving, Marco missed Emma terribly and looked at life as a lonely adventure. To make matters worse, his dog Jake died of old age, and as his father helped him prepare a grave under a big shade tree near the pond. He cried when he told Jake goodbye and thought his heart was breaking. He'd lost his enthusiasm and almost dreaded the rapidly approaching day when he'd be leaving. He and Emma had remained in touch, but he missed her more than she could ever know. It felt like emptiness, where what's outside looks wonderful, but inside, the content is missing. When he wrote letters to her, he always expressed hope they'd be together again, but before the end of that difficult summer, her letters trickled to a stop. She made no mention of feeling sorry and gave him no encouragement; it just ended.

On September 1, 1953, Marco carried his small suitcase and boarded a train for his trip to MIT in Massachusetts. He'd anticipated the trip for a long time, but he wasn't prepared for his awkward feelings, which were a mixture of excitement and terrible emptiness. Something had changed inside, and he wasn't sure how to deal with it.

THREE

$\mathcal{M}$arco arrived on campus feeling a bit dazed, but when Stuart Higgins introduced himself as his assigned mentor, he was immediately relieved. He'd already registered for a room in a residence hall, and Stuart was somewhat like his personal ambassador of good will. He certainly knew his way around the campus and took Marco through all the necessary steps of getting settled.

"This place is so big," Marco exclaimed. "How long did it take for you to find your way around?"

"It's easier than it looks," Stuart admitted, "but having some help for a few days removes the uncertainty."

When they arrived at his residence hall, it felt like a big, noisy hotel in stark contrast to the peace and quiet of his parent's farm. However, he settled in and was delighted to learn Stuart's room was on the floor above his. He also met his roommate, Kent Davis, who was a freshman with an interest in biology.

It seemed like a whirlwind as Stuart guided Marco around the campus. They took care of the required administrative details, attended a student orientation, did a walking tour, studied and marked a campus map, followed a maze of tunnels filled with students rushing from building to building, and finally enjoyed a satisfying lunch at the Forbes Café.

"I'll check in with you and probably see you quite frequently," Stuart explained in a proper collegiate manner, "but the main thing is to give yourself plenty of time to get to your classes. Keep your map handy and ask other students if you get lost."

"Thanks, Stuart. I think I have it figured out."

His roommate, Kent, also became a good friend, and when their first week of classes ended, they compared notes.

"I got lost twice," Kent confessed, "but MIT people are really friendly and helpful. I'd heard this school is just a bunch of nerds, but that's not what I've found."

Marco smiled and agreed! He'd arrived on campus feeling stressed and uncertain, but with Stuart's help, he already felt at home and had quickly established a routine. He especially enjoyed his math classes and more or less tolerated other required courses, which he thought were quite easy. However, it was definitely a change. The curriculum was a little more challenging, but he undertook his studies with ease just as he'd done in high school. On his first weekend, he spent some time in the library, took a leisurely walk around the campus to enjoy the fall weather, and then returned to his dorm to write a letter to Emma. He'd not heard from her for a long time, so he briefly described his experiences at MIT and then told her he missed her terribly. When he mailed the letter, it was a last-ditch effort to keep their connection; it was something he had to do.

Nearly three weeks later, he found her reply in his mailbox and rushed to open the envelope without regard for his other mail.

Marco,

I apologize for not writing, but my life has been topsy-turvy since graduating from Fresno High. My dad and mom are both working for my Aunt Beatrice and Uncle Phillip, and I've basically been on my own since moving here. I think I told you a little bit about this place in previous letters, but the life we enjoyed in southern Illinois is like another world. There are mountains in the distance, but Fresno is quite flat and hot. I like the palm trees, but otherwise, it's just a town surrounded by agriculture. I made a couple good friends, but now that we've graduated, my life has become a lonely mess. Of course, you're wondering what I mean by that, but there's no need to go into detail other than to say I'm kind of stuck. Part of it is that we're living in a four-room cottage on Aunt Bea's property, and it's like being cooped-up and stranded with no privacy. There's nothing here unless you like growing veggies! I suppose my parents expect me to show some initiative and either find a job or move out, but I don't really have the will to do either. I still paint, but my heart isn't in it anymore.

I know, this sounds like a sob story, so I'll quit complaining and say congratulations on your studies at MIT. When we were in high school, I was really happy in our relationship, but when I received your letter, it just reminded me we're really different. I've always known you're really smart, and I imagine you'll sail through your undergrad work and probably end up being a professor or something, but for me, I'll probably end up working at a local bar and trying to sell some of my paintings to supplement my income. You'll be notably successful, and I'll be notable loser. (Sorry for being negative again, but that's how I feel.)

This Stuart guy, who helped you get started at school, sounds like a pretty nice person. Where do they find people like him? There certainly was no one to help me when I arrived in Fresno. I could have used some help! It's a big high school, but once they had my transcript, I was basically on my own. Like I said, I made a few friends and did okay, but I was lucky to have made it through to graduation. It was a very lonely experience, and many times I thought how good it was when we were together back home.

You always say you hope we'll reconnect someday, and that would be great, but I doubt it'll happen . . . unless maybe you come to California. I can't ever imagine going to Massachusetts, and you'll probably move on to somewhere else anyway. I've had a couple of boyfriends, but now that I'm done with school, it's total isolation. You've probably got girls clamoring for your attention . . . I mean, how could it be otherwise? You're tall, good-looking and smart, so go figure.

Anyway, I thought you deserved a reply to your letter; however, I'm not in a very good place right now, so you probably won't hear from me again. I'd be blown away if you showed up some day, but I'll leave that to you. I'm probably just being sentimental, but knowing you was my only bright spot so far. However, it seems like a fading dream.

I wish you tons of success, Marco. Keep me in mind but don't dwell on what we can't have. It looks like I'm doomed to remain right here in Fresno. By the way, my aunt and uncle's last name is Phillips . . . Beatrice and Ed Phillips, and their place is called Phillip's Gardens. It's actually a lot more than a "garden," but that's what they call it. You're still in my heart, Marco, but I'd rather be realistic about ever seeing you again . . . I'd like to, but it's probably not going to happen. Good luck with your studies!

Love, Emma

Marco read the letter at least three times and felt encouraged in spite of her pessimistic conclusion. *I'm not giving up on you, Emma!* He folded the letter and placed it in a file where he kept his important papers and thought of it as his lifeline to someone very important.

~

"Your work is excellent, Mr. Jackson!"

His professor's comment was an honest assessment, and from what he could determine, he was doing very well. Unlike most students, he relished his studies and always did more than required. His interest in computer science was his motivation, and his innovative insights caught the attention of other teachers as well.

"I'd like to involve you in our analog computer research project if you think you could manage the extra time in addition to your regular studies," suggested professor Lee, who had become his advocate.

Marco was a bit stunned by the suggestion. He was just beginning his second year, and research projects were normally the domain of graduate work.

"Seriously?"

"Absolutely," professor Lee asserted. "You're a talented young man, and I know you have a keen interest in computer science."

"It would be fantastic," Marco replied without giving any thought to the ramifications. "When can I start?"

"I should be able to set it up by next week. I've already approached Dr. Zimmer about the possibility, so I'll call him and let him know you're interested." Marco looked at Dr. Lee with an incredulous expression but felt very honored. "It's a graduate-level project, so there may be some resentment of having an undergraduate involved, but I'm confident you'll be an asset to the work they're doing."

Needless to say, when he left the classroom that afternoon Marco was euphoric. His greatest wish was to find an entrée into computer science, and having a place on a research team would be a major step in that direction. That evening, when he joined his buddies for a beer, he was aching to tell them about his good fortune; however, he wisely kept the news to himself until he knew the results of his professor's inquiry. He did tell his ex-roommate, Kent, who had moved off-campus after his freshman year, and his new roommate, Kyle Eggers, who was sullen and a bit standoffish. They both seemed stunned he had been singled out to participate in graduate level research. Kent patted him on the back and shook his hand, but Kyle remained low-key.

"How'd you pull that off?" he inquired.

Marco smiled and shrugged. "Well, it's not official yet, but professor Lee is the one who suggested it."

"I thought research was a graduate thing. You're only in your second year, right?"

"Right! If Lee wants me to join a research team, then I want it too."

Kyle hunched his shoulders and raised his brow skeptically. "Good for you, I guess. There will be no such recommendations for me. I'll be lucky to just graduate."

~

*T*ime passed quickly, and Marco was so engrossed with his studies and his graduate-level project, he thought there couldn't be a better situation to be learning so much so fast. Unlike some of his friends, he relished his studies and had an insatiable appetite for learning. Dr. Lee continued paving the way for him to enroll in the right courses and to keep his eye on his goal.

Then one afternoon he picked up his mail, and his unimpeded progress hit an unexpected disruption when he opened a letter from home.

Dear Marco,

I was glad to read your good news, but I'm sad to tell you your dad has cancer. He's always been stoic and tends to keep things to himself, and unfortunately, he didn't tell me, or anyone what he was feeling. I guess he thought it would just go away, but as it turns out, its pancreatic cancer. I hate to burden you with this, but the doctors can't help him, and if you want to have some time with him, you'll have to make a trip home. I'm enclosing some money to pay for the trip, and I hope with all my heart your professors will understand.

Love, Mom

Marco's emotions surged, and his hands shook. He knew his dad's habit was to keep his feelings private, but he'd obviously made a big mistake this time. He read the note again.

My dad's dying!

Tears came into his eyes as he admitted the urgency, and regardless of the consequences, he knew he'd need to go home, so within the hour, he met with professor Lee and was relieved by his compassionate response.

"It's okay, Mr. Jackson! Family takes priority. I'll personally intervene to make sure your absence is understood." Marco was feeling emotional, and Dr. Lee noticed. "It's difficult news, Marco," he said with empathy. "My mother died from cancer, and I know from experience what it's like, so make the trip home to be with your dad. When you come back, you can resume your studies and everything will be just fine."

"Thanks, Dr. Lee! Thanks for being so understanding."

Professor Lee nodded. "I'm going to make another suggestion for you to ponder, while you're traveling."

Marco looked at him expectantly.

"You're an exceptionally gifted student, and I admire how you've continued your studies over the summer, so I want you to consider completing your undergraduate work in three years and then moving directly into our graduate program. I have a couple administrative friends, who will be happy to assist you with scholarships, and you can be one of our first and brightest in the field of computer science."

Marco managed a smile in spite of the stress over his dad. He knew without a doubt he wanted to do it. "I'm not sure how long I'll be gone."

"Time isn't a problem. Think it through, and when you return, come see me. Okay?"

Marco extended his hand in appreciation.

Dr. Lee reassured him, "I'll look forward to your return. Travel safely and be strong."

~

The farmhouse, with its three large maple trees protecting its north side, was accented in fall colors, and the weather was turning cold. There were more leaves on the ground than on the trees, and Marco savored the scent of fall and the bite of a strong north wind signaling colder days ahead. When he and his mother had pulled into the long driveway leading to the house, he felt the tug of memories and recalled many happy times when he and his dad had groomed the plants along the edge. He and his mother walked toward the house, and then he sat his small suitcase on the porch before going inside. While standing there, he scanned the horizon and thought of all the times he and Jake had roamed through the fields. Those were summer memories, and then he shivered from the cold and hurried inside. His mother had removed her coat and steadied herself against a wall beneath the coat rack. He sensed her sorrow as a nurse came out of the bedroom and quietly closed the door.

"He's in and out of consciousness," the nurse explained and then looked at Marco. "I'm glad you made it home," and then she reached out to embrace him. "Another nurse and I have been tending to your dad and trying to keep him comfortable."

Marco nodded his understanding.

"I gave him morphine just before you arrived, so I imagine he'll be sleeping for quite a while."

His mother reached for Marco's hand and led him into the bedroom. The window curtains blocked the daylight; so she left the door open to allow a little outside light into the room.

When Marco looked at his father, he noticed the hollowness of his face. Then reached down to touch his hand, and his mother sobbed softly.

"It's been days since he recognized me," she said, "but I stay with him as much as I can. He may not be awake, but I believe he knows we're here."

Marco leaned close to his father and kissed him on the forehead. "It's me, Papa," he whispered. "I'm home."

Various neighbors came and went, as Marco and his mother waited for the inevitable. He spent hours at his father's bedside, but he also took long walks, so he'd have time to think. He even walked to the pond and recalled how his dog Jake had taught him how to cool down at its shallow end. In his reverie, he recognized how much he'd changed. His time at MIT had given him a new perspective, but being at home made him very aware of how lucky he'd been.

"I think he's failing," said the nurse, who had been at his father's side during the early morning hours.

Aileen acknowledged her warning and hurried to his bedside, and then for one brief moment, Hank opened his eyes and looked directly at her before taking his final breath.

Marco, who was just finishing his breakfast, heard his mother's mournful cry and ran to her side. She was holding his father's lifeless hand and crying, so there was no need to explain the obvious. He embraced her, but he couldn't take his eyes away from his father's lifeless body. His death had come too suddenly. All that remained was the emptiness of knowing his father was gone forever. He stared at the lifeless shell of a man he'd respected and loved, looked compassionately into the anguished face of his mother, and wondered what else his life would bring.

"I was only twenty-one years old when I fell in love with him," his mother whispered. "He was an exceptional man, and we were side-by-side for over twenty-four years." She paused briefly and reached for Marco's hand. "We'd been married only a couple of years when you came into our lives, so it's been just the three of us for such a long time."

Marco put his arm around his mother to be supportive and suddenly realized death's intrusion had not only ended his father's life but also his mother's expectation of spending long years together with her beloved.

"I guess we never know what might happen," he lamented. "However, I hope I'll have the same kind of relationship you and dad have had for as many years or even longer."

"That's my hope as well," she agreed. "You'll know when you find the right person." She sighed. "Dad and I tried to give you a good foundation, and I want you to know he told me over and over again how proud he was of you."

Hank Jackson died on October 7 just two days after Marco arrived home.

~

$\mathcal{F}$riends and neighbors filled the small country church to its capacity. He remembered when he and Emma had been together. It had always been a meeting place for the farming community, a place where people gathered not so much for religion but for belonging.

Once again, he thought of Emma. Even as a young girl, she had already started painting and had done several watercolors of the white-framed church with its soaring steeple and steps leading into the sanctuary. Marco had gone to the church every Sunday when he was small but only periodically when he reached his teenage years. However, it was at the church where he and Emma had become friends.

"It's like a family," his father had suggested. "We come here from all over the county, and being together is one of the best things about this little country church."

His father and mother lived apart from their families, so friends and neighbors were like their brothers and sisters. It was *the* one thing about religious faith he couldn't deny. He'd always felt loved and respected by members of the congregation. It was his family as well.

Marco noticed his father's grave had already been prepared in a small adjacent cemetery, and he knew it was going to be difficult to stand there and say his final goodbye; however, when he and his mother entered the small sanctuary, they were inundated by love and support from their spiritual family. They were greeted and comforted repeatedly, and then an usher suggested everyone should be seated. Marco sat with his mother and her friends on the front row. with

The itinerant minister didn't have a long history the Jackson family, but he'd been their pastor each Sunday for the past five years, so Hank's death was his loss as well. He stood next to the casket, read the obituary, shared a passage from the

Bible and ended the service by inviting everyone to sing *Amazing Grace*, which brought tears to their eyes.

Hardy men from neighboring farms, lifted the casket and carried it from the church to the open grave, and as Marco and his mother walked slowly behind, he nearly gasped aloud when he realized the striking young woman standing near the door was Emma. She smiled when he recognized her, and he could hardly keep his composure. He wanted to immediately run to her and sweep her into his arms, but given the sanctity of the moment, he caught his breath and followed his mother to the graveside.

"Death is part of life," the minister intoned. "Some face it with fear, but none can escape the experience. Sometimes death comes prematurely, as in Hank's case, and for others it may wait for long years, but the secret is to live each day as though it's your last."

Marco turned to glance over his shoulder as he felt Emma's presence close by, and indeed, she stood just behind him and slightly to his left. He was nearly breathless as he moved his hand slowly from his side as though reaching for her, and when she touched his hand, he was flooded with emotion. He entwined his fingers with hers as the minister spoke his final words.

"It's with confidence of God's loving embrace on all of us that I now commend Hank Jackson into a host of unseen witnesses, who know the vastness of eternity and the peace of unconditional love. Dust to dust and ashes to ashes as his physical body returns to the earth and his spiritual being is surrounded by the eternal light of creation's dawn."

Emma slightly squeezed Marco's hand as the minister pronounced the benediction and the casket was lowered into the grave. It was a somber moment of great reverence. Then, led by his mother, they passed by the grave to toss flowers or smatterings of earth onto the casket. Marco followed his mother's example and then anxiously rushed to Emma's side.

"You're here!" he cried as he held his arms open to her. "I can't believe you're here!"

Emma smiled and folded into his arms. "I'm as surprised as you are."

"But you really didn't know my dad!" he exclaimed.

"My mom did. They were both members of this congregation, so she wanted to be here, and I wanted to come with her."

"But how did you know about my dad?" He released his hold on her, stepped back and held onto both her hands anxiously waiting for her to explain.

"Mom kept in touch, and when she heard about your dad, she told Aunt Bea she wanted to go home for the funeral. My dad agreed and told her a break would do her good, and when I heard her intention, I declared I wanted to be here too."

Marco pulled her back into his arms but restrained from kissing her. Others noticed, but everyone was talking, and most of them assumed it was a friend compassionately greeting him.

"I've missed you beyond reason," he declared. "When I received your last letter I was heartbroken."

"I've missed you too, Marco, but I've been trapped in a dumpy little 4-room cottage about twenty miles outside Fresno, and I honesty never thought I'd see you again."

He pulled her even closer and then escorted her to greet his mother.

"Oh, my, goodness, it's Emma!" his mother exclaimed and wrapped her arms around her.

Marco stood aside as they shared greetings, and then put his arm around his mom's waist and reached over to touch Emma's arm. "I feel reborn just seeing her," he said matter-of-factly. "When her family left for California, I grieved . . . just as I've been grieving after losing dad, but she's come home!"

His mother smiled knowingly and stepped back, so he and Emma could stand together. "And I'm glad to see you two together again."

Someone had been waiting their turn to talk to Aileen, so Marco took hold of Emma's hand and walked with her to the front steps of the church.

"Do you remember sitting here with me when we were kids?"

"Vaguely," Emma said and shrugged her shoulders. "I wasn't interested in boys," she added.

Marco nodded and smiled. "But you are now, right?"

She smiled and laid her head on his shoulder, and then she looked up at him, and he kissed her.

"I want more than this," she whispered. "We're staying with mom's best friend, who lives about ten miles from here, and in two days we'll be on our way back to Fresno, but I want more," she repeated. "I'm tired of letting fate keep us apart."

"I want *you*, Emma, and I've always wanted you; however, I'm not a believer in fate. There may be circumstances we can't control, but I refuse to lose you."

She felt encouraged, but in her heart she also felt it was beyond her to find a way.

People were returning to their cars, and Emma saw her mother walking away from the gravesite with Marco's mom. They paused and looked toward the front of the church. Then, to their surprise, Emma's mother walked directly toward them.

"Hello, Marco," she called. "I see you two have found each other."

Marco stood to greet Mrs. Downing, and Emma sat quietly waiting to see what would happen.

"It's good to see you, Mrs. Downing," he said, and she extended her hand in a gesture of neighborliness. "I was surprised to see Emma." Then he took hold of Emma's hand and encouraged her to stand. "I'm so glad you came."

Mrs. Downing smiled and shrugged her head to the side. "Well, your father was an exceptional man! He was loved and appreciated by everyone he met, so we needed to be here. We're all members of God's family, and after visiting with your mother, I know you've inherited the best from both your parents. I was pleased Emma wanted to see you again." She paused. "I imagine she's told you we will be returning to Fresno in a couple of days, and I understand you'll be returning to MIT. Congratulations for choosing such a fine school. However, Boston is a long way from California, so I imagine you two will remain apart."

Emma intervened. "It's not what either of us want," she declared tersely, "but it is what it is, at least for now." Then she surprised them by walking away.

Marco wanted to run after her but felt constrained to avoid being rude to her mother.

"Don't pay attention to her behavior, Marco. She can be immature at times. I know she never wanted to leave Illinois, and she's not been happy in Fresno. Her dad and I would like for her to go to college, but she says she's not interested, and the only thing that occupies her time is her painting and her part-time job waitressing at a little roadside café near the *gardens* where we live."

"I really want to be with her!" Marco asserted and even surprised himself by the abruptness of his statement. "It's not possible right now, but I'll find a way for us to be together."

"My, goodness, Marco, that's a rather bold assertion!"

He nodded his agreement and wrinkled his brow. "Well, I know Emma feels the same, so if you'll excuse me, I need to talk to her."

"By all means," said Mrs. Downing as she watched Marco sprint toward Emma.

She watched as he took hold of Emma's arm and brought her face-to-face with his determination. "I just told your mother I'll find a way for us to be together," he declared.

Emma laughed. "And how'd that go?"

He pulled her into his arms and whispered, "It's not possible right now, but I love you, and I'll find a way."

She sighed and hugged him tightly. "I love you too, Marco, but how long do you have in mind?"

"Trust me! It's not going to be very long! When I get back to school, I'm going to fast-track into a master's program on a full scholarship, and when I get my degree, we're going to be together."

She sighed. "It sounds like a long time, so are you asking me to marry you?"

Her question caught him completely off-guard, and his pulse quickened. "Yes," he exclaimed with all the boldness her could muster. "I'm asking you to wait for me."

"It'll be our secret," she whispered, "but don't make me wait too long."

FOUR

$\mathcal{A}$ mixture of an early winter rain and light snow blurred the landscape as Marco wistfully stared out the train's window. His thoughts were also a mixture of regret and anticipation. Mostly, he was remembering Emma and feeling intoxicated with his love for her. Her appearance at the funeral was such a total surprise; he could hardly believe it had happened. Her whispered words, "It'll be our secret," were like a treasure he would carry close to his heart until he could see her again. It gave him urgency to do as Dr. Lee had suggested and plow his way forward through a master's program.

Telling his mother goodbye had been difficult. She was facing great uncertainty in the isolation of their homestead in rural Illinois. She had reassured him the neighbors would help with chores, so she could manage, but he knew those promises would soon wear thin. He'd already concluded there'd be no way for her to keep the farm. However, she'd promised to take care of herself and to stay warm over the winter months, so for the time being there was no urgency. Then he thought of how the seasons had affected his life when he was growing up on the farm. Winters were always tough, but in early spring everything became reactivated, and there was plenty to do. He knew his mother would be faced with similar demands.

It'll be impossible for her to manage. She'll have to sell the place, and it'll be the end of our family's heritage.

The train slowed, and he felt a jolt when it shifted onto a siding and came to a complete stop. He checked his watch in anticipation of continuing to Boston as another train passed by on the mainline.

It'll be our secret.

Just thinking of Emma's words soothed his mind as he anticipated resuming his studies. He intended to immediately make an appointment to see Dr. Lee and then make plans for speeding up his academic schedule. However, he was already feeling excited to be one of the first to navigate into computer science; his imagination was working overtime. He'd been dreaming about such an opportunity for such a long time, and to think of it actually happening was his fondest desire. Somewhere during the transition he was confident he'd travel to Fresno and put an engagement ring on Emma's finger.

It won't be too long, Emma! It won't be too long.

~

*I*t was still raining when he stepped off the train in Boston. He paused, took out his wallet and checked to see if he had enough cash to take a cab or if he'd have to ride the bus. There was enough, so he signaled one of the cabbies waiting in line for fares. He always felt thankful to be shuttled from place to place in the big city. Everything moved too fast, and in his way of thinking it wasn't a good way to live. His lean muscular body and handsome good looks caused his friends to think he might be quite cosmopolitan, but to the contrary; Marco was proud to be a country boy looking forward to a future unlike anything he'd ever imagined.

~

"*It's* good to see you again, Marco." Dr. Lee said as he greeted him and asked if everything was okay at home. "How's your dad doing?"

Marco's face muscles tightened as he relived his emotions. "He died, Dr. Lee, but I was there to tell him goodbye."

"I'm so sorry, Marco. I'm sure it's painful. How's your mom doing?"

"She's fine," he said confidently, "but after the winter's lull, she'll be facing more than she can handle on her own. There are some big changes coming."

"Does that mean you'll be taking another hiatus from your studies?"

"I hope not!" he declared. "My hunch is she'll have to sell the farm and move into town where she'll have neighbors, and that's something she can handle on her own."

Professor Lee nodded understandingly. "Well, I hope it all works out to her advantage. Are you ready to knuckle down and make this accelerated program happen?"

Marco smiled broadly, pursed his lips and nodded energetically. "I'm ready!"

"I anticipated you would be, so while you were gone, I made some contacts and prepared a little *to do* list to get things started."

Marco scanned down the list and noted the names and phone numbers for a number of people, who would be helping him.

"Do I need to contact all these people?" he asked.

"Mostly, they'll be contacting you," professor Lee explained. "Just keep your eye on the goal and take it a step at a time. Everyone I talked to seemed excited for you to lead the way into computer science, so you're not going to be alone on this one."

"I'm excited, too. I've dreamed of it for so long. It's hard to believe it's actually happening."

"I'll be your main contact, and we should plan to check with each other at least bi-weekly. Any questions?"

"None I can think of right now."

Dr. Lee extended his hand in congratulations. "You can do this, Marco. You have many reasons to be proud."

~

*A*lthough Marco had little time for anything but his studies, he was incredibly energized by them. Each weekend he used Sunday as his day off, socialized with his friends, took care of his laundry, and sometimes ventured off-campus for a movie. He called his mother every week or so, and toward the end of the spring quarter, she told him about her decision to sell the farm.

"It was inevitable, Marco. The neighbors offered to help, but it would be a big imposition on their time. I've talked with a realtor about putting it on the market."

"It's a good decision," Marco agreed. "I was hoping you'd decide to sell."

"It feels like I'm violating the trust of the Jackson family," she lamented. "It's like giving up something historic and precious to our ancestors."

"However, things have changed, and without Dad, there's no way for you to manage the farm, so letting it go is the right thing to do." He paused. "Where will you live?"

"Harrisburg!" she replied with no hesitation. "I've already found a perfect apartment in Harrisburg where two of my best friends are living."

"Wow! That was fast!"

"Actually, I'm excited about it, Marco. That old farmhouse had served its purpose, and it's time for me to move on."

Marco laughed. "I love your spirit. I'm sure you'll be happy living in a place where you already have friends."

When the call ended, he was relieved. It was time for him to move on as well.

~

Dear Emma!

I hope you are remembering our secret and staying busy, so time passes quickly. You wouldn't believe how much is happening to me at MIT. In my previous letters I have explained the plan, and now it's been over a year, and I can finally see the light at the end of the tunnel.

When mom sold the farm, she generously started an investment account to cover my expenses and to establish a financial foundation for my future . . . and as you know, I'm hoping it will be our future together. I'm solidly engaged with the rigors of graduate work, but I've decided to take a short break this summer and find my way to Fresno. I'll be waiting anxiously for you to say, "Okay," so don't let me down. The actual dates can be flexible, but as soon as I hear from you, I'm going to put it on my schedule.

I could go on and on about the program I'm in, but that would be mostly boring, so I'll cut to the chase and tell you something exciting that's happened. IBM is recruiting me! As you may or may not know, IBM is a leader in the field of computing, and the recruiters have intrigued me with a very lucrative offer.

Anyway, write to me as soon as possible. I'm nearly delirious with my memories of you so don't keep me in suspense.

Love, Marco

Emma's reply came more quickly than he'd expected, and her letter began with capital letters and an exclamation mark: "YES!" He'd just completed the spring quarter and could hardly wait to coordinate his two-weeks summer break. He felt very privileged to have the option of time away and was reassured when professor Lee told him a vacation wouldn't slow his progress.

A number of things had happened in rapid succession. His mother had sold the farm just after the advent of spring, and she was ecstatic with the deal she'd received from an energetic young couple wanting exactly what she was offering. She also acted quickly to move and told him the apartment was wonderful.

"The farm sold for over $500,000," his mother had shared in her letter, "and I'm investing $300, 000 in an account for you and $200,000 in a separate account for me. When you're home sometime in the near future, we'll need to take care of getting your name on the accounts and deciding how you want yours administered. I know your dad would have wanted this as well."

Then, to his surprise, she'd sent him a check to cover his expenses, which was far more than he'd expected. The money made it possible for him to move off-campus and to also have the means for making his trip to see Emma. Of course, he also bought an engagement ring on credit with 24 months of easy payments, and that would be his surprise.

In addition, his studies had progressed phenomenally well, and when IBM recruiters made another offer, he had stars in his eyes. IBM was known the world over for its innovative typewriter technology, and now they were ushering in a new era with concepts for space travel, lasers, and the miniaturization of circuitry. They wanted people like Marco, who were on the cutting edge of computer science, and he was a very willing candidate.

"I usually caution against being too quick to accept offers such as the one they're making to you, but in this case, Marco, I think it would be to your advantage." Dr. Lee looked at him knowingly and arched his brow. "They obviously know who you are and have assessed your talents. Now it's mainly a question of what you want. You're going to emerge from our graduate program at the top of your class, so you can basically write your own ticket. Don't settle for too little. Know what you are worth and hold on until they make it worth your while."

Marco did exactly that, and just a couple of weeks before his trip to Fresno, he signed a letter of intent to work for IBM at a salary beyond imagination. Taking time to vacation in California seemed like a celebration, and he received complete support from all concerned. It was like being given carte blanche decision-making power over what would happen next. "Computers," he whispered to no one in particular. "Who would have thought?"

~

To even think about going to California was like a fantasy. Around campus, deciduous trees posed with their rich mantel of green against an azure sky, flowers bloomed, and the warmth of early summer lured everyone outside. For all the time he'd been at MIT, late spring and early summer had been his favorite time of year, and now with the prospect of seeing Emma, everything seemed brighter and more glorious. He'd never been to the West Coast before, but he knew the distance and the great varieties of scenery he'd be seeing along the way. Emma had agreed to the dates he'd suggested for his visit, but she had no idea what else Marco had in mind.

Planning his flight from Logan International was a nerve-racking experience. Marco had never learned to drive a car. His only long-distance travel had been by train, so as he looked at the airplane he was about to board, he relied on his intelligence to believe it could fly. He and Emma had negotiated his plan carefully. He would fly from Boston to San Francisco where she would meet his flight and drive him to Fresno in her newly acquired secondhand 1955 Chevy. (She had teased him about being his chauffeur, but he sensed her pride and independence.) They'd planned for him to stay for at least three days or maybe even a week, but he'd not shared his personal plan, which he would happily reveal once she was in his arms.

The engines on the big Douglas DC-7 roared to life after the ground crew pushed it away from the gate, and Marco felt his gut tighten. He had tried to imagine the experience, but it was already more than he'd anticipated. He calmed down a little as the plane taxied to the end of the runway before takeoff, but when the pilot revved the engines full-throttle, he doubted everything he'd ever learned about aerodynamics. Holding tightly to the armrests, the force of acceleration pressed him against his seat, and in a matter of minutes, the magic of flight enfolded him. He could hardly believe the perspective he had on the panorama below. As the plane banked and climbed toward its westerly course, he wondered how many more wondrous things would happen to him in the span of a few short hours.

~

Seeing Emma was breathtaking. She had shortened her auburn hair into a sassy fifties style and looked wonderfully relaxed in her Capri slacks and sandals. She always radiated soft beauty with her engaging smile, although she could also be feisty and moody, (as her mother had pointed out), but as she waved at him from a distance, he thought of her as his *earth angel,* which were words from his favorite song after going to college and being on his own. He waved and sprinted to meet her.

"You're so beautiful," he sighed, while scooping her up in his arms. "I really like your hair, but it took me a minute to realize it was really you."

He kissed her tenderly, and the noisy airport dissolved around them.

"I wasn't sure you'd ever come to see me," she said with a dreamy look in her brown eyes, "but I've longed to have you here for so many days, I've lost count."

"So many things have changed," he admitted, "and I've longed to be here with you as well." He kissed her again and hugged her so tightly, she gasped. "It's really warm here, or is it just the rush I'm feeling with you in my arms?"

"It's warm!" she agreed and motioned toward an exit. "I'm anxious for you to see my car."

He grabbed his suitcase with one hand and held tightly to her hand with the other, and as she led the way, he could hardly take his eyes off of her.

"It's the bright red Chevy," she said with pride and pointed toward where it was parked."

Marco stopped in his tracks. "Wow! It looks brand new! How did you get enough money to buy it?"

"That's my little surprise," she beamed. "I've been selling my paintings and doing really well."

He remembered her art and her skill in creating beautiful oils and watercolors, so he wasn't surprised people would want to buy them, but he wondered how they'd discover her work.

"How do people know about your paintings?"

"A gallery displays them, and the owner advises me on pricing, so I bought myself a car."

"Wow! Emma! You're not only beautiful; you're a successful artist as well. I remember seeing your paintings, and they were strikingly beautiful."

"It's been a bright spot," she said and raised her brow knowingly. "I had been holed up at Phillip's Gardens far too long, so my paintings and this Chevy have set me free. One of my goals is to teach you how to drive." She laughed and did a perfect pirouette playfully portraying her freedom.

Marco joined in her laughter and once again took her into his arms. "I want you to teach me everything, and I'm going to teach you what an IBM man knows how to do best."

"And what's that?"

"I'm going to teach you how an IBM man loves his woman."

She laughed joyfully and danced her way into the driver's seat for their trip to Fresno.

~

Their conversation covered everything they needed to say about their long absence from each other, and then, for the last fifty miles or so, Marco talked about their "little secret" and the expected conversation they'd need to have with her parents.

"Oh, I think they're expecting it, but it'll also be a conversation with Bea and Phillip," she suggested. "I really have two sets of parents now that we've become permanent residents at Phillip's Gardens. Aunt Bea has actually shown me more love than my mom. Don't get me wrong! I love my mom and dad, but if I need to talk to someone, I go to Aunt Bea."

He saw the Fresno skyline on the horizon, and it was getting hotter than he ever remembered.

"Man! I thought it was hot in southern Illinois," he declared. "How can you live here?"

"You get used to it, and if you don't mind, when we get to where we're going, I'm going to change into shorts and a halter top. It's my standard attire."

"I certainly *don't* mind! In fact, I'm looking forward to it. I've always wanted to see more of you."

He smiled in anticipation, and she noticeably perked up.

"We live on a huge farm, Marco, but our bungalow only has four rooms, so I told them you'll be staying in the air-conditioned comfort of our local Highway Inn Motel. They agreed it was the proper thing to do, but as you might imagine, they've innocently overlooked the fact that I'm planning on spending some time in the cool comfort of your motel room as well."

Marco blushed. Being intimate with Emma had always been his secret desire, but circumstances had never allowed it. In fact, he'd not given a second thought to where he might be staying, but he really liked her suggestion. It triggered something urgent in his emotions, and he knew he wanted her more than he could say with mere words.

When she pulled off the highway into the parking area of the motel, Marco felt his mouth go dry and his heartbeats thundered in his chest. Emma was acting with an air of confidence he'd never seen. She parked the car and motioned for him to follow her into the motel office, and then she stood aside as Marco approached the receptionist behind the counter.

"May I help you?"

"Yes," Marco managed to say in a somewhat lower voice than normal. "I'd like a single room with a king-sized bed."

"One night, or will you be staying longer?"

"It'll be at least three nights with an option of extending my stay if necessary."

"I have a ground floor room for $40. Would that be okay?"

He nodded yes.

"Are you a smoker?"

Marco shook his head no.

"Good! We try to keep a few rooms smoke-free, and this is one of them, so please fill out the registration." The clerk kept glancing at Emma. "It's just for one person, right?" Marco nodded and continued filling out the form, and then handed it to her. She noted he'd left blank spaces for the make and model car, and then she glanced at Emma again.

"She lives at Phillip's Gardens," he explained, "and it's her car."

"Whatever," observed the clerk as she handed him the room key. "Don't leave valuables in your room," she instructed. "Checkout is at noon on whatever day you decide to leave. Any questions?"

"Nope! That's all," Marco declared. "I'll just put my stuff in the room, and then we'll be on our way."

The clerk arched her brow and shook her head ever so subtly as they left the office and walked toward the car to get his suitcase.

Then Emma followed him to the room, and once they were out of sight from the overly curious clerk, she laughed and clapped her hands. "Did you see the look she gave me?"

"Oh, yeah," he agreed. "She probably thinks we're having a rendezvous."

Emma stepped closer to Marco and put her arm around his waist. "Well," she sighed.

He knew at that moment his next exceptional experience would be making love with Emma, so he quickly jettisoned all other concerns from his mind.

~

*I*t was more wonderful than either of them could have imagined. There was a bit of awkward fumbling as they discovered the delight of feeling their nakedness, touching the softness of intimate places and causing reactions only genuine love allows. As he cradled Emma in his arms, they both felt a bond so strong, they knew their love would conquer any foreseeable obstacles and carry them courageously into a future filled with promise.

She knew her parents were expecting her, so she suggested getting dressed and on their way.

Marco complied, but before they returned to her car, he produced the ring and asked her to marry him.

"It's time to reveal our little secret," he said as he placed the ring onto her finger, and Emma's eyes filled with tears.

"It's all I've ever wanted," she sobbed, "and in a day or two, it's going to be impossible for me to tell you goodbye."

"Then come with me," he pleaded. "You have a car, and I have the means. I think your parents will understand, and it's what I want with all my heart."

"Seriously?"

"Yes, seriously! It's been *my* plan all along. I can't stand thinking of another separation, and I don't want any more goodbyes."

She lingered in his arms and then whispered, "Yes!"

"Let me do the talking," he said, and she nodded. "This is the moment when we take charge of our life together, so let's go to Phillip's Gardens, where I'll politely ask your dad for your hand in marriage, but it's a done deal no matter what!"

FIVE

$\mathcal{A}$ seemingly endless two-thousand-mile drive from Fresno, across Arizona, New Mexico, Oklahoma and Missouri was a test of their endurance, but at every stop along the way it was a love fest for Emma and Marco as they tried to make up for all the lost time they'd endured over their years of separation. Marco felt he had finally found the missing piece of his life's puzzle, and he willingly admitted making love was better than any of his exotic ideas about computers, which caused Emma to laugh aloud each time he said it. She felt the same, but when he compared sex with computers, it was too much to take seriously. She'd been waiting and longing for Marco for so long there simply was no comparison. Now she felt fulfilled. They were so completely in love, everything blurred by comparison.

Marco had been wonderfully diplomatic with Audrey and David Downing, Emma's parents, and then equally so with her Aunt Bea and Uncle Phillip.

"I'll need to finish school before we get married," he'd explained, "but Emma and I have agreed we want to be together. We know it's a big decision, but Emma wants to go the Boston with me, and when it comes time for our wedding, we want to return to the little country church in southern Illinois where we met as children."

Her parents were reluctant to accept Marco's rationale, but Emma was twenty years old and far beyond the reach of their parental control, so with sadness, they gave their blessing and pleaded with them to check in periodically to ease their anxiety about the long road trip east.

"We'll be spending a few days in Harrisburg with my mom," Marco added. "It'll be the first time I've seen her since Dad died."

"Emma told us she sold the farm."

Marco nodded yes. "It was because there was no way for her to manage it on her own."

"And now she's living . . ."

"In Harrisburg," Marco interrupted. "She has a beautiful apartment and lots of friends."

The Downing's both smiled, and Audrey explained to Aunt Bea how Harrisburg is the nearest town to where they used to live.

Aunt Bea smiled, and the Downing's seemed okay with Emma's big decision, so to celebrate the occasion, Marco invited everyone to dinner, which turned out to be a buffet of over-cooked food at the Golden Corral. Emma added some sparkle to the otherwise drab interior of the restaurant with her brightly colored shorts and halter, and as they sat around a big table enjoying their meal, Marco put his hand on Emma's bare leg and smiled.

Before leaving Fresno, they made a quick trip to the gallery where Emma had a contractual agreement to continue her consignment of ten paintings, and the owner assured her he anticipated an increasing demand for her artwork. Marco was shocked as he admired her paintings on display and noticed they were selling for between $500 and $1,000.

When they left the gallery he simply said, "WOW! You should have bought a Cadillac rather than a Chevy. Those paintings of desert scenes are beautiful."

"I paint what I see," Emma boasted, "but it took a while for me to discover the beauty of this area. When I first arrived in Fresno, I was pouting and hiding my head most of the time."

"But those days are over," Marco counseled. "Having you at my side makes everything seem like a perfect picture."

She looked at him and rolled her eyes. "And you're my Adonis," she smiled. "I'm not sure what kind of picture you have in mind, but I agree; being together is too beautiful for words."

~

When they reached Harrisburg, the road-weary couple stopped to ask directions three times before they found his mom's apartment, which was located outside of the town in a newly developed area. He had called ahead to let her know they were coming, told her to watch for a bright red Chevy, and not to be surprised that Emma was with him.

His mother watched vigilantly, and when she saw them pull into the parking lot, she bolted from the front door of the building to welcome them.

Marco was first to receive her affection, and then she surprised Emma with lingering hugs and kisses on both cheeks. Marco was pleased, and Emma a bit overwhelmed.

"Oh, my!" she exclaimed. "Just look at you two. I don't think I've ever seen a more handsome coupled. Emma, you're so precious! I'm so pleased to see you again."

"Thanks, Mrs. Jackson!"

"Oh, my, goodness, let's end the formality. Call me Aileen . . . and Marco," she said with a big smile, "you can call me Mom!"

They laughed as she tugged on their arms urging them toward the front door.

"You can get your bags later. Right now, I want you to come upstairs to see where I live. It's very nice."

They followed her onto an elevator and exited on the fourth floor with Aileen motioning for them to follow her to her apartment at the end of a long hallway. When they stepped inside her corner unit, Marco was immediately impressed.

"This is really nice!" he exclaimed.

Emma quickly agreed. "It's so modern," she said as she glanced at the kitchen and then enjoyed the view from the living room windows.

"I know," Aileen beamed. "It's quite a contrast to the old farmhouse."

Marco joined Emma in the living room by the large windows, which faced a beautiful wooded area and a small lake surrounded by groomed trails and picnic areas.

"Do you walk the trails?"

"At least once or twice a week," she announced proudly, "and there's also an exercise room on the first floor."

"It's very nice, Mrs. Jack . . . I mean Aileen," Emma said as she returned to the kitchen area, where she admired the modern appliances and ample space. "How many bedroom are there?"

Aileen stopped short. "There are two bedrooms and two baths," she announced and then tapped Marco on his shoulder. "Do you . . . I mean . . . in terms of sleeping . . . do you . . .?"

Marco smiled and wrapped his arms around his mother. "Don't fret about it," he said with a smile. "One bedroom for us will be perfect."

His mother sighed rather loudly. Then she stepped back while still holding Marco's hand. "Do you remember what you said to me when your dad died?"

Marco wrinkled his expression trying to remember.

"We were talking about how Dad was too young to die, and I told you I treasured the years we'd had together."

Marco nodded as he recalled the conversation.

"And then you said you hoped you'd have the same and even more."

"Right! I do remember."

"And this young lady right here," she smiled and reached over to put her arm around Emma, "this young lady came immediately to mind. I just knew you two would find each other and be in love."

Emma felt overwhelmed and once again folded into Aileen's embrace.

"It's true! We are very much in love."

Then she held her left hand in front of Aileen so she could admire her engagement ring.

"Oh, my, goodness, I've not been very observant. It's beautiful! When's the wedding?"

"It was a mutual decision for Emma to come with me for the final phase of my master's program, and like we told her parents, we'll wait until I graduate and then get married."

His mother smiled and wrapped her arms around both of them. "I'm so pleased," she whispered, "so pleased."

When their hug ended, Marco noticed tears in her eyes and hugged her again.

"As I said," he repeated, "I want what you and Dad had, and I love Emma with all my heart."

"Well, why don't you kids get your bags and then maybe take a short walk by the lake while I make some lunch."

~

*L*ater that afternoon as they were reminiscing, Aileen seemed increasingly nervous. Marco noticed she was rubbing her hands in a stressful way and wasn't sure why.

"Are you okay, Mom?"

She looked at him sadly, continued fidgeting, and suddenly stood and went to her bedroom.

"Mom," Marco called.

"Just sit tight! I'll be right back."

When she returned, she was carrying a small metal box, which required a key to open. When she sat down, she placed the box on her lap and exhaled loudly. Both Emma and Marco looked curiously at the box and wondered what it contained.

"In order to move into this beautiful apartment, I had to do some downsizing, and it was very difficult for me to sell a lot of the things that made our home so special. Of course, when you do that kind of housecleaning, you rediscover all kinds of things, and Marco, this is very important. Your dad wanted to be here for this, but now he's gone, and it's up to me. You need to know I'm very nervous."

"What's in the box, Mom? What's going on?"

This box contains some personal papers I've been saving for you," his mother said with a tiny nod of her head.

Marco looked at Emma as though dreading she was going to reveal something embarrassing from his childhood.

Emma smiled coyly.

"I really don't know how to say this . . . and I hope you won't be angry with me, Marco, but you're our adopted child."

It was as though something had sucked all the air out of the room. Emma gasped, and Marco raised his brow in wide-eyed disbelief.

"What did you say?"

"We adopted you the day you were born," she added, "and you've been *our* beloved son from that moment on."

Marco jumped to his feet and threw his hands in the air. "And you waited all these years to tell me?"

His mother began sobbing softly, but he stood in front of her waiting for her to answer his question. Then she looked up at him and wiped tears from her eyes.

"Your father and I had agreed we'd tell you on your 21st birthday, but Dad died young, so now's the time, and believe me Marco, I wanted your dad to be with me. We agreed to wait until you were old enough to understand." She looked at him with a pleading expression and saw uncertainty in his eyes. "I've loved you from the moment I first held you in my arms, and your dad and I have treasured the joy you've brought into our lives, so please forgive me if I'm doing this the wrong way."

"But why now?"

"When you called and told me you and Emma were coming to see me, I knew it had to be now."

Marco sat down and cradled his head in his hands, while Emma stood and moved closer to put her hand on his shoulder.

"We could have told you when you were young," she explained, "but we thought it would be difficult emotionally when you were growing and acquiring your self-identity. We thought it would be better to wait until you were mature and better able to understand."

He slowly raised his head and wiped his eyes with the back of his hand.

Emma had never seen such tension in Marco and was deeply touched. She sat next to him and laid her head on his shoulder. Then she reached to hold his hand, as his mother came to his side and embraced both of them.

"Love is such a powerful emotion, Marco, and we've loved you unconditionally from the moment of your birth. What's inside this box doesn't change that at all."

"And where exactly was I born?"

"Well," Aileen sighed. "All the documents are in the box. You were born in the county hospital not far from our homestead," she explained, "and I'm sorry to say it wasn't under the best of circumstances. You know where the county hospital is? It's where we took you for a tetanus shot that time when you stepped on an old rusty nail near the barn."

"I know where it is!" he said tersely. "It's not a very impressive place to be born as far as I'm concerned, so who are my *real* parents?"

There was a sharp tone to his voice, and his mother grimaced. She took a deep breath and closed her eyes momentarily to collect her thoughts.

"Let's look at the contents of the box," she suggested and moved to the dining room table.

Emma stood and tugged on Marco's hand, so he reluctantly followed his mother to the table.

She used a small key to unlock the box and lifted its contents onto the table. "Here's your birth certificate," she said as she placed it in front of him.

He picked it up to read the faded text with Emma moving closer to see it as well. Marco traced his finger over each line of the statistical information.

Birth Certificate

Name of child: Marco Donato Conti, **Sex**: Male, **Race**: White

Date of birth: August 6, 1935, **Place of birth**: Saline County Illinois

Weight: 8 pounds 4 ounces, **Height**: 20.1 inches, **Hair**: black, **Eyes**: dark brown

Full name of mother: Frederica Teresa Conti, **Maiden name**: Frederica Teresa Rossi **Mother's place of birth**: Palermo, Italy

Mother's citizenship: USA, **Mother's residence**: Chicago Illinois Cook County
Full name of father: Antonio Valente Conti, **Father's place of birth**: Palermo, Italy
Father's citizenship: USA, **Father's residence**: Chicago Illinois Cook County
Name of attendant doctor: Richard Eggers, MD
Reported by: Martha Wagner, Nurse, Saline County Hospital, August 6, 1935

Marco's hand trembled as Emma took the certificate and placed it near the metal box. "Are you okay?" she asked.

He shook his head yes, but didn't feel like talking.

"It's okay," she said. "Think of your mom! It's difficult for her too."

He glanced at his mother, who was struggling to keep her composure, and when she reached to touch his hand, Marco wrapped his arms around her.

It took a while, but with Emma's help, he recovered and looked again at the birth certificate. "They were Italian!"

His mom shook her head yes, and he nodded knowingly.

"It says they lived in Chicago, so why was I born at the county hospital?"

Aileen raised her hands and shrugged. "I really don't know unless they were traveling when she went into labor."

"Well, this birth certificate answers one of questions; why do I have an Italian first name when my parents are Hank and Aileen *Jackson*? I've also wondered why I have dark hair and a darker complexion than either you or Dad? Now I know why!" Then he stroked his wavy hair and managed to smile.

Emma nudged him and arched her brow. "I've always known," she said playfully. "*Bell'uomo!*"

"And what does that mean?"

"Ah ha! For once I'm smarter than you!" She slapped his arm playfully. "It means *handsome man!*" she said with a big smile. "I learned it from an Italian couple, who worked at Phillip's Gardens."

His mother smiled. "*Bell'uomo!*" she repeated and continued sorting through more of the box's contents. Then she handed him a folded newspaper clipping. He read it twice to be sure he understood.

"My mother died giving me birth?"

Aileen nodded. "We were told she died shortly after you took your first breath, and that's why I think it must have been an emergency that required them to use the county hospital. We were also told that she and your father Antonio had agreed to the adoption in advance, but when she died, he wanted it to be immediate, so that's when we were notified."

Marco sighed trying to absorb so much information.

"Here's a copy of the adoption papers and a few other odds and ends relevant to your first year of life. I want you to have all of it. We thought about giving you a different name but decided your Italian name was too nice to change. Regardless, you are the beloved child of Hank and Aileen Jackson, and that will never change." She closed the box and sighed loudly. "I'm so glad you finally know."

However, Marco was still thinking about his birth father and reached to touch his mother's hand. "Is Antonio Conti still in Chicago?"

"I have no idea, Marco, and it's one of those things you may never know. However, even if he is, he has absolutely no legal connection to you, and I can tell you from our experience in adopting you, both he and your mother Frederica were obscure people. We never met neither of them, and the only evidence I have of their character came from a comment made by a nurse at the hospital."

"He's a lucky baby to be getting you and Hank as his adoptive parents. I fear what would have happened to him if his father had decided to keep him."

"And what did she mean by that?" Marco pleaded.

"I don't know, Marco, but by the look on her face, I could see she knew things about them she didn't want to tell us."

~

Their goodbyes were difficult! The day they'd arrived had been filled with joy and anticipation to share the good news of their engagement, but then everything shifted when his mom revealed his adoption. However, during the remainder of their stay, his emotions quieted down, and they talked briefly about wanting to come back to the little county church for their wedding as soon as his studies ended.

Aileen stood alone in the parking lot as they waved a final time before pulling onto the highway and turning east for the remaining thousand miles to Massachusetts.

"Italian, huh? I should have known!" Emma exclaimed. "There's no country boy, who can make love like you! I should have known."

They laughed loudly, and then Marco looked wistfully at the passing countryside. Harrisburg was quite a few miles from the farm where he'd lived, but Italian or not, he was leaving his home once again and hurrying to find his way into something new. Having Emma at his side was his only anchor.

She noticed his nostalgic expression and reached to hold his hand. He obviously had a lot on his mind, but she knew things were different now.

Marco responded to her touch, but his thoughts were about what he'd learned. He was feeling an intense need to know more about his Italian father.

I'd like to meet Antonio Conti, he thought. *At some point in my life, I'd like to look him in the eye and ask him why.*

SIX

When Marco and Emma arrived in Boston, he felt at home, and she felt uncertain, but the beauty of the surrounding area impressed her. She'd never seen a big university and wondered how he ever found his classrooms. His off-campus apartment was modest but adequate for the two of them, and within a couple of days they'd replenished the pantry and added a few pieces of inexpensive furniture to make it more livable. She was happy to discover he already had a full-sized bed and that there was a small storage room where she could set up her easels for painting.

"It's going to be perfect," she smiled, "and having me here will certainly change your domestic habits." To illustrate her point, she gathered up a few pieces of clothing, which he'd previously pitched onto a chair.

He noticed but motioned for her to stand with him at the apartment's one large window.

"I like this view looking south toward the river and the harbor."

She agreed.

Then he pointed to a well-used pathway, which disappeared into a grove of trees. "The campus is within walking distance, so I've managed quite well without a car."

They had arrived two weeks before the fall quarter and already the oaks, elms, and maples were displaying fall colors, so that afternoon they walked to the campus and spent a couple hours leisurely enjoying the quietness and just being together.

"There's a maze of tunnels running from building to building," he explained, "so students can get to classes without being exposed to the weather; however, at this time of year, it's great to be outside. It's so serene right now, but it won't be for long."

"It's beautiful," Emma agreed. "I see all kinds of possibilities for my paintings." She paused. "When will I meet your mentor, professor Lee, or are we keeping my presence secret?" She smiled and waited for his reaction.

"I probably should make an appointment to see him next week before classes resume . . . and yes, I'll proudly introduce you."

She smiled with satisfaction and took hold of his hand.

"You're going to be a part of everything I do, Luv, and I'm sure Dr. Lee will be impressed."

"Are you going to tell him about Antonio Conti?"

Hearing her recall his birth father's name startled him, and he let go of her hand. "No! I won't be saying anything about it, but believe me, it's on my mind. I won't have much time to fuss with it, but I'm going to find out who he is and where he is."

"I'm sure you'll find a way," she said and resumed holding his hand. "I know if it was me, I'd have to know."

Marco nodded and shook his head in agreement.

"I wonder if he looks like you?"

Marco suddenly jumped in front of her, posed like a male model and slipped on his sunglasses. "If he does," he laughed, "he must be devastatingly handsome."

Emma made a silly expression. "Oh, Lord! With your new Italian personality, I'll have to be constantly on guard."

He removed his glasses, stroked his wavy dark hair and smiled seductively. "You've got a real man on your hands, Luv, so you better treat me nicely."

~

"It's good to see you again, Marco. Did you have a relaxing vacation?"

Marco nodded, greeted his mentor, Dr. Lee, and then introduced Emma.

"This is my fiancé, Emma Downing. Emma, this is Professor Lee."

"It's delightful meeting you, Emma. I was unaware Marco had a fiancé."

"That would be true until recently when I asked Emma to marry me."

"My goodness! How nice," Dr. Lee said, while arching his brow knowingly. He nodded affirmatively to Marco and then narrowed his eyes to look at Emma. "You're a very lucky girl, Emma. Marco is an exceptional young man and certainly a gifted student."

"Yes, I'm aware, Dr. Lee. When we were in high school, he was at the top of our class."

"I'm not surprised. Everything I know about Marco is exceptional. Are you a student as well?"

"No, I'm an artist."

"I see," Dr. Lee said with a suspicious smile. "What kind of art do you do?"

"Oils and watercolors," she said confidently.

"How nice, and do you consider yourself a professional?"

Emma wrinkled her brow at what seemed to be a rather snobbish question, but Marco came to her rescue.

"Her work is very professional, Dr. Lee, and a number of her paintings are featured in a Fresno gallery."

"Fresno, so then you're from California?"

"So to speak," Emma reluctantly admitted. "I've lived there with my parents, but Marco and I are both from rural Illinois."

"Oh, yes! Marco has told me many times about his country home, but now you're here in the big city, and Marco is getting ready to make MIT proud of him as a leader in the emerging field of computer science."

Emma smiled nonchalantly.

"May I assume you'll be planning a wedding at some point along the way?"

Once again, Emma smiled and nodded, while Marco clarified their plans.

"Not until I graduate! I'm totally devoted to this graduate program."

Dr. Lee smiled and then extended his hand to Emma. "It's been wonderful meeting you, but Marco and I have some business to discuss, so would you mind waiting in the hallway?"

His request caught her off-guard. She glanced at Marco, shrugged and turned toward the door.

"Thank you, dear! We'll take just a moment."

She frowned at Marco, and Dr. Lee closed the door after she left the room.

"Don't let her become a distraction, Marco! We're putting you on a fast track for a good reason and it's going to be very intense, so I'm hoping you're ready to give it your full attention."

Marco wasn't sure he liked Dr. Lee's tone. "Emma isn't a distraction, Dr. Lee. She's patient and supportive, so I'm not anticipating any problems."

"I know, I know, but academic intensity can be very stressful, so I'm just sharing my concern . . . oh, and by the way, you need to finish your applications for scholarships. Please take care of that right away."

"I will."

"In addition, Dr. Simmons and Dr. Harlow want to meet with you to discuss some options for your thesis. I told them I'd arrange it as soon as you returned to campus, so that's another important item on your to-do list."

Dr. Lee handed him a slip of paper on which he'd written their names, numbers and the building where they had their offices. On the bottom of the paper he'd made a bold exclamation point indicating its importance.

"Any questions?"

Marco shook his head no and extended his hand to Professor Lee. They shook hands politely, and then he joined Emma, who was pacing in the hallway.

"Well, I hope you two got all your *business* things settled," she snipped.

"I'm sorry, Hon! I probably should have done this on my own."

"Right! Dr. Lee was very cordial up to a point, and then I felt I was given detention in the hallway."

She frowned and wagged her head, while making a snooty expression. He felt her anger but decided not to say any more about it. They walked in silence to the apartment, and it was the first tension between them. He didn't like the feeling.

~

Winter on the East Coast was especially harsh that year, and while Marco scurried from classroom to classroom, Emma was more or less stranded in the box they called their apartment. The view, which she'd admired so much in the fall, had turned into a snowy winter scene symbolizing the bleakness of her daily routine. Probably the best part of her day was enjoying a cup of coffee with Marco each morning before he dashed off, leaving her to fend for herself for long hours until he returned. Sometimes he didn't arrive back until six o'clock or later, so she devoted time each day to her painting but found it harder and harder to stay in a good mood. Sales of her paintings in the Fresno gallery were actually better than she'd expected, but when the owner asked her to send more of her work, she was embarrassed to have only one she'd finished. As she looked around her small workroom, she counted six she'd started and not finished.

It was snowing when Marco came home that evening.

"Hey, Em! What's for dinner?"

She looked at him and narrowed her eyes as he wiped water droplets from his glasses.

"It's in the freezer," she said sullenly.

He sensed her mood and tried to kiss her, but she pulled away.

"Do you love me, Marco?"

"Absolutely! I love you with a passion."

"Do you have any idea what it's like for me to be here all day with nothing to do?"

"Probably not," he admitted, "but there's not much I can do about it."

"What do you do all day?"

"I attend classes, do research in the library and write; it's all part of getting my degree."

"And then what?"

"I've agreed to work for IBM, so we'll get married and relocate."

She frowned. "Well, I'm bored."

"And I'm tired, so I'm going to get something out of the freezer for our dinner, and then I think we need to sit down and talk about this."

Emma didn't offer to help and instead went back to her painting room to put some things away and cover the painting she'd been working on for nearly a month.

Marco hanged around in the kitchen until he had warmed some pasta and leftover pork. "Let's eat," he called, and Emma reluctantly plopped onto the chair next to him at the table. They ate in silence, and when they finished he cleared the table and offered her a glass of wine. "Join me," he said and motioned toward the couch. She accepted the glass of wine, sat down and stared blankly at the wall. "You asked if I know what it's like to be in this apartment all day, and obviously, I don't, but I *do* know you're unhappy."

She looked at him and raised her brow. "I honestly didn't anticipate this."

"I didn't anticipate it either," he agreed. "Being in love with you is wonderful, and I thought we were doing okay, but Em, I don't know how to change my circumstances." He looked at her pleadingly, and she wrinkled her brow. "Academics have always been easy for me," he continued, "but this fast track program requires much more time than I thought it would. There's no end to the research and writing. I know I'm gone a lot, but there's nothing I can do to change it."

This time Emma looked up, and he sensed a little change in her mood.

"I feel trapped, Marco. I can clean this apartment in thirty minutes, the phone never rings, and all I have to occupy my time is my painting . . . and the moodier I feel, the less I want to paint."

He put his arm around her, and this time she wanted his embrace.

"I'm wondering if there might be an art studio close by, where you could spend time with other artists?"

"Maybe? I've never looked. Anything would be better than staying in this tiny apartment day after day."

"I wish we could afford a bigger place, but there's not much available in our price range. I know this one's like a little box, but being close to the campus is a real luxury."

She listened without comment, and then got up to refill their glasses.

Marco glanced out the window and thought it was snowing harder than before, and when Emma returned, she seemed in a better mood.

"I might look into the art studio idea. There has to be a community of artists here, and anything to spark my motivation to paint would be really good."

"I hope you do," he whispered, "and for the good of the order, I'm beginning to see light at the end of our tunnel."

"And what kind of light do you see?"

"I've had some serious discussions with IBM representatives, and I can hardly believe what they're offering. It's a global company, and as far as I know, I'll be able to choose where I want to work. They're really big in New York, but I'm not sure we'd want to live there. They're also in California and Texas, so the light at the end of this tunnel might be California, but not Fresno." He smiled and she rolled her eyes. "I'm thinking it might be Silicone Valley, where you'll be a notable artist and I'll be a pioneer in computers and technology."

"And is this light imminent, or flickering?"

"It's bright, Em! It's really bright! And I think we should keep an eye on it. As soon as I get my degree, we should take a break, go back to our little county church, have a fabulous wedding and then take a leisurely honeymoon. I'm ready to mount up and charge the windmills."

"Okay Don Quixote, I like your impossible dream, and while you're feeling so optimistic, I should tell you why I'm not drinking my wine; I think I'm pregnant."

Marco nearly dropped his glass but managed to set it down before leaping to his feet with a joyous shout. "Oh, my, god! Really?" Then he sat back down and pulled Emma into his arms.

"It's a maybe," she confirmed. "I've missed my period, so we'll wait and see."

He kissed her and sighed.

"However, my dear Italian lover, if I'm pregnant, then that light at the end of your tunnel is even more important than we thought."

The truth of it suddenly dawned on him and his expression changed. "You're right," he agreed. "Having a baby is both wonderful and scary."

~

$\mathcal{N}$early two months later, and after frequent trips to a campus clinic, Emma's pregnancy was confirmed, but there were some concerns over how she was progressing. Both she and Marco fell silent, when her doctor explained she might not be able to carry the baby to term. They hadn't said anything to their parents, so it was still a private matter, which left them shouldering the full responsibility. Marco was especially haunted by what his mother had shared about his birth and the trauma of his birth mother's death. He was reminded again of Antonio Conti, who immediately put him up for adoption as though he would be an inconvenience to whatever he was doing. All his thoughts prompted uneasy feelings, but for now, the best they could do was hope.

Emma found an art studio perfectly suited to her needs and met two artists about her age, who were meeting weekly, to paint and be supportive. They gladly welcomed her to join them. It was a godsend, and Marco was extremely pleased. He helped her pack her easel and a couple of canvasses, which she took to a workroom in back of the studio. When he met her two new friends, he felt a comforting sensation of relief just knowing she'd be involved in something meaningful.

However, early on a Saturday morning he awakened to Emma's cry of pain and rushed her to a clinic, where they assisted her through a miscarriage. She managed quite well but was devastated to lose the baby. Marco shook with emotion, while trying to console her and deal with his own feelings of loss. When the trauma ended and they returned home, he held her silently for a long time until her sense of calm returned.

"I'm so sad," he whispered, "but maybe it's for the best."

She nodded and kissed him. "We're just a couple of kids, Marco. We still need to get married, and there'll be a lot of time to start a family. I'm sad too, but I'm still thinking about the light at the end of that tunnel. I hope it's real."

SEVEN

*I*n spite of his intense schedule, Marco found time to do some research on Antonio Conti. He discovered a lot of history about various Italian families and was a bit overwhelmed when he realized the number of men named Antonio Conti. However, the most prominent and encouraging find was a certain Antonio Conti living in the Chicago area. Since Marco's birth certificate had listed Chicago as his father's residence, he assumed it might be him. He'd been keeping track of his research in a small notebook and carefully wrote down the details. However, for the time being, he had more pressing concerns, such as finishing his thesis, passing his finals and planning a wedding.

Emma's parents had recovered quite well from their financial woes and had purchased a small house near Phillip's Gardens, and Aunt Bea had enlisted Emma's dad into a partnership to essentially manage the farm. Emma had talked about their wedding plans nearly every time her mother called, and when they finally set the date, her mother proudly told her they'd be making the two thousand mile road trip in their new car. Of course, Marco's mom still lived in Harrisburg but was equally enthralled with the idea of reconnecting with all her friends at the little country church.

"She said they have a new car!" Emma exclaimed after talking to her mother. "I guess they've been doing very well since I left."

Marco smiled. "Speaking of cars, I'm wondering if your Chevy can manage another cross-country trip?"

"No doubt!" she boasted.

He rolled his eyes and looked at her over the rim of his glasses.

~

$\mathcal{M}$arco was awarded his Master of Science degree on June 5, 1959, and graduated with honors. With only a couple of weeks before their wedding on June 20, they were eager to leave, so he declined to wait for the graduation ceremony. It was like being caught up in a whirlwind. He and Emma had collaborated on his choice of location with IBM and settled on their facility in San Jose. He easily negotiated August 1 as his start date, which would give them time for a short honeymoon before the trip to California. He also received a generous signing bonus, and the check arrived on the day before they canceled their mail delivery, which seemed like a miracle. It was more than adequate to cover the wedding, the trip, and their honeymoon, which they agreed would be in Chicago. Emma knew Marco thought he might find his birth father in Chicago but gladly went along with his suggestion. She was giddy to finally be leaving their little apartment and kept remembering the "light at the end of the tunnel" Marco had promised. In addition to his signing bonus, she'd also received good news from the gallery in Fresno about a surge in sales of her paintings but told them to hold the money for her until things were settled.

"The long wait's over!" she exclaimed as they packed their belongings into a small U-Haul trailer attached to the rear of her Chevy.

Marco smiled and looked longingly at the now familiar apartment. "A new chapter is beginning," he agreed. "I told professor Lee goodbye last evening, and he was really grumpy because I wouldn't be here for the graduation ceremony. I think it's because he's the featured speaker, and intends to gloat over *his* success in integrating computer science into the graduate program."

"I hope he's forgiving," Emma said with a concerned expression.

"It's not a problem. He was gracious in wishing me success in San Jose and I didn't sense any ill feelings."

"Well, I'm glad he likes you. I'm sure he never liked me."

Marco scrunched his expression. "He's just an old academic. You have to get used to his abrupt style."

"Of course you'd say that; you were his star pupil."

"And he did a lot to help me. He's the one who secured my scholarships and coached me with my decision about IBM, so I owe him a lot."

"Whatever," Emma shrugged. "You're the one who made it happen. You made the right contacts, and you've wisely decided you want to marry me!" She flashed a devilish smile. "What more can I say, Mr. Jackson? Besides, you're an incredibly handsome Italian man with devastating dark eyes and sexy hair. How could you *not* be successful?"

She smiled teasingly, and as Marco put the last box into the trailer and then lifted her into his arms. "I think we're ready to hit the road," he announced after kissing her. "Do you think your shiny red Chevy has the right *stuff* to pull this trailer to Illinois?"

"Never a doubt," she claimed. "To Illinois and beyond! You're a lightweight, Marco, so get in and quit doubting my Chevy."

She had to use a parking lot for making a U-turn, but Emma bubbled with confidence as she maneuvered her car and trailer onto the highway.

"Our next stop is a little country church in southern Illinois."

~

*Th*e church accommodated maybe a hundred people if everyone sat shoulder to shoulder, and they knew it would be packed. Nostalgia filled the air as neighbors and distant friends enjoyed an opportunity to stand outside on a warm June afternoon anticipating a joyous celebration of love. Marco and Emma had come home, and many of their guests remembered them as children and reminisced about the good old days.

"We'll, we're not kids anymore," Marco explained. "We're both 24, and that's old enough to know what's what."

The older ones laughed and picked up on his humor.

"That's a good one, Marco, but it's good family values that makes our kids want to come home again," said elderly Mr. Jenkins. "My two children did the same and were both married right here in our little church."

Marco remembered, but now it was his turn, and he was relieved when the minister signaled them to go inside. Emma had remained sequestered in a small office near the main door of the church. Her father was totally caught up in reconnecting with friends and almost forgot he would be escorting his daughter down the aisle. However, once everyone was attentively inside, Emma's mother opened the door, and David Downing proudly took his place at Emma's side. Marco had not seen her since early morning, but as she approached the altar in her beautiful gown, he nearly burst with pride. He realized life allows us only a few exceptional moments, and this was clearly one of them.

~

*I*t seemed ironic that neither Marco nor Emma had ever been to Chicago; however, it wasn't unusual for rural families to avoid the big city. They left their U-Haul trailer and stacks of wedding gifts in temporary storage near his mother's apartment. With two small suitcases and their recently waxed red Chevy, they ventured into the metropolis. They'd made reservations for a hotel just south of Chicago's "Magnificent Mile" near the shores of Lake Michigan. Emma was sitting bolt upright and gripping the steering wheel, as she maneuvered through increasingly heavy traffic once they reached the city.

"Whew!" Emma exclaimed. "This is intense! However, the traffic's the same as in Boston! Who can live in such congestion?"

She skillfully found the hotel and sighed once they were parked. They got the suitcases and rode the elevator to the lobby. Marco was all business at the reservations counter. It was the first time they'd registered as Mr. and Mrs. Jackson. It seemed to give him a different attitude.

"Mr. and Mrs. Jackson," he said in a commanding voice.

"Yes, I have your reservation!" the clerk announced. "Here you are, and I see you're planning to be with us four days. Is that correct?"

Marco nodded yes and proceeded to fill out the form.

"We'll settle your account when you check out," she said with a big smile. "Enjoy your stay."

They declined a porter's offer to help with their bags, and Emma was especially pleased when they opened the door to their room. She immediately ran to the window and realized they had a partial view of the lake.

"This is really nice," she boasted. "Actually, it's about the same size as our place at MIT, but it's much less constrained."

Marco watched and waited because she seemed joyously happy.

"Since it's our honeymoon, shall we make a baby?"

Emma smiled and rushed into his arms.

"What a lovely idea, Mr. Jackson!"

After being together for such a long time, making love to Emma was certainly not new, but her playfulness was refreshing.

"Are you being serious or just playful?"

"Maybe both," she replied. "Now that we're married, I'm ready to try again."

"Absolutely," he agreed and lovingly carried her to the bed.

It may have been the novelty of being on their honeymoon, but for whatever reason, it was intense, and afterwards, as they lay in each other's arms, there was no need for words.

~

"It's a long shot," Marco admitted as they lingered over breakfast on their third morning at the hotel, "but I seriously want to check out a promising lead to find my father." He handed Emma the little notebook of research and pointed to an entry he'd underlined.

Emma looked at his notes with interest. "This one?" she asked and read the address: *Conti's Italian Cuisine,* 670 Michigan Avenue.

"It's not far from here, so I'd like to check it out."

"Let's do it," she agreed. "After all, it's our honeymoon, so we should go out for Italian."

He smiled, but inside, his gut was already tightening over the possibility of actually finding his birth father. Then he looked in the hotel's guest services book to see if the restaurant might be listed. The ads were listed by types of cuisine, and the last listing under "Italian" was indeed *Conti's Italian Cuisine,* so he dialed the number and asked for dinner reservations at six o'clock.

"Dinner for two at six," replied the perky representative. "And your name, Sir?"

"Jackson . . . Mr. and Mrs. Jackson."

"We'll see you at six, Mr. Jackson. Will that be all?"

Marco hesitated. "I'm interested in meeting Mr. Antonio Conti. Is this by chance his family's restaurant?"

There was a noticeable pause as the representative covered the phone and spoke in muffled tones to someone nearby. Then, when she took her hand away from the phone, she spoke in a more serious tone "Mr. Conti seldom greets guests in his restaurant. Would he know you for some reason?"

Marco fought his nerves and took a deep breath. "If he's the right Mr. Conti, I'm his son." The silence was deafening. "Hello! Are you still there?"

She made some nonverbal sounds, and Marco heard noises, which sounded like rummaging through things in a drawer.

"Yes, Mr. Jackson! Please forgive the delay. I needed to find my note pad, so if you'll give me your full name, I'll let Mr. Conti know."

"Just tell him *Marco Donato* from southern Illinois."

"I'll make sure he gets the message. We'll see you at six this evening."

He hung up the phone and looked at Emma with a surprised expression. "Well, that was interesting."

"I heard what you said," Emma whispered as though they were having a secret conversation. "What happened?"

"I think she covered the phone, because I only heard muffled voices. I imagine she was conferring with the manager, but then she came back on-line, asked for my name and said she'd let Mr. Conti know."

Emma looked at Marco wide-eyed. "What if he's really your dad?"

Marco nodded matter-of-factly. "If he is, I want to ask him a few questions."

EIGHT

Emma and Marco arrived at the restaurant around a quarter to six and were surprised when a doorman held the door for them.

"Buona sera e benvenuto!"

"Thank you," Marco said and Emma smiled.

Once inside, they immediately noticed the rich, authentic Italian décor and that most of the tables were occupied. Soft Italian music filled the room as all male white-coated waiters moved easily among the guests. A wonderful aroma of Italian cuisine filled the air, and Emma held tightly to Marco's arm feeling slightly uneasy about being among such sophisticated people. Although Marco had thoughtfully worn a sports coat, they were dressed casually in stark contrast to the more formal attire of other patrons.

"We're going to stand out like sore thumbs," Emma complained.

"We're fine, so don't sweat it."

"May I help you?" asked the hostess.

Marco's jaw dropped. She was his image of a Hollywood starlet, petite and flawlessly beautiful like a model. Emma noticed his reaction and took hold of his arm as though restraining him from being too interested. However, they both noticed her tight-fitting evening gown, her gleaming pearl necklace and her diamond bracelet. Then she smiled and looked directly at Marco waiting for him to announce their name.

"Mr. and Mrs. Jackson," he said in a rather high-pitched voice. "We have reservations for six o'clock."

She looked for his name in a small, palm-sized notepad, which she carried in her hand, and he noticed a bold asterisk next to his name.

"Come with me please."

Emma only noticed Marco's fixation with their hostess as she moved provocatively among the tables and led them to a very private corner partially obscured by brocade panels giving it the appearance of being a discreet meeting place. She held Emma's chair and then handed them their napkins once they were seated.

Crystal water glasses had already been filled and sparkled in candlelight on a table covered with white linen and set with fine china and sterling silver utensils. Their hostess waited until they had smoothed their napkins on their laps, and then she handed them leather-bound menus.

"Our special this evening is Veal Scaloppini, Mr. Jackson, and I must tell you, it's exceptional."

Emma waited for her to at least nod in her direction, but instead, she smiled at Marco and then sashayed back to her station near the entrance.

Marco fumbled with his menu, but out of the corner of his eye, he saw her discreetly smile at him before returning to her duties.

Emma tried to ignore their little exchange of glances, and then, as she scanned the menu, she fixated on the prices. All items were à la Carte with entrees beginning around $45 and higher.

"Marco! Do you have enough money for this?" she whispered.

He was also looking at the prices and whispered, "Yes! We're good!"

Emma rolled her eyes just as their waiter arrived with two bottles of Italian wine.

"Buonasera! Mi chiamo Aldo," he said and tapped his name badge. "Questi sono i nostri migliori vini Italiani."

Marco wrinkled his brow and shrugged.

"Scusami! Parlerò inglese! Would you prefer white or red wine?"

Marco quickly flipped his menu to the last page and noted the wine list, where everything was $65 and up, so he nonchalantly declined. "My wife and I prefer water," he replied and averted a scolding look from the waiter.

"Chiedo scusa, Signore, Compliments of the house," he said. "Do you prefer white or red?" Then he looked at Emma. "If I may, bella signora, I'll recommend the Pillastro!" He held the bottle for Emma to see. "Va bene!"

Emma nodded slightly, and Marco gave his consent as the waiter proceeded to open the wine and pour just a snippet into the glass for him to taste.

He complied and nodded yes, so then he filled their glasses before draping his napkin over his arm, bowing slightly, and properly returning to the kitchen.

"Compliments of the house," Marco repeated and raised his glass.

Emma cautiously followed his example and touched her glass to his, and then, just as they were taking their first sip, the attractive hostess with the diamond bracelet, returned.

"We're pleased to have you dining with us this evening, Mr. Jackson, and Mr. Conti will greet you at your table in just a couple of minutes." Once again, she ignored Emma, and as she walked away, she looked over her shoulder to once again smile at Marco.

"I think she likes you," Emma exclaimed, "and it appears we're going to meet Mr. Conti."

Marco felt his body stiffen. "This could be a mistake," he admitted, "and if it is, we may end up in the poor house if we have to pay for the wine as well as the dinner."

The words were no sooner out of his mouth than they saw an elegant Italian man walking toward their table. He was every bit the likeness of Marco . . . so much so, Emma audibly gasped. He was nearly the same height and build with wavy dark hair and a sparkling diamond stud holding his tie in place.

"Bouna sera!"

"Hello," Marco stammered and tried to stand.

Mr. Conti smiled and motioned for him to stay seated. "No! Si prega di rimanere seduti," he chided. "There's no need to be formal," and then he extended his hand in greeting. "I'm Antonio Conti, and you must be Marco."

Marco nodded yes, and Emma's eyes were still making comparisons.

"And may I have the honor of meeting this elegant young lady?" He reached to take hold of her hand, bowed, and then kissed her hand.

"This is my wife, Emma."

Conti bowed graciously a second time, and when he smiled at her, Emma felt her heart racing. He was an older version of Marco, and it was disconcerting.

Then Conti raised his hand and snapped his fingers, which signaled the hostess to bring him a chair. She responded quickly and did so with such grace it seemed scripted. Mr. Conti nodded and smiled at her as she did a slight curtsy and walked away with her swaying hips capturing Marco's full attention.

"And Marco, you mentioned to our receptionist you're from southern Illinois. Is that correct?"

Once again Marco nodded yes and felt his nerves tighten.

"And why would you want to bring that to my attention?"

Marco took a deep breath and paused briefly to take a sip of his wine.

Emma waited breathlessly.

"I was adopted at birth," he said as clearly as possible, "and my birth parents were named Conti."

Antonio stared intensely at Marco without saying a word, causing him to fidget with his napkin.

"And what was your birth mother's name?"

"Frederica!"

"And may God rest her soul," Conti exclaimed. "She was the love of my life, and I remember it well."

Emma suddenly broke her silence and said the obvious. "Is it true? You *are* Marco's birth father!"

"It appears I may be," Conti admitted. "There's a resemblance, don't you think?" Then he leaned closer to Marco so Emma could compare their features.

She was so caught off-guard she couldn't respond.

Marco felt a sudden surge of emotion, which was very hard to handle. He took another quick sip from his glass hoping to bolster his courage. "I have questions!" he said tersely.

"I imagine you do," Antonio interrupted, "but I'd prefer you ask those questions at a more appropriate time. For the moment, I have other business, which cannot wait, so I want you to enjoy your wine, and I highly recommend the Veal Scaloppini." Then he stood to leave. "I've enjoyed meeting you and your lovely bride, Emma." He bowed slightly as the hostess reappeared to retrieve his chair. "Enjoy your dinner, and I'll pick up the tab for this one. If you'd like to sit down and talk about those questions, you may arrange such a meeting by contacting my lovely associate Capricia." He handed Marco a business card and then walked away.

Emma noticed as he neared the front door of the restaurant, two rather tall men came quickly to his side and left with him.

Their hostess had returned to her place by the door, and as Marco looked at the card, Emma noticed his hand shaking slightly.

"Are you okay?" she asked and touched his hand.

He handed her the card without saying a word. She read the word "Capricia," which was followed by a telephone number, and then she noticed "The Outfit" printed below the number.

She handed it back to Marco and shrugged. "It's unusual to have only one name on a business card," she said with a confused expression.

"And it's even more unusual to have *The Outfit* listed without some sub-text saying what it means."

She took the card from him and looked at it again. "You're right! What's *The Outfit*?"

"I can't say for sure," Marco whispered, "but I think it's another name for *The Mob.*"

"The Mob?"

"The Chicago Mob . . . the Mafia," he explained. "I think Antonio Conti may be a member of The Mob."

Emma felt a shudder run the length of her spine. She was basically unaware of such things, but *The Mob* sounded sinister. Then she remembered his attire and how he'd been very European in kissing her hand. He also had a large diamond ring on his right hand, and he was wearing distinctive cologne, which was nearly intoxicating. Then it occurred to her that his suit was made with such detail it had to be an Armani.

"My, God, Marco! Are you seriously considering getting connected with this guy?"

Marco shrugged. "I have questions. I'd at least like to ask why he gave me up for adoption."

Emma rolled her eyes and wrinkled her expression.

~

The Veal Scaloppini truly was exceptional, and by the time they left the restaurant, Marco had studied the business card repeatedly.

Contact my lovely assistant and then what?

"Put the card in your wallet, Marco! Keep it as a memento! You've found your birth father, and if he's with the mob, I think you should leave well enough alone."

He did as she suggested, but he still wanted to know more.

~

They retrieved the trailer and most of their stuff from the storage unit in Harrisburg. His mother agreed to ship the rest of it after they were settled in San Jose. It was a sad goodbye, and she was already complaining about him being so far away.

"Maybe there's a way for me to come for a visit after you get established," she suggested. "If I ever have a grandchild I'm going to demand my rights."

There were smiles and hugs all around as they prepared to leave, and Emma unexpectedly reacted emotionally.

Aileen sighed. "You're the daughter I never had, and I love you with all my heart."

They waved vigorously as they drove away, and Marco was still debating why he hadn't mentioned what happened in Chicago, but maybe he would later.

The Chevy overheated south of Las Vegas, and they had to delay a whole day while having the radiator and water pump replaced. The mechanic especially liked Emma's car, and if there had been a way to do it, she could have easily sold it to him for a profit, but since there was nothing better available, they hitched the trailer to the car and were on their way

"No more breakdowns!" Marco demanded.

"We're good to go!" Emma exclaimed as she pulled onto the highway for the final leg of their journey.

~

Arriving in San Jose without a place to live proved challenging, but Marco placed a call to his contact person at IBM, and they were quickly rescued.

"I doubt that every new employee gets treated like this," Emma observed. "It's like you're royalty."

Marco laughed. "I'm not sure why either, but I kind of like the attention."

Not only were they rescued but also generously assisted in finding a suitable home, which would be conveniently located near public transportation, excellent schools and surrounded by some amazing community resources. They loved the house they found, and when it came time to make an offer, the realtor asked where he'd be working.

"IBM Research and Development," he announced proudly.

"Oh, my," she exclaimed. "I should have known! You're the Mr. Jackson from MIT."

"I guess my reputation precedes me," he said with a sheepish grin.

"Well, our real estate company has a close working relationship with IBM, and they always alert us when a new executive is moving into the area."

He hadn't heard the term *executive* mentioned before, so he reacted with surprise. "Well, thank you! You've certainly helped us find a perfect house, but I not sure how to manage a down payment because I have yet to receive my first paycheck."

"It's not a problem, Mr. Jackson. The company will secure your loan."

Emma looked at Marco with surprise and was beginning to wonder why. There were signing bonuses, lots of gifts from wealthy friends at the wedding, a honeymoon in Chicago, a meeting with someone from The Mob, and now he was being offered a secured loan from IBM without ever lifting a finger.

Who is this guy anyway?

Marco glanced at her and noticed her wide-eyed expression.

"Well, there you go," he said flippantly. "We love the house, so let's buy it."

~

What followed was a whirlwind of surprises. Marco's salary was in the six figures range with full medical and retirement benefits and a full month of vacation to be used at his discretion any time after his first six months of employment. Emma wondered what a person's expected to do for that kind of money and privilege. However, she adapted to the good life rather quickly and began making friends in her new community. She also found that being Marco's wife gave her an immediate entrée into spousal benefits such as the IBM fitness facility and a variety of social events where she met other "executive" women, who seemed to know every elegant shop and restaurant in San Jose. When she let it be known she was an artist, three women she'd met socially wanted to see her art and maybe have an opportunity to collaborate with her about finding a gallery. In less than two months she was introduced to a number of art studios, and then, on their six-month anniversary in San Jose, she was invited to do a private showing of her work at Baterbys, which also offered a caveat of introducing her art both locally and internationally.

Marco's work was also attracting international attention. He was clearly the executive leader on research and development into the rapidly growing world of personal computers, and every week or so he made the news. Emma was stunned to see an article in the New York Times proclaiming, "Notable achievements at Big Blue in the Emerging Field of Personal Computing," and then found her husband's name prominently referenced in the first paragraph. It was more than she expected in her relationship with an Italian boy from southern Illinois. Amidst all his acclaim, they maintained their loving relationship, and she felt privileged to travel with him on short trips to conferences and seminars where he was usually a featured speaker.

"I'm so proud of you, Marco. Who would have ever thought such a life would be possible for two country kids from Illinois?"

"It seems a bit surreal to me too," he admitted, "but I'm just doing what I love to do." He smiled and touched her hand. "I remember your reaction in high school when you looked at my books on computing."

Emma laughed. "I do remember that! I didn't know how you made sense of it then, and I still don't know how you make sense of it now, but I'm glad to be Mrs. Jackson! I'm just along for the ride." She slightly cocked her head to the side as though having an important thought. "Speaking of rides," she said with a challenging glance in his direction, "we're going to need two cars and you need to learn to drive!"

Marco looked at her with surprise. "Why?"

"Because I'm not always going to be your personal chauffeur. What if you need to take a company car and go somewhere? IBM doesn't provide chauffeurs."

"Couldn't I just take public transportation?"

"Come on, Marco! You can do this! Take driver's training!"

He finally agreed, and within a few months he had his driver's license and his own car. He not only drove to business meetings, but he also convinced Emma she should ride with him for a weekend in Sausalito, which meant driving on freeways through San Francisco and across the Golden Gate Bridge. She hesitated but agreed. When the weekend arrived, Emma was tense, but they made it safely there and back, and she praised him for his skillful driving. As he stood proudly beside his car, he aristocratically raised his brow and savored her affirmation.

"Then I guess I've finally passed my driver's test," he boasted and she nodded her approval.

~

*L*ife turned into a routine, which was so intense they hardly had time to be together, and after a particularly difficult day, Marco suggested having a glass of wine on the patio.

"I think everything is going well," he said, "but we're like ships passing in the night."

"Well, our little jaunt to Sausalito was nice," she said with a satisfied expression.

"Right! It was good, but I think I'm ready for a vacation."

"We've barely been here a year! How can you take a vacation?"

"I have a great team, so all I have to do is tell them I'm taking a couple weeks off. It's not a problem. How about you? Are you ready for a vacation?"

Emma stared down at her wine glass, and Marco noticed she hadn't been drinking at all.

"I've been missing my period again, and I have an appointment with my doctor tomorrow."

Marco looked puzzled. "Oh, dear," he exclaimed. "That's not the kind of vacation I had in mind."

She raised her brow and looked at him knowingly. "If I'm pregnant again, it'll be different from last time. It feels different, and we have excellent medical care, so we'll see how it goes."

"Then I want to go with you to your appointment. I want this to be our special occasion, so I'll take the day off."

She sat her glass aside and sighed. "It feels good that you want to go with me. Maybe it's a sign that we need to be together more and stay focused on us rather than just work."

Then she relaxed into his arms and nestled her head against his chest. "It's all good," she whispered. "I miscarried before, but it's different this time. Even without the doctor, I know we're going to have a baby."

He sighed and hugged her tightly. "I can hardly wait for it to be confirmed! Just like you said, it's a sign. It's a wakeup call."

"I think so too," she agreed, "and it was so much fun getting into this predicament."

She smiled seductively, and Marco smiled as well.

"It's really not a predicament, and you're right; making babies is a deliriously happy experience, which lasts only a few moments, but having babies changes life forever. I'm ready if you are."

~

*L*ater that night, Marco stood alone in front of their bathroom mirror, and as he stared at his image he remembered Antonio Conti. Then he fumbled in his wallet to find the business card Conti had given him and studied the single name "Capricia". *I wonder who she is?* His conversation with Emma left him with uneasy feelings. *If we're going to have a baby, what does it mean for finding ways to settle my questions about my father?* He carefully replaced the card into a protected pocket in his wallet. It was something yet to be pursued.

~

*T*he doctor smiled and nodded matter-of-factly when she showed Marco and Emma the lab results. "Everything is positive," she said. "If my calculations are correct, you'll become parents before the end of March next year."

On their way home, they both felt a sense of well being, but Emma was especially happy, and Marco thought she looked rather rosy-cheeked and bright-eyed.

"I'm feeling more energized than I ever thought possible," she exclaimed.

"I don't think you overheard," Marco said as they were turning into their neighborhood, "but I asked Dr. Denton if it would be okay for you to take a vacation."

"You're right! I didn't hear that, so what did she say?"

"She said yes," he exclaimed, "but she also said not to be gone too long. She wants you in for routine visits."

"Marco, you are so damn persistent."

"I know, but I can hardly wait to see my mother's expression when we tell her the good news."

"And that means a trip to Harrisburg, I guess?"

"And then after a few days in New York, it also means a trip to Fresno before coming home."

"You're like a school kid, who wants to brag about his achievements."

"I'm like a proud husband, who wants our baby's grandparents to know what's coming."

Emma smiled and hesitantly agreed but with the caveat of some careful planning and a confirmation call to her doctor.

~

Their plane touched down at Lambert International in St Louis at 11:55 a.m. on a warm summer's day in June. They rented a car for the drive to Harrisburg where they planned to stay a couple of days with Marco's mother, and then they would return to St Louis for a flight to New York. Neither of them had been to New York before, so they had big plans for doing all the touristy stuff if it wasn't too much for Emma's condition. They'd already booked a hotel in lower-Manhattan and had a couple sightseeing tours on their to do list.

It was only a short drive from St Louis to Harrisburg, and Marco's mother was ecstatic to see them. They'd checked in by phone, so she was watching for them and ran to greet them when they arrived. When Emma told her she was pregnant, she nearly burst with joy.

"Oh, my," she exclaimed. "I'm going to be a grandma."

Marco smiled, but then he recalled his sadness when he'd learned his birth mother had died on the day he was born. However, Emma literally glowed with health and vitality.

"It's good to see you, Mom!"

He almost wanted to say, *your adopted son is going to be a father,* but he censured the thought and hugged her as she continued wiping away her tears of joy.

They had a lot of catching up to do, but by the second day of their visit, their conversations were wearing thin. Emma busied herself by making phone calls to various galleries and then surprised Eileen by announcing the sale of two more of her paintings. Marco enjoyed her success, but each time she gained recognition, he slipped into a quiet mood.

I wonder how it's going to be with a baby in our lives. I'm a busy executive, and she's becoming a prominent artist.

Later, while still pondering his questions, he took a solo walk by the lake and enjoyed sitting on a bench; however, his concerns remained unresolved. Then, for some unknown reason, he opened his wallet and looked again at the business card Antonio Conti had given him.

I wonder if I'll ever know who she is? Then he saw Emma approaching and slipped the card into his pocket.

"What are you doing out here by yourself?"

"Oh, hi!" he said and scooted over so she could sit down. "I'm just day-dreaming."

"About what?"

"Oh, about becoming a father and wondering what my actual parents were thinking when I was born."

Emma shrugged and reached to hold his hand. "There are things you may never know, Marco."

"Except for my real dad," he countered. "He knows."

"However, he might not want to answer your questions!"

Marco shrugged. "I'd at least like to give him a chance to tell me the truth. When I think about our baby, I can't imagine just walking away when she's born."

"She?" Emma exclaimed. "How do you know our baby's a girl?"

Marco laughed. "Did I *say* she?"

"Yes, you said *she* very clearly, and I'd love to have a daughter too."

"Then that settles it! We're having a baby girl, and when we get back home, we'll have Dr. Denton confirm it."

"I wonder what Mr. Conti would say if we told him he's going to be a grandpa?"

"Well, that's another question I could ask him."

"You'll probably never know," Emma counseled.

Then Marco handed her the business card, which he'd slipped into his shirt pocket.

"I wonder who she is," he said pointing to Capricia's name.

"Don't get any ideas, Marco. Capricia needs to remain a mystery! I didn't know you'd kept the card."

"I did! It's wrinkled from being in my wallet, but you never know, there may come a time when I'll have an opportunity to call Capricia."

Emma grimaced! "I hope not."

She handed him the card, raised her brow and shook her head. "Keep it if you want, but let's stay focused on how an executive and an artist can be good parents to the their little girl."

~

New York exceeded their expectations. Marco's good income gave them the luxury of going beyond what most folks could afford, so they did the tours, tipped generously and dined at elegant restaurants. When it was time to leave, they still had a lot of things on their to-do list, but he promised they'd return after the baby was born.

"We've been gone a little over a week, so how are you doing? Are you ready for the final leg of our vacation?"

Emma stretched and sipped her morning coffee. "I'm feeling pretty good," she said confidently. "However, I'm ready to go home."

"What about visiting your parents in Fresno?"

"Maybe we could go home, rest up and then drive there."

"That's doable! It's only a two-hour drive."

"I'd prefer that! I'm a little weary of traipsing in and out of airports, so let's go home first."

"It's a deal! I'll book our flight."

Emma was clearly feeling her pregnancy, and Marco was aware of her moods. At the moment she was being cooperative, but he wasn't sure what to expect once they'd returned to San Jose.

~

*Th*eir plane landed safely at San Francisco International after bumping through some very rough air, which caused Emma to grip the armrests and stare blankly at the seat back in front of her. Marco put his hand on her arm, but panic had its way.

"Good lord," Emma exclaimed. "I may never fly again."

Marco sighed and felt her arm trembling beneath his touch.

"We're safely on the ground, so take a deep breath and relax."

She did as instructed but could hardly wait to exit the plane.

"I didn't realize it until now, but I'm really tired, Marco. I'm not even looking forward to riding the shuttle to the parking lot."

"You're a trooper, Hon! When we get to the car, you can recline the seat and rest on the way home."

"Home sounds really good! I thought I was going to be sick before we landed."

"Well, I'm glad we made trip, but it was a little presumptuous to put you through it."

She glanced at him, and when he opened the car door for her, she fell silent and rested uncomfortably on the ride home.

"I'm exhausted," she said after arriving and left Marco to deal with their luggage. "I'm going to take a nap."

He nodded and watched her fumbling for her keys to open the door.

Once they were inside, it seemed like the end rather than a pause in their journey.

I'm wondering if we'll even make it to Fresno!

NINE

Marco used the excuse of needing to return to his job on Monday in order to get Emma to agree to visit her parents in Fresno. On Friday evening, they'd just finished their dinner when she finally said okay.

"We'll make it a short visit," he promised. "We'll leave tomorrow morning, stay the night and return on Sunday."

Emma rolled her eyes as though completely uninterested, and he wasn't sure why. Her parents were not aware of her pregnancy, and he thought she'd be excited to share the good news. However, her moods were becoming unpredictable, and mostly he noticed her silence. Her favorite communication was to roll her eyes and twist her expression into a frown.

"We can travel light," he suggested. "Do you want to use your small suitcase?"

"Whatever!"

Apparently that means yes!

However, Emma made no effort to pack anything for an overnight stay with her parents, so Marco made the selections for her and packed both suitcases. When he returned to the living room, she was sprawled in her favorite chair and sound asleep.

It looks like we'll have a really fun trip.

Later, he awakened her and coaxed her to go to bed. She reluctantly complied and left him staring at a meaningless program on TV.

The next morning she complained about a backache and resisted his eagerness to be on their way. By default, he took care of everything including breakfast, which she tasted but pushed aside. He left her at the table, while he loaded the car, checked the windows and doors, and then ushered her into the car.

"If you're seriously not interested in making this trip, we can pull the plug on it."

"No, I'm okay! Let's just do it, and maybe I'll feel better by the time we get there."

Her judgment was partially true. He endured moody silence for the next 90 minutes until they arrived in Fresno, and then spent another thirty minutes locating her parent's home, which was quite a distance from Phillip's Gardens. However, she seemed to revive when he pulled into their driveway and her parents ran enthusiastically to greet them.

Emma straightened her clothing and fluffed her hair before embracing her mother and father.

"It's been so long, Em! We're so glad you're here."

David Downing proceeded to give Marco a manly hug and shook his hand vigorously. "You're looking great, Marco," he exclaimed. "I want to hear all about your work at IBM."

Once inside, Emma immediately plopped down in a chair, and her mother noticed her mood had changed.

"Are you tired, Em?"

She shook her head yes and then blurted out their reason for coming. "I'm pregnant!" she said unapologetically.

"Oh, my, god!" her mother squealed. "We're going to have a grand baby!"

Audrey ran to embrace Emma, and David energetically pumped Marco's hand as though congratulating him on impregnating his daughter. It was a happy time, and when their joyous behavior returned to normal, Marco added his assessment.

"She's doing really well, but we've just returned from a New York vacation, and I think it may have been a little too much for Em."

"Oh, my," exclaimed Audrey. "It's such wonderful news. When's the baby due?"

"Toward the end of March next year," Marco proudly announced as Emma remained seated and rolled her eyes.

"Oh, I can hardly wait," Audrey shouted and reached for David's hand to share her happy feelings.

The accolades continued until Audrey decided to prepare some lunch and make some tea. Marco thought Emma might get up from her chair to help her mother, but alas, she remained unmoved, and her behavior remained consistent into the evening. Marco provided most of the conversation and talked extensively about IBM, Emma's paintings and how they were looking forward to having a baby. However, when they were finally alone in their bedroom, Marco unloaded.

"You're about as much fun as a foggy day in San Francisco! What's going on? You've hardly said anything."

She looked at him and rolled her eyes without comment.

"It's difficult for me, Em. You could at least try."

"Try what?"

"Try to be somewhat social! Try to talk about anything rather than sitting there is such a sullen mood."

"Then you should be pregnant instead of me," she demanded. "I'm suddenly thinking that having a baby isn't worth the effort."

"That breaks my heart, Em! We were stunned but happy when the doctor confirmed your pregnancy. What's happened?"

"It's not worth explaining, Marco. I just feel lousy."

He took a deep breath and sighed. "Change into your PJ's, and I'll rub your back and help you feel better."

She shrugged but slipped out of her clothes and dug in her suitcase to find her pajamas. It was the first time he'd seen her nearly naked and noticed the slight swelling of her tummy and her fuller breasts. Then, after putting on her pajamas, she crawled under the covers and turned her back toward him without saying goodnight. He sat next to her and tried to stroke her shoulders, but she twisted away from his touch. It was a clear signal, so he sat forlornly as she slowly drifted into sleep.

Well, I tried, he thought. *Maybe she's right. Maybe having a baby isn't worth the effort.*

~

When Marco returned to his office on Monday morning, it was a reprieve. On Sunday evening, after returning home, Emma remained in her funky mood. She was refusing to eat and was showing signs of depression. He'd tried repeatedly to talk her into a better mood, but nothing seemed to work, so he silently committed to calling her doctor to explain the situation. He planned to make the call before noon, but in the meantime he relished the camaraderie of his team and the genuine excitement of catching up on their current projects.

"We've missed you, Marco, and it's been gangbusters while you were gone."

Kevin Hale, his friend and co-leader in R&D, preceded to review their progress and Marco did his best to absorb the details. It was an onslaught of data and excitement, which effectively brought him back on-board and diminished his concerns about Emma. However, he remembered to make the call to the doctor and was pleased with her compassionate thoughts about the ups and downs of emotions during pregnancy.

"She has an appointment to see me next week," she said, "and I promise to be a good listener. Believe me! Emma is certainly not my first distraught mother to be. We'll work it out, Marco, so you take care as well. With a little luck we'll deliver this baby and bring blessings into your lives."

He felt encouraged by her optimism, but when it was time to go home that evening, Marco continued working, and when Kevin rescued him they went to a local bar for a little one-on-one therapy. When he finally parked his car in the garage and went inside, Emma had already gone to bed, so the estrangement continued.

TEN

On March 27, 1961, which was a rather nice day in San Jose, Emma gave birth to Celine Aileen Jackson, a precious 7 pound 2 ounce baby girl with rather impressive dark hair. Marco and the attending nurses agreed she was a beautiful baby. When they placed her in Emma's arms, Emma radiated joy and contentment.

"She's perfectly beautiful," he whispered, and Emma smiled.

It was the beginning of a new chapter in their lives, and when they made phone calls to Celine's grandparents, it was a festival of joy. Audrey and David Downing had not seen Emma since their brief trip to Fresno, so they wanted them to come for a visit as soon as possible, and Aileen Jackson excitedly demanded they bring Celine to Illinois, as soon they were free to travel. Marco felt proud, and at the moment, he wanted nothing more than to keep the momentum going.

During Celine's first year, they took her for a short visit to Harrisburg, where Marco's mother fawned over her granddaughter as though God had granted an answer to her prayers. Then they traveled to Fresno, where the Downing's had an opportunity to be doting grandparents. Emma was more or less back to normal and was delighted with the love and happiness her child had brought into her life, and Marco beamed with pride as the father of such an adorable baby girl. He envisioned Celine becoming an amazing young woman and finding a career on the leading edge of science; however, Emma thought their daughter would naturally become an artist. Of course, those were dreams for Celine's future, but dreams for their marriage were not as clear or encouraging. Emma put her heart and soul into being a good mother, and Marco felt she was keeping her distance from him. There were "normal" times as well, but the excitement of being together was gone.

~

Time passed quickly, and Marco was very busy with his job. Each time Celine was down for a nap, Emma worked on her paintings. Just after Celine's first birthday, Emma was featured in an article because of her growing popularity as a west coast artist. She was elated, especially since caring for Celine left her very little time to devote to her painting. They were basking in the overdue recognition and enjoying frequent congratulatory calls in addition to invitations for Emma to display her art. It was a long awaited gift, which bolstered her ego and feelings of self-worth. However, Marco was also excelling in the field of computer science. Emma felt she could never rise above his executive status, and then his achievements became so notable he was listed among Time Magazine's 100 most influential people of the year. It should have been a time for mutual rejoicing, but in spite of their achievements, their relationship became more distant.

~

Celine was having a bad case of the terrible two's, which left Emma wondering how to cope without more help from Marco. He routinely left each morning to spend unreasonable hours at the office, while she had full the responsibility of keeping Celine under control. Marco would usually come home in the early evening around Celine's bedtime. By that time, Emma was nearly at her wit's end but looking forward to some moments of peace and quiet after putting Celine down for the night. When Marco arrived, Celine had usually just finished her bath and was powdery-fresh to greet her daddy, while Emma stood aside still dressed in her apron with sweaty strands of hair hanging over her eyes. Marco tended to ignore her and lavished his full attention on Celine. It was okay for a while, but Emma grew weary of his thanklessness and finally leveled him with anger.

"You really don't give a shit what I go through with this kid everyday."

He looked at her with surprise. "I beg your pardon?"

"It's true, Marco! I don't think you care at all. You leave the house every morning, including Saturdays sometimes, and go to the sanctuary of your office where everyone thinks you walk on water. It must be nice to enjoy your leisurely drive to work and to be surrounded by your friends, who enjoy the same things you enjoy. I spend mornings chasing after Celine and keeping her curious little hands out of everything, including coxing her to eat her food and not throw it all over the kitchen. I'm able to catch my breath when she's down for her nap, and then fight my way through until bath time, when I get her freshened up to see her daddy. During my long ordeal, you're enjoying your executive life style, and I don't think you care at all."

Marco bristled. "And what do you think I should do about it? I can't earn over a hundred grand a year by staying home to take care of Celine."

"I rest my case! It's just the way it is, but I damn sure think it's terribly out of balance."

He stared at her blankly and didn't know what else to say, so she turned away, ripped off her apron, forcefully took Celine from his arms and stormed into the bedroom to put their baby to bed. He thought she might mellow in the process, but when she returned, she directed him to help himself to some leftovers, and then went to their bedroom and slammed the door shut.

Marco knew she was right in her assessment of the situation, but he felt he was also right about the domestic cost of being an executive. He ate cold leftovers and then enjoyed a large glass of bourbon, while watching a game on TV. When he finally went into the bedroom, the soft glow of a nightlight outlined Emma's collapsed form surrounded by most of the covers, which she had pulled from his side of the bed. He knew there would be no virtue in trying to wake her or trying to soothe her feelings, so he quietly slipped into his pajamas and tried to put the tension out of his mind.

~

Celine awakened early the next morning and cried loudly for attention. Emma heard but groaned and pulled the covers over her head, so Marco lumbered into Celine's bedroom and did his best to quiet the storm. It actually worked quite well, and he managed to meet her needs and get her settled at the table for some breakfast before Emma finally shuffled out of the bedroom to see what had happened. Watching Marco's attentiveness amused her.

"Is this your compensating effort to heal the rift?"

He glanced at her and nearly reacted visibly to her haggard appearance.

"You obviously wanted to ignore Celine's crying, so I stepped up."

"Good job, Marco! This gives you a chance to see how easy it is. However, I'm confident you'll freshen up and be on you way at the normal time."

He glanced at the clock and realized he only had about 30 minutes to do exactly that, so without any explanation, he relinquished his time with Celine and hurried to the bathroom for a shower.

"I have a big meeting this morning, and if it goes well, we'll be enjoying a large bonus this year."

"If it goes well, I may be enjoying 30-40 minutes of free time to paint later today, and quite frankly my dear, I don't give a flying crap about your bonus."

Her words stung, but he didn't have time to talk about it, so he was out of the shower and on his way before Emma could wrinkle her brow to show her frustration.

~

*H*is meeting went well, and the bonus was no longer in question. Then, for the first time in a long while, Marco had some unscheduled time that afternoon and thoughtfully used it for himself. He would have normally gathered some friends for coffee and conversation, but instead, he shut the door to his office and rocked back in his chair to savor the moment. For some reason he checked his wallet to see if he had enough money to pay for a round of drinks during happy hour at the pub, and while checking, he pulled out the business card Antonio Conti had given him when they met in Chicago.

Capricia
702-312-4252
The Outfit

He'd looked at the card so many times its edges were worn from being forced in and out of his wallet. Each time brought back memories and his lingering need to find out more from his birth father.

It's been so long, I wonder if she would know who I am?

Then he thought of Emma's complaints and decided to make the call. A tiny surge of adrenalin tightened his nerves as he placed the card near his phone and touched the handset.

What harm can there be? I'll just ask how I might meet Antonio Conti again.

With that thought in mind, he dialed the number. It rang three times and he was ready to abort when a nearly angelic voice answered with a single word.

"Capricia!"

Marco softly cleared his throat. "Hi, Capricia, I'm Marco Jackson. How are you today?"

"I'm fine Mr. Jackson." Her voice was business-like and soothing. "Why does your name sound so familiar?"

"I'm calling about Mr. Conti. I'm his son."

There was a noticeable pause.

"Oh, my, goodness! Now I remember. You and your lovely wife met Mr. Conti at his restaurant a few years ago. How are you?"

"I'm doing quite well, and I'm surprised you know about the Chicago meeting."

She laughed softly. "I'm the hostess who seated you."

Marco memory did a fast rewind as he recalled the elegant and stunningly attractive hostess with a devastating smile. His recollection was clear, and he easily envisioned her loveliness.

"Oh, my, goodness," he exclaimed. "How could I ever forget you? I think my wife is attractive, but you were stunning in your white gown."

"Wow! You even remember the color. Thank you for the compliment . . . and if I may, Mr. Jackson, I must say I also remember how devastatingly handsome you are. In fact, you're like a younger version of Tony, whom I love with all my heart."

"You're kind! Anyway, he gave me your card and told me to call if I'd like to meet again, so I've decided to accept his offer."

"Tony will be ecstatic," she said softly. "However, it's been a long time, so I'll have to remind him." She laughed softly, and Marco could almost envision her smiling.

"I've been busy with life, but I really would like to meet him again because I have questions that only he can answer."

"Well," smiled Capricia, "I can arrange that whenever you're available. Are you planning to be in Vegas?"

Marco hesitated. "Vegas? I thought he was in Chicago?"

Capricia's laugh was playful and his vision of her smile teased him.

"We're from Chicago, but we've lived in Vegas for so long, it's truly become our home."

"When you say *we* I assume you two are married."

"Oh, my, goodness, no! I'm Tony's assistant. I love him with a passion, but only as his trusted friend. We've worked together so long, we're family." She paused. "Can you come to Vegas?"

"I have no plans to do so, but anything's possible."

"It would be wonderful to see you again. May I call you Marco?"

"Please! I wasn't sure what to expect, and I should have called a long time ago."

"No regrets, Marco! I'll tell Tony you called and that you'd like to see him again."

"That would be great."

"By the way, Las Vegas is a fun town, Marco, so if you come, I'll be your hostess."

"That would be an incentive. Thanks for being so gracious. I'm having good memories of you."

"I'm glad you called, and my, oh, my, you are so very much like Tony. Please call if you can work us into your schedule. Bye!"

He heard a "click" as the call disconnected and then he sat with the phone receiver in his hand until a loud signal from his phone reminded him to hang up.

Capricia! My, oh, my!

~

Marco's popularity over being featured in <u>Time Magazine</u>, caused an increasing demand for him to make presentations, and one day his company passed along a request for him to be a keynote speaker at a technology conference in Las Vegas. He could hardly believe the location. It seemed like an omen, which was an answer to Capricia's invitation. He quickly agreed to do it without conferring with Emma. It was after all, a part of his job to promote innovative ideas and to advance technology, so this would be just another conference.

"Hi, Capricia! It's Marco again."

"Oh, hi! Are you calling to say you're coming to Vegas?"

"It's ironic, but yes, I'll be attending a conference and would like to spend some time with Mr. Conti."

"Great, Marco! I just talked with him yesterday, and I know he'll be interested, so this will be perfect. We've been doing some background research on you after you called, and I'm pleased to tell you Tony's impressed with what you've accomplished. I think he's as interested in talking to you as you are in meeting with him. Also, I can hardly wait to see you again."

Marco's ego ballooned, but along with his fantasy of remembering Capricia, there was also an intense feeling of his real identity beginning to surface. It was the same feeling he'd had in Chicago when Conti greeted him. Even Emma recognized it, and he remembered she gasped when Antonio approached their table and she saw how much they resembled each other. He knew without asking he was looking into the face of his father. There was also an unusual feeling about Capricia. He remembered her affectionate glances, and just talking to her on the phone made his heart beat faster. He wanted to see both of them again.

"It's hard for me to believe this opportunity came along so quickly, but when I learned it would be in Las Vegas, I said yes immediately."

"It's perfect Marco. Tony will be very pleased."

There was seductiveness in her voice, and he knew she was encouraging him.

"I'm pleased as well, and I'm looking forward to it."

"When's the conference?"

"It's next month. It starts on Monday the 16th and ends on the 19th. I'll arrive on Sunday and probably leave for home the evening of the 19th."

"Is it okay for me to tell Tony about your schedule?"

"Absolutely! I have a presentation on the 16th but there's always time to slip away to see my father. I've been to these conferences before, and there are so many people no one notices if you're gone a while."

"Then I'll try to put you on his calendar for Tuesday the 17th and check with you again when you arrive. Tony has friends everywhere, so he'll know when you're arriving. In other words, we'll be expecting you."

"Great!" Marco said with confidence "I'll see you soon."

He envisioned her smile and waited for the call to disconnect. Something told him he'd crossed a line, but it was something he really wanted and had been thinking about for a long time. However, his moral backbone was twitching.

Days passed before he said anything to Emma. He was hoping to catch her in a good mood, but given the circumstances, her *good* moods were few and far between, so after a couple of weeks, he happened to arrive home at a reasonable hour and boldly made his announcement.

"I have an out-of-state conference coming up the week of the 15th."

"Where?"

"It's in Las Vegas."

She laughed mockingly. "Well, that should make the everyone happy. I'd be surprised if anything gets done."

"I'm on the agenda."

"I'm sure you are. You've become so important I hardly know you anymore."

"It's part of my job, Em. It doesn't matter where it's at; it's part of my job."

"Well, have fun," she said. "You're gone more than you are home anyway, so I'll be right here keeping Celine out of trouble and hopefully selling my paintings."

ELEVEN

Sometimes a brief moment in time changes everything, and meeting Antonio Conti had been one of those moments for Marco. It had especially changed his self-image, a change that was affecting his life dramatically. Although he'd moved on with his career, he'd never forgotten Conti's invitation to meet again. During the time between then and now, he'd more or less pushed the idea to the back of his mind, but he'd also frequently looked at Capricia's business card and wondered what would happen if he should call. When he finally decided to do it, it was stressful, but hearing her voice instantly brought back memories of her exquisite beauty and the excitement he felt when meeting his father. It had been a long time coming, but now he was on the verge of fulfilling his lingering desire to lay claim to his Italian heritage. When he left home for the airport, Emma was overtly casual. She'd managed to shout "Goodbye" from Celine's bedroom with no mention of love or good wishes.

~

The plane landed in Las Vegas on a blistering hot afternoon. His plan was to retrieve his luggage and go straight to the Sahara Hotel where his air-conditioned room would be his refuge during the conference. He remembered Capricia's comment about Conti keeping tabs on his expected guests, but had no idea she'd meet him at the airport. When he heard her call his name, he spun around in total surprise to behold a vision of loveliness.

"Marco," she called, and ran to greet him. "I'd almost given up any hope of ever seeing you again."

He wasn't sure how to react, but her smile and closeness invited a brief social hug. He wanted to speak but went mute with excitement. To say the least, Capricia was beyond beautiful. Her perfect body was so alluring he couldn't take his eyes off of her. She radiated sexuality. Her white Capri slacks revealed her perfect curves, and her cotton blouse added a touch of innocence. The fragrance of her exotic perfume made his head spin, and then he felt the softness of her black hair caress his cheek as she stepped away but continued holding his hand. He couldn't recall ever using the word "flawless," but it was the only word that came to mind when he felt the satin-softness of her skin and her delicate fingers holding his hand. Finally, she motioned toward the baggage claim sign, and they walked together.

"I assume you have luggage?"

"I checked one suitcase."

"My friends tell me you're staying at the Sahara. Is that correct?"

He wrinkled his brow questioningly. "Yes," he said with surprise.

She smiled. "I know they're hosting the conference, so I just assumed."

"My goodness! You almost know more than I do."

She smiled coyly and led the way staying slightly ahead of him, and he couldn't take his eyes off her. He wasn't the only one, because as they continued their walk toward baggage claim, every passing man strained to get a better look.

His suitcase was one of the last on the carousel, so he grabbed it and she directed him toward the parking garage. When they arrived at her white Cadillac, she opened the trunk for his luggage and motioned for him to get inside as she slipped behind the wheel. He was at a loss for what to say, so he turned toward her and touched her arm.

"Thanks for meeting me! I've never forgotten how beautiful you are."

It was a rather bold statement, and his voice was tense when he said it. However, she smiled graciously and sighed. "And I've never forgotten you," she said with a quick toss of her hair. "It's out of the ordinary for me to talk about my feelings, but I'm really glad you're here, Marco." Then she made a demure expression and smiled before starting the car.

He shielded his eyes from the sun as they emerged into daylight and sped toward downtown. A blur of buildings, cars, and people seemed surreal.

When they arrived at the Sahara, he noticed two valets greeted her as "Miss Parisi," and when she got out of the car to open the trunk, it caused quite a stir among people passing by.

"You surprised me by meeting me at the airport, but I'm really enjoying your personal attention."

"It's been my pleasure, Marco. I hope you have a great day tomorrow, and I'll leave a message for you about meeting Tony. I think it'll be Tuesday afternoon or evening."

He intended to pick up his suitcase and wave goodbye, but she opened her arms for another hug, and he felt her press firmly against him. Then she smiled and waved as she returned to her car. With the confidence of a woman who knows she's beautiful, she graciously allowed a valet to assist her into the car and then pulled away without looking back. Marco watched until she disappeared from view and went inside, where his senses were assaulted by the din of noisy people, clanging slot machines and loud music.

~

There was a flurry of activity on the first day of the conference, and Marco enjoyed the insights and energy from other attendees. He was one of the first featured speakers, which gave him immediate recognition and respect. He was in his element and quickly made connections with people interested in his work at IBM; however, he found it difficult to stay focused. Every time there was a lull in the activity, he thought of Capricia to a point of being obsessive. He had people lining up to talk to him about his role in the recent launch of a family of IBM computers using interchangeable software, but he grew weary of their questions. He also had people clamoring to hear about IBM's next big thing, but he wasn't interested to speculate. Because he had made news with various publications in journals, magazines and newspapers, people even wanted his autograph, but that grew old as well. His mind was on meeting his father, and everything else was fading into the background.

By the end of the day he was weary of having conversations. What he wanted most was to be left alone, but instead, he voluntarily had dinner and cocktails with two other presenters and tried to stay engaged with their ideas and enthusiasm. However, when they ordered dessert and after dinner drinks, he excused himself and wearily went to his room. It was just 9:00 p.m. when he dropped his satchel onto the bed and plopped down in a chair. He knew most conference goers would be going out on the town to gamble in the casinos and enjoy lavish shows, but he needed to be alone. Sounds from the street below faintly drifted into the silence, as he sat quietly in the darkness and watched flickering lights from neon signs dancing on the ceiling.

Finally, Marco turned on the lights, and after sorting through various papers and studying the next day's agenda, he called Emma. She had just finished her routine with Celine and surprised him by being quite cordial.

"So, how's it going?" she asked nonchalantly.

"I'm weary! It's been a long day."

"How was your presentation?"

It sounded like a "ho-hum" question, so he tried to tweak his answer to be more positive.

"It went really well, and I've been hounded by techies wanting to know more."

"Of course, Marco! You're a celebrity."

He ignored the comment. "How are you doing?"

"There's nothing new to report from here. Celine has been cranky. I think it's her teeth, so I'm glad she's finally asleep."

"I do appreciate what you do."

"Of course you do, but you're an executive, and I'm just a mom."

And I guess I'm a poor excuse for being a dad, he thought.

"Are you in your room? I'm surprised there's no background noise."

"Yep! I was invited to go barhopping, but I declined. I needed to get away from people and get some rest."

"Well, there are no bars and neon lights here. It's the same ritual with little or no time for my painting, and yes, I'm complaining!"

"You're amazing," he said. "You manage everything so well, and I'm aware of how privileged I am to be unrestricted in my work and to be gone so much."

"I'm glad you're aware; however, it is what it is, and I've accepted my role as a stay at home mom, and it's my job to soothe our cranky daughter. What's up for tomorrow?"

"It'll be another full day, and because my work has received so much publicity, I get cornered every time there's a little break in the agenda."

"Oh, my, it must be a burden to be so popular." She paused, and he grimaced. "Are any of your groupies beautiful young women?"

"Of course, Emma! I have a hard time knowing if they're attracted to my work or to my gorgeous physique." It was an attempt to be funny, and he hoped she'd laugh, but there was only silence. "Anyway," he continued, "I need to get some rest, and it sounds like you need to do the same."

"You've got that right," she confessed. "Enjoy tomorrow."

He was going to say, "Goodnight," but before he could, he heard a "click" when the call disconnected. Neither had said, "I love you," and it felt worrisome. In fact, saying, "I love you" had been missing from their relationship for a long time. Then he stared at the phone and thought about calling Capricia but wisely refrained.

~

Tuesday was more of the same with presentations, discussion groups and lots of technical give and take. Marco did his best to stay engaged, but his mind was on meeting Antonio Conti.

"Are there any messages?"

It was his fourth time at the registration desk hoping to learn when he'd be meeting his father. He was about to leave feeling disappointed, when a nearby attendant intervened.

"I just received this message for Mr. Jackson."

She handed the note to Marco, and he quickly unfolded it. Immediately he noticed Capricia's name at the bottom.

Marco! Tony would like for you to join him in his suite at 4:00 p.m. He's in the penthouse at the Stardust, which is only a short cab ride from the Sahara. Just tell the receptionist your name when you arrive.

Capricia

A feeling of well being rushed over him, and his mood changed instantly. By four o'clock, the second day would be winding down, and it would easy for him to slip out unnoticed. With a refreshed attitude he welcomed questions and conversations, and then at 3:30 he excused himself from his group and hurried upstairs to freshen up.

~

*I*t was still daylight, but the sun's rays were fading as the cab pulled into the casino's drive. Garish neon lights screamed for attention, especially on the big marquee advertising *Lido de Paris,* an "exotic extravaganza of topless showgirls." It certainly caught his eye; however, his mission was to visit Antonio Conti, so he tipped the cabbie generously and went inside trying to ignore the distractions. It was a din of activity, noise and cigarette smoke, but he pushed through the crowd and made his way to the front desk.

"Marco Jackson," he announced and noticed an immediate reaction in the clerk's expression.

"Just a moment sir," she replied and touched a small button near the edge of her workspace.

He hardly had time to think, when he heard a soft, seductive voice say his name.

"Marco! It's nice to see you again."

He spun around to face Capricia, who was now attired in a beige business suit with her flowing black hair caressing her shoulders.

"I love how you just appear out of nowhere."

"It's what I do," she said with a radiant smile. "Mr. Conti is expecting you."

"That sounds very formal. What happened to *Tony*?"

"To me he's Tony, but for you, he's Antonio. You may be his son, but it's best to be formal."

"I'll remember that. Thank you."

"The front desk has already notified him you're here, so if you're ready I'll take you upstairs."

She turned to lead the way, and he gladly followed. She walked slightly in front of him distracting him with her amazing body as they passed the main elevators and stopped at an unmarked elevator, which opened magically when she touched a small card to a sensor next to the door. After they stepped inside, she touched his arm.

"Tony loves convenience," she explained, "so the hotel installed this private elevator exclusively for his use." Marco noticed only two buttons, one next to an up arrow and the other for down, and it was whisper quiet. "His suite is his home when he's in Vegas. He's going to be pleased to see you."

When the elevator door opened, they stepped into a large atrium outside Antonio's suite. Marco was enjoying the lavish décor when his door suddenly opened, and Conti stepped into view.

"Marco!" he exclaimed. "I'm so happy you decided to come see me."

Then, instead of a handshake, Conti pulled Marco into an embrace. He responded politely, and when he turned toward Capricia, she had silently disappeared. Conti noticed his reaction.

"She's like a ghost," he chuckled, "which is a great quality in a woman. They appear at just the right time and then disappear when they're not needed." Marco smiled but didn't see the humor of it. "Come on in, and I'll fix you a brandy . . . unless you'd like something else."

"No, a brandy would be fine!"

Then he followed his father into the most lavish suite he'd ever seen. There was so much luxury it was beyond comprehension. Ultra plush carpeting cushioned every step, and the room's décor was extravagant in every detail. Beautiful paintings adorned the walls, and on a facing wall to the side of the windows, floor-to-ceiling mirrors gave the room an infinite dimension.

Conti walked to his bar to pour their drinks, added a tiny ice cube and handed it to Marco. As soon as the drink was in his hands, Antonio raised his glass.

"Here's to good health and relationships!"

Marco responded in kind and took a tiny sip. "Who are you?" he asked bluntly.

Conti smirked and chuckled. "I'm your father," he said in a confident tone.

"You're my *birth* father. My loving *father* died prematurely, and my *mother* is a plain-spoken jewel of a woman, who lives in Harrisburg, Illinois."

"Fair enough," Conti smiled and nodded. "I know who your adopted parents are, although I never met them. They're part of a painful memory from a long time ago. It's painful because your mother Frederica died after giving you birth." He tipped his head, swallowed his brandy and then glared at Marco as though waiting for him to acknowledge his loss.

"I've seen her obituary, but no one's ever explained why it happened."

"You mean why you were adopted?"

"Right! Was it planned? Was I that much of an inconvenience? What were you doing in southern Illinois? Why did you walk away?"

"Sit down, Marco. I need another brandy."

Marco did as Conti suggested and ran his hands over the luxury leather on the chair. Everything was beyond exceptional. He watched as Conti tossed down another drink and took another tiny sip of his own. Then Antonio walked to the windows with his back toward Marco and paused for a moment of awkward silence. When he turned to face him he narrowed his eyes.

"I don't have a good excuse for walking away." His voice revealed his tension. "Your mother, Frederica, was also a jewel of a woman, and she's the only woman I've ever loved unconditionally. She was also a strong woman, who allowed no room for discussion about having someone else raise our child, and I agreed for a variety of reasons."

"What reasons?"

"The most important one is that my business isn't a child-friendly environment."

"And what is your business?"

"The Outfit is in the business of making money, Marco, and sometimes it gets a little rough. At first, I made money in Chicago, and that's still the center of business for the Outfit, and now I'm making money in Vegas."

"And why were you in southern Illinois when I was born?"

"I had some business, which took me to New Orleans, and I foolishly thought your mother could handle the trip just fine, but I was wrong. On our way back to Chicago, she went into severe labor and we had to get help. I rushed her to the nearest hospital, which was the little county hospital where you were born. We had no choice, and within 30 minutes after you took your first breath, she took her last. It still grieves me to this day."

Marco nodded understandingly. "My mother showed me the obituary, but I didn't learn about my adoption until I was on my way to graduate school at MIT."

Conti nodded sympathetically. "Well, that would be none of my business."

"Why did you put me up for adoption?"

Conti shrugged. "In addition to Frederica's determined decision, I knew caring for a child would be a big mistake in my business, and I can tell you confidently, in this Outfit there's no way to live a normal life."

"And you say your business is making money?"

"That's as simple as I can put it. The Outfit is based in Chicago, but it's like a network. We have connections everywhere, and one of the most important is right here in Vegas."

"And what do you do here in Vegas?"

Conti set his glass onto a table and frowned. "There's no need for details, so suffice it to say we work with the casinos. In fact, we're connected to all the major casinos. They need what we do and it makes us a lot of money."

Marco stood and sat his unfinished drink on the table next to Antonio's glass.

"I still don't understand how you could just walk away from your newborn child. I have a little girl, and I can't imagine doing that to her."

He looked at his father over the rim of his glasses, but Conti remained unmoved.

"Don't be an arrogant smartass, Marco. Each situation is different. The past is the past and what happened is irrelevant now, so forget about it! Hank and Eileen Jackson gave you a good home and lots of love. I'm glad it was them and not me who raised you." He paused with a knowing expression. "There are always reasons for why things happen, and sometimes it's better not to know all the details. However, I'll tell you without apology; I'm not sorry about it! I could have never provided you a decent home like they did. Just look at you! You're strong and handsome just like I used to be in my younger days, and it seems you have good standards. I had the same muscular frame and the same good looks as you have, but I probably have different values. Frederica was a beautiful woman, and in some ways you remind me of her. I wish I had a picture to show you, but take my word; she was beautiful."

Marco turned toward the door. "I need to be going now. How do I find my way out of here?"

"Not to worry. Capricia will appear at exactly the right moment, but don't be in such a hurry, because I still have things to say to you."

Marco hesitated, and then an unnoticeable door on the mirrored wall silently opened, and Capricia swept into the room to stand next to Marco. She had obviously freshened up and added a touch of her wonderful perfume, which was nearly intoxicating. Antonio glanced at Marco as though confirming his description of her quiet nature. Then she took hold of Marco's hand, and Antonio smiled his approval.

"Before you go," he said in a softer voice and moved uncomfortably close, "I have something for you to consider."

Marco listened attentively, and Capricia slightly squeezed his hand.

"I've had my associates track down some details for me, and I'm fascinated to learn how smart you are." He smiled knowingly and Marco shrugged and waited. "I've learned you've been at the top of your class through all your years of education, and I'm inclined to think you genetically inherited Frederica's smarts." He laughed heartily. "You have my good looks and her brains." He laughed again, and Marco smiled. "I've also learned IBM had dibs on you before you graduated from MIT, and I understand they're paying you a pittance when compared to what you're worth." He waited for confirmation, but Marco resisted any urge to ask how he got hold of so much information. "I've also learned that gorgeous wife of yours does some really great artwork and sells a few paintings from time to time, but I'm going to repeat what I said, Marco. What you're making with IBM is a pittance. You could do a lot better."

Marco didn't like what he was hearing and began inching his way to the door, but Capricia lightly tugged his hand encouraging him to wait.

"You may not like it, Marco, but you and I are very much alike. I'd love to have you come to Vegas and work for me."

Capricia watched Marco's puzzled expression and caressed his hand with her fingers.

"If you're interested," Conti added, "all you have to do is let me know."

Then he resumed his normal posture with space between them and waited for a reply.

"I have no idea how that could be possible," Marco said with a wrinkled brow. "I'm into technology and computers, and I've already noticed you have neither in your gorgeous penthouse. There's no sign you're using any technology in your *business* of making money."

Conti laughed loudly. "I like your style, kid, but there are a lot of things about me you can't see. Anyway, I want you to take my offer seriously. I may be the cold-hearted son-of-a-bitch who walked away when you were born, but I'm holding my arms open to you now. I can help you make a fortune if you're interested, so take all the time you need to think it over. Talk to Capricia about it!" He winked at her and made a sweeping motion with his hand to call attention to her. "Hell, she knows more about me than I know myself. Anyway, you know where to find me, and all it takes is a phone call."

Then Antonio turned away, and Capricia nudged him toward the door, which opened as if by magic.

"It's nice seeing you again," Marco said in a constrained effort to be polite.

Conti nodded and gestured with his hand as Capricia ushered him into the atrium and onto the private elevator, which rapidly descended to the hotel lobby. She continued holding his hand as she guided him through the crowd, and when they were outside, she turned to face him and stood very close.

"It's been my pleasure," she cooed and brought his hand firmly in place around her waist. Then she kissed him on the lips. He was totally surprised and immediately aroused by her boldness. It was a very awkward but delightful moment, and he managed a weak smile.

"That was unexpected but wonderful!"

She smiled seductively and took a tissue from her purse to wipe a tiny smudge of lipstick from the corner of his mouth.

"Can I keep you a while longer and take you to the *Lido de Paris*? We can relax in the lounge until the eight o'clock show, and they'll let us in for free."

He hesitated, while still savoring her unexpected kiss and her exotic fragrance.

"I should be getting back. My first session is at nine tomorrow morning."

She made a pouting expression and then smiled.

"Okay, Marco. We'll have other times."

She waited politely, and he knew she'd welcome another kiss, but with aching reluctance, he let go of her hand and signaled one of the cabs lined up on the drive. The driver nodded when he told him "the Sahara," and then they sped away. He looked over his shoulder, and she waved still holding the tissue in her hand. His reaction to Capricia had been sexual from the moments they'd met, and he could still feel the softness of her lips touching his. He leaned back and closed his eyes. It had been more than he imagined, and he could still hear Conti's words in his head. It was so overwhelming he could hardly imagine the ramifications if he should decide to accept his offer.

"Here we are," said the cabbie as he extended his hand waiting to be paid.

Marco added a generous tip and went inside. It was a little past seven o'clock, so instead of going to his room, he found some conference acquaintances in the lounge and joined them for a drink. The alcohol burned its way into his stomach but took the edge off his anxiety. Three drinks later he'd crossed the line and couldn't stop. If it hadn't been for his "friends," he might never had made it to bed where he dreamed of Capricia.

~

𝒩eedless to say, when Marco finally awakened around noon the next day, his head was in pretty bad shape. He used the bathroom and paused to look at himself in the mirror. What he saw was so repulsive, he decided to order room service and skip the remainder of the conference. When room service arrived with his lunch, he placed a "Do not disturb" sign on his door and shuffled back to the bed.

God, I feel miserable, he moaned.

The food remained untouched until he awakened a second time around 3:00 p.m. He ate a few bites and sat forlornly in his darkened room. Bothersome thoughts filled his head and something disturbing was beginning to surface.

If there's that much money involved, maybe I can convince Emma we should move here? Las Vegas is a crazy place, but they have schools and art galleries the same as anywhere. What day is it anyway?

He shuffled through his papers until he found the schedule and slightly opened the drapes to see the print.

Oh, it's over tomorrow! Then he searched for his plane ticket and read it carefully as well. *Hum, I'm scheduled to leave at 4:00.*

He snapped the drapes closed again, finished his food, and then began the demanding task of making himself presentable. Later, on his way past the lounge, two friends chided him for being absent and then invited him to go with them to see Sinatra at the Sands. He accepted their invitation as a way of getting his mind off his father and Capricia. It turned into another late night, but he wisely limited himself to only a couple of drinks. On Thursday morning he packed his bags, had room service deliver his breakfast, and checked out at noon. He had a long wait at the airport, and when his flight finally departed, he had a strange sensation that he'd be coming back. How he'd make it happen was beyond speculation, but every time he thought of Capricia, it felt inevitable.

TWELVE

Marco returned home with uneasy feelings. During the flight he had time to mentally review the sequence of things that had happened. He'd only made one call to Emma, and after seeing Antonio, he'd basically dropped out of the conference nursing a hangover and fantasizing about Capricia. He sensed a storm brewing. With such mixed emotions it wasn't going to be easy facing Emma. When the plane passed over San Francisco, he had a momentary calm feeling, but it quickly passed. Once the wheels touched the runway, it was like facing the rumbling turbulence he knew was coming. Since he'd parked his car at the airport, it was only a matter of collecting his bags and making the short drive home. Emma was probably aware of the approximate time he'd arrive, but given her recent moodiness, he didn't expect a warm welcome. The contrast between her frustration and Capricia's radiant smile teased him to concentrate on one rather than the other.

He had so completely succumbed to Capricia's charms, he knew it would be impossible to hide his indiscretions from Emma, and although he'd rehearsed his explanation over and over again, it was doomed to failure. When he pulled into his driveway, there were no signs of life anywhere, so he rang the doorbell a couple of times to signal his arrival and then used his key to go inside.

"I'm home," he called after letting himself in the front door. "I'm here!"

The silence was deafening. He went immediately to Celine's room and found everything perfectly in place as though she hadn't used her bed or her toys.

"Emma? Are you here?"

A quick check of the house quickly answered his question, and when he went to the bedroom he found a note.

Marco! Celine and I left on Thursday morning for an impromptu visit with my parents in Fresno. I figure if you can go to Las Vegas, then I should have the same privilege. I thought you'd at least call more than once, but your thoughtlessness is just another sign of the strain we're under. Your boss, Mr. Kerns, called late on Wednesday afternoon saying he'd been trying to contact you with no success and wondered if I knew why. It's like a psychic hunch, but something tells me there's something going on, which you don't want me to know, and the more I thought about it, the more desperate I felt. I feel trapped here with Celine, and since you're never around to help, I decided to go to Fresno where I know my mom will help and give me a breather. At this point, I'm unsure how long we'll stay, but please don't try to contact me. I feel exhilarated just getting out of this house, so you're on your own. I want you to know I can't stand uncertainty, and I don't like being deceived, so keep that in mind as you continue working your deals. I know you'll come home and wonder what I'm trying to prove, but taking Celine and going to my parent's is my way of coping.

If there's something you need to tell me, I'd prefer hearing it in person, but it'll have to wait until I regain my balance.

Emma

He read the note a couple of times before placing it back on the nightstand. But he wasn't surprised. Emma's sensitivity had surfaced before, and even without saying it, he knew she'd sensed a change in his relationship with her. His emotions were tangled.

The emptiness and quietness inside the house was dramatically different from Vegas, but in a way, it felt soothing. However, he was overwhelmed with feelings of sadness because Emma's indictment was accurate. She said his job was too demanding, and she was right; he was gone more than he was at home. Then, on top of everything else, he'd initiated contact with Antonio, and one thing led to another. In fact, after his brief phone conversation with Emma on Monday night, he'd not thought of her again until on his way home.

I've been thoughtless just as she says, but I just can't see a way to turn this thing around.

With that thought in mind, he went to the cupboard in the kitchen where he kept a few bottles of wine and reached way to the back to retrieve a half-bottle of bourbon they'd bought when entertaining friends from his team at IBM. He poured more than a double shot and added a single ice cube. Then he went into the bedroom, read Emma's note again and then stared at the phone. The little phonebook lay next to the phone, but she'd specifically asked him not to call. The bourbon caused him to relax and he thought of Capricia. As soon as she came to mind, he felt for his wallet and stared at the phone again.

Don't do this Jackson! It's too soon.

With each sip of his drink, his resistance diminished, but instead of calling, he slipped into a funky mood and gave in to his memories.

Antonio's offer is unclear, but I could become a wealthy man! The alcohol effectively blocked his recollection of the Outfit being the Mob. *He likes me! I imagine he'd be delighted if decided to work for him.*

Then he thought of Capricia's kiss and her intoxicating fragrance. He remembered her pouty expression and her teasing smile. *My god, she's a beautiful woman!*

Then tears filled his eyes.

"Millions?" he said aloud in the emptiness of the bedroom and took another bold sip of his drink. The effects of the alcohol were fuzzing his brain, but at the same time he was aroused by memories of Capricia.

She has such a teasing, pouty expression. God, how I wanted to spend the night with her!

He had nearly finished his drink and began pacing. *It's the Chicago Mob for god's sake. Conti is a mobster! Do I really want to be a part of the mob?*

He stopped in front of the phone and nearly picked up the receiver, but then he took the last swallow of his drink and shifted his attention to his empty glass. The booze was really affecting his judgment and his thoughts were jumbled. He felt deeply conflicted over what he wanted and what seemed possible. Once again he stared at the phone and then focused on his pathetic image in a mirror above Emma's dresser. Agony and confusion had etched deep lines in his brow, and his sorrow weighed on him so heavily, he bent forward with his face nearly touching Emma's letter and wept. Tears stained the letter, so he picked it up and wiped it with a tissue causing the ink to smear. The blurred ink seemed symbolic, and when he used the same tissue to dry his eyes, ink also smeared onto his face. He let go of his empty glass and staggered into the bathroom where he tried to wipe away the ink stains.

"Marco! You're a fucking mess," he declared to his image.

Of course, there was no one to hear his condemnation or to give him any reassurance at all, so then he wandered back to the kitchen, refilled his glass and staggered to "his" chair in the living room. The house was lifeless and desolate, and he was clearly drunk. His only connection to any semblance of decency was the tear-stained note from Emma.

When the phone rang, he literally jumped up and nearly knocked over his chair trying to find the receiver.

"Hello, this is Marco."

"Hey, buddy, it's Kevin. I wasn't sure if you'd be home. How was it?"

He did his best to sound sober but didn't manage very well.

"Yeah, I just got home. How are you doing?"

"Great!" Kevin declared. "Are you okay? You sound a little out of it."

"Well, if you must know, I just finished a double shot of bourbon on an empty stomach."

Kevin laughed. "It must have been a hard week . . . huh?"

"You have no idea!"

"Well, anyway, productivity has improved in your absence."

His statement shocked him, and then he heard Kevin's teasing laughter.

"Very funny! Very funny, but I know better."

"No! I'm just joking! Hey! We're looking forward to your return on Monday. I'll bet you have a ton of stuff to share."

"I have a few things, but I'm sure you won't be surprised if I tell you IBM is way out in front of the rest of them."

Kevin laughed heartily. "There's no doubt about that! I'll bet all the stuff you've written made you a celebrity at the conference?"

Marco thought about it and stared at his nearly empty glass wishing he had more.

"I had gropers . . . I mean *groupies* following me around."

He swallowed the last of his drink and glanced toward the kitchen.

"What about those Vegas show girls, Marco? Did you take any pictures? I hear they have topless show girls!"

He was past the point where he could think straight, but Kevin's comment reminded him of Capricia wanting him to join her for the *Lido de Paris*. Then he mumbled some incoherent words about her, which made no sense to Kevin.

"What did you say? You're mumbling. How much bourbon have you had?"

"I said I didn't take any pictures of her."

This time, Kevin heard him clearly.

"Pictures of who?"

"Oh, it's nothing Kev. No pictures, but lots of memories."

Kevin didn't pick up on it, but Marco was dangerously close to a confession, and he was drifting aimlessly and slurring his words.

"Okay buddy," Kevin concluded. "Put the bourbon away, and we'll see you on Monday."

Marco was about to say, "Okay," but the call disconnected before he could get the word out. However, he completely disregarded Kevin's advice and went straight to the kitchen for another refill. He knew he was already drunk, but regardless, his numbness felt better than his reality.

~

Waking up alone was terrible, but in addition, he also had a terrible headache, which amplified his loneliness. There was hardly any food in the refrigerator, so once his head quit throbbing, he went to a nearby café for lunch, which he barely touched, and then he made a trip to a grocery store for some frozen dinners. In one way, having Emma and Celine gone was a reprieve, but being completely on his own was not his forte. Their absence was only delaying the inevitable, or at least he assumed that to be the case, and when she returned, it would be crunch time.

On Sunday evening he had more bourbon and as before, it was a little too much. Once again, he lost control and slipped into melancholy. He shouted at the TV for its lousy picture and paced from room to room. Then he began pleading aloud with Capricia and emotionally declared his gnawing hunger to be with her. His confession unleashed some deep sobbing and feelings of betrayal. It was like losing everything he'd ever claimed to be important, so he cursed his situation and also shouted at an imaginary Antonio Conti to get the hell out of his life.

Finally, he was nearly exhausted when he suddenly envisioned Emma staring at him and shaking her head in despair as his beautiful daughter Celine ran to him asking, *"What's wrong Daddy?"* He cursed the silence and banged his fist on the table, but nothing changed, so he kept drinking until the bottle was empty, and then he sprawled on the bed and wept. Of course, there was no one to hear his anger and no one to see his tears. At best, there was privacy, so in painful loneliness, he finally closed his eyes and tried to make the bad thoughts go away.

About an hour later, he staggered into the bedroom, fumbled his way into the adjoining bathroom to pee and then vomited into the stool. When he splashed cold water onto his face, it was more shocking than helpful, but it afforded him a chance for another look into the mirror. What he saw frightened him.

What's happening to me?

The alcohol had opened the floodgates and a rush of emotions blocked his ability to reason his way out of the dilemma he'd created. He waited in front of the mirror as though expecting a transforming miracle, but none occurred, so he teetered back to the bed, sprawled face down and finally went to sleep.

~

$\mathcal{M}$arco awakened just before 10 o'clock and reared up his aching head to look twice at the clock.

"Oh, my, god," he said aloud. "I'm screwed!"

His mouth felt dry and gummy, so while taking a quick shower he allowed water to pummel directly into his mouth and tried to soothe his aching head. There was no time for anything like a leisurely cup of coffee or to wait until his headache subsided. He thankfully found clean clothes in the closet, took a couple of aspirins and hurried to dry his hair before rushing out the door. At 11:15 he dashed into his office, greeted the secretary and then hurried to the lab to face the music from his confused team members.

"I blew it guys," he lamented. "Vegas caught up with me and some bourbon put me down for longer than I anticipated."

His fellow team members responded with raised eyebrows and then smiled coyly at his dilemma. Kevin stepped forward and took hold of him by the shoulders.

"So, Mr. Straight and Narrow, what's happened to you?"

Marco wasn't ready to make a confession, so rolled his eyes and pushed a few stray hairs back into place.

"I'm okay, and I wish someone would say, welcome home!"

"Oh, is that all you need? Okay! Welcome home, Marco," four of them said in unison.

Then Kevin leaned closer and whispered, "Director Kerns is waiting for you in his office."

He seldom talked with Kerns, who typically allowed him complete freedom as long as he provided periodic status reports on their projects. However, when he looked towards Kerns' office, he had a funny feeling in the pit of his stomach.

Kevin noticed his ashen look and watched him slowly walking toward the office. Marco glanced over his shoulder and saw Kevin arch his brow in an attempt to be sympathetic.

"I really apologize for being late this morning," he said immediately after entering Kerns' office. "I guess I'm kind of fumbling my way back into my routine."

"You certainly don't look like one of _Time's_ most influential men; however, I'm not concerned with your late arrival," Kerns said rather tersely. "What most concerns me is your absence at the conference on Wednesday."

Marco's eyes revealed his panic as images of Antonio and Capricia flashed through his mind.

"Yeah, I skipped out on Wednesday," he confessed, "but I can explain why . . . and I have a ton of materials from the conference if you're interested."

Kerns scrunched his expression. "Are you aware of the cost of sending you to Las Vegas?"

"Yes, Sir! I'll have a complete expense summary on your desk by Wednesday."

"I'm not talking about your expense report, Marco. IBM paid your registration fee, paid for your room at the Sahara, and paid the airfare in addition to what you'll submit on your expense report. It's unfortunate you somehow decided not to honor the company's investment to send you there."

Marco remained mute and knew Kerns was right. There really was no excuse.

"If I had to describe a model employee," Kerns continued, "I'd describe you, but something's changed, Marco. After repeated calls to your room on Wednesday, I finally called the hotel's concierge hoping to get a message to you, and was informed you had a *Do not disturb* sign on your door and no one had seen you. Quite frankly, I was very concerned for your well being, so I called Emma to ask if she'd heard from you and was discouraged when she said you'd only called once on the day you'd arrived." He looked directly at Marco and waited.

"My birth father is living in Las Vegas," Marco explained. "I've finally reconnected with him and I thought seeing him was important."

"You've never mentioned you were adopted."

"I know! It's a rather long story, but that's why I missed some of the conference, and I apologize."

"Emma didn't mention this when I talked to her."

Marco nodded. "She doesn't know."

"What do you mean she doesn't know? She doesn't know you were adopted?"

"She knows I was adopted, but she doesn't know anything about me visiting my father in Vegas."

"Sounds unusual to me," Kerns said and wrinkled his brow. "I can't understand why you wouldn't let Emma know what you were doing, but I guess that's none of my business. Anyway, your absence concerns me. I know you're an executive in this company, but regardless, consider this a warning! Any questions?"

There was no reason to linger or say anything more, so Marco left the office and rejoined his team. They paid no attention to his return, but in a private moment, he pulled Kevin aside and told him to be ready for anything. Kevin knew

Kerns was fired-up, so he looked at Marco with a questioning glance.

"What's going on?" Kevin asked.

Marco rolled his eyes and nodded towards Kerns' office. "It didn't go well."

"Is there anything I can do?"

"Just continue being my friend! I have some heavy things to sort out."

"Okay!"

What happened in Las Vegas has taken its toll, he thought. *I'm not sure what happens next?*

~

Other than Kevin and a couple irritating solicitations, there'd been no calls to break the silence, so when the phone rang at nine that evening, it startled him.

"Hello!"

"It's Emma! How is my executive husband?"

Emma's voice was as subdued and non-confrontational. She totally surprised him.

"I'm so glad you called."

"Just to be fair; I'm not coming home, but I thought I should at least call and see how you're doing."

"I'm fine! How's Celine?"

"There's no change! She keeps me and Mom busy."

"You totally surprised me by leaving."

"I surprised myself, but I had reached the end of my tether."

"What can I do to make it better?"

"That boat left the dock a long time ago, Marco. You know why as well as I do; you've been preoccupied."

He had no reasonable counter to her accusation, so he paid his dues with silence. She waited and thought he might argue the point, but instead he changed the subject.

"Changes are coming at IBM."

"Really? I haven't heard anything about it."

"There's nothing official, but I've heard rumors we might have to relocate."

"Lots of things *could* happen, Marco, but I prefer to deal with what is rather than what might happen. Speaking of what is, I need some money, and if you've got a decent bone left in your body, you'll send me some."

"It would be easier if you'd just come home."

Silence.

"Send me some money, Marco. You're responsible for Celine as much as I am."

"Fine! I'll do it, but I need to know what you're planning? Are you making this separation permanent?"

"I'm not sure. It's better here than it was there."

He stared into the emptiness around him and sensed it might get worse. It was as though she'd pulled the plug on their relationship, and it would be up to him to reconnect it. However, as the weight of her indecision pressed down on him, the allure of Las Vegas grew stronger. For a brief moment he thought about telling her he'd seen his father again, but he knew it would only complicate things further, so in the seconds that followed, he made another half-hearted appeal.

"I hope it's not permanent. I'll call you if anything changes."

"I'd rather not be bothered, Marco. We're getting along fine, and Mom is delighted to help me with Celine. I've already reconnected with the gallery in downtown Fresno, and they're excited to have me back in the area. In fact, my paintings are still selling, and with Mom's help I can at least have a few hours each day to paint. Anyway, enjoy your unfettered life with your IBM buddies. I may call again someday, but don't hold your breath."

He was about to say, "I'll look forward to it" when she hung up and disconnected the call. He held the receiver in his hand as though she'd just cut his lifeline, and his loneliness suddenly felt more oppressive.

~

*I*n addition to Emma's ultimatum, there really was uncertainty at work. Marco's team members also knew something was amiss, and it reminded him repeatedly of the fragile nature of his relationships. There was tension between him and Kerns, and Kevin was increasingly becoming the contact for their projects. Part of his frustration was because Capricia still dominated his thoughts. He found it hard to concentrate on the work he was doing. Every night at home was increasingly lonely, and it was just another sign of a steady unraveling of his life. In his solitude, he pondered his father's suggestion and frequently thought about turning his back on everything and taking a chance with good fortune in Las Vegas. He was also drinking more than he should and felt the clock was ticking.

The following weekend, he decided to drive to San Francisco. He would normally have avoided going into the city, but since it was Saturday with no major sports events scheduled, he decided it would be better than being bored at home. He really had no purpose going there other than creating a diversion, so after a brief jaunt at Fishermen's Wharf and a fairly decent meal at Fog Harbor, he headed back to San Jose. The drive was uneventful but long enough for him to think things over. Of course, he had many things on his mind, and mostly he thought about Capricia. There had been no actual threat of losing his job at IBM, but given what had happened, Kerns was treating him differently and he'd already lost his enthusiasm, which had previously motivated him, so his thoughts were less about work and more about what might happen if he said yes to his father. The thought of doing that always caused a surge of anxiety. If he said no, it would require a major effort to mend his broken relationship with Emma and an end to his fascination with Capricia. He tried to lean in favor of Emma and Celine, but his desire to be with Capricia was stronger.

"I've brought this on myself," he whispered aloud as though explaining his dilemma to an unseen listener. "I'm the one who made contact and ignored my better judgments." He knew saying yes to his father would cause a dramatic turn in his life, but he was inclined to do it, and by the time he parked in his driveway he'd decided he'd make a quick trip to Las Vegas the following weekend. His purpose would be to meet with Antonio and give him an answer, but more honestly, he wanted to see Capricia.

~

On Monday when he arrived at his office there was a note on his desk to meet with Kerns for lunch. He assumed he meant lunch at noon, so his anxiety increased throughout the morning as he obsessively watched the clock, and then around 11:45 he noticed Kerns talking to his secretary and checking his watch, so he straightened things on his desk and hurried to be on time.

"I assumed you meant at noon," Marco said as he entered Kerns' office.

"Right! Actually, I don't recall mentioning the time, but we always break for lunch at noon." He glanced at his watch again and closed a document on his computer. "If you don't mind, we'll just eat in the executive dining room."

"Fine!"

When they entered the dining room, the hostess immediately took them to a quiet table near the windows away from other diners. Then she handed a menu to Marco and unfolded his napkin.

"The food's good," Kerns suggested as he tapped the menu in front of Marco. "I usually have the Quesadilla, and the waitress already knows that's what I'll want."

"Then, I'll have the same."

Kerns glanced toward the waitress and held up two fingers. She nodded and smiled.

"I want to talk to you about what's going on, Marco? It seems Las Vegas has caused a big change in you, so I'm wondering if you're willing to tell me about it."

Marco reached for his water and nearly knocked over the glass. It wobbled, but he caught it before it tipped. His mind was racing to think of what to say, and Kerns simply waited.

"It's rather personal," he confessed, "and Las Vegas is not the only cause."

"Say more about that."

"Well, my birth father is a very wealthy man, and he wants me to work with him."

"Hum, that's interesting! What kind of business is he in?"

"He runs a network of businesses closely connected to the casinos."

"Such as?"

"I don't know the details, but he thinks I could be a real asset if I'd join his team."

"Doing what?"

Marco's mind raced to answer the question and reminded him he had no idea what his father was suggesting.

"Probably data management," he said weakly.

"It's your thing! Are you interested?"

"Yes, but I'm also uncertain. I really like working here; however, it would be a chance for me to patch together some missing pieces of my life." Kerns nodded as though inviting him to continue. "You mentioned you weren't aware I'd been adopted, and I didn't know either until I left for graduate school."

"Hum," Kern's mumbled. "I can only imagine how shocked you were. It had to be a jolt to your self-image."

"The jolt was learning my real mother died giving me birth and that my real father didn't want to keep me."

Kerns took a deep breath and arched his brow. "And you said you reconnected with your father in Las Vegas, so how did you find him?"

"My birth certificate listed his residence as Chicago, so I did some research and when Emma and I were on our honeymoon in Chicago, we met him at his restaurant."

"And what about the Jacksons, who adopted you?"

Marco smiled. "They're exceptional. They gave me a good home and loved me unconditionally; however, my dad died from cancer when I was at MIT."

"Are you still close to your mother?"

"I don't get a chance to see her too often, but yes, she's very important to me."

The waitress arrived with their Quesadillas and refilled their water glasses. Kerns paused to savor a few bites while the food was hot, and Marco did the same.

"Well," he said between bites, "this explains a few things. It sounds like you've been on an emotional roller coaster, so are you *seriously* considering working for your birth father?"

"It's an option, but I'm unsure. It would be a major decision with lots of ramifications."

"What about Emma? How does she feel?"

Marco visibly grimaced. "I really don't know, because Emma and Celine have moved out. When I came home from Vegas, she'd gone to stay with her parents in Fresno."

"My goodness! Are you having problems?"

"It's frustration mainly. Celine's a handful, and I'm gone too much."

"Interesting!" Kerns mumbled and kept eating. "When I called her to inquire about you, she told me you'd only called once. Women are temperamental, you know."

Marco wrinkled his brow and shrugged. "Yeah, I know! Anyway, right now she's temporarily living with her parents, and I'm not sure if she'll be coming home."

Kerns finished eating and pushed his plate aside with one slice of his Quesadilla untouched. "Tasty," he exclaimed, "but it's always more than I can eat."

"It's very good," Marco agreed.

Kerns smiled and took a drink of water. "Well, what you say is very interesting, Marco. Personal problems are tough, so I'm not surprised you're feeling conflicted. However, while we're on the subject, you might also want to know IBM may be closing down operations in San Jose. I've refrained from making any announcements about it because nothing's been decided, but with what you've just told me, you may want to keep it in mind."

Marco's expression revealed his surprise. "I hardly know what to say. I'd heard some rumors, but I thought everything was secure with IBM."

"The business is secure, but change is inevitable. If a move happens, our employees will still have their jobs, if they're willing to relocate. Anyway, I'm just giving you a heads up, and I hope you can get yourself back on track and do whatever you need to do to settle your issues."

The waitress returned, Kerns signed the tab and then glanced at his watch. "I've got a meeting, so thanks for trusting me and letting me know what's going on."

They stood. Kerns shook Marco's hand, and it was over. As he watched his boss leaving the dining room, he wasn't sure if he was feeling good or bad, but it occurred to him he might have unwittingly received a gift from his boss. The possibility of relocation would be a reasonable way to bridge the chasm, which seemed to be growing wider every day. As he walked back to his office, he was convinced that making a quick trip to Vegas would settle some of his questions.

~

On Friday he called Capricia.

"I'm coming to Vegas for the weekend."

He expected her to shout for joy but instead he got the third degree.

"Why, Marco?"

"Because I can't stand another day without seeing you."

He meant it to be playful, but she reacted.

"Don't be too casual, Marco. What about your wife and daughter?"

"They've abandoned me. When I arrived home, Emma had taken Celine and gone to stay with her parents in Fresno. I've not seen her since, and my mind's in a quandary over Antonio's suggestion."

"Do you mean his suggestion about coming here to work for him?"

"It's also about seeing you again. You've been on my mind constantly."

"Jesus, Marco! I don't know what to say, but I need to be clear with you. You're married and you have a kid! Have you talked to her about it?"

"No!"

"Are you planning to leave her?"

It was an unnerving thought, which sent a shudder down his spine. "Not at the moment," he replied, "but I feel I need to talk to Tony to settle my mind."

"Don't call him *Tony*, Marco. He's *Antonio* until he tells you otherwise."

There was a noticeable pause

"What about this weekend? Is it okay if I come?"

"Do you want me to make an appointment for you to see him?"

"Yes."

"Can you be here before noon, so you can meet with him at four?"

"It should be easy."

"Then call me when you have your flight scheduled, and I'll pick you up at the airport."

"I'm eager to see you again."

She paused, and he waited.

"I do care for you Marco, but this wife and kid thing scares the hell out of me."

"It scares the hell out of me too, but for two days I want to set my fears aside."

"I hope you've thought this through."

"More than you know. Let me set up my flight, and I'll call you again in an hour or so."

When he hung up the phone his heart was racing with anticipation. It was like watching a line of dominos tumble in sequence. One thing was leading to another.

~

*T*rue to her word, Capricia met Marco at the airport. He spotted her immediately, as she was creating quite a stir among other male passengers with her baby blue outfit consisting of shorts and a loose-fitting tank top exposing her exquisite waist and tummy.

When he rushed to greet her, several men watched enviously before being jerked away by their wives. She folded into his arms, and he inhaled her intoxicating fragrance. He had feared she might be standoffish, but the warmth of her embrace erased any lingering doubts. When she tilted her head up and looked expectantly into his eyes, he kissed her and tried to keep his emotions under control. He had longed to see her again, and then she whispered something unexpected.

"It's selfish, Marco, but I've really been hoping you'd come back."

He didn't want to let her go, but when he did, she continued holding his hand. People walked around them, and other men slowed their pace as they passed by.

"We need to be on our way," she suggested. "Do you have a checked bag?"

"No! Everything's in my backpack, so I'm ready when you are."

"Ready for what?" she teased.

"If you have to ask, then I fear you may be an imposter."

They laughed, and she tugged on his hand to lead the way. It was the same routine. When they arrived at her car, she opened the trunk for him to store his bag and motioned toward the passenger seat as she slipped beneath the wheel.

"Did you make a hotel reservation?"

He shyly shook his head no, and she arched her brow.

"I assume you're not going home until Sunday evening."

He nodded. "My flight isn't until eight o'clock."

"Well, you can stay at my place. I have an extra bedroom."

She smiled, and he agreed, while trying to be platonic, but inside, his heart was racing.

"If it's not inconvenient, that would be great. Maybe we can have dinner together?"

"Antonio knows you're here, so he's first on the list," she said and glanced at her watch. "Your appointment is at 4:00, so we can catch a light lunch and maybe have a drink before then if that's okay."

"Great! Do you have someplace in mind?"

"Yes, we'll go to the Stardust. It's where I live."

He'd been there before to meet his father, but he was unaware she lived there as well. However, there was no doubt about it when she drove directly into the parking garage and pulled into a private stall with her name permanently displayed on the wall.

"Wow," Marco exclaimed. "You really do live here."

She smiled. "The parking space comes with my suite."

She turned off the ignition and as they got out of the car, she explained the arrangement. "My place is at the other end of the penthouse hallway. Between Tony and me, we occupy the entire top floor."

Marco had questions but decided to be polite and not ask.

"Would you like to go upstairs and freshen up?"

"I'd love to. Lead the way."

She walked ahead of him as he idolized her beautiful legs and sexy outfit. They passed the main elevators, just as they had done in the lobby, and with a wave of her tiny card, an unmarked elevator opened and they stepped inside.

"It's the same elevator we used when you were here last time," and as he turned to face the door, she took hold of his hand and laid her head against his shoulder.

The whisper quiet elevator rose swiftly, and when the door opened he immediately saw the door to Antonio's penthouse and noticed a tiny red light glowing next to the door.

"It means he doesn't want to be disturbed or he's not home at the moment. My place is down the hall."

He willingly followed her down a rather long hallway, and once again she waved her hand past a sensor and the door to her suite opened as if by magic.

"Well, don't just stand there," she teased. "Come inside."

It was similar to Antonio's suite with luxury beyond his imagination. He stood mesmerized for a moment, and then she motioned him toward her bar."

"What'll you have, Mr. Jackson?"

"I'll have a bourbon with just a little ice."

She poured a generous amount, added an ice cube and then prepared another for herself.

Then she raised her glass. "Let's drink a toast to a lasting friendship, Marco."

She touched her glass to his and then he nervously took a large swallow and waited as it burned its way to his stomach.

"Oh, my," she exclaimed. "Let's slow you down a little. You need to be sober when you meet Tony, and in the meantime, let's just relax on the couch and stare at the desert."

She laughed, and he refrained from drinking too much too fast. The couch was plush, and she was right about looking at the desert. Along the "Strip" there were glaring neon signs and lots of excitement, but on the backside the desert gave a stark reminder of the desolation around the Vegas oasis.

"There's not much of a view," she added, 'but that's okay because I want you to look at me instead."

She patted the cushion next to her, and when he sat down, she laid her head on his shoulder and caressed his arm. He felt like he should say something, but words failed him, so he took another bold sip of his bourbon. He could feel the warmth of her skin, and everything about her was so sensual, his resistance ended and after setting his drink on the table, he enfolded her in his arms and she willingly kissed him so deeply he immediately wanted her. Their kisses lasted a while, and her unspoken invitation caused him to lift her in both arms and carry her into the bedroom. She offered no resistance whatsoever, as he removed her clothes and marveled at her flawless beauty. She looked like a sculpted goddess, and he'd only dreamed of such perfection. She twisted beneath him in perfect rhythm with each thrust, and he was drawn into ecstasy beyond earthly bounds. Then, after she'd consumed him, she soothed his tension with tender kisses and allowed him to explore her body in ways he'd only dreamed.

"Well, I'm guessing you won't be needing the guest bedroom for your overnight stay?"

She smiled, and he let out a sigh of exhaustion. Then he glanced at the clock on her nightstand and realized he had about an hour before his visit with Conti. However, when he turned toward her, he wanted her again. This time it was rapidly intense. She shuddered beneath him, and he sobbed with passionate tears as he collapsed on her totally expended.

~

At two minutes until four o'clock precisely, Capricia took Marco to visit Antonio. He immediately noticed the tiny light beside the door was now green. Capricia waved a small card over the sensor and stood aside, so Marco could be first inside. Conti came to meet them.

"Marco! It's good to see you again! Capricia tells me you're here for the weekend, and I can tell by looking at her, she's pleased."

Capricia smiled, and Marco grimaced.

"If it's okay with you, my dear, I want Marco to myself for a few minutes."

She nodded demurely and disappeared through the mirrored door, which was nearly invisible until opened. Light from outside flashed from its surface when it opened and like the wisp of a soft breeze, Capricia left the room.

Conti watched Marco's expression and smiled. "She's beyond beautiful, don't you agree?"

He certainly did, and was still fixated on the mirrored door, which had blended perfectly into the wall of mirrors. Conti waited.

"Yes, she's unbelievably beautiful," he exclaimed and turned to look directly at his father.

"Yes, well, anyway, let's get to the business at hand. I assume you've thought about my offer, so what's your decision?"

Marco felt his gut tighten. "There are lots of ramifications," he stated in a business-like tone. "I'm inclined to say yes, but I'm not sure what you're asking me to do."

"Fair enough," Conti agreed. "I could give you details, but the main question is are you willing to work for the Outfit?"

"I guess you're assuming I know the *Outfit* is the Chicago Mob?"

Conti grimaced. "That's an unfortunate label, Marco. Personally, I never refer to our organization that way. The Outfit is like a family. We have members of our family in many places. It just so happens our roots are in Chicago, but as you know, I'm permanently here in Vegas. Sure, I go back to Chicago from time to time, but this is my home, and like I told you last time, we're providing a service to the casinos. They pay us for our services, but it's also to their benefit. Without the Outfit, this place would go belly-up."

"How so?"

"Las Vegas is about entertainment, Marco. People come here by the millions. They love gambling and the lavish shows, so the Outfit guarantees their success. It's our network that makes it happen. If everybody's being honest and playing by our rules, it's bonanza time."

Marco knew the casinos passed a percentage of their revenues to the Outfit, but he was yet to learn the amounts of money involved, so he nodded as though he understood

"If I say yes, you'd expect me to live in Vegas?"

"Jesus, Marco, it's a great town. Everybody who works for me loves it." He smiled knowingly. "Hell, I know you work for IBM, but I'm going to be frank with you, Marco. There's a lot more to life than having a regular job. I know what you do, and I know you work your ass off for about 110k a year . . . plus benefits, of course, but that's chump change. I could give you that much a month and set you up to live in a suite like this one. You'd love it!"

"Well, I also love what I'm doing now," Marco countered. "It's pretty damn good for a farm boy from southern Illinois."

"And that's what intrigues me about you, Marco. Most of my guys are goons from Chicago. They have a tendency to be in trouble with the law and shit like that . . . but you're my flesh and blood, and as innocent as a warm spring breeze. In addition you're smarter than probably anyone I have working for me. My, god, you've been at the top of your class, educated at one of the best schools in the country, you're on Time's list of 100 most influential people, so why wouldn't I want you to work for me?"

Marco frowned and hesitated. Conti shrugged.

"We own this town, Marco. Nothing happens in Vegas without me, and we're making all those casinos out there on the strip glitter like gold."

"Right! It appears you do very well."

Conti laughed loudly. "You have no idea!" Then he paused and moved uncomfortably close to look Marco directly in the eye. "Like I said before, you remind me of myself when I was your age. You're my biological son, and I know the chemistry that makes you tick. I know you have a good job at IBM. I know you have a pretty wife and a gorgeous baby girl. I know you're gifted intellectually, but I also know you want what I'm offering. If you decide to stay at the shallow end of the pool, I'll respect your decision, but I'm offering you more than you can imagine. You'd be able to help your wife succeed as an artist. You'd be able to help your little girl get the kind of education she deserves and put her into the very best schools. You'd be able to live well for the rest of your life."

Conti was so close to him, Marco knew his eyes and expressions were giving him away, but he still hesitated, so Conti backed away and laughed.

"We're too much alike, Marco. I can see it in your eyes. Are you hesitating because of Emma?"

Just the mention of Emma's name nearly sent him into shock. "Sure!" he replied forcefully. "She doesn't know I'm here talking to you."

"But she's already taken your daughter and gone to live with her parents in Fresno."

He flashed Marco a kind of coy smile, and Marco wrinkled his brow wondering how he knew such details.

"She'll come back!" Marco said frankly.

Conti rolled his eyes. "It's always hard to figure out what women want." He smiled knowingly. "I imagine it's hard to know for sure what she'll do."

Marco made a nonchalant expression that revealed his uncertainty.

"Well, it's okay if she's not interested in Vegas." Conti said with an innocent shrug, and then he walked to his bar. "Would you like a drink, Marco?"

"No! I'll pass."

"Okay, but I need a drink." Then he poured a single shot into a glass and swallowed it without blinking. "We know Emma likes art, right?" Marco raised his brow and waited for him to continue. "Maybe we could set her up with her own gallery or something like that?"

"Where?"

"Wherever she'd like. We could make her an offer she can't refuse." Then Conti glanced at the mirrored door through which Capricia had disappeared. "She lives just down the hall," he said with a knowing smile.

Marco immediately recalled having sex no less than an hour before and felt he was blushing. Antonio noticed.

"I'll tell you what, Marco. I know it's a big decision, but I think you should seriously consider joining me. We can put it on hold for a while, if you want you to ponder it . . . let's say for maybe thirty days of so, and then let me know."

Then Conti touched a button on his phone, which signaled Capricia, and when she came into the room, Marco felt his heart beating faster. Of all the things his father had said, one thing lingered in his mind, *"She's here!"*

Capricia walked quickly to Marco's side, took hold of his hand and led him to the door.

"Have fun this evening you two," Conti called as they left his suite. "Dinner's on me! Capricia knows!"

Marco glanced over his shoulder and saw his father standing with his hand raised to wave goodbye.

He responded with a halfhearted wave, and as soon as the door closed behind them, Capricia motioned toward the other end of the hallway. He didn't hesitate an instant. In fact, they nearly ran down the hallway.

Capricia waved her card over the sensor and opened the door to her suite. He followed her inside and watched the door close silently behind him. She suddenly disappeared from view, but when he turned the corner toward her bedroom, she'd removed her clothes and was waiting for him on the bed. He'd thought he'd already memorized her goddess-like body, but soft light from her bedroom window accented her exquisite form and caused his heart to beat faster. He remembered the word "flawless," and it remained the only adequate word to describe her. As she waited for him, she appeared as smooth as a work of art with no blemishes or imperfections of any kind, so he quickly removed his clothes and lowered his muscular body over her. With only a slight movement of his hips, she received him and rhythmically matched his movements in complete submission. The sweetness of making love with Capricia was an experience of ecstasy beyond his wildest fantasies. She consumed him and took all he could give. Then she moaned and cried out in ecstasy, as they passed a point of no return and climaxed together before lying exhausted in each other's arms.

After their lovemaking ended, Capricia kissed Marco in ways he'd only dreamed, and in his euphoria he did the same for her. Finally, they rested, until she bolted from the bed and ran to the bathroom. When she returned, she was wearing a soft see-through negligee, which excited him even more.

"Are you real Capricia, or is this some kind of out-of-the-body experience?"

She smiled and snuggled next to him. Her touch was irresistible and within minutes, he wanted her again. This time she straddled his body and teased him to the point of release and then relaxed before resuming her rhythm. He enjoyed her control, but then he forced her to continue and quickly brought her to an explosive climax.

"Enough is enough!" she laughed. "There can be no more of this until morning."

"I thought we were going out for dinner," he complained.

"We should do that, but we only have to go downstairs. I know the Maitre d', and we'll be treated royally. Are you hungry?"

"I'm totally depleted. Maybe some food might help."

"Okay! Get cleaned up and dressed, and before we leave I want you to tell me your decision."

"Do you mean about working with Antonio?"

She waited as he entered the shower.

"It's still undecided. He's given me thirty days to make up my mind."

Capricia groaned and banged on the shower door. "Marco! Don't toy with me! It should be obvious I want you here."

He smiled at her through the fogged glass. "If it was just for you, there's be no doubt, but it's major. He's asking me to upend my life."

She stormed out of the bathroom and sulked until he was dressed and ready to go.

"I thought it was a done deal," she complained. "Otherwise, I wouldn't have been so submissive."

He pulled her into his arms and kissed her.

"Submissive is good," he said with a big smile. "You just have to give me time to work this out."

~

On his flight back to San Jose, Marco was fairly resolved that he would decide to work with his father. He clearly knew it would be a life-changing decision to join the Chicago Mafia, but he naively assumed he would somehow remain aloft from its sinister darkness and simply be working with his father in some kind of computer-related job that had nothing to do with crime. His motivation was mostly driven by his hunger to be with Capricia. Each time he thought of her, he fantasized about their erotic ecstasy, and with each fantasy he felt serious guilt. At the moment he had absolutely no idea how he would tell Emma, but at least he still had a few days to sort it out.

THIRTEEN

"*H*ello! This is Emma."

"Hi, Em! It's Katie at Fresno Art."

"Oh, hi, Katie! What's up?"

"We're on a roll, Girl," Katie exclaimed joyously. "I just sold two of your paintings."

"Which ones?"

"The smaller one called *Harvest* went for $1,500, and the big *Country Landscape* of Oak trees and a road bordered by a split-rail fence sold for $3,700. One buyer wanted both of them."

"Wow, that's great news."

"But I'm not done yet!"

"There's more?"

"Well, you know I've had the gallery listed with Century 21 for nearly three months."

"Unfortunately, I'm aware of your plans to sell, so please don't tell me you've found a buyer."

"You're going to be surprised, Em!"

"Just tell me! I can handle it!"

"It's a rich business man from Chicago . . . and here's the surprise . . . he knows you."

"Are you kidding me?"

"Absolutely not! He knows you by name, and my agent told me he wants to buy the gallery and have you manage it."

Emma's mind swirled with confusion.

"I don't know anybody from Chicago," Emma declared. "Who's the mystery man?"

"I don't know who he is, but he must have a ton of money, because he's made an offer, which is nearly $10,000 higher than I expected."

"Who is he, Katie? Can't your agent give you a name?"

"I'll put you on hold and check with her. She probably has a name. Stay on the line."

Music played, while Emma was on hold, and her head was spinning trying to figure out who would know her from Chicago.

The music ended and Katie came back on-line. "His name is Conti. It's Antonio Conti."

Emma felt the blood drain from her face.

"Are you sure, Katie?"

"Yes, I'm sure! Do you know him?"

"It's Marco's birth father."

"Your husband's?"

Emma was at a loss for what to say. "Forgive me, Katie, but this is a jolt to my emotional balance. I know you're happy to have a buyer for the gallery, but this guy Conti is primarily responsible for wrecking my marriage."

Katie paused, while trying to absorb what Emma was saying, and it rapidly deflated her joyous news.

"Oh, my," she exclaimed, "I had no idea what the connection might be. However, on the upside, I'd love to have you managing the gallery. You're our best selling artist, and there'd be none better than you to make this place a success."

"You're kind, Katie, but there's more to this than having a buyer for the gallery. I don't think you need to know the details, but I suspect Marco has had something to do with this, and it really upsets me to think he'd sink so low to think he can buy my favor."

"Oh, lord, Em, I had no idea."

"No, it's okay. I understand, but just to be clear; I have no intention of managing the gallery, especially if Antonio Conti owns it. I want nothing to do with him."

"Oh, dear, I was afraid this was too good to be true."

"Is it a firm offer?"

"Yeah, I think so, but my agent says it's contingent on having you manage it."

"It's not going to happen, Katie. I'm sorry!"

"I'm sorry too, Em! I can tell by your tone it's a sensitive issue. I'll talk to my agent and see how she wants to handle it. I'm assuming when Conti hears you're not interested, he'll withdraw the offer."

"I'm sorry, Katie, but I think I know what's going on here, and I really don't like it."

"Well, at least the good news is you've sold two more paintings."

"That's great! I can use the income: however, as far as Conti is concerned, I'm going to call Marco and ask what's going on."

"Okay, Em! We'll stay in touch."

~

Marco had left the hot sun of Vegas and returned to foggy San Francisco Bay Area. The contrast made him shiver. The fog also caused a gloomy darkness inside the house, which matched his mood. Because of traffic, it had been a longer drive than he'd anticipated, so he buffered himself with a glass of wine and flopped into his big recliner. The message light on the phone was blinking, but he intentionally ignored it. He needed time to think about a whole bunch of things.

When the phone rang, he'd nearly fallen asleep. He glanced at his watch and wondered who would be calling at 10:00 p.m.

"Marco! What in the hell have you done?"

Emma was riled beyond anger and screamed her question so loudly he had to hold the phone away from his ear. He'd been hoping she'd call, but he'd forgotten her feisty temper.

"What I've done is sit here for weeks waiting for you to call." He tried to speak calmly and wanted to remind her she'd left him and not the other way around. However, it didn't work.

"I've called repeatedly, but since you're never home, I'm surprised you even answered this time!"

"I'm a busy person, so why are you screaming at me?"

"I got a call today from my friend Katie, who runs the Fresno gallery, and she told me your *father,* Antonio Conti, has made an offer to buy the gallery and wants me to manage it for him."

She paused to let the information sink in, and he was caught totally off-guard.

"Jesus, Marco! Are you so frigging desperate you've resorted to mob tactics? What in the hell is going on?"

His facial muscles tightened as fear thundered in his brain. "I have no idea," he confessed. "I'm as surprised as you are."

"Oh, for god's sake," Emma shouted. "I find that hard to believe!"

His thoughts were in hyper drive, but he was at a loss for what to say. "I have no idea what Conti wants. It's certainly not my idea."

"Whatever! I don't really care who's idea it is, but the sheer audacity of thinking I'd want to manage a gallery owned by Antonio Conti is completely ludicrous."

"It's not my idea, Emma!"

"Well, there has to be a reason, Marco, and I don't accept your plea of innocence. What have you done? Why does Conti think he can buy my favor? Have you been in contact with him?"

He could feel the shift in her tone and could tell she was getting emotional. He remembered Antonio saying something about helping her with a gallery, but he certainly didn't expect this.

"I really don't know," he repeated. "Maybe he wants to extend an olive branch. Hell, I don't know what he wants."

Emma sniffed and didn't reply, so he waited as she blew her nose, but when she returned, she fired off another set of indictments, which were far more personal.

"You're pretending to be innocent, but it's not working. You must have had contact with him, and you know why he's doing this, but you're not telling me! What's happened to you Marco? What's happened to the loving guy I married?"

"I'm right here in San Jose waiting on you and Celine to come back home."

"Bullshit! That's not going to happen! You've not been there the whole weekend. What have you been doing? Don't you ever check your messages? No one could find you when you were at that stupid conference, so what else is going on? You made one stinking phone call to me and then disappeared. What's happening, Marco?"

She paused, but he knew this wasn't the time for truth telling.

"I can't take it, Marco. That's why you came home to an empty house. I decided if you don't care, then I don't care either! What's happened to you? Are you in cahoots with Antonio Conti? He's a mobster, Marco, and I don't care if he is your birth father. Why is he offering to buy an art gallery and trying to seduce me into managing it for him? Why would he do that? Good lord, Marco, is this some kind of a carnival game where I get a stuffed teddy bear if I'm a good girl?"

He knew what he should say but didn't have the guts to say it, so he continued the charade.

"I don't know what to say, Emma. I'm not in cahoots with Antonio, but I have talked to him. IBM's going to move to another location, and he wants me to come work for him." He could almost hear the dull thud of his words landing on Emma's consciousness. "I guess he thought you might enjoy having your own art gallery. Hell, I imagine he'd even set you up in Vegas if you wanted."

"Vegas? What in the hell does Vegas have to do with it? Good, god, Marco! Do you know how absolutely absurd that sounds? Do you honesty think I'd be interested in having the Chicago Mob funding my art career?" She paused for a deafening moment of silence. "I can't believe what you're telling me, and how come Vegas is suddenly a point of interest!"

"Conti lives in Las Vegas."

Emma audibly groaned. "Jesus Christ! Have you gone completely out of your mind?"

"He's offering way more than I could ever earn at IBM."

"Oh, Jesus, Marco! You're such a fool. When Celine and I left San Jose, I wasn't sure what was going on with you, but now it seems obvious. You've reconnected with your father and you're selling your soul!"

He heard her sobbing, but could tell she wasn't finished because she was stuttering to find the right words.

"You can't have this thing with Conti and still be my husband!" Her words were bold and cutting. "If you're stupid enough to do something like this, then this is goodbye."

He felt defensive but couldn't find words to retaliate. There was silence and more sobbing before she lashed out again.

"It seems very strange to me that you'd decide to do this out of the blue, but I hope you're realizing how angry I am about it. I want nothing to do with Antonio Conti, so if you're choosing him, it's on your shoulders not mine. I'm also speaking for Celine, and I hope you understand what you're losing." There was more sobbing as her words burned their way into his brain.

"Goddammit, Marco! What's happened to you? I bet there's more to it than Conti, but that's just a hunch, and it hurts more than you'll ever know."

He was going to say, "I haven't made a decision yet," but before he could speak, he heard a "click" as she hung up on him. The phone felt hot in his hand. He'd anticipated her anger but wasn't prepared for such a blistering attack. He hung his head in despair.

Antonio miscalculated her strong will, he thought, *and for that matter, so did I.*

When he put down the phone, he wished he could reverse course but didn't have the courage to do so. The darkness outside was like the darkness inside, and it was descending over him relentlessly.

Marco had purchased another bottle of bourbon and felt the need to break its seal. He noted it was nearly 11:00 p.m. when he poured his drink. The silence felt oppressive, so he carried his glass into the bedroom where he sat forlornly on the edge of the bed staring into the mirror behind the dresser. His reflection revealed more than he wanted to see. His jowls drooped, his eyes were moist with tears, and his shoulders slumped as though burdened with a tremendous weight. If someone could have asked directly, he would have said he loved Emma, but his actions revealed otherwise. Capricia had taken her place. Her sensual sexuality could arouse him instantly, something Emma could also do but not as well. In other words, Emma's rejection was no match for Capricia's embrace. He was torn by his conflicted feelings, but he'd already gone over the edge.

Any person with a normal conscience would say I'm a son-of-a-bitch, and I'd be defenseless.

He drank until his glass was empty and then turned toward a wall, refusing to look at his image any longer. Thoughts of Celine caused him to break down in tears. Not being able to see her and hold her in his arms was beyond painful. He looked at his empty glass and sobbed uncontrollably. His prospects were not as promising as he'd hoped. The alcohol clouded his reasoning, but he mumbled aloud that he was going to be with his father regardless of the cost.

It's probably not a wise decision, but I've got to do this.

He knew he would need to resign from his job with IBM, and he was already regretting it. Finally, he set his glass aside and rolled onto his side. Shadows on his bedroom wall seemed sinister, and the darkness seemed an ominous reminder of the life he was choosing. He moaned aloud in emotional pain and wondered why he'd ever give up his marriage, his daughter and his job, but then he thought of Capricia and cried out her name. He'd never felt so impotent and vulnerable. It was like being caught in a whirlpool, where the force drawing him down was stronger than his resistance.

"Help me!" he cried, but his only consolation was to blot out his vulnerability with more alcohol.

FOURTEEN

*M*arco resigned from IBM and moved to Las Vegas taking only a couple of suitcases filled mostly with personal items and a few clothes. Antonio had told him he could get what he needed once he got settled. He'd sold his car to a co-worker and arranged to have the exterior of the San Jose house maintained, but when he locked the door, he wasn't sure when or if he'd ever return.

More than likely I'll have to come back someday and sell this place.

He waited forlornly on the front porch until the airport shuttle arrived. The cheerful van driver wished him a good morning, but he only nodded and tried to smile cordially. As the van pulled away, he looked wistfully over his shoulder and realized he was literally leaving it all behind.

"You'll have unlimited funds to buy whatever you need," Antonio had said, and then he'd given him a thousand in cash to use during his transition.

He was leaving his neighborhood, his wife, his daughter and his job at IBM. It seemed very final.

There's no turning back now.

The van thudded over every bump on the road, and he wondered if it was symbolic of what was ahead.

~

*H*e had called Capricia just before leaving, and she was ecstatic over his decision.

"Antonio wants me to live at the Tropicana," Marco explained.

"I know," she said. "It's very upscale. They're renovating your suite."

"I can hardly imagine living in a casino hotel."

"It'll be great, Marco. Tony said he wants you to have the best."

"Are you going to meet me?

"Absolutely! I'm aching to see you."

~

Capricia was with Antonio, and he could tell she was happy but anxious.

"Something tells me Marco has stolen your heart."

"Maybe?" she said playfully. "He's incredibly handsome and very kind."

Antonio laughed. "He'll be a novelty on my team. All my guys act like a bunch of bums. Marco's smart and acts like a real gentleman."

"It's genetic, Tony. He's smart like you!"

Antonio smiled. "He looks a lot like me too." Then he winked at Capricia and kissed her on the cheek to show appreciation. "He probably gets his smarts from his mother, but maybe a little from me, too."

Capricia smiled and gave him a hug.

"You're my angel," he said with a big smile, "and Marco better treat you good if he wants to keep me happy."

Capricia glanced at her watch and saw it was time to go, so she gave him another hug and hurried out the door. She'd never felt this way before, but as Antonio had said, Marco had captured her heart.

~

As the plane began its final approach for landing at McCarran International, Marco wondered if he was making a big mistake; however, Capricia had encouraged him to just accept his natural status as Conti's son, be honest and do what he was asked to do. However, he still wasn't sure what that would be. He also wondered how other associates working for his father would accept him. He'd already concluded they wouldn't be as accepting as Capricia. Then he thought of Emma and Celine. Before leaving, he'd called to explain, but she didn't answer, so he left a short message.

Sorry I missed you, but I want you to know I'm moving to Las Vegas to work with my father. I know you'll think I'm crazy but it's what I want to do. I'll keep sending money every month, and I'll try to call you once I'm settled.

When the wheels of the plane touched the runway, he opened his bag and splashed on some cologne in anticipation of meeting Capricia. She'd been rather blunt and told him their relationship would never be anything more than sexual, but he felt something had changed. Of course, they'd made love, but the last time they'd been together, she'd told him what she liked best was when he held her in his arms.

He looked nostalgically out the window as the plane taxied toward the terminal and then felt a surge of excitement. He could hardly wait to see her.

"Welcome to Las Vegas," announced the flight attendant. "Local time is 4:06. Please remain seated until the plane stops and the captain has turned off the seatbelt sign. Thanks for flying American, and have an enjoyable evening."

When he walked off the plane, Capricia ran to him like a schoolgirl in love.

After lingering in a long embrace, they retrieved his bags and went directly to the Tropicana, where a bellman greeted him by name and took command of his luggage. The staff had obviously been briefed about their newest resident guest, and with Capricia at his side they recognized him the moment he arrived. He thought he would need to go to the registration counter to get his room assignment, but the bellman politely led them toward the elevators without saying a word. Capricia smiled and motioned for him to follow.

"I don't even know my room number," he complained.

"Trust me," Capricia smiled. "It's not *just* a room, and the staff knows exactly what to do."

He was still a bit baffled, but she held his hand as the elevator rose swiftly to an unmarked top floor where the doors opened to an elegant foyer of complete privacy. The bellman led the way down a short hallway to an impressive doorway. He touched a sensor by the door with a small card, and it opened as if by magic. Then he handed the card to Marco.

"Just keep the card on your person, Mr. Jackson. The door automatically locks when you leave, so just touch the card to the sensor when you arrive."

Capricia beamed and Marco clutched the card as though it was his lifeline. Then he stepped inside onto ultra-plush carpeting and realized his suite was similar to Antonio's and Capricia's. There were several spacious rooms, one of which was a large living room with big windows overlooking the lights of Las Vegas. Then down a joining hallway he discovered a mega-sized master bath with a glass shower stall and marble counters accented with fresh flowers and costly toiletries. Just steps away from the bath, he entered a bedroom big enough to live in, and was overwhelmed at the extra big bed covered with pillows and a brocade comforter.

"Antonio said it would be special," Capricia cooed. "And just look at that bed! Shall we give it a try?"

The bellman ignored her comment, and when Marco handed him ten dollars, he bowed graciously and closed the door on his way out. Capricia had been serious! She tugged on his hand, slipped out of her clothes, and crawled to the middle of the bed. In the soft light of the bedroom, she appeared as a Greek goddess waiting for her Adonis.

"Hold that thought," Marco called. "I'll be with you as soon as I use the bathroom."

In minutes he returned to her waiting arms as she raised her knees and cried out with joy when he pressed against her.

"Oh, god, Marco, I've missed you."

He had no words, as she greedily demanded all he could give. Their lovemaking was so intense, Marco literally collapsed at her side trying to catch his breath. He realized in that moment he'd given up everything for her. He was there at the invitation of his father, but his decision was really to be with Capricia. It was gratifying and terrorizing at the same time. As he rested at her side, he realized he had abandoned his safe harbor and moved into the turbulence of uncharted waters. She nestled in his arms, and he sighed. He savored the intimacy, caressed her satin smooth body, and inhaled her intoxicating fragrance, but when he tried to see beyond the moment, his anxious feelings returned. Whatever followed such ecstasy would undoubtedly take him further into the darkness.

~

Capricia spent the night, and at seven the next morning, she was up and about making calls for room service and brewing fresh coffee.

He finally managed to slip on a robe and wander into the small kitchen to stand next to her. "What's the hurry?"

"We have lots to do!" she said and gave him a quick kiss. "I'm taking you to Tony's tailor who will measure your amazingly muscular body for a new wardrobe, and then I'm going to introduce you to the Tropicana staff and in particular to the ones charged with keeping you happy. Then Tony wants to see you at eleven, so breakfast will arrive soon and we'll get started!"

"Wow! Are we going to the Stardust to meet Antonio?"

"No! He's coming here and wants to see how the renovation turned out, so you need to be here before eleven. He's dependably prompt."

"Is there a doorbell? How will I know he's here?"

Capricia smiled. "It's like magic," she explained. "You'll get a call when he's on his way up, and I'd suggest meeting him when he steps into the atrium. I know it seems very private here in your new penthouse suite, but believe me! Tony's the boss and expects to be treated respectfully."

Marco hurried to shave, shower and get dressed, and by the time he was finishing, their breakfast had arrived. They dined comfortably, but Capricia kept pushing to keep him on schedule.

The tailor was cordial but very business-like. When Marco asked what would be in his wardrobe, his question caused the tailor to stop and wrinkle his brow.

"It's not a concern, Mr. Jackson. My staff and I will take care of you."

"Will I get a new suit?"

This time the tailor frowned. "There will be three or maybe four, suits Mr. Jackson. You'll received everything a gentleman needs including monogrammed underwear, if that's what you're asking."

Marco reacted with a surprised smile and decided not to ask any more questions. When he returned to the waiting area, he looked at Capricia and raised his brow showing his surprise.

She smiled, and when the tailor left, she asked: "Do you like him?"

Marco wrinkled his expression. "He doesn't appreciate questions."

"I know," she laughed, "but he's a damn good tailor."

Then they toured the Tropicana where he met his personal aide, Lila, who was middle-aged but very attractive. She explained how things worked and that whatever he needed the staff would do their best to provide.

"We're paid handsomely to take care of you, Mr. Jackson, so never hesitate to ask."

Then they went on a whirlwind behind-the-scenes tour of the hotel before returning to Lila's office where she spent the next 20 minutes making notes about his likes and dislikes. She explained that they'd be taking care of his housekeeping, his wardrobe and making contacts at his request.

"Antonio is a good friend of mine," she explained, "and he's advised me quite explicitly about what he wants for you." She smiled and patted his arm. "Speaking of Antonio, he's informed me he's coming to visit you at eleven this morning, so I'll give you a call when he arrives. I'd suggest you greet him when he steps out of the elevator."

Between her and Capricia, I've learned that meeting Antonio at the elevator is protocol.

~

Capricia left around 10:30, and he waited patiently until minutes before eleven when the phone rang.

"Hello."

"Good morning! This is Lila! Mr. Conti has just arrived, so please go to the elevator to greet him."

He glanced at his watch. It was exactly eleven o'clock, so he hurried to the elevator, and when the doors opened, Antonio stepped out and wrapped his arms around him like a father welcoming his son home.

"Hey, Marco! Look at you! My, god, you're a handsome devil!"

Then he hugged him again. His embrace conveyed genuine affection, and Marco graciously responded without words. Then they walked to his door, which Marco opened with his *magic* card and motioned for Antonio to go in ahead of him.

Antonio smiled and nodded his approval when he saw what had been done. He glanced into the bedroom, where the bed was still disheveled, and then smiled again, while patting Marco on the back.

"They did a great job with this place! Calvetti Construction has done a lot of work for me, and they're amazing with interiors."

"Thanks for being so generous," Marco said in a subdued voice. "It's so luxurious."

"You're my son, Marco! You deserve the best, and I've already put out the word that you've joined the family."

Marco felt another flutter of anxiety. The "family" meant the mob, and that was his lingering concern. He knew of course, there would be others in the Outfit, who would be meeting him and sizing him up, and he was fearful. He slightly shuddered at the thought of being scrutinized by a bunch of thugs, but this was his new reality, and Antonio had probably boasted about him a little too freely.

"I see you've had breakfast," Conti smiled, while pointing to the leftovers. "I told Lila to take good care of you."

Marco nodded, while Conti kept looking things over.

"She'll get anything you need, so don't hesitate to ask."

"She's already been helpful," Marco agreed.

"Yeah! She's great!"

The Conti went into the kitchen and called to Marco over his shoulder. "I'm gonna pour you some coffee, Marco, and maybe you can sit over there by the windows, while I tend to a little business matter."

It didn't sound like it was open for discussion, so Marco took his coffee and did as he was told, while Antonio fussed with his tie, flexed his arms and then reached for the phone.

"Yeah, Lila, Tony . . . hey, listen, I want you to tell D'Angelo to bring Mantino up here right away, Capisce? Yeah, now!" Then he hung up the phone, straightened his tie again and smiled at Marco. "It's just a little personal matter Marco. It won't take a minute."

Marco had no idea what he was suggesting but could sense his nervous tension, and then he heard someone knocking at his door. Conti motioned for Marco to remain seated and quickly opened the door to let two men inside. They stood before him like soldiers, and Marco also stood to see who had entered the room.

"Mantino, you're a son-of-a-bitch, but you probably know that already!" One of the men bowed his head and stared at the floor, while the other man waited stoically for Conti to continue. "You know I value loyalty, isn't that right?" The man looking down nodded slightly. "So, look at me Mantino!" He used his hand to lift Mantino's face and squeezed his jowls. "How much did you take, maybe 100 grand? You greedy bastard! I guess you think we don't pay you enough; is that right?" Mantino tried desperately to avoid eye contact, while Antonio continued squeezing his face. "Maybe you took more than a hundred, you asshole! If I knew where she's buried, I'd piss on your mother's grave . . . do you hear me?"

Mantino finally jerked his head free from Antonio's grip and looked away.

Marco watched and fought a feeling of nausea churning in his gut.

Mantino looked a little pale.

Then Antonio pinched the flesh of Mantino's cheek and slapped him playfully. "You sly bastard! You know the money doesn't belong to you, right?"

Mantino nodded.

"I'll tell you what we're gonna do, Mantino. D'Angelo's a good man, and he'd gonna take you for a little ride and give you some time to think about what you've done. What's the name of those big birds D'Angelo?"

"They're Vultures, Tony!"

"Yeah, that's it!" Antonio confirmed. "He wants to show you some of them big birds called Vultures."

The blood drained from Mantino's face, and Marco suddenly realized what Antonio was saying. His knees nearly buckled, so he decided to sit down.

"I'm gonna give you one last chance to be honorable, Mantino. LOOK AT ME! Did you take the goddamned money?"

Once again, Mantino looked down and didn't answer.

"Jesus!" Antonio screamed. "You ain't even got the balls to admit what you did." Then he gave Mantino a little shove and turned his back on him. "Get him outta here, D'Angelo!"

The muscular man held tightly to Mantino's arms and pushed him into the hallway.

The door closed silently behind him, and Antonio went straight to the bar, poured a generous amount of whiskey and downed it in one swallow. Then he walked to the windows to stand next to Marco. He stood with his feet apart, tightened his fists and continued fussing with his tie.

Marco turned to look at Antonio and grimaced.

"It's about loyalty, Marco. That's all I ever ask. I want my people to be loyal." Then he sat down.

"What just happened?" Marco asked and looked pleadingly at Antonio.

Conti laughed uneasily. "I've just created a job opening for you."

"Mantino's job?"

"Well, it used to be his job until the son-of-a-bitch double-crossed me . . . but hey, it's a perfect match for your skills!" Then he laughed uneasily and put his arm around Marco's shoulders.

"I don't like the way it feels," Marco said and looked away.

"Yeah, I know, and I'm sorry you had to witness this on your first day. It's never easy, and I know you're probably a little shocked, but I'm telling you Marco, the Outfit never tolerates cheats and liars. Once you get squared away, you'll be dealing with some pretty tough people, and there's just no way to avoid it. You have to be strong . . . and even more than that, you have to be honest. If you ever find out someone's not playing by the rules, I expect you to tell me."

"What's going to happen to Mantino?"

Conti squinted his eyes and leaned toward Marco.

"Look at me, Marco! I'm an honorable man, and I'm sorry I walked away when you were born, but you're important to me, and I plan to take good care of you. I've not said that to you before, but I want you to know. I'll take care of you!"

"Yeah, but what's going to happen to Mantino?"

"Mantino's history! He took over a hundred grand of the Outfit's money, so now he gets his due. Don't worry about it. D'Angelo's a good man, and he'll deal with Mantino."

Then Antonio walked toward the bar and started pacing.

"Once in a while these things happen, Marco. You'll get used to it. I invited you to work with me because you're my son, and I know you're an honorable man, but you'll get used to the way we do business." He smiled knowingly. "You have a lot of your mother's characteristics, so we're going be close, Marco. I know you'll be loyal, because you and me . . . we got the same blood running through our veins. This luxury suite is just the beginning. I'm gonna take good care of you, Marco, so don't forget, we're family! Just relax and let me prove it to you. Capricia has already told me you're solid, and by the way, she's also going to take care of you . . . if you know what I mean." He smiled and made a knowing expression. "Anyway, now that Mantino's out of the way, I'm going to show you where our Outfit keeps its money, and you're gonna take a look at the system we're using to keep track of it."

"What kind of system?"

"It's a computer system, Son, so it's right down your alley."

"Computers? I didn't know you have computers."

"Yeah! We have computers, but I don't know a damn thing about them; anyway, I know you do, so maybe you'll have some ideas about making our system work better. I'm putting you in charge of keeping track of our money."

Antonio paused and looked extremely pleased, but Marco was suddenly feeling a tremendous burden settling over him. He'd just witnessed a mob boss sending a man to his death and now he was essentially telling him he'd been chosen to take his place.

"I'm really glad you're here, Marco. I think everything's going to work out just fine." He winked and nodded smugly. "Did Capricia get you squared away with my tailor, Giuseppe?" He glanced at Marco for confirmation. "He's the silent type but one helluva tailor. You're gonna love the suits he'll make for you. There's none finer."

Marco smiled weakly and accepted Antonio's handshake.

"I'll just have another quick drink while you freshen up, and then we'll go on a little field trip to check things out."

Once again, Marco sensed it wasn't open for discussion, so he did as he was told. Within minutes he followed Antonio to the elevator, which rapidly descended to the lobby of the Tropicana, where they were joined by an entourage of three muscular soldiers impeccably dressed in expensive silk suits and wearing very dark sunglasses. He consciously looked down at his own casual attire and felt weak in their company.

"Are you ready to go, Tony?" one of them asked, and Antonio nodded.

Various hotel employees stepped aside to clear the way for them as they marched through the lobby and then outside where two very sleek black sedans waited to whisk them away in air-conditioned comfort to an undisclosed location on a less traveled street somewhere in Las Vegas. Marco sat next to a very big man, and once again felt he was descending into darkness. Antonio had assured him, but he felt vulnerable and out of place. The physical size of the man next to him made him feel small. Although Marco had a lean, muscular body, he knew he'd be no match for the guy's brawn. Things moving way too fast.

The car rounded another corner and then slowed.

Darkness is a metaphor, Marco reasoned. *It's mysterious and frightening. It's like fog, which get thicker and thicker until there are no visual markers and no way to tell what's coming.*

FIFTEEN

Marco was in the lead car with Antonio, while the others followed in a second car, and there was absolutely no communication of any kind. Their driver, a slender man with Italian features, obviously knew where Antonio wanted to go and drove rather recklessly through traffic turning corners so fast, Marco had to hang on to a center armrest to avoid slipping on the leather seats. The muscular man next to him seemed immune to the force of gravity and only leaned slightly as they sped to their destination. The car's dark windows made it difficult to see, but within minutes both cars pulled into a parking area in front of a white, stucco building with a covered walkway accented by a fountain and marble statues. The drivers hurried to open doors for their passengers.

Antonio led the way and was greeted politely by various staff people as he walked quickly toward a doorway, which opened electronically leading to a stairway. Marco hurried to keep up and quickly went down the stairs with the others behind him, and then Antonio entered a code to open a second door, which let them into a large dimly lit room. He removed his sunglasses and realized they were in a vault-like room beneath the very private Italian American Club somewhere on the backstreets of Las Vegas. He immediately felt the controlled temperature and lack of humidity, and most unusual of all, there were floor-to-ceiling stacks of banker boxes carefully arranged on wooded pallets filling more than half of the space in the room.

Antonio waited with his three impeccably groomed soldiers, while Marco looked around. In one corner of the room there was a well-appointed office with two computers setting side-by-side and two large file cabinets next to a wall. He tucked his sunglasses into his pocket and walked past the others to take a closer look. During his time with IBM he'd watched the rapid development of personal computers, but this was the first time he'd actually seen a setup outside of IBM where computers were in use. He quickly surmised they were networked, and then studied the monitors, which displayed spreadsheet data similar to programs they'd developed at IBM.

"Computers!" he said with a smug expression to Antonio, "and lots of banker boxes!"

"It's like our own Fort Knox," Antonio boasted. "It's too risky to use banks for handling large sums of cash, so we set up our own little cash management system. It's a little antiquated, but this is our vault."

"And those boxes . . ."

"Are full of cash," one of Conti's soldiers interrupted. "Only a few of us are ever privileged to be in this room, but the boxes are filled with cash."

Marco tried *not* to act surprised, but he was nearly overwhelmed by such a claim, so he reached to touch one of the boxes and noticed its lid had been sealed with tape.

"I'm confused," he said and looked at Antonio. "How can you manage this much cash without some kind of banking transactions?"

"We have connections," Antonio explained. "I'll fill you in on the details later."

"It's crude," Marco said unapologetically. "What's preventing a thief from tunneling into this room and taking your money?"

Antonio and his three goons burst into laughter.

"There are no thieves in Vegas but us," one of them boasted and the others continued laughing. "Besides, if any stupid-assed dude ever decided to break in, he'd spend a month of Sundays trying to penetrate the walls and floor of this place. When Tony calls it *Fort Knox*, he's not kidding."

Antonio smiled smugly, but Marco shrugged.

"What about Mantino? It seems he found a way."

The soldiers stiffened and clenched their fists, but Antonio motioned for them to be at ease.

"Mantino was my manager in this room, Marco. I trusted him to be loyal, but he decided to be a smartass and thought he could get away with stealing our money."

Marco listened and slightly nodded his head.

"Nobody breaks the rules!" Tony proclaimed with a clenched jaw and narrowed eyes.

"And what are the rules?" Marco challenged. "I haven't heard much about the rules."

The soldiers glared at him as though he might be crossing a boundary, but Marco looked directly at Antonio and waited for an answer.

"You and I are gonna talk about the rules, Marco, but I can tell you straight-up, the Outfit has ways of watching over things, and everybody, who works for me knows the rules.

There's no need to talk about it now, but before you come back to this room, you'll know the rules."

Marco noticed an angry look on the faces of the three soldiers, and he sensed they didn't like his questions or Antonio's soft approach with him.

"I apologize for asking, " he said, while looking directly at the three soldiers. "I guess I'm just nervous being around this much money."

Antonio laughed. "You'll get used to it, and you're gonna be amazed at how we run things."

He nodded, but his nerves were rattled. He knew Mantino had paid with his life for breaking the rules, and now he was being asked to take Mantino's place. It was as though life and death were suddenly hanging in the balance.

"How about it, Son?" Antonio asked loudly. "Do you think you can manage this?"

"With a little coaching, I think it might be a *cool* job."

The three soldiers burst out laughing.

"He sounds like a fucking high school kid being asked to manage the senior prom," one of them said.

Antonio immediately grabbed him by his lapels and pulled him within inches of his face glaring into his eyes. "Don't mock what Marco says, Veneto! Maybe you should learn to say *cool* instead of *no shit.* Maybe you should keep in mind that Marco's my kid. Capisce?"

"I apologize, Tony. I was just being stupid!"

Conti released him and nodded his acceptance of the apology. Then he looked at Marco.

"They're from Chicago, Marco. You just have to forgive them. They're smart, but they don't know good language when they hear it." He smiled and patted Marco on his shoulder.

Marco smiled weakly, but he also noticed the cold angry look on Veneto's face.

"Okay, I think we've seen enough," Conti announced. "Let's go upstairs and have a drink."

Veneto gave Marco another angry look as they followed Antonio out of the room, and when the door shut behind them, it made a solid "thud" followed by a loud "click" as a lock automatically secured the vault. Marco looked up and noticed a red light glowing inside a glass sign above the door. It illuminated a single word: ARMED!

~

When he returned to the Tropicana that evening, Marco went straight to his private bar and poured some bourbon over ice. He had acted cavalier during the visit to the mob's money vault, but found it difficult to accept what he'd learned. There was no longer any doubt "the Outfit" was stealing cash from the casinos, and all those boxes of money he'd seen contained the illegal bounty. As he dropped a second ice cube into his drink, he thought again about darkness.

It's a room full of the mob's money, and he wants me to manage it. He also thought of Antonio's three soldiers, who stood like stoned-faced statues. *God, they're intimidating, and I'm an outsider, who has a non-Italian last name.* His presence at Antonio's side seemed an anomaly. The others had earned their place within the family, and he was a young upstart, who just happened to the boss's kid. It was okay because it gave him an advantage, but then he remembered Veneto and shuddered. He obviously didn't like the way Antonio was favoring him and stared at him with anger. *I would never want to be alone with him or to confront him about anything.*

He took his drink and walked to the windows to face the fact there'd be no turning back. What he'd experienced so far was in the shadows and he knew the seriousness implied by all of it. On the street below he saw the intensity of Las Vegas' nightlife with inebriated tourists overcoming their inhibitions.

They seemed oblivious to the mob manipulating everything. What he'd seen at the Italian American Club was the sobering reality of how the system worked. The sight of all those boxes of money symbolized the mob's total control.

He finished his bourbon and turned to look at the lavish interior of his penthouse suite. The alcohol had settled his nerves, but he still had questions.

Who lives like this?

Before leaving the club, Antonio had given him more money, all in hundred dollar bills. He had no idea how much money he'd receive or when he'd receive it, but it was beginning to dawn on him that Antonio's promise of making him a rich man was already beginning. He really didn't need more cash, so he put it into a safe in his room and kept out a thousand to open a personal checking account. Since arriving, he'd paid for nothing. He had the luxury of a car and driver whenever he needed it, his expensive tailor-made suits and shirts would magically appear in his master bedroom closet within a few days, he had an open tab at restaurants and bars according to Lila, he could depend on having a well-stocked bar, which could easily lead to over indulging.

"I'll give you money every month," Conti had told him, "and if you don't need it, just store it away for later."

I wonder how long it can last?

He went back to the bar with the intention of pouring another shot of bourbon but decided against it. When he looked at his image in the mirror behind the bar he realized his innocence was already turning into hardness. In fact, he was still wearing his sunglasses without knowing why, so he removed them and looked himself in the eye. The decency, love, and family values he'd treasured during his youth had been replaced by Tony's single request: "Loyalty, Marco. That's all I ask! I need to be able to trust you."

"My life has changed in a single day," he said aloud lamenting what had happened since his arrival. He had turned his back on Emma and his beautiful daughter and foolishly wallowed in his lust for Capricia. He had willingly accepted his new status as Antonio Conti's son and marveled at the opulence of his new surroundings. He had freely accepted a major responsibility of managing millions of illegal mob money, and had already started stashing cash into a safe in his room. "All this in a single day," he said again.

While he was standing in that room filled with the mob's money, something began changing inside him. He'd joined the *Outfit*, which was manipulating everything in Vegas, including the police and some Nevada officials, who were willingly turning a blind-eye to the mob's activities. Now he was a part of it, and instead of saying, "I can't do this," he simply nodded and smiled as though it wasn't a big deal.

"Do you think you can manage this?" Conti had asked, and instead of saying, "I want no part of it," he simply said with a little coaching, it should be a *cool* job. He wasn't being true to himself and was too easily accepting a major responsibility with the mob.

He frowned at his image in the mirror, poured another shot, downed it in a couple swallows and felt beads of sweat on his forehead.

~

*M*arco was feeling deeply conflicted and wanted to get away from the loneliness of his spacious penthouse, so he splashed some cold water on his face, combed his hair and returned to the spacious but noisy lobby of the Tropicana. He stood among the crowd trying to decide what he'd like to do, and then, with angel softness, Capricia surprised him by wrapping her arms around him. He spun around to lift her into his arms as hotel workers paused to admire their loving display of affection. She was a picture of loveliness. Unlike before, she was wearing a gorgeous soft yellow evening ensemble of silk slacks with matching heels and an elegant top, which accented her perky breasts and lustrous hair. She was so striking she literally caused a momentary hush to come over the crowd in the lobby.

"And why are you dressed so elegantly?" he asked and kissed her softly.

"Do you remember I offered to take you to the *Lido* at the Stardust?"

He nodded.

"Well, tonight's the night!" she said with a gleaming smile.

He hesitated. "I'm not sure I'm free to go. Antonio was unclear as to what's expected."

"It's okay! I've already talked to him, and we have his blessing."

"Do you run his life?"

"More or less, and he loves it."

He released her from his embrace and stood back admiring her. "You're so beautiful."

She smiled. "Do you need to freshen up?"

"If I'm going to be with you, I think I better at least change my clothes."

She grabbed his hand and pulled him toward the elevators. His special card sent the elevator past the other floors to the top floor of the Tropicana where no one else was allowed to go. Capricia held his hand and laid her head on his shoulder during the short ride to the top. Then they stepped out of the elevator into the surreal privacy of the penthouse foyer and walked hand in hand to his door, which opened in a whisper when he touched his card to the sensor. She smiled knowingly, raised her hands and did a pirouette through the doorway before seductively coaxing him inside. He followed but stopped suddenly as the door closed behind him.

"What's the matter, Marco?"

He seemed thoughtful, and she noticed the serious look on his face.

"I was here with Antonio, D'Angelo and Mantino this morning. They were standing right here next to the door."

Capricia shrugged her shoulders. "I know what happened," she said sullenly. "Mantino should have known better."

"Antonio said he stole some money."

"Over a hundred grand, Marco! He was being stupid."

"I heard Antonio tell D'Angelo to take him for a ride and show him the vultures."

"That means D'Angelo whacked him! That stuff happens all the time, but the smart ones know better than to break the rules. Mantino knew there'd be consequences."

"So, D'Angelo killed Mantino?"

Capricia made a nonchalant expression and shrugged again. "He knew he'd never get away with it."

"What about the police? Don't they arrest people for murder?"

She frowned and wagged her head. "It's better not to ask about such things, Marco. I try to ignore it . . . it's just the way things are done."

He shuddered and shook his head. "It's very disturbing!"

"Of course it's disturbing! Tony doesn't like it either, but he's the boss, and when somebody screws up, he has to deal with it. Tony's a good man, Marco, but like he says, loyalty is everything, and Mantino broke the rules."

"You're being very matter-of-fact!"

"Forget about it, Marco. It's none of your business."

He arched his brow and stared at her with a questioning look. "I've heard about things like this," he complained, "but I've never witnessed it. I wonder why Antonio brought Mantino here to confront him"

She shrugged and hunched her shoulders. "Maybe to make an impression, but it's none of your business, Marco. Forget about it! Just be truthful and loyal and you'll stay out of trouble."

He hesitated but seriously considered her advice.

"Right! I'm going to take a shower, so feel free to fix yourself a drink."

Marco also shaved and groomed himself with some expensive lotion and cologne before wrapping a towel around his waist and then walked past Capricia to select some clothes.

She watched and followed him. "You may not know it, Marco, but you are devastatingly handsome. A girl like me can get all a flutter real quick."

To make her point, she walked toward him licking her lips. He was immediately aroused. Then she kicked off her shoes and let him watch as she slipped out of her slacks. When she turned to face him, he loosened his towel letting it drop to the floor, and the only thing between him and absolute ecstasy were her silk panties, which he slowly removed and then lifted her to receive him. She wrapped her legs tightly around him as he carried her into the living room where he sat down on the couch, so she could be in control. As always, having sex with Capricia was an erotic dive into ultimate pleasure, and with the glittering lights of Las Vegas as a backdrop, his concerns about mob tactics vanished from his mind.

~

In the days that followed, Marco and Antonio had many conversations about managing the mob's money, which he'd seen in a subterranean room at the Italian American Club. He learned the rules, which could be easily summarized by Conti's repetitive insistence on loyalty. He also learned about the mob's activities, which included collaboration and money laundering with the Teamsters' Union, prostitution, bootlegged booze and what Antonio called "skimming" cash from the casinos.

"Money flows in and out of this room everyday, Marco. You'll get used to it. I'm going to set you up with our contacts, and it'll be your job to maintain our cash flow. I'll depend on you to account for what comes in and what goes out. D'Angelo's going to work with you for a couple months or so. He'll help you learn the system. I want you to take a critical look at how the system works, because I think you can come up with a way to make it work even better. D'Angelo is gonna identify all our key players, the ones we are trusting to bring in the cash, so learn their names and get to know them. I want you to keep close tabs on all of them, and if you see anything suspicious, you let me know."

It was difficult for Marco to hear these things and not feel nervous. Antonio sensed he was a little overwhelmed, so he kept reassuring him and reminding him he'd take good care of him, which made it seem okay in spite of the questionable things he described. He repeatedly told him the "system" works because of the cooperation between the casinos, the police, the politicians and the Teamsters.

"It's a syndicate, Marco, and my job is to manage what goes on in this town. I try to make it good for everyone involved. You can ask anyone you choose, and they'll tell you the same thing. We make good things happen in Vegas, and as long as everyone cooperates, it works. They're all happy because they make more money because of us."

Marco could hardly believe it, but Antonio made it seem reasonable.

"It's a great big system," he added, "and I'm the one who holds it together. That's why I had to deal with Mantino. When somebody fails me, I have to deal with it."

Marco nodded and Antonio patted him on the back. "We earn our respect, Marco, and I'm proud to have you working with me."

However, Marco felt there was another side to his life that didn't earn respect. When listening to his father's explanations, he felt closely identified with him and had a sense of camaraderie, but frequently he longed to see his daughter Celine and wondered how she would think of him someday. He also thought of Emma and felt he deserved no respect from her. It was only in the context of his new life in Vegas that he felt confident. It was only when Antonio bolstered his ego that he felt any kind of personal power.

After a couple of tries, he finally connected with Emma, and when she answered the phone there was no respect in her voice.

"I tried to call our San Jose number," she said tersely, "and received a message that the number is no longer in service, so I assumed you'd followed your stupid inclination to go to Las Vegas to be with your father."

"I did," he admitted, "and I left a message for you. I thought I should at least let you know where I am, and that I'm setting up a checking account so I can keep sending money to help with expenses."

"Are you planning to stay there or is this just a temporary bout with insanity."

Her words hurt, but he maintained his composure and tried to be honest about it. "I'm not sure what will happen, but for the time being I'm here."

He thought she might have other hurtful things to say, but instead he endured an awkward silence. He waited.

"I've got nothing more to say, Marco. We're still married, and you're still Celine's father, but that's as far as it goes. I can't imagine why you'd want to give up everything to work for the mob, but I guess that's your business. I can't shake the feeling there's more to it than being with your father, but for the time being I'd rather not know."

"I'll send a check each month, so let me know if there's any change of address."

He waited for her to reply, but instead he heard a "click" as she disconnected the call.

Hearing her voice caused a longing, but there were things to do and people to meet, so he quickly put his mind on matters at hand.

~

During the weeks and months that followed, Marco overcame his nervousness and began enjoying his prestige and power. His impeccable tailored suits were outstanding and Capricia repeatedly told him he was the most handsome man she'd ever known. He did as he was told and settled in to help his father in his business of making money. People involved with the operation respected him, and when he talked with them he felt powerful. He skillfully managed the inflow and outflow of cash and did so without too much concern about the amount of money under his control. He kept track of millions, and toward the end of each month Antonio would give him large sums of cash for his personal use. He had no idea where his personal money came from, but he enjoyed having it and being generous. The more he tipped employees the more he endeared himself to them.

It was always the same when Antonio handed him more money.

"Here you go, Marco. This should take care of your needs for a month or so."

The money was mostly in one hundred dollar bills, and always tax-free. He regularly set a portion aside to deposit into his checking account, and then he'd put the rest of it in his safe. It seemed a bit ironic to be receiving cash from Antonio, while trying to keep track of millions flowing in and out of the basement vault at the club. There was never a record of Conti's payments to him, at least none he could track, and since he was responsible for managing the money, it made him nervous. The ritual had gone on for months, so one day during a private moment, he asked his father.

"Where do you get this cash you give me?"

Antonio scowled slightly. "Don't worry about it. You're working for me, Marco, so I pay you with my personal funds. Just enjoy it and don't worry about it."

He tried not to worry, but the more thoroughly he learned the system the more he saw potential troubles. He interacted frequently with his contacts from the Teamsters and felt the whole thing was a crooked as a dog's hind leg; however, as he'd been repeatedly instructed, he didn't question anything. Since he really didn't need the money, he kept stashing it in a safe, which the hotel provided in his room, and by the time he and Capricia celebrated his first anniversary of being in Vegas, his safe was nearly full. He hadn't counted it for quite a while but decided it was time to ask Lila if she could get him a larger safe.

"Absolutely," she said. "How much larger do you have in mind?"

He tried to be tactful. "Well, I have a lot of important papers and personal items to keep secure, so I'm thinking it should at least be the size of a four-drawer file."

"Oh, my, that's a challenge," she said uncomfortably, "but I'm sure I can find one somewhere in this town. Do you want it installed next to the existing one?"

"Yes, that would be perfect . . . and by the way, I'm assuming this will be handled discretely by people you trust."

"Oh, absolutely, Mr. Jackson! We're here to serve you, and as I've told you many times, Antonio is my *special* friend. I would never arrange anything that might damage our relationship."

"That's good to hear."

"Indeed! Is there anything else?"

"Nothing . . . unless maybe you might want to come to see me."

She laughed teasingly.

"Will that be all, Mr. Jackson?"

"Thank you, Lila. Have a good evening."

~

*B*y the time he'd reached his third anniversary, the larger safe still had room for more, but the question of what to do with his money was becoming an interesting problem. His life had taken on a certain rhythm, and Antonio had held true to his word of protecting him.

Marco became known for his suave good looks and statuesque physique. His habit was to stand apart from the others. Giuseppe the tailor complied with his requests for an adequate wardrobe and made at least ten suits of the highest quality with plenty of monogrammed shirts and expensive silk ties. His trademark sunglasses were always his finishing touch before leaving his suite, and despite criticism from Capricia, he never took them off unless they were making love.

"You really like this mob-thing, don't you Marco?"

He stroked his hair and adjusted his glasses. "I've got to look good," he explained. "My job depends on respect, and you don't get respect if you look like a bum."

Capricia smiled. "But you could at least take off those damn sunglasses, so you could see me better."

"I see you just fine, and you should talk so critically about my appearance. Look at you! Your perfection is beyond question, and the only time I see you a bit ruffled is when we wake up after a hard night . . . but even then, you are flawless."

She blushed, and then, while putting her arms around him, she pushed his sunglasses up on his forehead. "I love looking into your eyes," she cooed.

"I love it too," he agreed, "but these are prescription glasses and now you look fussy."

She laughed. "Get used to it farm boy. My vision is 20/20, and you look delicious."

He treasured Capricia's playfulness, but every morning, as he prepared to make his rounds to the casinos, he groomed himself impeccably.

Over a period of months as he made routine contacts with members of the Outfit and certain key players managing the casinos, everyone accepted his carefully coiffed appearance, and Antonio especially noticed.

"You make me proud, Marco!"

Then Antonio would throw his arms around him as though endorsing him as a model soldier in his family. Others took it as a clear sign of their father/son bond and slowly accepted Marco as one of their own.

"I wasn't sure about you when I first met you," Veneto explained, "but you're a fucking genius Marco. You make this organization run like clockwork."

Marco took his compliment in stride, but Veneto, who was in a partnership with a front man running Caesar's Palace, was on Marco's radar as an important part of an interesting dilemma. He had first noticed it in his interactions with people at Caesar's Palace, but for the time being it was only a gnawing suspicion that Veneto might be running a double-skim, which allowed him to pocket some of the cash.

Marco had applied his intelligence to learning everything about the mob's skimming operations. He made it a point to know all the players on a first name basis, and they all trusted him. He had free access to the counting rooms at each casino and was fascinated by the piles of cash that passed through their hands. The money the mob skimmed was just a normal way of doing business, and when they counted the profits, large sums of 100 dollar bills were handed to designated representatives of the Outfit and packed into large attaches, which were then transported for temporary storage in the vault at the Italian American Club. Marco knew exactly how much was received and distributed. He also knew how the skimming operation was done with no oversight. It was free money, and as he soon learned these large sums of cash were above the law and never taxed. His job was to keep track of millions, which passed from the casinos and were then stored temporarily before being "laundered" through the Teamsters and other faux businesses. He tracked it carefully as large sums of cash were flown in boxes and locked luggage to mob contacts in Chicago, Kansas City, Milwaukee, and Cleveland.

As Conti had told him many times, loyalty and trust kept the system working and when everyone cooperated, it was beneficial to all concerned.

When he first noticed what he thought might be Veneto's double-skim, he wasn't sure it was actually happening; however, it was part of his job to find out. Veneto had accepted Marco's friendship and was trying to be very collegial about everything; however, when he dropped by Caesar's Palace, he noticed everyone, including Veneto, overplaying the welcome. He was suspicious of such gracious attention and tried to look beyond it to see what might be the cause. Actually, he had good relationships with all his contacts and was treated well everywhere he went, but the Palace raised concerns. The staff thought it was just his favorite place to hang out, but he made it his business to be there frequently for other reasons.

Caesar's Palace was a ten million dollar mega resort, which had been built in the early '60s with a loan from the Teamsters. It added a touch of the Roman Empire to Las Vegas. Everything that happened there was extravagant, so Marco always enjoyed his visits but watched carefully and made it a point to look behind the scenes.

The "Counting Room" was off-limits except for certain people, who worked there. Marco had been in the counting room a couple of times and knew the routine. There was an obscene amount of cash stored in the room and more coming in all the time, so those who counted and bundled the money had plenty to do. At one end of the room was what the workers called the "drop box," a safe-like cabinet literally stuffed with cash. It was money deliberately set aside and unaccounted for as though it didn't exist. Periodically, a dignified member of the Outfit would enter the casino carrying a large, empty attaché case. He would walk past casino patrons and armed guards into the restricted area and then into the counting room. Everyone ignored him as he opened the drop box and proceeded to fill his large case with cash, and then he would walk out of the room, nod knowingly at the guards, pass freely through the hotel lobby and slip into a waiting sedan. It was an expected way of doing business, and Marco knew all the details. He especially knew how money was "skimmed" from all major casinos, and at Caesar's Palace, there was an anomaly .

On one occasion when he was relaxing in the lounge, he saw a member of the Outfit go into the restricted area carrying *two* attaché cases, one large and the other a medium size. At first, he wasn't concerned, because he knew the drill; however, when the man came out of the restricted area he was only carrying the large attaché. Of course, Marco wondered why, and then he saw Veneto enter the restricted area. He watched and waited for him to come out, but after an hour and a half, he gave up and left. He would have completely forgotten about it, except for the fact that the next day he needed to stop by Veneto's office, and the first thing he saw was the medium-size attaché on a chair with Veneto's suit coat carelessly thrown over it. He knew it was the same attaché and assumed it was full of cash.

The mob's skimming operation depended on the willingness of hotel staff, armed guards and parking valets to look the other way. It was routine business, but Marco had witnessed a break in protocol. Veneto had somehow arranged a way to skim his personal share as well.

Shortly after he'd seen the attaché case in Veneto's office, he greeted him when he arrived and invited him to have a drink with him. Veneto glanced at his watch but agreed to a short conversation, while being completely unaware that Marco wanted to talk about how things were going in the counting room.

Veneto reacted in an uneasy manner.

"Why are you asking?"

"It's my job," Marco explained. "I'm the guy who keeps track of the money."

Veneto arched his brow and made a knowing expression. "And as I've said before, you do a helluva job, Marco! I think Antonio's very happy with how you keep track of things."

"Some of it is hard to account for," Marco suggested. "The whole system depends on honesty and dependable loyalty."

Veneto quickly drained his glass and twisted in his chair.

"Yeah, I suppose it's pretty challenging to be handling all that cash."

"Right! It's challenging, and I'm thinking some of it probably slips through the cracks."

"Not here at the Palace!" Veneto exclaimed in a defensive tone.

Marco nodded and slightly shrugged his shoulders.

"Come on, Veneto! I'm sure it happens, and you probably know about it. Since it's my job to keep track of the money, I'm feeling concerned."

This time, Veneto bristled and looked at Marco through anger-filled eyes.

"I hope you're not accusing me of something serious."

Marco shrugged and adjusted his dark sunglasses, which he wore constantly regardless of being inside or out.

"If you're not doing anything *serious*, then there's no need to be concerned."

Veneto glared at him. "I've grown to like you, Marco, but I'm not liking the tone of what you're implying. When I first met you, I thought you were a smart-assed kid taking advantage of Tony, but I've watched you and learned to respect what you do; however, I'm going to be straight with you. You need to keep your fucking nose out of my goddamned business. The Palace is my baby! You're welcome here whenever you choose to come, but don't start accusing me of things you don't really know."

Marco shrugged and adjusted his glasses again. "Well, Veneto, my business has a lot to do with your business, so I'm just saying if you're not playing by the rules, don't think you're above my scrutiny."

Veneto picked up his glass and slammed it down on the table. Then stood abruptly and glared at Marco.

"You're just a punk kid, Marco, and the next time you come here, you may not be so welcome."

Marco raised his brow and made a nonchalant expression but sat calmly without over reacting. Veneto was clearly threatening him, but he'd had been around long enough to be confident when confronted by tough guys.

"It's not a matter of being welcome," he explained. "I'm just doing my job."

Veneto reacted to his soft-spoken challenge and lowered his face within inches of Marco's nose.

"You may think Tony's the only one who knows everything, but I also know things too, you asshole! What's the name of that pretty wife of yours? Oh, yeah, now I remember. It's Emma! That's her name isn't it? I understand she took your daughter Celine and ran out on you. That must have been hard on your fragile ego! Where was it she went? Oh, yeah, she's with your kid in Fresno! Is she still living with her parents, or is she on her own now? I know all about it, Marco, and I've got friends everywhere, who will do whatever I ask them to do, so if you're feeling like a smartass, who knows everything, you should forget about it!"

Veneto pulled back, and it was one of the few times Marco was honestly glad to be wearing dark glasses; otherwise, Veneto would have seen the fear in his eyes.

"Capisce?" Veneto snapped before turning and walking away.

There was a heaviness that settled over Marco. Just hearing Veneto recall Emma and Celine's names completely unnerved him. To even think something might happen to them was unbearable, and he knew it wasn't an idle threat. He remembered his first run-in with Veneto. There had been tension between them for a long time, which had slowly healed, and now they were at odds again. This time it was far more serious.

~

*T*here had been only a couple of contacts with Emma. Marco had tried to call her a number of times, but she seldom answered the phone. The last time he'd talked with her, she told him to quit calling, and that Celine had quit asking about him. She'd meant for her words to hurt him, and it worked. Now he wondered if Veneto would seriously threaten her and Celine or was it just a warning to intimidate him from saying anything. Time passed with no more exchanges between Marco and Veneto, but he knew the dilemma would only become worse. Unfortunately, he also knew there'd be a time very soon when he'd have to tell Antonio.

~

*I*n preparation for the inevitable, Marco waited unnoticed in the lounge at the Palace on three different occasions, and when a member of the Outfit walked past carrying two attachés, he discretely took pictures. Then, he took more pictures, each marked with the date and time, when the man returned from the counting room carrying only the large attaché. It was too obvious.

Planning to tell Antonio was excruciating, and on the day he actually presented the evidence, Veneto was completely unaware. Antonio was very somber as he listened to Marco and sorted through the pictures. Veneto had always been one of his most trusted soldiers and Conti took it personally. He glared at Marco and furrowed his brow, but after looking at the pictures, there was little he could do except grimace.

"You realize it's breaking my heart," he pleaded with Marco.

"I know, but you've always told me to be upfront with you about what I know, and believe me, I've agonized over this one."

Conti tightened his facial muscles and continued shaking his head as though denying the truth of it. Marco wasn't sure what he might do, and it startled him when his father slammed his fist on his desk and spewed a string of obscenities.

"Go to the bar, Marco, and have a drink, while I deal with this."

He did as he was told and looked over his shoulder to watch his father through his open office door. Antonio angrily grabbed his phone.

Oh, my, god, he's calling Veneto!

However, it was out of his hands now and all he could do is hope for the best. Then to his surprise, two of Conti's biggest and most muscular soldiers rushed out of the back room of the club and into Conti's office. They'd obviously been summoned. Marco heard a lot of shouting and cussing, which ended with a loud demand.

"Get over to the Palace and bring the son-of-a-bitch to me!"

The two soldiers literally ran past the bar and out the front door of the club. Marco hadn't touched his drink and sat terribly still. Tension filled the space around him.

~

The trip from the Italian American Club to Caesar's Palace and back to the club took around thirty minutes, so Marco waited as he'd been told to do. When the two soldiers forcefully escorted Veneto into the club, Marco tried to look away, But Veneto saw him and shouted an obscenity.

"You little prick!" he yelled, and Marco ducked his head to avoid his eyes.

Tony's door had remained open the entire time, and what happened during the next dreadful minutes would burn its way into Marco's memory. It caused him to think about what he'd already witnessed. There was life and death darkness inside the mob. It also caused him to question why he'd ever decided to be a participant, because there was still an imprint of decency in him, a recollection of the values instilled in him during his childhood and a heartache over what he'd left behind.

The heated words exchanged between Veneto and Tony quickly reached a boiling point, and when Conti showed him the pictures and told him about Marco seeing the attaché in his office, Veneto raised his voice so Marco could hear.

"That son-of-a-bitch may be your kid, but he's history in my book. He's going to pay for this one."

Tony countered with an equally loud confrontation.

"You're in no position to be making threats, Veneto. You're the son-of-a-bitch who's made a really bad decision, and it's going to be the last decision you'll ever make. I'm gonna ask you to look at me and be honest. Are you taking money?"

"It happens in every one of your goddamned casinos, Tony, so if you're gonna fuck with me, you're gonna have a line at your door. Sure, I've taken a little money on occasion. Why wouldn't I? It's all unaccounted for, so it's no big deal."

Tony squinted his eyes and shook his head in denial, but Veneto had left him no options.

"You know the rules, you bastard, so don't tell me it's no big deal. I trusted you and you failed me, so it's over! Get rid of him," he commanded his soldiers. "Get him the hell out of here!"

Marco turned his back to avoid watching as they forcefully led Veneto out of the club, and as soon as the car pulled away, he left his drink on the bar and had his driver take him back to the Tropicana. He felt sick inside and worried if he'd be able to face Antonio because he knew the grim fate Veneto would face within the hour. He walked into the hotel lobby feeling the weight of what happened. Veneto would be executed and he was the cause. His emotions were reeling.

Honesty can be fatal, he thought. *The same thing could happen to me if I ever crossed Antonio. One slip up and it's over.*

He felt dizzy when Lila greeted him, so he only nodded and went straight to the elevators. She noticed. Once inside his suite, he immediately picked up the phone and waited for her to answer.

"Yes, Marco, how can I help you?"

"I need to place a call to my wife, Emma," he said in a shaky voice.

"I'll connect you to an outside line and dial the number for you."

"Thanks!"

"Once you've finished the call, Marco, I want you to come downstairs and talk to me."

"Hum, okay," and then he waited.

Emma's phone rang three times and then she answered.

"It's me," he said.

"I told you to quit calling."

"I know, but I needed to know you're okay."

"Any why wouldn't I be okay?"

"It's complicated," he explained, "but some stuff has happened, and I have reason to be concerned."

"Marco, you amaze me! What kind of *stuff* are you talking about?"

"A threat," he said matter-of-factly. "I had a run-in with one of my father's goons, and he implied harm to you and Celine."

She was silent for a moment, and he wasn't sure what had happened, but then she said what he'd dreaded most.

"Someone was watching the house last week and I wondered what was up. At first, I made nothing of it, but then Celine came home and told me a bad man was following her. I freaked and called mom. She told me to call the police, so I did, and they started patrolling our neighborhood. The car never returned, but if it had something to do with you, it makes me sick!"

Marco sighed. It was the most Emma had said to him in three years, so he was clinging to every word.

"I'm sorry if I was the cause," he confessed, "but now the situation has been resolved, so I just needed to hear your voice. I'm glad you answered the phone."

"Good lord, Marco, it almost sounds like you care."

It was her trademark caustic style, but he countered by seizing the moment.

"I do care! I've always cared! I know I've been an asshole, but if anything ever happened to you and Celine, I'm not sure I could handle it."

"Well, my goodness! Have you had some kind of religious experience?"

"Not since the day we were married, but maybe you can drop your guard for just a moment and accept the fact I still have feelings."

There was a long pause and he sensed she might be crying; however, she quickly recouped and came back to say the obvious.

"It's been a long time, Marco. Saying you still care doesn't heal the rift."

This time he paused and faltered for words, so she waited and was nearly ready to hang up when a question occurred to her.

"Are you ever coming back?"

Her question thundered in his brain and he wanted to say yes, but it was impossible. Instead, he framed a diplomatic reply.

"I can't predict the future."

"I should have expected that," she lamented. "Anyway, Celine and I are fine and managing quite well. I actually like being in Fresno and I've got a real good thing going with my paintings. Celine is in Kindergarten, and that's the news from here. Don't get into any more situations, because I don't want anything to do with you or your mobster father. Bye!"

The call ended so suddenly, it left him with a ton of frustration, but at least it quieted his panic. When he hung up the phone, the little message light started blinking, so he picked it up again and heard Lila's soothing voice.

"I heard what happened to Veneto," she said without mincing words, and there was no need to ask for more information. "Why don't you come downstairs and see me?"

Her compassion triggered his emotions, but he managed to say, "Okay," and when he put the phone down, he went to his bar for some alcoholic fortification. The booze burned all the way down his throat but soothed his troubled feelings. However, he resisted a second shot.

Why did I ever come to Vegas in the first place?

Then he thought of Capricia and knew the truth of his decision. He hadn't seen her in days, but it occurred to him that she would also know what had happened. In the same way she comforted him, she also comforted Antonio, but there was no way of knowing the real relationship she had with Tony.

Lila has become a really good friend, he silently admitted, as he gathered his wits before going downstairs. *She comforts me in an entirely different way.*

~

To celebrate the beginning of their fourth year together, Marco arranged a special evening with Capricia at the Tropicana. As the most important resident of the hotel, he had good relationships with many of the staff, and when he told Christie, the lounge manager, what he had in mind, she was delighted.

"We'll make it very special, Marco. We'll serve her favorite cuisine and serenade her with violins," she beamed. "I love arranging these special occasions. We'll set it up so everyone's who's with us that evening will know you're celebrating, but it will be especially tailored for you and Miss Parisi."

The *special occasion* happened exactly as Christie had promised and lasted into the wee hours of the morning. As they prepared to leave the lounge, Capricia kissed him and whispered, "Thank you."

"We're like a married couple having an anniversary," he whispered.

"Not quite," she countered. "As far as I know, you're still married, but not to me."

He grimaced.

"And do you know what, Marco?" she asked rhetorically, "I really don't give a damn."

He was a bit shocked but said nothing.

"We're at a really good place right now," she added. "I did my best to soothe Tony's feelings over what happened with Veneto, and I love the fact that you had the courage to clear the slate with him. What I feel when I'm with you is far better than marriage anyway. I mean, just think about it. We've been sitting at this table for over three hours. We've enjoyed an amazing dinner and had violins serenading us. What more can a girl ask? Did you ever do anything this special for your wife?" She arched her brow expectantly, but he refused to answer. "My, god, marriage is so over rated, and this has been such a wonderful evening, it's way better."

He smiled, and she picked up her wallet and motioned for him to follow her out of the lounge. Christie watched and waved, and then Capricia surprised him by giving Christie an enormous hug. He smiled and mouthed the words, "Thank you!" as they left. Then Capricia took hold of his hand and pulled him toward the elevators.

"Where are we going?"

She turned to look at him and arched her brow. "To bed," she said with a playful frown. "I'm tired."

~

Time had been a good teacher for Marco, especially in his job of managing the mob's money. He'd earned the respect of most of Antonio's soldiers and had also earned the respect of important people outside of the *family*. He'd learned how the Teamster's Pension Fund was being used to launder money and make multi-million dollar loans, and he had routine contacts with important people to make frequent transactions. They respected him and always related to him on friendly terms; however, he knew their respect was mostly because they identified him with Conti.

His relationship with Antonio was back to normal, and he knew Capricia had been instrumental in healing the issue over Veneto. They kept in touch but essentially Antonio allowed Marco to manage on his own. As their trust deepened, Antonio would often invite him to be at his side when meeting politicians and other important people. Marco took it in stride and began loving the feeling of power he had with his father. Antonio also took him deeper and deeper into the mob's sordid affairs, which were part of the system. He learned to accept a variety of activities keeping the enterprise afloat. In addition to skimming cash from the casinos, there was prostitution, kickbacks from entertainers and illegal businesses such as supplying alcohol to an insatiable market. Other members of the mob also invited him to participate in all male parties where sex and dark perversions seemed perfectly acceptable. There were drugs, if desired, and as always, alcohol flowed freely. It was hard for Marco to resist, especially as his taste for alcohol was becoming constant. It was a life with no shame, and the more he drank, the more he lost control.

~

When Marco reached his fifth anniversary with the mob, he foolishly celebrated by attending one of those perverted parties and sank to a new low. He drank so much he was completely out of control and finally had two friends carry him to a restroom, so he could throw up. Then his friends carried him outside and told his driver to take him "home," which had become his affectionate name for his suite at the Tropicana.

Lila was shocked when they brought him into the lobby and watched his friends trying to help him stand upright. She rushed to help, but they waved her off and carried him between them toward the elevators. They rummaged in his pockets until they found his keycard, dragged him to his front door and finally managed to get him inside. Then they proceeded to put all the booze into a cabinet beneath the bar, locked its door and hid the key. When they left, he was sprawled in a chair near the windows and they hoped he'd sleep it off.

Marco was awake but terribly drunk, so the best he could do was watch the patterns of light flickering on the ceiling. His head was spinning and his conscience was under full assault.

Good god! What's happened to me?

He sat helplessly in his stupor until nature forced him to stand and stagger into the bathroom to pee. He barely made it and unfortunately missed the stool, while trying to catch his balance by leaning against the wall. As he unsteadily wobbled back toward his chair, he noticed a little red message light blinking on his phone.

"Hello," he mumbled when Lila answered. "My little message thingy is blinking."

"Thanks for checking in with me, Marco. Miss Parisi would like you to call her. She says it's urgent."

"What did you say?"

"Capricia wants you to call her. It's urgent."

"Okay! Thank you," he mumbled in slurred tones.

"Call her right away!"

"Okay! I'll do it right away!"

He dropped the phone onto the table and steadied himself against a wall. He was a long way from sober, but he'd heard the word "urgent," so he picked up the phone and tried to dial Capricia's number from memory.

"Do you want an outside line, Marco?"

"Oh, hi, Lila! Are you still there?"

"Would you like for me to dial Miss Parisi?"

"Yes, please do it for me. It's so dark in here I can't see the numbers anyway."

"Stay on the line."

"Is she home?" he asked in an impatient, unsteady voice.

"Just hold on, Marco. Her phone is ringing now."

SIXTEEN

"*I'*m in trouble, Marco!"

"What happened? Did you get too sassy with Tony?" He snickered because he thought it was funny.

"Are you drunk, Marco?"

"Maybe a little," he admitted with a slur.

"Then I'm coming over there to force-feed you some black coffee."

"Just knock three times, and I'll let you in." He snickered at his playful suggestion, but it didn't set well with Capricia.

"Oh, for god's sake, Marco! Why now? Go wash your face with cold water, and I'll be there in fifteen minutes."

He was about to say, "Okay," but she hung up on him. However, he thought the cold-water idea was a good one, so he managed to do as she'd suggested. The water shocked his system, but he continued until he began feeling better. After drying his face with a towel, he stared at his blurred image in the mirror. He knew it would be a while before the effects of the booze would wear off, and admitted his normally handsome face was a mess. He did a couple more splashes over the sink and then pressed the towel against his eyes enjoying its softness and hoping some of the redness would go away. When he went back into the living room, he passed his well-stocked bar and wondered what had happened to all his booze, but when his stomach lurched in resistance, he really didn't give a damn. He still hadn't turned on any lights, so he wobbled through the darkness, plopped down in a chair and waited.

His phone rang three times before he managed to answer.

"Capricia has arrived," Lila explained. "Would be okay to escort her to your suite?"

"Absolutely," he agreed, and within minutes she knocked softly at his door. Since he was still carrying the towel, he wiped his face again and opened the door.

Lila watched briefly and then politely hurried back to the elevator.

"Good, god," Capricia exclaimed. "It's like a dungeon in here. I suppose you're hibernating in the dark because you're hung over?"

Her indictment irritated him, but it was true, so he motioned to her, and she followed him to the chairs by the windows.

"Are you sober enough to listen to me?"

"Yeah, yeah, but please speak softly."

Instead of talking, she stood behind his chair and massaged his temples hoping it might help. He moaned with satisfaction and patted her hand.

"I've not seen you for a few days, so I'm sorry to be in such a mess."

"I'm the one in a mess," she countered, "and I need to tell you what's going on, so listen up."

He straightened his posture as she kept massaging his temples.

"Tell me! I'm listening."

She paused, and he felt her fingers tighten.

"I'm in really big trouble!"

Then she moved in front of him and knelt on the floor to look up at him in the flickering light of the neon jungle on the street below. Marco did his best to focus and tried to straighten his posture to be more attentive.

"I met a guy, who really lays on the charm, and . . ."

He cupped her face in his hands and stared into her eyes. "Oh, god, please don't! I can't take it if you're going to dump me."

"Marco! Just shut up and listen." She swatted his hands away from her face and glared at him. "He's charming, but this isn't about dumping you!"

Marco sighed and exhaled loudly like a deflating balloon. "I don't ever want to lose you, Capricia."

"Don't get all sentimental on me . . . just shut up and listen! This guy came to see me at the Stardust, and we had a couple of drinks in the lounge. He seemed to know a lot about me, and I just thought it was because he was a secret admirer, but he got me talking, and he was really curious about people I know in the Outfit. I probably said too much, but he was really sweet and very casual, so I thought it was okay."

"I don't like the direction this is going," Marco complained as he massaged his forehead trying to soothe his headache. "I hope he didn't put the move on you."

"Stop it, Marco! Just listen! Around ten o'clock he said he needed to be going, but asked if it would be okay to use my phone. It seemed strange to me, and I pointed to a public phone, but he shook his head no and said he needed privacy. It really caught me off-guard."

"And . . ."

"And like a dumb ass, I said okay."

"Oh, Jesus!" he moaned. "You took him upstairs?"

Capricia nodded and then whispered: "It was just to use my phone."

She flashed an innocent look accented by the ever-changing lights filtering through the windows. It was just enough light for Marco to see the concern in her eyes.

"Good God, Capricia! Don't you know better? You're undoubtedly one of the most beautiful women in Vegas! Don't you know about being careful?"

She looked down but reached out to hold his hand.

"I'm smarter than you think . . . anyway, I opened the door to my suite and then waited outside the door, while he used the phone! It's on the little table just inside the door, so I just held the door open and waited."

He squeezed her hand. "And then what?"

"I couldn't hear anything he said, but he was on the phone for at least five minutes, and then I took him back to the lobby and told him goodbye."

"And that's it?"

"Well, he said he'd like to see me again, but it's not going to happen!"

"Then why are you in big trouble?"

She hesitated and rubbed his fingers. "Because he put a listening device in my phone. Every call I've made since my stupid mistake has been monitored, and it's really bad, Marco. It's really bad!"

"And how do you know about this listening *device* he put in your phone?"

"It's been over a month, and Antonio started picking up clues from some of his guys, so he sent a couple of his men to my suite to check my phone, and they found a device inside."

"I assume they removed it? Did it solve the problem?"

Sure! They removed it," she exclaimed, "but it gets worse, Marco. I'm in big trouble."

"You mean Tony's not very happy this happened?"

"Oh, you can say that again! He was really angry and warned me about being so stupid, but the worst part just happened two days ago, and I don't even know if Tony's aware of it."

"Aware of what?"

"I've been subpoenaed to testify before the Nevada Gaming Commission."

Marco felt his head spin for reasons totally unrelated to his over consumption of alcohol.

"Oh, my, god!" he exclaimed. "Oh, my, god!"

Capricia began crying.

Marco pressed his hands against his temples. "When?"

"It's scheduled for next month."

"Are you going to tell Tony?"

"I'm telling you and pleading for help."

Marco struggled to his feet and lifted her into his arms. She continued crying, and he honestly didn't know what to say. He knew the Gaming Commission was beginning to tighten the screws on the mob's activity, and he also knew Tony would never allow her to testify, so he held her in his arms for a very long time. Finally he bent forward and kissed her.

"Whew! You really have bad breath."

He released her and unsteadily hurried to the kitchen to find some mints, and this time he flicked on some recessed lighting that cast a warm glow into the living room.

"Come back, Marco! I don't give a damn about your breath. Just come back and tell me you love me."

It was the first time the word *love* had been spoken between them, and he dropped the roll of mints in reaction. Then he hurried back into the living room and joined her at the windows looking forlornly at the lights below. Then he wrapped his arms around her.

"I do love you!" he whispered. "We've not used that word before, but when I'm with you, it touches my soul, and I hope you feel the same."

"I love you too, Marco! Maybe it's the seriousness of the moment that brings it to mind, but I've loved you for a long time."

Assured by his mint-freshened breath, he turned her around and kissed her tenderly.

"It's not going to end well," she said and kissed him again. "I know how these things work, and I know it's not going to end well, so can I stay the night? I'm scared."

He held her in his arms as though never wanting her to leave.

"Of course you can stay . . . you can stay forever if you want."

They spent the next hour or so talking about her dilemma and trying to get him sober. Around midnight they were both feeling better, so before going to bed, he invited her to take a shower with him, and by the time they'd consumed more than a fair amount of the hotel's hot water, they were lost in a very steamy sexual encounter, which was more unique than functional. After drying each other, he carried her into the bedroom and began caressing her with his hands until she begged him for more. For a few intense moments, they forgot about what they were facing.

~

Capricia stayed close to Marco's side for the next few days and nights, and by the following weekend she was a nervous wreck because she'd heard nothing from Antonio. Marco, on the other hand, crossed paths with him at the Italian American

Club. He had greeted him in the same manner as had become his custom, but there was a noticeable difference.

"How's it going, Marco?"

"Fine! I was just heading downstairs to tend to business."

"Great! Keep a close eye on it."

He preceded downstairs to the vault wondering if Antonio knew about Capricia's subpoena. It was the first time he'd seen him since Capricia had told him, and he sensed some tension. Then, as he was checking data on the computers, he noticed the names of two county officials, who had each received ten thousand dollar payments as gifts in appreciation for their support and cooperation. It wasn't unusual, because he'd seen similar entries before, but in this case he quickly identified the two officials as members of the Gaming Commission. *Something's going on,* he thought, *and Capricia is probably right. It's not going to end well.*

~

Capricia had left her car in a reserved space in the hotel's parking garage. It had been parked there since the night she'd rushed to rescue him from his drunken binge. He'd gone to the Italian American Club each morning, leaving her on her own, so everything seemed normal. However, they both knew she needed to stay secluded.

After one of his trips to the club, he checked in with Lila, greeted a few employees and then went directly to the elevators. While riding to the top floor, he felt uneasy about some bits and pieces of hearsay from trusted friends, who suggested Tony was making frequent contacts with two guys from the gaming commission.

If that's true, then maybe he's working things out.

When the elevator doors opened, he was also remembering some scuttlebutt he'd heard about members of the New York Mob and the Cleveland Mob doing business at the Tropicana. Lila had told him to be aware, and she also mentioned that Tony knew about it, too.

"It's becoming a fact of life in the openness of Vegas," she'd said, "but it worries me. The federal government has investigators here."

When he touched his card to the sensor on the door of his suite, he wondered if anyone was watching.

I think I'm becoming paranoid. Why would anyone be watching?

Once inside, he told Capricia what he'd learned, and she turned pale.

"It's serious, Marco. The feds are making no attempt to hide their interest in mob activities, so it's time to be vigilant."

"I saw Tony!"

She grimaced. "Did he say anything?"

He shook his head no. "He was busy."

"Did he talk to you?"

Marco wrinkled his brow. "He just told me to keep a close eye on the money. I felt he was a little subdued."

"I'm really nervous, Marco! I've had zero contact with him, and the tension's killing me."

Then she went to the bar to pour a drink.

"Where's all your booze?"

"I think the guys put it away and hid the key, but I just so happen to have another key right here."

He dangled a small keychain, opened the cabinet and replenished his bar. Capricia proceeded to help herself.

"Do you want a drink?"

He declined.

"There's not been even one message from Tony. I know it's this subpoena thing, because I'd normally hear from him two and three times a day."

"Maybe he's just busy with all the stuff going on," Marco observed, trying to pacify her feelings. "Lila told me the Feds have invaded Vegas, so Tony's probably staying out of sight."

Capricia sipped her drink and pouted.

"It has to be more than that, and I'm really nervous," she repeated. "I don't like it at all."

Then Marco called Lila and asked her to send up some sandwiches for their lunch, and when room service knocked on the door, Capricia jumped with a look of panic. Her glass was nearly empty, and when she looked at the food, she pushed it aside.

Marco ate his sandwich and then stood beside her at the windows to watch hoards of tourists beating the heat by hurrying from one air-conditioned casino to the next. Then he thoughtfully took her empty glass and returned it to the sink. When he turned around, she was standing near the door clutching her purse and fidgeting to touch up her lipstick.

"Are you leaving?"

She nodded. "I need to make a quick trip to my place to pick up some clean clothes and to check one more time to see if there might be any messages."

Marco nodded, and she kissed him.

"I'll be back in a flash," she said with a teasing smile. "I love you," she added and then opened the door.

"I love you too, so don't be gone too long."

The door closed with a soft click, and he sat down near the windows to wait for her return. In a matter of minutes, a loud explosion rattled the windows and shattered his peaceful mood. He leaped to his feet to look down at the street in front of the hotel. Just feet from the driveway he saw the burning remains of Capricia's white Cadillac. Injured people littered the street and sidewalk. Sirens wailed as police, fire trucks and aid cars responded to frantic calls for help. Marco realized what had happened and crumpled onto the floor screaming in tormented agony.

SEVENTEEN

During his 36 years, Marco had never suffered a major emotional trauma. When his father, Hank Jackson had died, it was difficult, but nothing had ever torn his emotions so violently until now. As soon as he saw the smoldering ruins of Capricia's car, the shock nearly stopped his heart. A wave of panic and trauma rushed over him. It literally brought him to his knees. There was no need to hurry downstairs to intervene. The car had obviously been rigged to explode within minutes of her starting the engine. It was just enough time for her to pull out of the parking garage and onto the street.

"Why, why, why?" he cried out in agony. However, he knew why! It was obviously intended to silence her.

It took quite a while for him to regain his composure, but when his profound sadness moderated, rage took its place. When he finally found the courage to look out the window again, emergency workers had already transported the wounded to hospitals, and a tow truck had lifted the twisted steel of Capricia's car onto its flat bed to take it to a police garage as evidence. The blast had disrupted everything, and police tape fluttered in the wind around the entire area. Marco's mind was whirling, and his anger boiling. Within minutes he pushed his way through a crowd of onlookers and hailed a taxi about a half-a-block away from the scene.

Antonio could have been anywhere, but since it was nearly noon, Marco knew he'd probably be at the Club for lunch, so in a fit of blind rage he directed the driver to take him there. He stormed into the Italian American Club, where Antonio was sitting alone at one of the tables. He stood when Marco burst through the door and braced himself to intercept him.

"You bastard," Marco shouted, and ran headlong toward him.

Marco was nearly a foot taller than Antonio and still had the muscular frame of a young man, so Antonio felt he had no choice but to reach for his gun.

"Take it easy Marco!" he shouted, but Marco ignored the warning and lunged at him. Antonio turned his shoulders to block against the blow, but they collided with such force it sent both of them falling backwards. Conti sprawled onto a table, and Marco tumbled onto the floor. Then, as they struggled to their feet, Marco shouted another obscenity and lunged toward him a second time.

"You cowardly bastard," he cried with saliva dripping from the corners of his mouth. He hit Antonio full-force, just as he brought his gun into view, and in an instant before they collided, Marco saw the gun. When his body slammed into Antonio, there was a sickening "pop" as a single shot from the revolver dropped Antonio to his knees. The gun skidded across the hardwood floor.

On his way down, Antonio screamed at Marco. "D'Angelo did it, Marco! It wasn't me!"

Then Antonio's head rolled to one side and blood oozed onto his suit where the bullet had nicked an artery. Marco stood over him with his fists clenched and tears running down his cheeks.

"I don't give a damn who rigged her car! You run this operation and nothing goes down without your word."

Antonio couldn't answer and held his hand over his bleeding wound.

The commotion quickly brought two of Antonio's soldiers bursting from a backroom into the lounge. They saw Tony on the floor and Marco standing over him. One immediately ran to the phone to call an aid car, the other one hit Marco on the jaw so hard he sprawled onto the floor.

As Marco's legs crumpled beneath him, he saw little dancing stars in his head, and then everything went black.

~

*H*elp arrived quickly, and the EMT's stopped the bleeding and stabilized Tony, while his soldiers watched helplessly. They lifted him onto a gurney and immediately transported him to Valley Hospital where he was placed into intensive care.

When Marco regained consciousness, Las Vegas police officers informed him they were arresting him for attempted murder. Still dazed by the blow to his head, he looked up at the soldier who had knocked him senseless, and noticed he was nodding his agreement. Marco was having a hard time remaining conscious as the officers carried him outside and forcefully dumped him into the backseat of a police car. He nearly fell over onto the seat as they snapped handcuffs onto his wrists for the short ride to the Clark County Detention Center. In addition to his state of confusion, he had a pounding headache and thought he was dying.

"Where are you taking me?" he managed to ask.

"You're going to jail for attempted murder!"

Everything blurred again, and within seconds they sped away from the Club with the siren wailing. He'd never been arrested before, but after seeing the smoldering ruins of Capricia's car, he honestly didn't care.

They came to a sudden stop in front of the center, and he was forcefully pulled out of the car. Once inside, they took his fingerprints and snapped a series of mug shots before pushing him down a hallway and into a cell. When they closed the door, he screamed obscenities at the officers. The absolute violence of Capricia's death and his assault on Antonio had ripped the moral fabric in his brain, and his only relief was to shake the cell door and continue screaming.

Of course, no one listened to his distress, so he finally gave in to exhaustion and sat on the floor. The isolation and starkness of his cell tortured him even more. He felt totally defeated. Finally, he struggled to his feet and looked at his image in a tiny metal mirror above a stainless steel sink.

What in God's name is happening?

Memories swirled in his brain like a dark storm. He knew the answer to his question. He had willingly come to Las Vegas, fallen in love with a beautiful woman, witnessed mob violence such as he'd never imagined, tried to brutally beat his father, and now he'd been arrested and charged with attempted murder. It was despairing. His rage was the outcome of the accumulating darkness into which he'd fallen, and when he'd heard the gunshot and watched Antonio crumple to the floor, he felt himself falling into a bottomless abyss. He was in a state of hopeless desperation and seriously wondered if he'd ever find a way out.

~

*U*nknown to Marco, Antonio Conti had survived and was receiving emergency care at the hospital. His condition was critical, but they were doing their best to keep him alive. Salvatore Bacciarelli, one of the Outfit's lawyers, came to Marco's cell to inform him. He looked Marco directly in the eye and shook his head.

"You really fucked up, Marco! I know you're angry at Tony about what happened to Capricia, but what were you thinking when you attacked him?" Marco said nothing. "It was D'Angelo, who wired her car! Capisce?"

Marco's rage returned. "I don't care who wired her car. Nothing happens in Vegas without Tony's approval, so in my mind he's the one who killed her."

Bacciarelli shook his head and sneered. "It's complicated, Smartass! You think you know what happened, but you really don't know anything. She was going to testify before the Nevada Gaming Commission, and it couldn't be allowed. The Outfit's having a hard enough time dealing with what's going down in Vegas, and if we're not careful, the feds are going to put the screws to all of us."

"Why should I care?" Marco shouted with clenched fists. "And besides, I don't know what the hell happened when Tony's gun went off. I don't remember even touching it. I saw the gun when I hit his arm, so I think he accidentally shot himself. I sure as hell didn't pull the trigger."

"That's important," Bacciarelli confirmed. "We can use that information, but you need to get your head out of your ass and realize you're in serious trouble."

Marco had nothing more to say and shook his head bitterly.

"Look, Marco! I know you had a thing for Capricia, but goddammit, her testimony before the commission would have split the mob wide open. I know you're naïve about things like this, but there's no way we could allow her to testify, and when D'Angelo told Tony it couldn't be allowed, they had a big argument but D'Angelo won."

Marco couldn't believe what he was hearing.

"You can explain it however you want, but Tony killed Capricia, and he might as well killed me too. Capricia was my world, and now she's gone. I don't really give a damn what happens next."

"Well, I'm sayin' you should give a damn. This stuff happens all the time, and you just have to get over it. I'm sorry about Capricia, but you need to buck up and quit bitching."

Marco squinted his eyes and looked angrily at Bacciarelli.

"Get the hell out of here and leave me alone. I don't need you or any of your explanations."

Bacciarelli turned to leave. "By-the-way, Tony wants to see you," he said matter-of-factly. "He's really in bad shape, but he told me to bring you to the hospital."

Marco looked at him wide-eyed with surprise. "Why?"

Bacciarelli sneered. "Because he's still the Don of this family, so if he says bring you to the hospital, then that's what we're gonna do."

"I'm in jail! I can't go to the hospital!"

"Leave that to me! We still have friends on the Vegas police force, so I'll arrange it. They'll probably escort you, but I'm telling you, you're going to the hospital real soon, so get your head around it."

Marco went mute, and Bacciarelli motioned for the guard to let him out of the cell. When the door "clanged" shut, the locks snapped automatically, and then the lights in the cellblock dimmed. He'd left his watch at the Tropicana, but reasoned it was probably around 10:00 p.m. His emotions were a mess as he paced the floor. Each step he took increased his frustration, and then he thought once again about Capricia, and began sobbing uncontrollably.

~

$\mathcal{A}$t some point in the darkness, exhaustion forced Marco to close his eyes and sleep. He'd been fighting his emotions, so sleep was sporadic. A thin mattress provided his only physical comfort, and sounds from other detainees rattled his nerves; however, he managed to dream, and for the first time in a long while, he dreamed of Emma. She appeared and then disappeared. When he saw her, it startled him and caused him to sit bolt upright with his eyes wide open. In the darkness of his cell, he thought he saw her waiting for him and then he realized it was only an unusual pattern of light filtering in through glass block windows near the ceiling.

What's happened? Why have I so foolishly sacrificed everything? Emma where are you? Is Celine okay?

Sweat beaded on his forehead as panic invaded his soul. "I never wanted it to turn into a disaster," he said to the darkness. "I never really wanted to lose you and Celine," he pleaded. "It's my fault! Can you forgive me?"

Of course, it was pointless, because Emma had clearly drawn the line between them and there would be no answers to his pleading questions. However, remembering was important. As he continued watching a moving pattern of light on the walls of his cell, he had thoughts of dying and shook with fear.

This cell is miserable. What's going to happen to me?

He stood and began pacing in circles, and then it suddenly occurred to him the darkness was symbolic of what had happened to him, and the flickering pattern of light on the wall seemed symbolic of his fading hope.

~

"Come with me, Jackson," the cell guard commanded. It was still dark outside, and he'd been rudely summoned. "You've been given a little reprieve to visit the man you shot."

Marco glared at the officer, but there was no option but to go with him. Before leaving the cell, the guard snapped handcuffs onto his wrists and forcefully pulled him into the corridor. Once they exited the cellblock area, Bacciarelli suddenly appeared along with a second officer, who escorted them to a plain white van waiting just beyond the front door. Marco was forced to sit between the two guards, and Bacciarelli sat in the front passenger seat for the short ride to Valley Hospital. When they got out of the van, one of the guards draped Marco's suit jacket over the handcuffs, so he would be less conspicuous. However, when they went inside the hospital, everyone within view stopped and watched the procession.

"Tony's in the ICU," Bacciarelli explained. "We'll only be allowed a few minutes with him, so don't go crazy on me!"

Marco glared at him as he was tugged along down a long corridor. When they reached the ICU, the nurse in charge reminded them to keep it brief, and the guards more or less pushed him to his father's bedside. Tubes and wires hung from many places on Tony's body, and he could barely open his eyes, but he managed to do so and slowly focused on Marco. Then he lifted his hand motioning him closer. Marco's gut was churning, but he managed to lean closer and looked directly into Antonio's eyes. He could only speak in a whisper but he managed to say Marco's name.

"Marco!"

His weak and raspy voice startled Marco, and then Antonio struggled to touch his hand. His first reaction was to jerk away, but then he saw desperation in Antonio's eyes and allowed it.

"I know you're angry," Antonio whispered, "but please forgive me. I'm sorry! I should have never had you come here."

Marco stared at him and realized this might be his dying wish. He was still angry and didn't feel any forgiveness, but from somewhere deep inside, he felt a need to at least try, so he nodded a couple of times, and Antonio squeezed his hand.

Then Antonio motioned to Bacciarelli and to one of the officers. Marco stepped aside as they leaned down to hear what he wanted to say.

"Listen to me! Marco didn't shoot me, so let him go!"

His voice was barely loud enough for Marco to hear, and he gasped in surprise.

Antonio repeated his request. "I said let him go! He didn't do it! I accidentally pulled the trigger, and I goddamned didn't mean to do it. The force of him hitting my arm pushed the gun against my ribs, and it accidentally fired, so let him go!"

Marco felt a surge of emotion and a tiny ray of hope. Bacciarelli and the officer looked at each other and then the officer said, "Okay, Tony! We'll work on releasing him."

Tony reached over to pat Bacciarelli's hand and nodded to be sure he'd been understood.

"Okay, Tony. It's what you say," and then Antonio closed his eyes for a moment to show his appreciation.

There was a brief moment when Marco wondered if his father was still alive, but then he suddenly opened his eyes and motioned to Marco to come closer. When he leaned down near Antonio's face, it was to hear something that would change his life forever.

"This life is no good for you, Marco! You're better than this, and now I'm speaking to you as your father. You've never really been a part of the Outfit, so get the hell out of it with my blessing."

It was like seeing a tiny ray of light penetrating his darkness. He felt a flood of emotion as Antonio struggled to lift his head slightly to look directly at him.

"It's okay!" he said in his broken voice, and as Marco watched his expression become more peaceful, he saw tears in his father's eyes. "Bacciarelli knows what to do, and by god, if anyone ever lays a hand on you, they better be ready to meet their Maker."

Tony looked at Bacciarelli, who nodded to acknowledge the request.

Then Tony reached to take hold of Marco's hand, and this time Marco gripped his hand affectionately as Antonio closed his eyes. He continued gripping his hand, and after maybe four difficult breaths, he forced his eyes open and struggled to speak again.

"I know you've accumulated a lot of money," Antonio whispered, "so pack it up and get the hell out of Vegas. Go home and reclaim your life, Marco. There's nothing here except more grief, so go home and put your mind and heart into something that counts."

Conti's breathing seemed more labored, and the nurse watched anxiously from the foot of his bed. She indicated it was time to leave, so Marco fought through his emotions to speak.

"Thanks, Dad!" he whispered, and Antonio faintly smiled, which touched Marco emotionally. He felt tears welling up in his eyes.

The nurse became more insistent as Antonio continued gasping for air, but when she tried to intervene, he refused to let go of Marco's hand and shook his head slightly. He seemed to have one more thing he needed to say, so Marco leaned closer knowing it might be his final words.

"I loved her too, Marco, and when D'Angelo told me what he'd done, I slapped him upside the head and cried like a baby." Then he squeezed Marco's hand. "I want you to know I loved her too." Marco fought back his tears and tightened his grip on his father's hand.

Then Antonio surprised Marco by pulling him even closer and kissed him on his forehead. It caught him completely off-guard, especially when he realized it was Antonio's final act. He released Marco's hand as his eyes rolled back in his head, and with one more raspy sound, he took his final breath.

This time, the nurse forcefully pulled Marco away from the bedside and immediately coded the emergency. Other nurses and technicians rushed in to help, but all the monitors attached to Antonio's body had flat-lined.

Intense sadness swept over Marco as he and the others stood helplessly by the door as one of the doctors recorded the time of death, and then it was over.

"I'm sorry," the doctor said on his way out of the room, and then the nurse lifted the bed sheet over Antonio's face.

~

They waited in total silence for a few moments and then left the room. Once they were in the hallway, one of the guards removed the handcuffs from Marco's wrists and had a brief conversation with Bacciarelli about coming to the station and signing an affidavit regarding Antonio's statement of an accidental shooting.

When they returned to the van, Marco was invited to sit in front seat for the short ride to the Tropicana, and when the van stopped, he saw Lila smiling at him from the doorway. He looked at the officers, and they nodded it was okay for him to get out. It felt as though a little more light had come into his darkness.

Bacciarelli also got out of the van and stood very close to look directly at him.

"I assume you're taking Tony's advice and going home?"

"I'm still in a daze, but, yes, I think it's time for me to leave! Everything I cared about is gone," he lamented, "so Tony's advice sounds good." It was the first time he'd called his father "Tony," but now it had become very personal.

"Then I'll let the others know," Bacciarelli said matter-of-factly. "I don't want to add insult to injury, but I think you need to know the others always questioned having you here. Tony was adamant about making a place for you, but none of the rest of us thought it would work. You're a frigging genius, so why waste your life with a bunch of guys like us?"

Marco wrinkled his brow and frowned. "I came here because I really wanted to be with my father," he explained. "It's hard to say why, but I wanted it more than anything. I never thought it would be the way it turned out to be, and now I feel torn inside over all the stuff that's happened, so maybe going home will help."

"Like Tony said, 'You're better than this,' so I'm telling you to take whatever you need . . . including the money, and book your flight to wherever the hell you lived before coming here."

Marco rubbed his forehead thoughtfully and tried to get his mind around what was happening. Bacciarelli slapped him playfully on his shoulder and looked at him with a knowing expression.

"I'll take care of the details," he said, "and we'll do what Tony wants. D'Angelo will immediately step in as the new Don for our Las Vegas family, but it'll never be the same. We all loved Tony, so it won't be easy."

"Yeah! I understand! I'm never going to forget what happened here today. I feel like I've been given a second chance."

Bacciarelli patted him on the shoulder again and nodded smugly.

"I'm telling you, Marco, the stuff that's coming isn't going be pretty, so you're lucky you won't be here to see it. It's going to be a damn roller coaster ride, and it's a good time for you to get the hell out of Dodge. I'll talk to D'Angelo and square things away, so there'll be no need to be looking over your shoulder. What happened in the ICU is unprecedented. Nobody ever walks away from the Outfit, but Tony has set you free, and that's something I've never seen before."

~

Marco watched the van pull away and suddenly felt very alone. Then he went inside, smiled cordially at Lila, walked straight to the elevators, and after arriving on his unmarked floor, he stood for a few moments in the foyer with some very mixed feelings. The reality of what had happened was settling over him as a mixture of excitement and sadness. The darkness was ending, but there was still a lot of uncertainty ahead.

Once inside his penthouse, he looked toward the windows and immediately remembered his painful agony when Capricia had been murdered. He had avoided looking down at the street where it had happened. He could almost envision her standing in front of the windows and remembered how he'd put his arms around her and that they'd finally said, "I love you!" He shuddered and felt emotional. If someone had told him he'd be heartbroken, he wouldn't have believed it; however, now it was time to set his heartaches aside and get on with the rest of his life.

Standing forlornly in the luxury of his extravagant suite, he paused to look into the mirror behind the bar. This time, when he ran his hand over his face, he felt weary. His stress was nearly gone, but when he looked again, he wondered how he would manage trying to reclaim his life.

Will I ever have a chance to be with Celine again? He took a deep breath and sighed. *How's it possible to start over?*

Then he poured a snippet of whiskey into a glass and glanced at his image one more time. Strangely, he thought he saw Antonio's face and pleading eyes in his own image, and then he wept.

EIGHTEEN

*L*as Vegas was always remarkably calm in the early morning. Residents and visitors usually ventured out of their air-conditioned cocoons around 10:00 a.m. to begin their daily search for food and entertainment. Marco had done the same many times, but the breakfast buffets offered too many high cholesterol foods, so he generally used room service, which included the bonus of hearing a cheery "Good morning, Marco," from Lila.

"I was so relieved when you returned to the hotel yesterday," she said.

"I assume you heard what happened."

"Unfortunately, yes, and I'm very sad to lose Tony. I feared for you as well, Marco."

"Thanks, Lila!"

"How can I help you this morning?"

"I'll have the *Heart Healthy* breakfast, and if it's not too inconvenient, I'd like a small bottle of brandy to go with my coffee."

"It'll be on its way shortly," she said with sparkle in her tone. "Will there be anything else?"

"No! That will be all . . . unless you'd like to personally bring me my breakfast, so I could cry on your shoulder."

She paused. "Well, as much as I'd enjoy doing so, I'm afraid it's against the hotel's rules. However, I must ask if you're okay?"

"Yes, I'm okay! However, I'm also very sad."

"I know your heart must be broken."

Her intimate comment caught him completely off-guard, and a flood of emotion rushed over him. He choked up, and the long pause was noticeable, but she waited.

"It's true, Lila! Losing Capricia has made my world tragically lonely, and then when Tony died I . . ."

"I'm truly sorry, Marco. She and Tony were friends of mine as well."

"Thanks for understanding!" He took a deep breath and regained his balance. "Are you sure you can't bring me my breakfast? I'd be happy to see you."

She laughed softly. "Oh, Marco, you're such a tease, but I'll always have a smile for you when you pass by. Okay?"

"You're special, Lila. Thanks for being my friend."

"Bye!"

The call ended, and within minutes his breakfast arrived. He tipped the bellman and went immediately to the bar where he opened the brandy and added some to his coffee. After breakfast, he had another, while catching up on local news. There were numerous reports about the FBI investigations into mob activity, but no mention of Capricia or Antonio's death.

~

Marco was suddenly faced with nothing to do but prepare to leave Las Vegas. It was hard to concentrate on anything else. Going back to San Jose was going to be traumatic. The company he'd engaged to take care of his property had sent letters every six months to advise him about things needing to be done to keep the house from falling into disrepair. They usually added little bits of information about the neighborhood and told him the house was weathering his absence quite well. However, each time he thought about it, he remembered Emma and Celine.

I wonder how they're doing and if I'll ever see them again.

It was going to be like falling backwards, and he already dreaded the feeling.

He finally found the courage to look down from his window, and as he watched people in their endless hustle from cars and vans to escape the heat, he stared at the place where Capricia's life had ended. It had been very hot that day as well, and he shuddered when he remembered the carnage. It had literally torn his emotions to shreds.

Her memory's going to be with me for the rest of my life.

Then he remembered standing at Antonio's bedside. When he'd asked forgiveness, it had triggered a sudden change in Marco's feelings. Something had awakened in him. It was a moment when everything he'd ever treasured came roaring back to the surface, and it was Antonio's request that had caused this rush of feelings, which had become a transforming moment. When Antonio had whispered he'd also loved Capricia, Marco felt a seismic shift he couldn't explain.

"It was truly amazing," he whispered into the silence. "I would have never expected it, but I treasure what he said."

Now, in the cool air-conditioned comfort of his lavish penthouse suite, he looked wistfully at the busy street below.

His broken heart and cluttered memories would become souvenirs from Vegas and most notable would be the moment when forgiveness found its way into his heart. Being in Las Vegas had begun innocently but had rapidly pulled him into the mob's web. Capricia's intoxicating beauty had burned its way into his heart, but now she was gone. Tony was also gone, and learning to forgive had burned its way into his soul.

It's redemption, he thought. *It's a chance to begin again.*

He turned away from the windows and went into the bedroom where he kept an inconspicuous envelope of pictures in the back of this top dresser drawer. There were a couple pictures of his friends at IBM, but most treasured was his picture of Emma and another one of Celine. He held their photos and felt a yearning in his heart because he knew they were still part of his life. He and Emma were still married, and why she hadn't officially dumped him remained a mystery. However, he knew it was his foolishness, which had caused their separation. His irrational need to be with his birth father and his lust for Capricia had caused permanent damage.

There are so many broken pieces, I wonder if it's actually possible to reassemble my life?

He finally returned the pictures to the envelope and then wearily returned to the bar to check his coffee pot, which he'd already emptied, and the brandy was gone as well.

"Go home and reclaim your life!"

He remembered the look on Tony's face when he'd struggled to say those words. It had been a simple suggestion but one he'd desperately needed to hear. Now it was up to him to make it happen.

~

After a quick shower, Marco dressed in casual clothes and started sorting through what he'd take with him. He had accumulated a lot of stuff over five years, some of which he wanted to keep and some he'd need to leave behind. His plan was to sort it out and then ask Lila to arrange for help with the packing. Ironically, his biggest challenge was going to be the cash in his two safes.

I know there's around three million, he thought, and I a*lso have quite a bit in my checking account, but there's no way I can put this much cash into a bank, so how does one move three million in cash without raising suspicion?*

The thoughts kept coming, but none solved the money problem. He also had closets full of expensive clothes, which he called "the trappings of his mob life," so he planned to take as much of it as possible.

It's going to be really strange, he thought. *I've never faced anything as weird as this.*

In Vegas, if he needed anything, it was provided, but now he'd be returning to an everyday world where you do everything for yourself. It was almost too much to anticipate, but he knew Lila would send help and offer advice.

I wonder if I should tell her about the money? Probably not!

He opened both safes to study his *problem.* The money was mostly in stacks of $100s and there was more than he'd ever dreamed of having. Antonio had warned him to be discrete, so he'd used some of it to feed his checking account, and stashed the rest.

I guess I'll have to purchase two metal suitcases with locking straps, and carry it home as checked baggage.

Just thinking about it made him nervous, but then he realized how lucky he was to have such a unique problem.

I'll also need a couple wardrobe suitcases, so I can pack my suits, shirts and shoes. I wonder if Lila can help me get what I need?

After sorting lots of his things onto his bed, he was suddenly overwhelmed by the thought of going home.

"It's clearly redemption," he whispered aloud and realized the word was foreign to his vocabulary. *I used to hear about redemption in church, but I never thought it could happen in Las Vegas.*

The thought energized him.

"That's it!" he said aloud. "Tony has given me a second chance." Then he picked up his phone and waited for Lila to answer.

"Yes, Marco, how may I help you?"

"I'm going home, Lila!"

"Oh, my, goodness! Are you not happy with the way we're treating you?"

He laughed. "You've spoiled me, but it's time to pack up and leave Vegas behind."

"Because of Capricia and Tony?"

He paused and took a deep breath. "Because before Tony died, that's what he told me I should do."

"Tony was your father . . . right?"

"Yes, he was! He's the reason I came to Vegas . . . and of course, Capricia, too."

"Well, my friend, I've been hanging around the mob for a long time, and I can't recall ever hearing about anyone just packing up and leaving, and that's a cold, hard fact." She laughed softly. "No one ever just walks away, Marco."

"I know! It's unprecedented."

"You can say that again," Lila sighed. "Tony did you a real favor. I've already heard D'Angelo has taken your father's place, and without Tony's blessing . . . I'm just saying."

"I understand. Do you also know Bacciarelli?"

"I do! He's a lawyer."

"Right! He'll be responsible for settling everything when I leave."

"Oh, there's no question about that. One thing I can say about the Outfit is that I've never had to beg for their accounts to be settled." He heard her sigh. "I'm going to miss you, Marco. I consider you my friend, so I hope everything works out really good for you. If there's anything you need, please ask."

"As a matter of fact, I need suitcases," he declared with a chuckle, "and I'm sure you'll know where to find exactly the kind I need."

~

"You're lucky I'm driving a big car," said his driver, after filling the back seat and the trunk with his luggage. Dino, who had loyally shuttled him from place to place during his time in Vegas, had become a dependable friend. "You're also lucky to be getting out of here," he declared with a knowing glance. "I never helped anyone escape the mob before. You're a lucky SOB!"

Marco smiled at his casual characterization of his final trip to the airport. "I'll take that as a compliment."

"You damn right! It's a compliment! You were also lucky to have won Capricia's heart! I guess that counts for something." He puckered his face into a smug affirmation. "Anyway, I'm driving you to the airport, and you're leaving the rest of us to wallow in the quagmire of what's coming. Jesus! I'd like to be in your shoes, Marco."

Marco tilted his head thoughtfully. *I really am lucky. Nobody just walks away from the mob.*

When they stopped next to the terminal building at McCarran International, Marco took a moment to thank Dino, and when he reached to shake his hand, Dino pulled him into an embrace.

"I'll miss you," he said, "but not too much."

They both laughed as a porter started putting Marco's luggage on a cart for baggage check.

"Be real careful with those bags, and there'll be an extra $20 for your kindness."

The porter smiled, and Marco watched his special suitcases until they were correctly tagged at the counter. It occurred to him there might be another redemptive moment in the making if everything was still intact upon its arrival in San Jose.

~

*K*evin Hale, Marco's co-leader on the R&D team at IBM had faithfully stayed in touch, so when he told him he was coming back to San Jose, Kevin agreed to meet him at the airport. As his plane descended toward San Francisco International, it passed through layers of fog and he realized how much he'd missed the Bay Area. He wondered if he'd recognize Kevin. It had been five years, and he remembered Kevin was already going bald when he'd last seen him. Also, he'd not mentioned the amount of luggage he was bringing, so he hoped he might be driving a station wagon or at least a full-sized car.

"Welcome to San Francisco," beamed the in-charge flight attendant. "Local time is 4:15 p.m. Please remain seated with your seatbelt fastened until we've stopped at the gate and the captain has turned off the seatbelt sign. We wish you a good evening in the City by the Bay."

As he made his way from the gate to baggage claim, he felt anxious and hoped his two special suitcases had safely passed through the baggage system, and as he walked toward the luggage carrousel, Kevin spotted him and waved his arms above his head calling his name. Marco hurried to greet him and gave him a heartfelt hug.

"Hey, man, I didn't think you'd ever come back. What happened? Did you lose all your money in Vegas?"

"Hardly, but it was time to come home! Five years of helping my father in his business was more than enough. I needed to leave the desert for the natural air-conditioning of Frisco's fog."

"It's good to see you, Marco! Just look at you! You're still tall, dark and handsome, so it looks like that desert sun was good for you."

"Yeah, you're mostly right. I'm dark because of my Italian parents, and *handsome* is a judgment or at best a genetic gift from my parents. I'm a younger version of my father. As far as the desert sun is concerned, I'll take this cool Bay Area climate any day. Oh, here are my bags."

Marco proceeded to retrieve suitcase after suitcase, and when he'd gathered all of them, he glanced at Kevin and noticed his wide-eyed expression.

"Lordy! It looks like you brought everything including the kitchen sink!"

Marco smiled. "I should have warned you, so what are you driving?"

Kevin dangled his keys. "It's a big one ton *Jimmy* custom pickup," he said with a pleased expression. "And it looks like it's a damn good thing I didn't drive my wife's Honda." He laughed and hurried to intercept a luggage cart just being returned.

"You're a good man, Kev! Be real careful with those two metal cases. They contain some of my treasures from Sin City."

Kevin smiled and winked knowingly, and when the last bag was on the cart, he led the way to his gleaming red pickup.

Marco whistled. "Man! You're not kidding! It's a piece of art."

Kevin unlocked the shiny bed-cover and helped load Marco's stuff with room to spare. Then Marco paid the parking fee, and they were on their way.

"I assume you kept the house?"

"I did! However, I'm not sure how livable it'll be after sitting idle for five years, but if you don't mind, I'd like to go there and off-load my luggage. I hid a key before I left, and Emma has the other one. I'm confident she's not going to be there."

"Did she divorce you?"

"No! As far as I know, we're still legally married, and my little girl, Celine is probably quite a young lady by now."

"Man, Marco! It must be hell to have been separated from both of them. I always thought Emma was a perfect wife and mother, so I can only imagine how you feel losing her."

"You're right, and it's my own damn fault. Choosing to go to Vegas was more than she could tolerate. I'm too young to admit it, but my heart has already been broken a couple of times."

Kevin took the San Jose exit and remembered his way to Marco's house. When they pulled into the driveway, he waited until Marco found the key and held it high when he returned.

"It was right where I left it. Let's take a look inside and see what's left of the old place."

The sun still glimmered in the West providing just enough light to see their way inside even though there was no electricity.

"Man, it smells musty in here," Kevin complained. "I'll bet there's no water either."

"You're right, so all I want to do is off-load my luggage, and then, if you'd be so kind, I'd appreciate it if you'd take me to a motel. Once I have a room, then I'll buy you a drink, so we can catch up on what's happened during my absence."

Kevin agreed with the caveat of not being gone too long. "Cathy and the kids expect me home by nine, but that should be enough time to have a beer and knock around some memories."

"By the time you need to leave, I will have enjoyed at least two beers and settled my mind on a couple of things I need to know."

In addition to finding him a decent motel, they also stopped at a nearby car rental, so Marco would have a means of transportation. All things considered, it had been a smooth transition. Kevin wanted to know what it was like living in Las Vegas, but Marco had other things he also wanted to know.

"What's happened with IBM?"

"The rest of the team stayed with the company," Kevin told him, "but they had to move to new locations."

"But you're still here!"

"Yeah, because Cathy has family in the area. I was offered a job in New York, but she wanted to stay here, so I went job hunting and accepted a really good position with Intel. It's a great company, Marco, and they're moving like gangbusters with microchip technology. They just recently introduced the first commercially successful DRAM silicone microchip, and it looks like the sky's the limit."

"It sounds like you did the right thing."

"It's the best job I've ever had, and if you're interested, here's the name and number of my friend who's in charge of recruitment."

He quickly wrote the name and number on the back of a business card and handed to Marco.

"Well, that answers one of my questions," Marco said, while putting the card in his wallet. "I've been wondering where I might find a job, so maybe you and I could be working for the same company . . . once again."

"Yeah! Give him a call! They're looking for people with your skills."

Marco finished his beer, and Kevin needed to leave, so they promised to get together again as soon as possible.

"I'm glad you're back, Marco. I've never really understood what you did in Vegas, but it always seemed out-of-character for you. It's good to have you back where you belong."

They shook hands, and then Kevin gestured toward his shiny red truck with a big smile. Marco smiled smugly and waved goodbye.

~

Before the weekend, Marco had resurrected his house, reestablished his residency, set up three checking accounts at different banks, invested a reasonable sum of cash with a reputable stock broker, paid cash for a very nice used car, and contacted a few friends, who happened to still be living in the area. It was nonstop, but the pieces fell together quite nicely until loneliness caught up with him. It was difficult being in the house where he had been comforted by Emma's love and laughed playfully with his daughter Celine.

I wonder how she's doing?

He sat down at his kitchen table with a glass of bourbon and thought of the many times Emma had joined him at the table.

I wonder when I'll see her again?

His thoughts prompted lots of memories, which made him feel even worse, and it wasn't long before he'd consumed two glasses of booze. As the alcohol blurred his reasoning, Marco started slipping into a very dark place filled with regrets and self-pity. Haunting images of Capricia teased him, and he was deeply conflicted with his concerns for Emma. As he continued drinking, he also thought about the deathbed moment he'd had with Antonio, which was haunting to say the least. Then he thought of Dino's surprised observation about leaving the mob.

How's it possible to be part of the mob and then just walk away?

The alcohol was feeding a mixture of uneasy recollections and anxiety-ridden uncertainties about his future. He finally pushed the bottle aside and held his head in his hands.

Coming home may not be as good as I thought.

His hiatus in Vegas had been a fool's folly, which had cost him dearly. He remembered how Capricia had said it so precisely, "There's fantasy and reality," she'd explained, "and it's always a question of which is stronger." At the moment, he wasn't sure which was more appealing. The bourbon had effectively numbed his loneliness, but he was drifting like a rudderless ship. He wasn't grounded or guided by anything anymore.

I'm just dangling in uncertainty and chasing after things like a feather being tossed by the wind. Of course, I'll have to start over, but the real question is, do I have the will?

NINETEEN

*Th*e letter arrived three weeks to the day after returning to San Jose. He nearly overlooked it while sorting through other more demanding notifications about things relevant to his house, his car and his bank accounts. However, when he saw the name, Audrey Downing on the return address, he dropped everything and grabbed his letter opener.

Marco!

I have no way of knowing if you'll receive this, and since Emma literally threw out all her connections to you . . . including phone numbers, I've decided to send this to your San Jose address and hope it will be routed to you. It grieves me to tell you Emma isn't doing well. She's become reclusive and angry. We've tried everything possible to help her, but whatever it is that's bringing her down, it seems beyond our ability to help her. Celine is seven now, and Emma has basically consigned her to our care because she spends nearly all her time at her art studio, which adjoins a gallery in Fresno. Her artwork is exceptional, but her personal life is a mess.

I would gladly invite you to intervene, but she's been adamant in her decision to never let you back into her life. I try to stay out of her wants and needs, but I've heard her blaming you for the way things are, so I just want to be honest about it. She's never been specific, but sometimes she mentions your Las Vegas life as connected with crime and an illicit affair with another woman. It grieves me to hear her talk like that because it feeds her anger. I think it looms as a barrier to ever reconciling your relationship with her, and it makes me feel sad. As I understand it, you're still married, so as long as that's true, I feel we're still connected as well. I wish I had some kind of magic wand to use, but it is what it is, and there's not much I can do except tell you what's going on. I'm not asking you to come here or to do anything. I'm writing because I think you should be aware.

Celine is a beautiful little girl. She's very bright and loves school. I'm hoping there'll be a time when you can be with her. I'm not sure what's going to happen with Emma, but your little girl is going to want to see her daddy someday, and I'm hoping you'll help make that possible. She's perfectly safe with us, and we're in love with her beyond all measure. We were just talking about it the other day when we realized by the time Celine is eighteen we'll be ready to retire. Emma is doing well with her paintings. They are in demand and priced high. She's sold enough art to be able to buy a house, and she lives a very comfortable life, but Celine mostly lives with us, while Emma does her thing.

On a personal note, David and I hope you're well and living the life you want to live. We care about you, and wish Emma would as well, but as I've said, she's become reclusive and angry, so we're doing what we can to help her work things out.

Lots of Love,

Audrey

A flood of feelings rushed over him. It was his first and only communication from Emma's mother, and he tried to remember the last time he'd seen either of her parents. Her comments about Celine really bothered him. Their separation was his fault. Even though she'd walked out on him, he'd been the cause. Granted, he hadn't worried about either of them during his hiatus in Vegas . . . especially when he was with Capricia; however, as he re-read Audrey's letter, it triggered lots of guilt. Sadness overwhelmed him, and then he decided to have another drink to soothe his feelings. He poured a double shot and drank it rather quickly. As the alcohol blurred his thinking, it was one of those times he wished he could undo some of his ill-fated decisions.

~

"*O*h, hi, Cathy! It's Marco!"

"Hi, Marco! Welcome home! How does it feel to be out of the desert heat?"

"It's good! I love the Bay Area. Is Kev home?"

"Sure! Hold on, and I'll get him."

There was a long pause, and then Kevin greeted him in a lighthearted but scolding tone.

"Are you calling to tell me you're going back to Vegas?"

"No! I'm staying put, but I'm wondering if Cathy will let me borrow you for a couple hours?"

"House repairs?"

Marco smiled. "No! Emotional repairs, maybe? I'm having a bit of a struggle, and you're my only close friend."

Kevin paused. "I'm honored to be your close friend, but I'm no counselor."

"I just need to talk to someone, and you're a good listener."

"What's going on?"

"Well, we should sit somewhere comfortable and have a beer or two, and then I'll attempt to answer that question."

"Let me check with Cathy." He muffled the phone, and then, when he came back online, he suggested a brief delay. "Tomorrow's Saturday, so what about having lunch and a couple beers tomorrow?"

Marco agreed to a time and place, and then bolstered himself for another evening alone in a house, which contained too many memories. There was still plenty of bourbon, but he knew drinking made him sad, so he had a Pepsi instead and spent an hour watching his new TV. Regardless of the mindless entertainment, he kept fighting memories. He repeatedly thought about his past five years and replayed his happy moments with Capricia. However, every time he thought of her, he also relived her violent death, and then deep sorrow consumed him. That single horrific memory was stuck in his brain and kept dragging him down, so ignoring his initial resistance, he turned off the television, went to the kitchen, where he poured a drink. He sat passively, while waiting for its numbing effect and continued replaying the tragedy in his mind.

It really doesn't matter that D'Angelo was the one, who wired her car with explosives! Antonio knew! He had to know! Nothing ever happened without his go ahead. He took a couple more swallows of his drink and fought back tears. *But he asked my forgiveness!* Then he remembered his father's pleading look. *I said okay, but it still haunts me. Why did Capricia have to die? Why was it so violent? But Antonio said he loved her too, and I believed him.* His memories were so unsettled, and he knew there were no reasonable answers. Then he tipped his glass and felt the alcohol burn its way into his soul. When the final drop was gone, Marco stared at the empty room around him.

He said that when D'Angelo told him what had happened to Capricia, he wept.

It was such a painful memory, Marco also wept. He sat with the empty glass dangling in his hand and continued weeping until he had no more tears.

~

*O*n Saturday, Kevin tried to be upbeat and a bit playful, but Marco was in a serious mood. He didn't feel well, primarily because he'd refilled his glass two more times the night before and had gone to bed in a drunken stupor feeling terribly depressed.

"I have a headache," he complained. "I'm drinking too much."

Kevin scrunched his expression and shook his head. "It's easy to do," he agreed. "Being alone doesn't help."

Marco nodded. "Being alone sucks, but it's mostly because of what happened in Vegas," he said rather boldly, "and I'm hoping you can help me sort it out."

Kevin arched his brow and looked doubtful. "I'll listen, but I found out a long time ago that sorting things out is a personal responsibility."

Marco nodded. "You're right, but having a friend, who will listen helps a lot. Let's order a sandwich, so we can sit awhile without being bothered."

Kevin agreed, and after nearly two hours, Marco had summarized his Las Vegas story, including what had happened between him and Capricia, her tragic death, and then his emotional account of Antonio's final words. Kevin had listened faithfully and tried to be compassionate, but when Marco finished telling him, he was overwhelmed."

"It's an amazing story, my friend. It's shocking really, but what are you asking from me?"

Marco frowned slightly because he wasn't sure about what he wanted. He poured his remaining beer in his glass and then stared at the bottle as though an answer might suddenly occur to him.

"I guess I'm trying to figure out what's next. Do you have any suggestions?"

"Well, what do you want to be next?"

Marco frowned again. "I'm not sure. I felt a very strange sensation when Antonio looked at me just before he took his final breath. It occurred to me it was like redemption."

"That's a powerful word, Marco."

Marco twisted his expression to admit the irony of such a thing, and Kevin seemed to agree.

"It's redemption because he saved your ass from being with the mob for the rest of your life."

"I know!"

Then Kevin noticed tears welling up in Marco's eyes.

"Hey, buddy, it's okay!" he said in a comforting tone. "Consider yourself lucky and be thankful you had the presence of mind to come home."

Marco smiled faintly. "Thanks," he said and reached out to pat his friend's hand. "It's the first time I've tried to describe what happened, so thanks for listening."

Kevin smiled and nodded. "I think you've been through a lot, Buddy, but it's over now."

Marco nodded and wiped his eyes. "I'm still carrying the baggage, but I guess it's time to reclaim my life."

"It sounds like a plan," Kevin agreed, "and with that said, I need to be going."

When they stood to leave, Marco gave Kevin a hug and then watched him walk away.

Outside, the sun had broken through the overcast, and it seemed like a good omen. He walked to his car feeling a lot better than when they'd arrived.

No matter what I call it, it's about reclaiming my life, and that's exactly what I need to do.

TWENTY

Emma's loneliness and anger had steadily increased since their separation. She knew it had been an anger-driven decision, which had put her life in limbo. Caring for Celine had been demanding, and without her parents helping her, she would probably have had a breakdown. She had been terribly distraught, and her suspicions of Marco had left her feeling uncertain, angry and unattractive. She knew he'd gone to Las Vegas to reconnect with his birth father, but she also suspected there was more.

On Friday evening she went to her parent's home, and her mother wanted her to stay for dinner, which she was glad to do. Then after dinner, her mother poured them a glass of wine.

"I really need to get going," Emma announced. "I have a ton of laundry to do and tomorrow's going to be a busy day."

"Well, at least have a sip or two of your wine," her mother suggested. "I have something I want to share with you." Then she began fidgeting with an envelope.

When Emma glanced at it, she saw the San Jose return address and narrowed her eyes.

"I sent a letter to Marco," Audrey explained.

Emma bristled. "You did what?"

"I'm sorry, Hon, but your dad and I still care about him, so I thought I'd at least try to touch base with him. It's been a long time."

"And . . ."

"And he sent this brief reply saying he's back home in San Jose."

Emma stood so suddenly it startled Celine, who was coloring one of her storybooks.

"Can't you leave well enough alone? I want nothing to do with Marco!"

"I know," her mother conceded, "but I wanted you to know he's come home."

"Well, thanks for sharing," she said caustically. "Come on Celine! Put your book and crayons in your bag, and tell Grandma goodbye."

Celine did as she was told and kissed her grandmother on the cheek.

"I'll be back on Monday," Celine said with a confused expression. "Bye, Grandma!"

"Bye, bye, sweetheart! Mind your mama!" She paused, while Emma took her untouched wine to the kitchen. "By the way, Emma, try to remember that Marco's Celine's daddy."

Emma shuddered and frowned before politely kissing her mother goodbye and ushering Celine out the door. Then, once she was on her way, she fought back tears. She'd always blamed Marco for leaving her and giving in to his fascination with Antonio Conti, but in her heart of hearts, she also knew it had been her decision to pack up and leave San Jose. It seemed a long time ago, and indeed it had been, but for all those long years until now, she had remained adrift in an ocean of ill feelings. Her parent's willingness to help with Celine had been a godsend, but even so, she'd felt increasingly lost and uncertain.

On the drive home she kept hearing her mother's reminder about Marco being Celine's father, and indeed, she knew his connection with her would be forever. The fact they were still married loomed over her life, but any thoughts of reconnecting with him were ridiculously crazy.

~

Celine loved being with her grandparents, and Emma overplayed their generosity by taking lots of time to sequester herself in her studio. For a while, she'd also had a part-time job, but when her paintings gained public notice and started selling for thousands of dollars, it was addictive. She had been upfront with her mother and told her of her success. There had been constant encouragement for her to take all the time she needed, and it had worked. Her income made it possible for her to buy a modest house and to rent a studio in a chic storefront gallery in the artsy part of Fresno. Of course, it required more time to keep her small enterprise running, but with the help of her parents she managed quite well. However, memories hovered over her like a dark cloud and always made her sad.

Celine noticed. "What's the matter, Mommy?"

"Oh, nothing, really! I'm just thinking."

"About what, Momma?"

"Never mind, Celine! What difference does it make?"

Celine shrugged. "Were you thinking about my daddy?"

Her question startled Emma.

"Do you remember him?" The question just bubbled up and spilled out without warning, and then she noticed Celine's tiny, curious smile.

"Un huh, but maybe not actually!"

Emma smiled. "You were just a little girl the last time he was with us."

"I've seen a picture of him holding me in his arms, and Grandma said he's in San Jose."

"Grandma talks too much."

"Where's San Jose?"

"It's in California, Hon, but please, no more questions."

"Okay!" Celine said obediently, and Emma sighed.

However, after she finished the laundry, she read a story to Celine before putting her in bed, and as soon as she went to sleep, Emma had an unexpected decisive moment. She had just put on some music, slipped into her pajamas, and was having a glass of wine, when it occurred to her she should end the uncertainty over Marco.

I've had enough, she mused. *There's no reason to be living in limbo. If he's moved back to San Jose, then I should put an end to it.*

She hurried to get her business card file and began sorting through the cards to find the one she'd received from Terrance Colton, an attorney, who had helped her set up her business.

"Terrance, it's Emma! I hope it's not too late to be calling."

"Well, my goodness! This is a surprise," Terrance replied. "No, you're not interrupting at all. I'm just sitting here in my office working with some documents, which need to be filed on Monday. What's up?"

"Do you handle divorce and child-custody cases?"

There was an awkward pause. "I do, and of course I'm wondering why you're asking?"

"I'm still married," she said matter-of-factly, "but we've been apart for a long time."

"And . . ."

"And I'm tired of being in limbo, so I need a lawyer."

~

Marco received the certified mail envelope on the same day as he received his first and only letter from Emma since their separation. When he saw "Barnes and Colton, LLP," on the envelope, he suspected its contents before opening it. However, Emma's letter seemed more important, so he opened it first.

Marco!

You should receive this at about the same time as you receive a letter from my lawyer, which will begin a divorce proceeding. When I think back over our history, it's hard to believe I've waited so long before taking this step, but it's time. Mom surprised me with your letter, and told me you'd returned to San Jose, so I knew this decision must follow. Celine's welfare will undoubtedly be affected, so we'll need to appear in court to set the terms for her custody and care. I don't want to be adversarial, but we need to deal with this. My main concern is for Celine's welfare and her loving relationship with my parents, but I'm also ready to break this impasse.

I've been in limbo for far too long. My amazing parents have helped me cope, and they have been primary caregivers for Celine. In spite of our long separation and my poor mothering skills, our daughter has become an amazing child even at such a young age. I've already seen signs she's gifted much in much the same way you're gifted. She excels academically; she's physically beautiful, and she has social skills far beyond her years.

I've asked my lawyer to set a court date, and I'm hoping you'll honor the proceedings and be present without impunity. Celine will probably be shy in your presence, but I know she'll respond positively to you. She treasures a picture of you holding her in your arms, so she'll be excited to meet you for real. It will be difficult for me to see you again because I loved you deeply before you turned away from me; however, it's time for both of us to move on with our lives.

Emma

His hand was trembling as he placed the letter onto the table and then opened the other envelope. Its contents were very legal and left no doubt about what would follow. The court proceedings were set for August 13, 1973, which would be just a few days after his 39th birthday, so he marked his calendar and planned accordingly.

Although he had talked periodically with his mother during his time in Las Vegas, he felt compelled to let her know he and Emma would be divorcing. After exchanging a few pleasantries, he boldly announced what was going to happen.

"Emma and I are getting a divorce."

Silence.

"Oh, dear," she finally said in a weak and broken voice. "When calls from Emma ended, I suspected something was wrong. Oh, dear," she repeated. "This breaks my heart. Why, Marco?"

He thought carefully before answering. His mother knew he'd gone to Las Vegas to connect with his birth father, but he had protected her from knowing anything about his affair with Capricia.

"It was the long separation and uncertainty," he explained. "After Celine was born, things changed in our relationship, and Emma couldn't accept my need to connect with my biological father. For that matter, I didn't understand it myself, but you'll remember I told you about meeting him and how he wanted me to work with him."

"Yes, I recall, but I don't remember what kind of work he was doing."

"It doesn't matter, Mom. I told you about his connection to the casinos!"

"Oh, yes, I do recall that, but Marco, I never understood what he did with the casinos."

Marco was trying to be diplomatic, but with every question he was being drawn dangerously nearer the truth of what had really happened.

"It was management, Mom, and when I went there, I worked with all the electronic files."

"I have no idea what you're talking about, and besides, what does that have to do with leaving Emma?"

"She didn't want any part of it," he said rather bluntly. "You remember I told you she took Celine and went to be with her parents in Fresno."

His mother sighed, and he could hear her frustration. "I suppose I'm never going to see Emma again? And what about Celine?"

"A divorce can sometimes be a healing experience," he suggested. "Emma and I are not angry at each other . . . well at least I'm not angry with her, but she's decided she doesn't want to be married to me any longer."

He paused and thought he heard his mother crying. He waited and then heard her sniff and clear her throat.

"I'm old, Marco, and this makes me cry. I can't imagine traveling anywhere, so how will I ever see Celine again?"

She raised her voice when asking the question, and he heard her frustration.

"I don't have an easy answer to that, but I'm facing a similar dilemma. How can I stay connected to her as well?" He paused, but this time his mother waited for him to continue. "I told you that Antonio, my birth father died." Again he waited, but she said nothing, so he stopped trying to explain. "You and Celine are my only family, and I desperately want to stay close to both of you."

"Then you'll have to come to Harrisburg," she said in a demanding voice. "I'm having a really hard time walking, so I'm not going anywhere. You'll just have to come here."

"I agree," he admitted. "It's been a long time! Telephone calls are good, but visits are better."

His comment seemed to quiet her mood, and then she became more practical.

"I can only imagine how Celine's going to feel with her mommy and daddy going their separate ways."

"I can't predict what she'll feel, Mom, but I'm hoping for the best."

"I'm so sorry this is happening, Marco. It makes me very sad."

"I know! I feel sad too, but I also have a feeling it's going to be okay."

"I hope so! Please come to see me, Marco, and bring Celine if you can."

"We'll just have to wait and see what develops."

He thought she'd say okay and end the call, but instead he heard her sobbing again, so he waited.

"I'm sorry, Marco, but this makes me very sad. I know you'll do your best, but . . ." She paused, and he wondered what would follow. "You've changed, Marco!"

Her comment caught him off guard. He knew he'd changed, but he thought it was in a good way.

"What do you mean?"

"I don't know what's happened, but I just feel it; you've really changed. Whatever happened to the innocence of our life on the farm? When I remember those days with you and your dad, it warms my heart, and after Dad died, everything's changed. There's been a lot of loneliness in my life. Do you feel lonely, Marco?"

It seemed a rather sudden question. "Of course I feel lonely and at times I also feel anxious."

"Then you should come see me," she pleaded.

"It's not a good time right now, Mom."

"Then when will be a good time? I'm getting old, Marco, I can't wait too long."

"We'll find a time, Mom, and I'll call and let you know."

He felt uneasy making promises, but before he said, "Goodbye," he promised again.

~

$\mathcal{M}$arco had been living comfortably without a job. He made routine cash deposits into several accounts, and so far no one had raised any concerns. Everything was going well, and he felt relatively secure. His invested funds were doing very well, and as he calculated the returns on his money, he anticipated it would be adequate to see him through for quite a long time. However, he was also beginning to see he needed to earn an income. It was really a question of his purpose in life, and not so much about making money. Regardless of feeling *secure*, he was drifting aimlessly. Then he remembered Kevin's reference to his recruiting friend at Intel.

I really should make the contact and get serious about finding a job. I need to earn an income, so why not go for a job at Intel?

Unfortunately, his moment of inspiration fizzled, and he didn't follow through. He just didn't have the gumption to do it because he was drifting through a maze of raw emotions, and now he was facing the stark reality of divorce. Whenever he thought about Emma, he remembered how long they'd known each other. It was hard to reconcile their long relationship with how foolish he'd been in violating her trust. Just thinking about a divorce made him anxious; however, he knew he'd probably survive. Putting everything else aside, his agenda for the moment was to face Emma and hopefully reclaim Celine's love and affection.

At times, it was nearly impossible to think about losing Emma.

Maybe she'll change her mind, but the letter from her lawyer was very final, so he repeatedly had to grit his teeth and take a deep breath to clear his mind. In addition, it was even more difficult for him to admit he'd never see Capricia again.

My life's becoming an empty shell.

Marco wasn't sure his broken heart would survive.

~

Kevin had called a couple of times to ask if he'd followed through with his recruiter friend at Intel, and finally Marco told him straight up it would be a while before he intended to look for a job.

"Okay! I won't ask again! You're lucky to be able to take your time."

"I am lucky," Marco asserted. "I made good money while I was in Vegas, but one of these days I'll need to go back to work. It's just that I have some things that need to be settled before I get back into the grind."

Kevin seemed to understand. "What's going on?"

"Emma is divorcing me."

"Hum," Kevin sighed. "I'm sorry to hear that. Are you okay?"

"Yeah, but I'm thinking I might take a vacation."

"Hey, Marco, you've already been on vacation. You had five years in Vegas! Wasn't that a vacation?"

Marco laughed. "No! It was just the opposite. There was way too much stress to call it a vacation."

"I thought you said you had an easy job."

"The job was easy but there were other factors. My father' business was connected to some of the biggest casinos, and I had to deal with some very powerful people."

"And what was your job again?"

"I was his assets manager!"

"And what about your relationship with that woman? What was her name again?"

Marco hesitated. Memories of many nights of ecstasy flooded into his brain.

"Capricia," he said, "but that was stressful too, Kev. It's hard to explain, but I kind of lost my way, and now that Emma has filed for a divorce, I just need to get away and get my head together."

"Where will you go?"

"Certainly not to Vegas, but actually I haven't given it much thought. I just need some alone time."

"Sounds fair," Kevin concluded. "I'll tell my recruiting buddy, Pete, to keep you on his *maybe* list. He already knows who you are, so whenever you get around to it, landing a good job with Intel should be easy."

~

*M*arco occupied his time by steadily making more cash investments of his money and did so discretely to avoid raising any suspicions about always dealing in cash. He also began doing some volunteer work and was surprised by how satisfying it was to be helping others. He'd been reading a newspaper and saw a request for volunteers to help a charitable organization with data management, so he'd made the contact on a whim and got the job. For two days each week he volunteered and loved it. It was a perfect match for his background and skills.

"You're really good at this, Marco," said another volunteer with whom he worked. "I like helping people. If I had the means, I'd love to set up a foundation for helping kids become computer literate."

"You know, I've had similar thoughts," Marco agreed. "Maybe it's something we could collaborate on someday."

His coworker smugly agreed. "I'll keep it in mind. I'd love to join an effort like that."

"It's a good idea, but now's not the right time."

It had been a casual conversation, but it planted a seed.

Someday, he thought, *someday maybe.*

At the moment, Marco had other concerns on his mind. With his pending divorce looming on the horizon, there were other bridges he needed to cross before embracing such lofty ideas.

Before the end of the week he'd registered to attend a seminar at a retreat center in Big Sur. Its theme was self-awareness, which seemed like something he needed to do. On Sunday afternoon he made the drive to Big Sur with great expectations. Miles away from the city, he enjoyed the tranquil beauty of the coastline and the Santa Lucia Mountains.

Why haven't I ever done this before? It's so beautiful and relaxing.

The setting along the California coast at Big Sur was more than he'd anticipated. It was a revelation. He was overwhelmed by the natural beauty and serenity. When he checked in, he received a schedule of activities and moved into his room where he enjoyed one of the most restful nights that he could remember. The sounds of nature and the solitude reminded him of his boyhood home.

"Devote yourself one hundred percent," said the retreat leader. "This retreat can change your life."

It was both a greeting and a challenge, which he accepted graciously. He listened and managed his entire stay without consuming any alcohol, and in the process he met a number of new friends, who were on a similar quest as his own. In addition to plenty of time alone, he enjoyed a variety of small group meetings and many enlightening classes, which gave him good insights on how to reassemble some of the broken pieces of his life. It was a perfect preparation for the endings and beginnings he was facing, a time for finding a new perspective. When his two-week stay ended, it was hard to leave.

~

*A*lthough time is constant, August 13 seemed to come faster than anticipated, and Marco's retreat-induced tranquility ended as his anxious anticipation returned. He wondered how Emma would greet him and what it would be like to hug his beautiful daughter again. He felt assured that David and Audrey Downing would welcome him, but he was uncertain how he'd relate to them after the debacle of his ill-fated sojourn in Las Vegas. He anticipated some awkward moments but was actually quite eager to see Emma, in spite of the circumstances.

The day before the proceedings, he drove the 200 miles from San Jose through Stockton, Modesto, and Madera, arriving in Fresno around three o'clock. He'd made reservations at a downtown hotel relatively close to the courthouse and planned to return home no later than the weekend. He'd shared his arrival information with Emma's mother but anticipated no contacts with anyone until the 13th. However, when he arrived at his hotel, the clerk politely handed him a message.

Meet me at eight in the hotel's lounge. Emma

He read it twice to be sure, and then went to his room with great curiosity about why she wanted to meet with him. It was past four o'clock, and he was hungry, so he ordered room service. Then he helped himself to a couple tiny bottles of alcohol, which were available in his room. During the remaining time before eight o'clock, he agonized over what seemed to be an unusual way to begin divorce proceedings. However, he was also excited, so he was groomed and ready when he went to the lounge at around 7:50. She wasn't there, so he was tempted to order another drink but refrained in favor of having a clear head. At 7:55 he began fidgeting, and for the next few minutes he sat nervously waiting for her. At eight o'clock sharp, when she walked into the lounge, he felt his heart pounding. Emma had always been attractive, but as light from the foyer silhouetted her in the doorway, it was a breathless moment. His mind swirled with memories. She was wearing her hair in a shorter style and was dressed stylishly in a matching ensemble, which could have been featured in any glamour magazine. She spotted him, and he stood to greet her.

"Marco," she said with poise and confidence. "It's good to see you again."

He was at a loss for what to do, so he leaned awkwardly forward and kissed her on the cheek. As he did so, he inhaled the fragrance, which Capricia always wore and nearly lost his balance. However, he recovered quickly and managed to say, "You look amazing!"

"Well," she said with a teasing smile, "I want you to know what you're losing."

He slightly raised his brow and nodded toward her chair. When she sat down, she crossed her ankles in a perfect modeling pose and smoothed her skirt, which amply revealed her shapely legs.

"Would you like a drink?" he asked, and she nodded without saying what she'd like. Then he remembered her preference and motioned to the waiter. "She'll have a Glenlivet, and I'll have a Jack Daniels, both straight up."

"I'm impressed, Marco! Your exotic nights in Vegas haven't dulled your memory."

Once again her words had a slight sting to them, but he ignored it and smiled.

"It's good to see you," he said as they waited for their drinks to be served.

She smiled and opened her wallet.

"I want you to see this picture of Celine on her birthday." She handed him her wallet, so he could look at it. "She has your hair and my good looks."

Again, he arched his brow and let it pass. However, he was amazed at how Celine had changed.

"She's beautiful, and I remember you said she's also very bright."

"I guess we know where she gets that, but I must tell you she's rather artistic too, which is my genetic imprint."

He returned her wallet and waited for her next comment, but instead, she said nothing as she nervously scanned the room. Then she looked at him and smiled knowingly.

"Okay, Emma, what's the agenda? We're going to court tomorrow to end something neither of us thought would ever end, and you seem intent on making me squirm over losing you, so is that why we're meeting?"

"Oh, Marco, please don't be so petty. Can't we just enjoy a drink together and remember good times?"

He looked down just as the waiter brought their drinks.

"Do you want to run a tab, Sir?"

"No! Just add it to my room." He held up his key, so the waiter could note the number.

Then Emma raised her glass and waited for him to do the same.

"Let's drink a toast to memories."

He lightly touched his glass to hers, and for a few moments, they sat in silence.

"Together with no impunity," he said quoting her request in the letter, which had accompanied the divorce papers.

She laughed nervously with a more serious expression and slightly tossed her head to the side.

"Yes," she said. "That's what I hope, and if you still have even a shred of the character you once had, we will have a very civil procedure tomorrow, *with no impunity,* and all legal matters will be settled."

He nodded and sipped his drink. "No regrets?"

"Yes, I have regrets goddammit, but it is what it is!"

Her angry volley caught him off-guard, but then he noticed tears and handed her his handkerchief. She refused his gesture in favor of a tissue she had in her purse.

"Sorry," he added, "but I had to ask."

She looked at him with a furrowed brow and tightness in the skin around her eyes.

"I gave you my heart and my soul, Marco, and to this very day I still cannot say for sure what you've done, but I know something happened, which made you want to run away to Las Vegas. I know you said you wanted to be with your father, but I think you had another itch you needed to scratch. As a woman, I just felt it, but I guess it doesn't matter if I understand it or not, because here we are. It is what it is!"

He listened without reacting and knew exactly what she was implying. He'd been foolish and had turned his back on everything that had been good in his life just to satisfy his lust for Capricia and his fascination with his father's lavish lifestyle. She suspected it but had no evidence of his indiscretion. However, the memories had seared their way into his emotions, and suddenly he needed his handkerchief to blot his tears. Emma noticed and knew she'd touched a nerve. It was the finality of what would happen the following day that had suddenly pushed its way to the surface.

"I'm glad to see you still have feelings," she said as though handing him another indictment. "I hope you're feeling what I've been feeling for the past five years. I've cried until I have no more tears. Hell, yes, I have regrets. I loved you with all my heart, and if magic were possible, we'd just forget about it and be happily in love again, but there's no such magic, Marco. There's only reality, and what we used to enjoy is simply no longer possible."

He looked at her pleadingly, but she shook her head no. Then when he started to speak, she held her finger to her lips and made a schussing sound for him to be quiet.

"Don't say it!" she demanded. "Tomorrow, we're going to put this behind us, set up some new rules, and then move on. I fully anticipate you'll slowly reenter Celine's life, but our so-called marriage will end tomorrow. I imagine we'll remain friends, and that there'll be times when Celine will be our neutral zone; however, it's time to move on. Oh, and for the good of the order, Marco, I want you to know I forgive you. I hope you'll find ways to reclaim your life."

He was stunned. In no way had he anticipated such a deliberate summary and ultimatum. Ironically, he agreed with her, but what shocked him most was how she'd used the same words as Antonio. It was as if she'd confirmed his death wish for him to reclaim his life. He wanted to speak, but words failed him. Then he tried to make eye contact, but she turned away from him, finished her drink, stood and walked away.

TWENTY-ONE

*Th*e most memorable part of the divorce was when he walked into the courtroom and Celine shyly smiled at him. Emma had done a good job coaching her about seeing her father, but her smile revealed her eagerness. He made eye contact, and she approached him.

"Are you my Dad?"

Marco nodded yes and smiled. "I've missed you! Can I give you a hug?"

She hesitated but then hugged him politely, and he immediately noticed she had Emma's eyes and teasing smile. In that brief moment with Celine, he received a gift he'd treasure for the rest of his life.

He also received hugs from Emma's parents, who were genuinely glad to see him again, while Emma sat demurely with her lawyer waiting for the proceedings to begin. He'd never conceived of a divorce hearing being a pleasant experience, but it appeared everyone was being quite civil.

The hearing was straightforward and matter-of-fact. Her lawyer presented the case and clearly established the terms of agreement, and when it was over, he felt it had been quite amicable.

Celine glanced at him frequently, but Audrey took her hand as they told Marco goodbye; however, as they walked out of the courtroom, she waved and smiled, leaving him with another precious memory.

While her lawyer organized his papers, Emma took the opportunity to also say goodbye.

"Thank you!" she said and touched his hand. "I'd like to stay in touch."

He nodded, and she smiled.

"I like the settlement, and I hope you feel the same." Then she looked at him for confirmation, and he nodded slightly. "Your financial support will make a big difference." She glanced at him knowingly. "I hope it seems fair to you."

He managed a slight smile and nodded yes.

"Celine will be going back to school, and her friends will probably hear all about what happened here today."

"I imagine you're right. She's a treasure."

"I think you need to reconnect with her, and I'm sure Mom and Dad will be happy to have you visit anytime, so don't be shy about asking."

It felt like she was giving him a "to do" list, but he also felt encouraged, and she was being cordial.

"I imagine we'll be together from time to time to share in Celine's accomplishments, but right now, it's time for both of us to move on."

"I agree," he said boldly to break her monologue, and then he took hold of her hand.

She looked down at his hand holding hers, raised her head, and looked directly into his eyes. "I really don't hate you,

Marco. I hate what you've done, but I see through your crusty façade. You're still Marco."

He slightly squeezed her hand, and when she smiled, he kissed her on her cheek. It was a moment to treasure, a moment they would both carry with them for all the years to come.

~

Sundown in Fresno brought a refreshing breeze, which gave promise of an enjoyable evening, and when Marco returned to his hotel there was lightness in his step. All of his fidgeting and anxiety had been for naught.

I'm actually a lucky man, he mused. *Emma has been more than gracious, and she knows she's still important to me . . . and I'll treasure Celine's smile for the rest of my life.*

On his way past the registration desk, he told the clerk he'd be leaving in the morning, and that he'd like to settle his account to expedite the process. There were no calls or further messages, so when he was in his room, he opened one of the little bottles of bourbon from his in-room bar, enjoyed a nightcap, and then had a wonderfully restful sleep. Ironically, he felt amazingly free and unfettered.

~

On the drive back to San Jose, Marco did a lot of thinking. He felt amazingly good, which wasn't what he'd anticipated.

I would have never thought a divorce could be so civil. We were so agreeable. It was just a matter of signing some papers.

He'd treasured seeing Celine again and smiled broadly when he remembered how she'd waved at him as she left the courtroom. He was also thinking about how he could rebuild his relationship with her and tried to envision her as a young woman.

I wonder what she'll do with her life.

Then he thought of how Emma had forgiven him, and had to admit it was a gift that would sustain him.

He stopped for gas in Modesto, and as he watched the spinning meter on the pump, it prompted another thought about how quickly time was passing. The divorce was clearly a turning point, which seemed to be a part of a continuing process he'd called *redemption*. He recalled Antonio's words: "Reclaim your life," and now he was another step closer. These were moments in time, and as Emma put it: *"It's time for both of us to move on."*

During the remainder of his trip home, he felt emotional. He was sad for how he'd turned away from Emma and Celine, and each time he thought of her saying, "I forgive you," he felt like he might break down in tears.

"Forgiveness is an important part of redemption," he whispered aloud as though trying to convince her he was finally getting his life back on track. He knew there were still many more things that would need to happen, but he had just taken a big step in reclaiming his life.

As he neared the turnoff for San Jose, he had firmly resolved to make it happen, and the first thing would be to make contact with the recruiting guy at Intel.

Marco parked in his driveway, then went inside, and as soon as he shut the door, there was a momentary rush of feelings and memories. His strongest feeling was satisfaction. He carried his suitcase into the bedroom, changed into comfortable clothes, and then went to the kitchen to make some tea. As he was looking for a teabag, he noticed his remaining bourbon and thought how easy it would be to skip the tea and have a drink, but he refrained.

If it's going to be a new day, then I have to deal with it in a new way.

~

"*I'm* excited to put you on Intel's payroll," exclaimed Pete Dawson, Kevin's friend, who managed recruitment for the company. "I know about your work with IBM and the recognition you received as one of <u>Time Magazine's</u> 100 most influential people. You're one of a kind, and if you accept my offer, you can work with Kevin, who has constantly bragged about being your trusted teammate at IBM."

"Kevin and I have a good history," Marco boasted.

"I know he'll be pleased if you sign on, and in a very short time, I'd like to see you leading some of our best research and development."

Dawson smiled and handed Marco a folder containing a job description and outlining the starting salary and benefits.

Marco opened it and was overwhelmed.

"This is very generous, so thank you, and yes, I'm looking forward to working at Intel."

The handshake lasted longer than expected, but Mr. Dawson was clearly excited to welcome Marco's expected contribution toward the company's goals.

"Intel is synonymous with Silicone Valley, and we are poised to dominate the industry."

He smiled and watched for Marco's nod of agreement.

"It's good to join a winning team," Marco said in response to his hearty welcome.

"We're doubling our growth every year," Dawson beamed, "and your work will be on the leading edge of this company's future."

"I look forward to it," Marco said, "but I have to admit my interface with Intel's product line will take some time. Microchip technology will be new to me."

"It's okay, Marco. We need your ability to be a visionary. Intel is going to be the driving force behind a global technology revolution. We have all kinds of technicians making microchips, but it will be people like you leading the way."

"I appreciate your confidence, and I'll do my best."

~

On his first day on the job, Kevin came to welcome him.

"Here's to old times," Kevin said and then hugged his friend.

"You'll have to lead the way, Kev. I'm the new kid on the block."

It was a joyous reunion.

On the following weekend he invited Kevin and Cathy to get a babysitter for the kids and join him in a celebration of his new career opportunity. They were delighted, and Kevin repeatedly said it was like old times. Over the hours of their enjoyable evening, they reminisced and laughed a lot, which was cathartic; however, it was the first time Cathy had been included in a conversations about Marco's ups and downs, so she did her best to absorb his history. Then at one point before their evening ended, Marco mentioned his divorce from Emma. They already knew, and they were sad, but when he told them about how amicable it was, Cathy was wide-eyed with surprise.

"I've never heard of a divorce, which has a happy ending," she exclaimed. "Who ever heard of divorcees kissing when the proceedings ended?" She laughed playfully, and Marco smiled. "I remember Emma," Cathy said with a wistful look. "She always impressed me as a very special and talented woman. I also recall she's beautiful."

Marco smiled knowingly.

"It's all of the above," he agreed, "and part of the reason I feel so positive about our divorce is exactly what you've described. We're both looking forward to a positive future."

Kevin stared at him playfully. "You realize, of course, all three of us are facing a midlife celebration with black balloons and morbid jokes."

"I know," Marco admitted, "but I'm seeing it as a transition, which sets a new course." They smiled coyly, but he could see they agreed. "Actually, I'm looking forward to what's ahead."

"Wow!" Cathy asserted. "You have good thoughts, Marco, and I think Kev and I are right there with you. We've talked about this many times, and the road ahead looks very promising."

Kevin nodded his agreement. "I'm really glad you took the job," he added, "and I'm looking forward to the next phase as well."

Then they raised their glasses to toast their future, and Marco put it into words. "This is for good friends, a new job, fantastic children and to a positive future."

Marco could almost hear Antonio's words echoing in his mind: *"Go home and reclaim your life,"* and then, when he remembered Antonio's final breath, tears filled his eyes.

~

Marco's work at Intel was everything he'd hoped it would be, and much in the same way he'd succeeded at IBM, he took the lead as an innovator and visionary, which was what he'd always dreamed of doing.

Another big change came shortly after he started his new job. He put his house on the market and moved into a condo closer to his work. It was refreshing to live in a new space and to leave the memories that lingered in the rooms where he'd been with Emma and Celine.

"It feels invigorating to live in a new place," he explained to Kevin. "I love the light, airy interior in my condo. It's kind of symbolic of the changes in my life."

Kevin had joined him on his balcony overlooking a wooded area, which gave it a park-like setting. "I like it too, Marco. Your house was okay, but it was too big and too empty."

He invited other friends to visit his new home as well, and as the months turned into a year, he felt extremely lucky to be leaving his past behind and finding satisfaction with how things were going.

~

*H*is first vacation came in his second year with Intel, and he could hardly wait to go back to Fresno for Celine's ninth birthday. Although he'd been having telephone chats with her nearly every Friday since the divorce, she persistently begged him to come see her. Emma had encouraged him to rebuild his relationship with his daughter, but Celine was the one insisting they needed more than his phone calls.

"Come for my birthday," she pleaded, and when he said yes, she was elated.

"Will Mom be there?" he asked nonchalantly.

"Maybe," she answered in a sly, doubtful tone, "but it doesn't matter. Grandma says I can have two parties," she boasted.

He agreed and told her he'd take some vacation time to be there. Of course, he also checked it out with David and Audrey, and they were happy with his decision.

"I thought you'd visit frequently," Audrey observed, "so coming to see Celine is long overdue."

"I really want to get reacquainted with her," he said. "Unfortunately, I've been too focused on my work at Intel, but now's the time, and I'm looking forward to it. Do you think Emma will be there?"

"Well," she said, "she's talked about Celine's birthday, but as far as we know, she's not made any plans. Why don't you give her a call?"

He immediately felt anxious but gladly wrote down her number, which was a new entry on his phone list. "I'll think about it," he said. "I don't want to overstep our agreements."

"Let us know when you're coming," Audrey suggested. "You're always welcome in our home."

~

*H*e nearly completed dialing Emma's number three times but hung up before her phone rang. *She'll probably be angry her mom gave me her number.* However, he finally threw caution to the wind and waited nervously as the phone rang. When Emma answered, his voice nearly failed.

"Hello!"

"Emma, it's Marco!"

It was the dreaded moment. Would she disconnect the call or scream at him for calling, but to the contrary, her response was quite pleasant.

"Oh, hi, Marco! I won't ask how you got my number, but what's up?"

He exhaled and collected his thoughts. "I'm longing to see Celine," he confessed, "so I'd like to visit her for her birthday."

"That would be nice. I know you've been calling her quite regularly, and each time you call, she says, 'Why doesn't daddy come see me?' so I'm sure she'd love it if you could be here for her birthday."

"You're very kind. Thank you! I've been really nervous about it."

"Not to worry . . . my brave ex-husband! You're still loved."

"Then it's okay?"

"Sure! Why not? Her birthday is March 27, but I'm sure you know that already."

"Absolutely! I'm taking vacation time."

"Which means you must be working?"

"I am! I have a great job with Intel."

"Congratulations! I know about Intel. I've heard it's a good company."

"And how about you?" he asked. "Are you willing to share Celine's birthday with me?"

"I may stop by . . . assuming it'll be at mom and dad's place, but it really should be your special time with her."

"Are you doing okay?"

"I am," she confirmed. "I can hardly believe how many paintings I've sold, so everything's good."

"I'm glad I called," he said softly.

"Yes, it's good to hear from you, Marco. I'll look forward to a quick hello while you're here."

"Later! Take care."

"You too," she said, and then the call ended.

He felt refreshed. It was his first overt effort to test the "friendly" terms of their divorce, and it had gone quite well.

Sometimes I feel like a damn fool for being so stupid and losing her.

TWENTY-TWO

An air of cordiality surrounded Celine's birthday and it helped Marco more than he could tell. As promised, Emma stopped by, and Celine paid close attention to how her mother and father interacted. She understood they were divorced, but when they hugged and talked politely, it made her feel happy. Emma had just sold one of her most expensive paintings, so she was feeling optimistic.

Celine loved every minute with her dad, and he treasured his time with her. The party ended too quickly as far as he was concerned, but he managed to collect enough happy memories to last until the next time. Best of all, he'd remembered his camera and had taken plenty of pictures, which would fill his new photo album. He'd also managed to take a couple pictures of Emma, which he planned to keep in his private envelope of memories.

~

With over 300 days of sunshine during the year, the climate in San Jose is wonderful year-round, but during the summer it's warm. Marco loved it. He invested himself in his work, made many new friends and virtually eliminated loneliness from his weekends. There were many things to do, and friends often invited him to events and outings in the area. He seldom had any alone time, and when fall rolled around, he was looking forward to the end of another successful year feeling very positive about his accomplishments.

The Thanksgiving holiday took on special meaning as Marco joined Kevin and his family for a traditional Thanksgiving dinner. The food and celebration reminded him of his boyhood in Illinois. He remembered being especially fond of Thanksgiving dinners around his family's big table. His parents always invited lots of friends to join them for the holiday feast, and his mother took extra care to set a festive table. Unlike California, it was usually cold during November in Illinois, so his dad took special care to have a fire in the fireplace, and his mom prepared a wonderful mixture of cinnamon and spices to heat on the hearth, which filled the house with its aroma. As he savored a final bite of pumpkin pie and sat back to enjoy his coffee, he thought of how important those traditions were and regretted he had no family so he could carry them forward. The laughter and conversation in Kevin's home touched a need in his life and reminded him he'd promised his mother he'd try to bring Celine to visit at Christmas.

As soon as he returned home, he called.

Emma answered the phone and seemed a bit surprised to hear from him.

"What's up, Marco?"

"I'd like to take Celine to spend Christmas with my mother in Harrisburg."

His request was met with a rather long pause, so he waited politely.

"Christmas has always been a special time for us," Emma complained. "Mom and dad make a big deal out of sharing Christmas with family and friends, and it's become such a tradition, I'd hate to see it interrupted."

"But Celine is also my mother's granddaughter. It's only fair for her to get to know her other grandmother as well."

"And how are you planning to travel? It'll be in the middle of winter, which is no big deal here, but Illinois can be very unpredictable in late December."

"I love your motherly concern, Emma, but you know I'll protect her with my life. We'll fly to Chicago, and then I'll rent a really good 4-wheel-drive car for the trip to Harrisburg. We'll stay through New Year's and then fly back to Fresno."

There was another long pause.

"Well, maybe," Emma said reluctantly. "I guess it's only fair, and I'm sure Celine will jump for joy if I suggest she can take a trip with you."

"I'm sorry for the short notice, but is it okay?"

"Probably, but give me some time to think about it."

He smiled. "How long?"

Emma hesitated. "I've been seeing someone, Marco, so if I say yes, then I may be spending Christmas with his family."

Marco wasn't sure what to say. He'd more or less anticipated she'd meet someone, but in just an instant he realized he'd secretly been holding onto her as though she would always belong to him in some strange way.

"Say something, Marco!" she demanded.

"Well, I'm not sure what to say. Who's the lucky guy?"

"Oh, you don't really need to know, but there's one thing I think will surprise you."

"And what's that?"

"He's just moved back to Fresno after spending the last five years in Las Vegas."

He nearly laughed but restrained the urge.

"You're right! Who would have thought?"

"He's in real estate, and during his years in Vegas he made lots of money. He's filthy rich, Marco!"

"Well, I'm rich too," he chided, "and I'm probably better looking."

He laughed, but she didn't seem to find it funny.

"Anyway," she concluded and returned to the issue at hand, "I'll check with Mom and Dad because they watch over Celine more than I do, and then I'll talk to her. I'll let you know in a couple days. Is that okay?"

"Sure! I'll look forward to your decision."

When the call ended, Marco felt a surge of excitement. He wanted this with all his heart and was pretty sure Emma would say okay.

"It'll be my chance to be her father again," he said aloud, "and Mom can be a doting grandmother."

~

When Emma called again, she agreed, and Celine was super excited to be making a trip with her dad to see her Grandma Jackson. However, on Tuesday of Christmas week, Marco's phone rang just before 6:00 a.m. and startled him awake.

"Hello!"

"Are you Marco Jackson, Aileen Jackson's son?"

"Yes, who's this?"

"Thank goodness! I guess I've been dialing wrong numbers. I'm Mary Cavanaugh, and I've been your mother's caretaker for the last two years. She's gravely ill, Marco."

"What's wrong?"

"She has severe pneumonia, and we've put her in the hospital. I wish I could say otherwise, but we're concerned she might not make it."

His heart sank, and his emotions fell from euphoria over taking Celine to see her grandmother to despair over the news he was receiving.

"Oh, dear," he exclaimed. "I was planning on bringing her granddaughter to see her at Christmas, and now . . ."

"And now, I think you should try to get here as soon as you can."

"Is she able to have visitors?"

"For very limited times, and they're taking lots of precautions with masks and gowns, but I'm being honest about her condition. When I left the hospital last night, she wasn't showing any signs of improvement."

"I'll make arrangements and come right away. Is there anything else you can tell me?"

"What's your daughter's name?"

"Celine! She's nine and a half years old."

"Aileen has been asking for her! She kind of drifts in and out, but I've heard her asking for Celine quite a few times."

"I promised her," Marco explained, "and she was very excited to think about having us visit her for Christmas."

"Oh, my," Mary sighed. "Things often don't go as planned." She paused. "I'll look forward to meeting you Marco. When you get here, go directly to General Hospital, and I'll give them a heads up that you're coming."

"I may still bring Celine."

"That would be wonderful. Travel safely."

When the call ended, there was no time for indecision, so he called Emma even though it was quite early. She said a groggy, "Hello," and waited.

"Emma! It's Marco! I just got a call from Harrisburg, and my mom's very ill."

"Oh, good, Lord, Marco! Are you serious?"

"She's in the hospital with severe pneumonia."

"What about your trip?"

"I need to move it up one day. Can I still take Celine with me?"

"She's in school until Thursday."

"Can we take her out of school a day early, so she can see her grandmother?"

"Oh, Lord! Let me get my robe on. Wait just a minute." She returned out of breath. "I just checked the schedule, and they only have a half-day on Thursday, so it's probably okay."

"I'll take that as a *yes*! I'll make an adjustment on our flight, so we can leave Fresno on Wednesday, if that's okay?"

"Okay, and I'm really sorry about your mom. Are you okay?"

"Yeah, I'm good but rattled. My mom's been asking for Celine, so I'm glad she'll be with me."

"Okay," Emma agreed. "I'll call my mom and let her know what's going on. She'll have Celine ready for whenever you get here."

"I think there's a 4:00 p.m. commuter, which gets to Fresno around 4:45, so if you could bring her to the airport, we'll meet there and then catch the next flight to Chicago."

"Okay! I've got nothing scheduled Wednesday, so I'll coordinate from this end and have her at the airport in time for the flight. Call me as soon as you have it confirmed."

"Thanks, Emma. I still love you."

He realized the second he'd said it that it wasn't okay, but he honestly meant it. However, Emma didn't answer, and he heard a "click" when she disconnected the call.

~

$\mathcal{M}$arco hustled, and it worked. It was a fast and furious day, but he made the flight to Fresno, and then at 6:00 p.m. on Wednesday, their plane touched down in Chicago. With Celine holding tightly to her dad's hand, they hurried through the airport, picked up a rent-a-car and were on their way to Harrisburg by seven.

"You know Grandma is very sick," he said and watched Celine nod yes. "Do you think you'll remember her?"

"Mom has her picture sitting on her dresser, so I think I'll remember."

Hearing her mention the picture gave him a little surge of hope. It was like telling him there's still a connection.

It was dark when they arrived, so they hurried to the hospital, inquired about the room, and took the elevator to the third floor. As they were walking down the hallway, Mary Cavanaugh ran to greet them.

"You must be Marco," she said and shook his hand. "And this attractive young lady must be Celine."

Celine smiled and shook Mary's hand as Marco introduced Mary as her grandmother's friend.

"I'm so glad you're here, Marco. She's not doing well, and the doctor is honoring her advance directives not to intervene." She made a sad expression and shook her head. "She stopped eating and drinking yesterday, so I'm afraid it's not good news."

Celine listened and watched her father's expression change to sadness.

"She's in room 318," Mary added, and motioned toward the nurse's station. "We'll have to wear sterile gowns and masks." Then as they prepared, Mary looked at Celine and told her what to expect.

"I was just with your grandma, Honey. She was awake and seems to be resting peacefully. She's been waiting for you to arrive, so I know she'll be glad to see you."

Celine nodded and blinked her eyes to hide some tears, so Marco intervened.

"Thanks for taking care of her, Mary. The last time I talked to her on the phone, she mentioned you by name and told me how lucky she was to have you helping her."

"She's a sweetheart," Mary beamed. "You have a wonderful grandmother, Celine! Let's go in to see her."

~

Aileen Jackson died peacefully at 3:00 p.m. in the afternoon on December 24, just one day before they'd hoped to be celebrating Christmas with her; however, for at least twenty minutes before she took her final breath, she held tightly to Celine's hand and was able to say, "I love you." Celine was captivated by what was happening to her grandmother, and Marco struggled to keep his composure.

When Celine suddenly felt her grandmother's hand go limp, it frightened her, and she looked at Marco with a grimacing expression.

"What's wrong, Hon?"

She lifted her grandmother's hand and then let it drop just as a nurse rushed into the room to check the various monitors. Marco felt a wave of emotion when he realized the monitors had flat-lined. He looked at the nurse, who slowly shook her head and then lovingly placed Aileen's hand under the covers.

"Is Grandma sleeping?" Celine asked, while looking at her father.

Marco felt a profound sadness as he shook his head no and reached for Celine's hand. "She's gone, Hon."

Celine stepped back from the bedside and fought back her tears. She jerked her hand away from Marco as though he should have done something to save her.

"Why didn't the doctor come and help? Why did they let Grandma die?"

"Grandma had told the doctor not to do anything more," he explained. "She wanted to see you and me, but she'd already told the doctor to let her go."

Celine started crying as Mary put her arm around her, and then Marco broke down in tears as well.

"It's very sad," he said in a voice broken by emotion, "but I'm so glad we were with her before it happened." Then he leaned forward to kiss his mother's forehead and whispered, "Goodbye".

Celine watched as Mary continued comforting her. Then she said, "Grandma's gone!"

Marco wiped his eyes and realized she was making a statement rather than asking a question, so he nodded yes and reached to hold her hand again. This time she took hold of his hand tightly, and he quietly sighed. "Grandma waited to see you, and I'm so glad we got here before she died."

"I'm going to miss her very much," Celine said matter-of-factly.

"I'm going to miss her too," Marco confessed. "I'll also miss her very much."

Celine had stopped crying and smiled.

"You probably can't remember," Marco said, "but when you were just a baby we came here to visit Grandma."

Celine had a questioning look, which confirmed she had no memory other than the picture of her grandmother.

"I feel bad that I was gone as you were growing and changing," he confessed. "Grandma would have loved having you visit, but since I wasn't there, it didn't happen."

"It's okay," Celine said maturely. "I bet you have lots of memories of her, don't you, Dad?"

"Oh, sure," he agreed. "I have wonderful memories from when I was a little boy. We lived in a wonderful old house on a farm, and Grandma and Grandpa Jackson loved me just like Grandma and Grandpa Downing love you."

"Mom showed me a picture she painted of your farmhouse," Celine announced proudly. "I really liked the big windmill."

Marco laughed. "That old windmill made a *clickity-clack* sound, and when I went to bed at night, I'd listen to it, and let it sing me to sleep."

Celine smiled and looked once more at her grandmother, and then she tugged on Marco's hand.

"Did you tell Grandma goodbye?"

Marco smiled and nodded. "Yes, I did! How about you? Did you tell her goodbye?"

Celine motioned for him to bend down, so she could whisper in his ear.

"Grandma told me she loved me, and then she said she had to go, so I told her goodbye."

It was endearing to hear her perspective, and when the nurse stepped into the room to remind them it was time to leave, Celine turned one last time to wave goodbye to her Grandma. The nurse smiled, and Marco savored the moment as a reminder of what's truly important.

~

*I*t was cold, but thankfully there'd been no snow or ice on the day when Marco and Celine entered the church for the memorial service. It was chilly inside, and Celine only had a jacket, so she shivered and mentioned how nice it would be to go back to where it would be warm.

A small group of friends sat mostly toward the front of the sanctuary, and Marco remembered his wedding day. One older couple asked why Emma wasn't there, and he avoided the truth by saying she was with her family. Celine overheard and looked at him doubtfully.

It was a simple memorial service, and Celine seemed fascinated, but when she realized her grandma would be buried in the ground next to her grandpa in the cemetery next to the church, it frightened her. There had been no previous occasions to learn about such things, so Marco explained what would happen, and she relaxed a little. However, as they stood by the graveside, he felt her tension, so he put his arm around her to comfort her, but as it sometimes happens, he was the one who felt comforted to have her at his side.

When the memorial ended, and as they were walking away from the grave, Celine surprised him with an unexpected comment.

"Thanks for being my dad," she said with a big smile.

Marco was so filled with love he thought he would burst. Having her with him had prompted a lot of remembering and caused him to realize the importance of family. He would have preferred celebrating Christmas with his mother, having a special dinner and opening gifts, but her illness and death had brought him closer to Celine. He knew without a doubt he was slowly reclaiming his life.

She's a lot like Emma, he thought, *and even though we're divorced, I'm still in love with both of them.*

Celine ran ahead toward the car, and he was so proud, it touched his heart.

Love is forever, he thought, *and Celine is a gift of love.* Then it suddenly dawned on him he'd been hoping to reclaim his identity as her father, and that was exactly the gift she was giving him. *I'm Celine's father, the son of Hank and Aileen Jackson, and the biological son of Fredericka and Antonio Conti. I've come home to reclaim my identity.*

Celine waited for him to open the car door, and then he helped her inside.

Thank God she could come with me.

As they drove away from the little country church, he wondered why he'd been so willing to surrender everything to be with Capricia and Antonio, but now, with Celine at his side, he felt he was slowly reclaiming what he'd nearly lost for good. As he pulled onto the highway for the short ride back to Harrisburg, he remembered Antonio's final words, and when he glanced at Celine sitting next to him, it was finally settled. She was helping him understand how *redemption* works.

"It's a process," he said aloud as though making an announcement.

"What did you say, Daddy?"

He smiled. "Oh, nothing, really! I was just thinking out loud."

Celine shrugged, but without knowing it, she was his affirmation, and it was changing his life. Being with her was beginning to heal his brokenness.

~

When they arrived in Fresno, Celine rushed into the arms of her Grandmother Downing, and Marco's joy could not be contained. He smiled and laughed heartily.

"Oh, my, precious Pumpkin," her grandmother beamed, while giving her a welcoming hug, "I've missed you so much, and your mother has missed you, too. We'll be interested to hear all about your trip to Illinois.

"Where's Mom?"

"She'll be here in exactly one hour to give you lots of hugs and kisses." Then she glanced at Marco. "Can you stay?"

Marco smiled. "No, I'll need to be going, but Celine has some wonderful stories to tell, so everyone might as well settle in and get ready to listen."

"As always, Marco, it's wonderful seeing you again. I'm sorry about your mom, but having Celine with you must have made it very special."

Marco nodded and nearly choked up. "It's hard to explain how special! I'll treasure these memories for the rest of my life." He smiled and gave Audrey a big hug. "Tell Hank I said, hello, and when Emma gets here, give her a hug for me."

Audrey smiled and nodded. "You've been through some difficult days, Marco. It's good to see you smiling."

"It's part of the process," he explained, "and she's helping me more than she knows." Then he pointed at his daughter, and Celine rewarded him with another smile. "I'm reclaiming my life, Audrey. All the pieces are falling together, and it's wonderful!"

"I'm glad," Audrey said with a satisfied smile. "Hank and I are glad to still be a part of your life. We must promise to never lose contact."

"I agree, and we must also make an effort to see each other more often."

He opened the car door and Celine ran over to give him a goodbye hug.

"I wish you could stay until Mom gets here."

"I know! But it's better if I go. It's just good to know she's happy." Then he waved at Audrey. "Hugs and kisses all around . . . I've got to be going."

As he pulled away, Celine waved goodbye, and in one more tender moment, she nudged his redemption another notch forward.

TWENTY-THREE

*T*ime passed so quickly, it was hard to keep track of milestones along the way. Marco continued making routine calls to Celine and was delighted when she told him how well she was doing in school. He'd also returned to Fresno a number of times to maintain their father/daughter connection, but he noticed major changes around the time she turned fifteen.

Another milestone was when he received an announcement from Audrey that Emma had married Eddie Slather, whom she described as a wealthy real estate broker.

"He's really nice, Marco. I think you'll like him."

It had been years since the divorce, but hearing about her marriage nearly knocked him for a loop. The finality that Emma had chosen another man instead of him brought him face to face with his own loveless life. He was still single and so completely tied to his work, he'd pushed his social life out of the way. Emma had remarried, and he was still suffering from a broken heart. It was like the power of love was ignoring him.

"You should have seen Celine at the wedding, Marco. She was Emma's maid of honor."

"I hope to see some pictures," he hinted. "I know it's none of my business, but I'd love to see Celine, and of course, I'm curious to see Mr. Slather."

"I'll tuck some pictures in my purse and share them the next time you're here." She paused. "Speaking of next time; will you be coming to see us anytime soon?"

He knew it had been a long time, but coincidently, he'd been thinking about Celine again and wondering if she'd give him a warmer reception next time.

"I'm considering it," he declared. "This summer I have a business trip to LA in August, and I've been thinking I could work in a side trip to Fresno on my way back."

"Celine would love that. She'll be graduating from high school before you know it, and she's already changed into quite a beautiful young woman! Where does the time go?"

"I'm embarrassed it's been so long since I've seen her, although we talk regularly on the phone, I've noticed she has less and less to say, so I'm really hoping to see her this summer." Marco paused thoughtfully. "I agree with you that time passes too quickly."

"Well, don't feel bad about it. You're still young, and Celine still talks about you frequently. She thinks you're the best dad ever."

"How about her new father-in-law?"

"She likes him, but he'll never be able to take your place." Then she laughed softly, and Marco felt a wave of relief.

"I think Celine knows I love her with a passion, so I'm glad to hear you say that."

"Well, it's true! We all love you. Anyway, life just keeps happening, and we do the best we can." She paused. "Celine's gifted like you, Marco. She's at the top of her class, and you'll be very proud of the way she's become so mature."

"Oh, there's no doubt about that! I just hope she's not too full of herself."

"Oh, no, she's very grounded! School counselors wanted to put her in an accelerated program, but she declined in favor of staying in the same class as her friends. Her mom and I are trying to coach her on how to deal with the attention she's getting, but I can tell you for sure, she's going to be very successful."

Marco listened and remembered when he'd opted to stay with his friends during high school.

"Anyway," Audrey concluded, "there are some big things coming, so stay tuned."

"I will."

"Stay in touch about your summer plans. If you can come in August, we'd love to see you."

"Okay! I'll talk to you soon."

~

After disconnecting the call, Marco had a lot on his mind, not the least of which was that Emma had remarried. He tried to imagine her with another man and then felt bad. His love for her had lingered in spite of everything that had happened. Hearing about her marriage seemed to finalize their separation. On one hand, he was truly happy for her, but on the other hand, it caused him to face his loneliness. Since his affair with Capricia, he'd never even thought about being with another woman, and in all honesty, there'd really been no good opportunities. However, after talking with Audrey, he wondered why.

Why is there such a big empty space in my life? The older I get, the fewer options I have.

~

$\mathcal{M}$arco anticipated his birthday. *If I visit Celine this August, I will have just turned forty-six, and the clock's ticking. If Emma's remarried, then why should I still be wallowing in loneliness?*

His thoughts cast a spell of melancholy, so he decided to take another look at the pictures he'd accumulated. The envelope bulged, and as he spread the pictures on his bed, each one brought back a ton of memories. He kept sorting them until he found a dated picture of Celine, and when he tried to imagine the changes Audrey had described, it was impossible to think of her as a young woman. She would always be his little girl. Then he placed Celine's picture next to one he had of Emma and admitted she had Emma's beautiful features. As he started placing the pictures back into the envelope, he held onto the one of Emma and felt an unexpected surge of emotion.

She's moving on, and I'm still looking at pictures and living in the past. Oh, well, it's my own doing.

Then he picked up his treasured picture of Capricia and realized he was feeling less attached to her than before. He remembered telling her he loved her, but when compared to Emma, it was his out of control sexual urges more than genuine love.

It was a long time ago, he thought, *and there's really no reason to remain lost in the wasteland of failed relationships. I think I finally agree with Emma: "It's time to move on."*

He scooped up the remaining pictures, put them into the envelope and then left his bedroom feeling resolved to get on with his life.

I'll call some friends and propose getting together! I need to take the initiative! However, the friends he called were busy, so he spent a rather moody weekend with nothing to do. *Okay! On Monday, I'm setting a new course. It's time!*

~

Ellie Simmons worked with another team at Intel, but he'd gotten to know her during break times when everyone went for coffee in the cafeteria. She was one of many friends, but whenever he and Ellie happened to sit together, they swapped stories about their projects and laughed easily. There were also times when they shared more personal things like what they enjoyed doing outside of work, and over the course of a year, he realized he was actually looking for her and intentionally wanting to sit with her. It was a very pleasant relationship, so on his designated Monday for setting a new course he watched for her, and motioned for her to join him. As soon as she had her coffee, she pulled out the chair next to him, sat down and gave him a polite hug. He loved it and suddenly realized he really liked her, so before they finished their coffee, he took decisive action.

"Would it be too bold to ask you to have dinner with me?"

She visibly blushed and averted his eyes, but when she looked up, she smiled. It was like light breaking through his darkness.

"I thought you'd never ask," she said demurely. "I'd love to have dinner with you."

A cleansing feeling of joy swept over Marco as he nervously negotiated the time and place. It was like feeling a fresh spring breeze, which made him very hopeful. When their break time ended, she hurried to be on time for a team meeting, and he was left standing in a daze.

Jackson, he thought, *you're a fool to have waited so long.*

For the first time in a long while, Marco looked forward to the coming evening. They'd agreed to meet at five, have an early dinner, and then let the evening set its own course. Although he'd never noticed before, her work area was on the same floor as his, and they'd agreed to meet by the elevators, so around a quarter to five, he watched for her and found it difficult to concentrate on anything else. Five o'clock was actually later than his normal quit time, so he'd already put his things away, and when he saw Ellie walking toward the elevators, he hurried to catch up to her.

"Things are kind of quiet around here at five o'clock," he observed.

She smiled, and he had an immediate flashback to Capricia. He quickly dismissed it, but as he stood next to her, Capricia came to mind again. Ellie was a much more mature woman than Capricia but equally captivating in her jeans and loose fitting blouse. She blushed, and he realized he was staring, so he had to consciously create a diversion.

"Normally I'd already be on my way home, but this evening, five o'clock feels refreshing." He glanced to see if she agreed. She nodded and smiled. "Going to dinner with you sure beats going home and choosing something from the freezer."

"We must lead similar lives," she suggested. "That's exactly what I do about 90 percent of the time. It's either a frozen dinner or leftovers."

They laughed, and he felt encouraged.

When the elevator doors opened, they stepped inside and stood mutely watching the floor indicator, while they descended to the lobby. When the doors opened, there was noise from people in the lobby, which softened their awkward silence; however, once they left the building, she became playful and deliberately teased him by walking really fast toward her car.

He caught up and took hold of her arm. "Let me be the chauffeur," he demanded and turned her toward his car.

She willingly changed directions and let him guide her.

"We'll come back to get your car later."

"Oh, my," she exclaimed. "Is this your car?"

He smiled and proudly opened the door of his Audi sedan for her.

"I don't know much about cars," she admitted, "but this is really nice." She smiled and arched her brow. "I'm glad we're not going in my Toyota. It pales by comparison."

He happily accepted her compliment and thought she might be a bit frugal, because just like him, she had to be earning an impressive salary.

"Would it be okay if we have dinner at *Wings*?"

"I don't think I've ever been there."

"It's the only Chinese restaurant in historic Japan Town, and as a matter-of-fact, it's on a street named after me," he teased.

"Marco Street?" she asked in astonishment.

"No! Jackson Street!"

"Is that your last name?"

He smiled and nodded.

"I didn't know your full name," she admitted. "My last name is Simmons."

"I know," he said with a smile, "I saw it on your employee's badge."

"Well, so much for my powers of observation," she laughed. "I've been so caught up with your good looks, I've never noticed your name badge."

She was being playful, but the way she looked at him when she admitted her oversight, he knew she meant it.

"You're kind, Ellie. I love your playfulness!"

Then they pulled onto the street and accelerated toward downtown.

"Keep your eyes on the road, Marco. I'm putting my name badge in my purse, so now you'll have to rely on your memory. It's S-I-M-M-O-N-S," she teased.

Marco actually laughed heartily for the first time in a long while.

~

After dinner Marco and Ellie went to a nearby lounge and stayed longer than either of them intended. On their way back to his car, he held her hand.

They playfully chatted about their coworkers on the way back to Intel, and when he pulled alongside her car in the parking lot, he thought about kissing her, but it seemed presumptuous, so he settled for an affectionate hug and said, "I hope this is the first of many times together."

"I'd like that!" she beamed. "As I said before, I didn't think you'd ever ask . . . but I'm very glad you did. I'll see you at work in the morning."

He waited until she was safely inside her car, and when exiting the lot, they turned in opposite directions.

Being lonely is my own doing, he thought, *but I think those days are over.*

~

Marco's LA business trip and his side-trip to Fresno took an entire week, and he missed Ellie terribly. He called her every evening, and she graciously listened to his summary of what he'd been doing. However, before ending the call, she said the same thing each time: "Please hurry home, Marco. I miss you." He had nearly forgotten the beautiful feeling of being with a woman, and by Friday he wanted nothing more than to be with her.

"I miss you too, Ellie. Even being with my daughter doesn't take my mind off of you."

He called her the minute he arrived in San Francisco, and she agreed to meet him for dinner at a restaurant near his home. As they dined by candlelight he could hardly take his eyes off of her.

She's wonderfully poised, he thought. *Maybe it's because we're older and more mature. I like the fact we're taking our time. It feels good to move at a slower pace.*

Compared to his urgent sexual intensity with Capricia, time seemed to be a welcomed companion with Ellie. They were slowly getting to know each other, and each time they were together, they were more trusting, so during one of their more serious conversations, he told her about his time in Las Vegas and his love affair with Capricia.

When he finished sharing, she reacted by saying, "It's hard to believe such a thing actually happened. It's like something you'd see in the movies, but I can see how deeply it's affected you."

"I apologize, Ellie! I shouldn't have burdened you with my story."

"No, it's okay, Marco. I'm glad you told me. I want us to be open and honest, but five years with the mob in Las Vegas is kind of scary. It's hard to believe, because I'd never characterize you that way. You must have scars from what happened."

He immediately felt her compassion.

"Until you came along, I hadn't realized how much damage those years had done. When I came back to San Jose, my spirit was broken and I've been terribly lonely, but then I met you!" He smiled and looked at her tenderly. "I've enjoyed every minute we've been together."

Ellie listened, but what he'd explained about his exploits in Vegas had changed her mood. When he told her goodnight that evening, it was different.

"I feel like I've burdened you," he said.

"Oh, not really! However, it's been our first serious conversation. I feel you've trusted me, and it's put me in a serious mood."

"It's a bit one-sided," he suggested. "I still need to learn more about you."

"All in good time, Marco." Then she leaned into his arms affectionately. "For the moment, I feel very honored that you've trusted me with your story. We'll get around to mine at another time."

"Thank you!" he said, and then he kissed her. Unlike the passion, which had consumed him with Capricia, kissing Ellie was like a soul experience. She responded tenderly and remained in his embrace a long time. *We're taking our time, and that's okay.*

~

*H*is relationship with Ellie grew stronger, but at times he wondered if he was taking her for granted. However, as she often said, "There's no urgency. I just love being with you, Marco, and I feel time's on our side."

"Speaking of time, I should tell you I'm planning to go to Fresno to attend Celine's graduation, and I'm thinking you should go with me."

"That's very thoughtful of you," she said with a teasing smile. "I assume your ex-wife will be there?"

He nodded and arched his brow knowingly.

"And I imagine her husband will be there too," she chided, and he rolled his eyes. "However, I will decline going with you. It needs to be your special father/daughter time."

"You're so very special, Ellie. You're transforming me."

"Hum," she exclaimed. "I didn't know that."

"And that would be my fault," he admitted and held his arms open to her. She gladly snuggled closer. "I think I'm hooked on you!" he whispered.

"Hum, I didn't know that either."

"I'm going to really miss you."

She smiled and hugged him tighter. "I'll miss you too! When we're together, I feel safe and secure."

"And that's the way it should be," he admitted. "It's comfortable being together."

"I don't think you know my fears, Marco. You've told me your fears, but I've not shared mine."

"Such as?"

"Such as how vulnerable I feel. I put up a brave front, but I feel anxious, and that's one of the reasons the pace of our relationship is so slow."

He pulled her even more tightly into his arms and heard her sigh.

"There's no need to feel anxious, Ellie. We're not in a hurry, and nothing will get in our way. That's a promise!"

She sighed again and seemed to relax.

He thought she'd say more, but instead she nestled in his arms in silence. With Ellie, whatever was still ahead was definitely worth waiting for.

~

Celine's graduation was a youthful celebration, which made Marco feel old, but he loved being there. As Ellie predicted; it was a major family event including their extended family and lots of friends. When he arrived in Fresno, he checked into his hotel and then called Audrey.

"Oh, Marco, I'm so glad you're here. Celine can hardly wait to see you, so here's the plan."

She went over all the details and told him to wear a suit and tie for her big graduation dinner, which she described as a buffet at the Holiday Inn on highway 41.

"I don't know all the people she's invited, but there are over a hundred. Emma's rich husband is footing the bill, and it all seems a little over the top to David and me." She paused. "Oh, by the way, did I tell you we're retiring?"

"Congratulations! I hope it's the beginning of a whole new chapter in your lives."

"I can hardly wait, Marco!"

"Well, it's a good time to do it. Emma's married, Celine's graduating and moving on, and you and David have a lot of good years ahead."

"Thanks, Marco! When I think back to when we left Illinois, I can hardly believe where we are today. However, we're so used to farming and living in Fresno, I doubt we'll be making any bold moves."

"Time will tell," he chuckled. "Time will tell . . . Okay, I'll see you this evening. What time?"

"We're going to be there most of the afternoon, but you should come around six o'clock. That's when people will be gathering, and the buffet begins around six-thirty or so."

When the call ended he glanced at his watch. It was 3:45, so he had plenty of time before showering and getting dressed. The only drawback was being in a motel room.

He arrived at a quarter to six, checked his appearance in the car's vanity mirror, got out, straightened his shoulders and moved toward a crowd of smokers having one last cigarette before going inside.

Audrey was right! Who are these people?

"Daddy!" Celine's voice rose above the crowd as she ran to him. It was a love fest, and try as he might; he couldn't avoid a few tears. Too much time had passed since he'd last seen her.

"Wow! Just look at you! You're beautiful!"

She smiled and snuggled into his arms. "It's major!" she exclaimed. "I know it's just high school graduation, but to me it seems like crossing the Grand Canyon."

"It's important," he agreed, "but there's a lot more coming."

"I know, and it's happening so fast. I've already been accepted into UC's pre-med program on a full scholarship."

"Holy Moly!" he shouted and held her at arm's length to comprehend her announcement. "When you say *fast,* you're not kidding. I assume Mom knows?"

"Why don't you ask her? She's standing right behind you."

He released Celine and turned to see Emma standing about two feet from him. She smiled knowingly and gave him a polite hug.

"Hi, proud Papa," she said with a big smile. "It looks like we did good with this one," and then she reached to pull Celine into her arms. "I'm very proud of her."

Then Emma stepped back and turned to a balding man standing a couple of feet from her. "Marco, I want you to meet my husband, Eddie Slather."

Eddie stepped forward confidently and shook Marco's hand.

"She told me you have an amazing head of hair, and as you can imagine, I'm jealous."

He smiled, and Emma shook her head.

"It's what's in your heart and not what's on your head," she scolded and looked directly at Marco.

He got the message but took a deep breath and recovered nicely.

"Maybe the next time we're together, I'll introduce you to Ellie."

Emma raised her brow and twisted her expression. "Ellie?"

He smiled smugly. "Ellie Simmons works with me at Intel."

"Oh, I see," she observed and lifted her chin with a slight nod of sophistication.

Celine noted her mother's expression and stepped in to redirect attention to her.

"Okay you guys! This is my party, so let's have everyone move toward the buffet."

They did as instructed, and by the time Marco returned to his hotel, he'd been affirmed over and over again as a lucky SOB to have a daughter like Celine. The accolades came from well-meaning adults but also from her classmates. He felt extremely proud, and possibly most important was the fact that Celine would be going to school just across the bay from his home in Silicone Valley.

The graduation ceremony was a festival, which was nearly out of control, and Marco felt the strain from his generation gap. However, he was bursting with pride when Celine received her diploma.

He had greeted lots of people he didn't know and had enjoyed the novelty of watching Emma interacting with Eddie, but he was also feeling a little weary by the time the festivities ended.

He's nearly bald, he mused and ran his fingers through his hair. *He's good looking, but he's nearly bald.*

Marco knew his vanity was showing, but he couldn't help himself.

She'll miss my Italian flair, he smirked, *and I know I'm going to miss her seductive smile.*

Actually, he was less bothered by Emma's marriage than he'd thought he would be. Then he suddenly thought of Ellie and realized how much he was missing her. All his comparisons were for naught. Ellie was beyond compare, and when he closed the door to his room, he could hardly wait to call her and share the details.

"I've been bursting with pride over Celine," he boasted, "but more than anything else, I've been missing you."

"That's mutual," she admitted. "Tell me about your ex and her husband."

"He's nearly bald," he said with a chuckle. "However, they seem happy together."

"Well, that's good." Then he heard her sigh. "Please hurry home, Marco!"

"I have a flight at eleven in the morning, so how about dinner? I'd like to go to *Wings* to remember our first date."

"I'd love to do that!"

"Great! We'll have dinner at seven and then linger over a cocktail or two. It's about time for us to get serious about our relationship, don't you think?"

She laughed. "I've been serious about our relationship for a long time. I'm just waiting for you."

"I deserved that," he admitted, "so let me rephrase: It's about time for *me* to get serious about our relationship."

"I can hardly wait," she laughed. "It's overdue."

~

*D*uring dinner, while on their special date at *Wings*, they talked about how special it was being together, but Marco was still holding back on his promise to get serious about their relationship. It would have been a perfect time to propose marriage, but there were still some memories standing in his way. It had been a wonderful evening, which ended with a lingering kiss and a soft-spoken "Goodnight!"

Ellie has remarkable patience, he thought. *I should have popped the question.*

~

About the same time as Celine began her internship at San Francisco General Hospital, Apple Computers introduced the Macintosh personal computer, and Marco's work took on an even greater significance. The industry was moving at light speed. He still had a tattered copy of his 1963 <u>Time Magazine</u> in which he'd been recognized, but now technologically *significant* people were commonplace. Countless people were routinely doing amazing things in the world of personal computing, and change was coming faster than he'd anticipated. He admitted his age was becoming a factor, and whenever he read about new and very talented young people, they were obviously eclipsing his talent, so he began thinking about other ways to engage with life.

Over the years, he had successfully invested over two million dollars, patiently parceling his cash into unsuspicious amounts, while working with his broker to develop a balanced portfolio. Intel's benefits gave him the luxury of also growing a significant 401K, which would work in tandem with Social Security to provide a very comfortable retirement income.

Then one evening after an enjoyable dinner with Ellie, he felt restless after going home and searched for the folder he'd compiled when he'd been volunteering. He found it in the back of his file cabinet, and inside he found a business card from Gary Hartshorne. On the back of the card he'd written, "Interested in creating a foundation to help young people."

~

"Good afternoon! Hartshorne and Peters! How may I help you?"

"I'm Marco Jackson calling from San Jose. May I speak with Mr. Hartshorne?"

"Are you a client, Mr. Jackson?"

"No, I'm a friend."

"Thank you, I'll forward your call."

"Marco! This is a surprise! It took me a minute to remember, but then I recalled our volunteer work"

"Hi, Gary! I still had your business card in my file."

"The receptionist said you're still in San Jose."

"Yes, I've lived here for a long time, and I'm thinking about what's next after Intel."

"It's a great company. I'm in San Francisco, so I'm your neighbor. What's on your mind?"

It's a whim, Gary, but do you remember our conversation about setting up a non-profit foundation to help underprivileged young people?"

"Absolutely! It was my idea and you heartily agreed!" He laughed.

"That's true," Marco admitted, "so do you remember I said I'd like to consider setting up a foundation someday?"

"I seem to recall you saying that, so have you started one?"

"Not yet, but I think it's time, so I'm wondering if you were serious about it."

"Of course, and it just so happens our firm does that kind of legal work."

"Then this call is serendipitous," Marco said with a smile. "If you're willing, I'd like to proceed."

"Come see me, Marco! We'll talk about what's involved and if it looks possible, I'll help with the legal work pro-bono. Once we have the details worked out, I may also invest in it."

Marco jotted down the address and made the appointment.

Sometimes it seems like fate is also a factor in redemption.

~

The Jackson Foundation started small but experienced significant growth from contributors, who shared the vision.

Gary invested substantially and then networked with some of his professional friends to attract them as investors. Because of increasing national attention on science, technology, engineering and math (STEM), he made those disciplines a part of the foundation's mission. He wanted to focus on the personal lives of students pursuing their dreams. Every time he thought about how his life had changed, he was thankful for people, who had helped him along the way, encouraged him, and provided ways for him to succeed. With the foundation up and running, he felt he'd been reborn.

As he prepared to celebrate with Ellie, he finally admitted he was in love with her.

"It's true," he said as he held her in his arms and lovingly kissed her. "I love you with all my heart, and I never thought I'd ever say that again."

Ellie smiled and returned his kisses. She'd waited a long time but had never lost faith in Marco's promise.

"And I love you too, Marco! I love everything about you! Of course, I also love the fact you are devastatingly handsome, so now you know I have a streak of vanity in my character."

"Ah, you're just trying to make me feel good."

She smiled and winked. "I want you to listen carefully, because I have something important to tell you! I mostly love you for who you are, and as I've listened to stories about your life, I think your character is a reflection of how you were raised by your loving parents."

He knew he was blushing a little but waited for her to continue.

"I also love you for being so honest with me about your successes and your mistakes. When you told me what happened to you in Las Vegas, it came as a jolt, but I appreciated you trusting me. I can see how it has shaped who you are today."

She smiled, and he wanted to kiss her, but she still wasn't finished.

"Another thing I love about you is your passion for helping others. I think your vision for this foundation is phenomenal. In fact, I think it's such a great idea, I want to be a part of it." She took a breath and arched her brow expectantly.

He looked at her with deep seriousness. "You *are* a part of it, Ellie."

"Of course, but what I mean is I want is to invest money in it and be your partner."

"Well," he exclaimed, while holding her at arm's length, "the Jackson Foundation is always open for new investors, so what do you have in mind?"

She looked at him and smiled seductively.

"There's something about me I've never told you, Marco."

"Really! And what's that?"

"I know you think I'm too frugal, but I'm a very wealthy woman."

His expression went blank.

"But you drive an old Toyota and live in a modest rental! What do you mean? How can you be wealthy?"

"I like living modestly, but what you see doesn't accurately account for who I am."

"Are you going to fess up or keep me guessing?"

"Well, first of all, I need to remind you of something you already know. I'm a California girl, who came to the Silicone Valley from my family's estate in Napa Valley where my parents ran a very successful winery. As you know, my parents are deceased, and I, as their only child, have zero interest in running a winery, so I sold it for an unbelievable amount of money, which I've invested. If you want specifics, I'd have to contact my broker because the amount changes daily; however,

I'd like to join you as a significant contributor to the Jackson Foundation, because I love you and cherish your passion to help young people."

His expression revealed total surprise, and he was speechless, so he wrapped his arms around her and held her quietly for a rather long time. She sighed deeply, and when he finally recouped, he said the first thing that came to mind: "Should we get married?"

His question caught her completely off-guard, but she recovered nicely. "It's an option! Would you like to marry me?"

Then they laughed their way into a wonderful decision they'd wanted to make for a long time.

"When?" he asked

"Right away!" she replied. "We're both getting too old to put it off any longer."

"We can have a simple wedding at the retreat center in Big Sur."

"I'd love that!"

They were deliriously happy and couldn't stop smiling.

~

They told a few close friends, and Marco let Celine know, but other than that, they managed to have a very discrete and private wedding. Ellie contacted her friend, a retired clergyman, Timothy Cline, who agreed to do the ceremony if they'd pay for his stay at the retreat center.

On August 17, 1983, Marco and Ellie said their marriage vows, and Marco told her she had helped him finally understand the power of love.

"It's been a slow process for me, Ellie, but being in love with you has allowed me to reclaim my life. There have been times when I've felt completely lost, but no longer."

She smiled and snuggled closer to him, but he still had more to say.

"I think we have what I've longed for all my life. It's the same kind of love my Mom and Dad shared when we lived on the farm in Illinois. I remember telling Mom I wanted what she and Dad had found, and now it has come true."

"It's true for me as well, Marco. My story's quite different from yours, but I've been longing for love like this all my life, and now it has come true."

~

Reverend Cline went home after the weekend, but Marco and Ellie stayed in Big Sur for another week after their wedding, and other than making love until they were both exhausted, they took long leisurely walks and talked about how the rest of their lives would make such a significant difference for countless underprivileged children.

TWENTY-FOUR

$\mathcal{M}$arco was a changed man. He told Kevin being married to Ellie was as good as it gets. "It took me a while, but I think I finally made the right decision."

"I have no doubt, my friend. You look content and at peace with the world."

"It's hard to put into words, Kev, but my loneliness is gone, and those restless nights filled with confusing dreams have ended"

~

$\mathcal{E}$llie and Marco established a rhythm in their lives, which was good. They were both in their late-forties but thankful they still had many years ahead. There were times when he looked back and wondered how he'd managed to navigate through his impulsive foibles and come to such a good conclusion. In moments of reverie he recounted significant events along the way, but one thing stood out more than anything else. Learning about his adoption had changed his world so dramatically it was like a line of demarcation. On one side of the line was his innocence, and on the other side his shame. When he returned to San Jose after five years in Las Vegas, he was carrying a lot more baggage than his suitcases filled with clothes and cash.

Sometimes I wonder what would have happened to me if Antonio had decided to keep me rather than put me up for adoption. Fate has definitely played a role.

By the time he turned 50, he'd seen both sides. His achievements were notable, and he'd experienced what most could only dream, but his success was contrasted by his fall into the darkness of organized crime, where he'd lost his perspective and his decency.

If it wasn't for Antonio's forgiveness, I may have never found my way back.

However, he did what few have ever done and walked away from the mob and did so with his father's blessing.

I've always called it my redemption because it allowed me to begin again.

And now, with Ellie at his side, Marco felt whole and finally free from the darkness.

Everything prior has been like a dress rehearsal to ensure the final scene will be perfect.

~

The years accumulated, and to celebrate their 10th anniversary, Marco arranged a special evening, which included dining at *Wings* where they'd had their first date. Following dinner, they went to the same lounge to reminisce about old times. To their surprise, there was a pianist and a dance floor, so they danced to some dreamy music, which was perfect for their style.

"It's perfect," he whispered as the song ended.

Ellie smiled and led him back to their table, where they enjoyed one more drink before going home.

"No regrets?" she said with a questioning look.

"None with you, but I still have regrets about my sojourn in the desert. When I look back on those years I see my flaws and how broken I was."

"It's never perfect, Marco. We all have flaws, but the real question is what dominates the changing scenes? We can dwell on our missteps and failures, but if they don't dominate our entire lives, then we look past them to focus on what's right and good."

"You sound like a philosopher," he chided. "However, you're making a good point, and I really like where the script is taking us."

In fact, it really was perfect. They were doing exactly what they'd planned, and Marco repeatedly reminded himself that redemption takes a while; however, he thanked Ellie a hundred times over for being a dominant force in changing his life.

~

The Jackson Foundation prospered and exceeded their expectations. Its progress was like reading a really good story when you know the best is yet to come. As the size and complexity of the foundation increased, they hired people to manage the details and moved their offices into a new building not far from their condo. Marco had explained the foundation's vision so many times he had it memorized.

What started as an altruistic idea has grown into a clearly defined enterprise to build bridges for underprivileged children, who need a fair chance to enjoy equal educational opportunities.

Each time he gave his presentation there would usually be two or three more investors, who wanted to join the effort. Typically, there would also be questions, so his staff had prepared a very slick brochure explaining how the foundation was achieving its purpose.

Grants from the Jackson Foundation work in tandem with existing schools, which are serving black, Latino and low-income students. We offer personalized tutoring and guidance programs for emerging fields of technology. The foundation has made significant investments in teachers and leaders, who work to intervene in self-defeating situations and to provide professional learning opportunities designed to increase student motivation

He carried a handful of the brochures everywhere he went and tried to be a constant ambassador for the foundation's growing success. Ellie was equally engaged and most of their weekends were devoted to promotions and other foundation business before returning to their jobs at Intel on Mondays. They had become a dynamic duo with endless energy, but there were moments when they could see the effect it was having on their lives. The weeks and months rolled into years and they were constantly pressed for time. He wanted to spend more time with Celine, and they tried to have a few weekend getaways, but there was very little free time on their schedules.

"We've created a thriving enterprise," Marco said with a sigh, "but I'm thinking it would be a lot easier if we were retired from Intel. It's way too hard keeping up with the increasing demands."

They were having their morning coffee when he made the suggestion and he thought Ellie would resist; however, as it so often happened; they were on the same track.

"Actually," she said, "I've already thought a lot about this. My thirty-year anniversary is almost here, and I think both of us would be better off if we only had one job instead of two."

"I didn't know you'd been with Intel 30 years."

She confirmed it with a knowing glance. "I'm one of the pioneers. Although it's hard to admit, I'll be 59 next year, so I think it's time."

"Then I should retire too," he said matter-of-factly. "Although I look very young, I'm almost a year older than you, so let's make it a mutual decision."

Ellie looked surprised but nodded her agreement.

"I didn't think I'd ever hear you say that, but I like it! We can have a big retirement party."

~

"*N*ext year" seemed a long time away, but Ellie's 30th year came faster than either of them had anticipated. She announced her retirement and then challenged him to follow through on his agreement to do the same. He hadn't anticipated how difficult it would be, but on Friday of that week, he went to HR and started the process.

"Were you serious about having a big party?"

"Absolutely! What better excuse do we have?"

"Where?"

"At Intel! They owe us a party after all we've done for them."

"Who authorizes retirement parties?"

"You do, Marco, or have you forgotten your executive management status."

"Can I authorize yours as well?" he teased.

"Come on, Marco. Just call and set the date."

It seemed a little unusual to be setting up his own retirement party, but he did as Ellie suggested and found an open date at the end of May.

"Call Celine and let her know," Ellie suggested. "Maybe she'd like to attend."

~

Celine's phone rang four times before she answered, and she seemed rushed.

"Celine, it's Dad. Do you have a minute?"

"Oh, hi, Dad! Sure! You caught me on my way out, but I've got a few minutes. What's up?"

"I'm retiring."

"You're not old enough to retire."

"Thank you, my dear, but you know better. Ellie's been with Intel for thirty years, so she says it's time."

"Well, congratulations."

"Can you come to our retirement party?"

"When?"

"It will be in two weeks on May 31."

"Oh, my, god! Are you serious?"

"Why? Is that a problem?"

"Mom and Eddie will be visiting on May 31."

"Well, then, bring them along."

He turned to Ellie and whispered the situation. She looked surprised but nodded okay.

"Well," Celine hesitated. "I'll mention it, but I have no idea what she'll say, so I'll have to call you back. Tell me what time and where?"

He quickly shared the details, and told her goodbye. When he put the phone down, his head was spinning.

"I certainly didn't expect that," he said to Ellie.

"Don't worry about it," Ellie countered. "Life takes some funny turns sometimes."

"You've never met Emma and Eddie, have you?"

"No, but it's bound to happen sometime, Marco. They're probably just as curious about me as I am about them."

~

*H*is department at Intel reserved a large room adjacent to the cafeteria for their party, and they were overwhelmed with many good wishes from coworkers and friends. He and Ellie stood hand-in-hand, while greeting their friends, and then they raised their glasses to toast friendships and new beginnings.

Celine had told him Emma was hesitant but agreed to drop by for a few minutes. However, the party was well under way when he glanced at the clock and wondered if they'd changed their minds. Then, just as the formalities were ending, Emma, Eddie and Celine quietly slipped into the room. His heart beat a little faster when he saw them, and then he took Ellie by the arm and marched boldly to meet them.

"Sorry to be late," Celine apologized. "There was a collision on the freeway, and we sat in a traffic jam for nearly thirty minutes."

"It's okay," Marco said and then he smiled at Emma. She fidgeted.

"This is my husband, Eddie Slather," Emma said with a directive glance at Ellie.

"And Emma, I want you to meet my wife, Ellie," Marco beamed.

Everyone shook hands and bowed slightly. Although it was an awkward moment, they were polite, and when Emma greeted Ellie, she glanced at Marco, raised her brow and smiled. No one seemed to know what to say next, so Ellie excused herself and hurried off to meet other friends, and the brief encounter ended as quickly as it had begun. Marco scanned the room and thought briefly about joining Ellie, but Emma seemed to be waiting for a moment when they could speak privately. He glanced at her, and she motioned for him to step aside.

"Whew!" she exclaimed. "I wasn't sure how that would go."

He smiled and nodded. "I'm as amazed as you are. When Celine told me you'd be visiting, I couldn't believe the coincidence. It's good to see you, Em."

She hugged him politely and smiled. "It's serendipitous! I certainly had no plans to attend your retirement party." Then she glanced toward Ellie, who was still chatting with a co-worker. "You married a beautiful woman."

Marco blushed a little.

"She's very special! However, you're special too."

Emma arched her brow and frowned slightly, but then she surprised him.

"Sometimes my heart tells me I should have been more willing to endure your bad choices, but looking back, it seems we've both found a way forward. It appears love has rescued us."

Marco agreed. "You're right," he admitted. "However, a lot of things have happened including some heartaches."

She looked at him with a slight nod and a knowing expression.

"Yes, I know, but this is now and not then. Are you happy?"

It was unexpected, but it was a perfect question.

"Yes, I'm happy, and I think my darkness has finally ended."

"Celine said you don't see each other very often, so has she told you she's going to be on the staff at the hospital where she did her internship?"

Marco reacted with surprise. "No, I didn't know that, but that's wonderful news."

Emma smiled and agreed. "She's unstoppable." Then she touched his arm. "I've heard about your foundation. Does Ellie know you're using mob money to fund it?" Her eyes twinkled, and then she raised her brow suspiciously.

"We have no secrets, Em, and besides, Ellie has more money than I do."

"Oh, I see," she said. "It appears the gods are smiling."

He wasn't sure if she was being spiteful or playful, but as she turned to leave, she smiled.

Ellie noticed Emma was maneuvering toward the door, so she hurried to rejoin them.

"Sorry to have been pulled away," she apologized. "I have thirty years of friendships in this room, but it's very special to have you and Eddie here."

"Thank you, Ellie."

Once again, it was an awkward moment, but then Eddie and Celine returned, and it was a perfect time for saying goodbye. There were social hugs and handshakes, and then Celine led the threesome out of the room. Marco felt relieved and gave Ellie a quick kiss before going with her to meet more friends.

Indeed, he thought, *it appears the gods are smiling.*

~

*A*fter their retirement, working with the foundation became an obsession for Marco and Ellie. Their enterprise kept growing by targeting geographical areas of need, and after years of hard work, it had grown into a national effort, which attracted scores of investors.

As Marco often said, " It takes tons of hard work, but the years of growth and success have made it all worthwhile."

He concentrated on building networks to help students in their transition from near failure in high school to highly motivated postsecondary schools and career training programs. Ellie especially loved working with emerging programs such as S.T.E.M, which gave her many opportunities to use her technical and mathematical skills. They literally had no time to look back and long for the "good old days". They were enormously happy in making the foundation their life's work.

"It's so satisfying," Ellie said when talking with friends. "The foundation was Marco's idea, but I'm on-board one hundred percent, and I can't think of anything I'd rather be doing."

During the next few years they enjoyed the privilege of traveling to different cities where the foundation had offices, and with each visit they received accolades for the way in which their work was changing lives.

It became repetitive, but after each one of their on-site visits, they returned home with more stories to tell. Ellie always said the same thing: "What more could we ask?"

~

The Jackson Foundation gracefully sustained them through their 60s and 70s and gave them enough youthful energy to remain fresh and high-spirited as though they would live forever. However, aging changed their perspective. Marco had typically been cavalier about his enthusiasm and energy, but when he finally faced the fact that he was nearing his 80th birthday, he leaned on Ellie's wisdom, poured her a glass of wine and motioned toward the couch.

"We need to talk," he said and took his place beside her in front of their decorative fireplace, which seldom if ever warmed them with an actual fire.

"Why do we even have a fireplace, Marco? We never use it."

He handed her the wine and smiled. "Did you hear what I just said?"

"What?"

"I said: We need to talk."

"About what?"

"About getting old and passing the torch to those who are still young and vital."

"Oh, Marco," she said with a frown, "if we stop doing what we're doing, we'll just crumble like dried flowers. Working with the foundation keeps us young."

"I know," he agreed. "I feel the same, but I think slowing the pace would be good."

"Why? Do you have something else in mind?"

"In fact I do!" he exclaimed. "I have a bucket list."

She looked at him and wrinkled her brow.

"What could you possibly want that you don't already have?"

"We've never traveled! I'd like to go to Europe, and I think it would be fun to spend some time in exotic places like Hawaii or Tahiti."

"Oh, Marco! You *are* a dreamer. What will happen to the foundation, while we're gallivanting on your bucket list excursions to *exotic* places?"

He wrinkled his brow and shook his head.

"I have no concerns about that. Our staff already runs the foundation, and we can still be on the Board of Directors."

She sipped her wine and paused thoughtfully.

"It's never crossed my mind, but maybe you're right." Then she laid her head on his shoulder. "Actually, I kind of like the idea of traveling." She paused and suddenly looked up at him. "You know what I'd really like to do?" It was a rhetorical question, so he waited expectantly. "I'd like to go back to Napa Valley and show you where I lived when I was a little girl."

He raised his glass in an impromptu toast. "You know, I've had the same thought. I'd like to show you where I used to live. I've often wondered if the old farmhouse is still standing. I'd like to show you the pond where I used to go skinny-dipping with my dog Jake."

She laughed. "Oh, my, goodness! I think we're beginning to sound like two old duffers."

He smiled and sipped his wine. Although he didn't mention it, he'd also been thinking about going to Las Vegas just to remind himself of that episode in his life. It was a fleeting thought but clearly an urge.

I wonder if Lila still works at the Tropicana?

However, there was more to it than that. For some reason it was bothering him that his experience in Las Vegas was unknown by their current community of friends. They were both known for their philanthropic work, but in his old age he was feeling a need to let people know there was more to his life than that. Nobody knew about his dark period except Ellie and Kevin.

There's a before and after in my life, he thought, *and talking about it openly is like the final piece of my redemption.*

Ellie sat quietly sipping her wine with no idea what he was thinking, so he decided to fess up.

"What I did in Vegas still haunts me."

She turned her head, looked up at him and rolled her eyes.

"What did you say?"

"You heard me! I'm bothered that my friends really don't know about my dark period."

"Oh, Marco! Your life isn't defined by what happened years ago!"

"I know, but sometimes it feels like something I'm trying to hide."

"Anyone who knows you well would never say that," she scolded.

"You're very kind; however, I keep thinking I need to reconcile my past with my present. I want to be completely transparent and speak openly about my history. I want our friends to know how my past has shaped my present."

She smiled knowingly and then frowned.

"I just think you're having a hard time facing your 80th birthday. Is that's what's going on?"

He looked at her and scowled.

"Maybe! Turning eighty is no small matter. It adds urgency."

"Urgency for what?"

"To ask for forgiveness."

"Oh, dear! Forgiveness from whom?"

He tightened his facial muscles and twisted his expression.

"I guess it's forgiveness of myself, mostly."

"Oh, Marco," she pleaded. "Think on the bright side. You've done so much good, so why dwell on what happened years ago?"

He sighed. "That's easy for you to say, but I'm not at peace with my life like you are. I still have vivid memories of what happened in Vegas. People only know me for the second half of my life and . . ."

"And," she interrupted, "you're an exceptional person, so why is it necessary to reveal your past sins? You're not obligated in any way to . . ."

And then he interrupted her. "I know I'm not obligated, but there's more to me than my last 40 years reveals. I'd like my friends to know who I really am."

"And why's that so important, Marco? If doing good things required confessing all our mistakes, people would have to stand in line and take a ticket to enter the confessional."

He looked at her and frowned.

"How did you become so wise?"

Then he set his wine aside and wrapped his arms around her. She smiled and pressed her head against his chest.

"It's in my DNA," she said with a soft laugh. "I fell in love with an amazing guy named Marco, and everything I know about him is completely honorable. You may feel a need to forgive yourself, but I'm here to tell you, people already know who you are."

He kissed her and then ambled off to his office to catch up on some administrative stuff for the foundation. When he finished, he rocked back in his chair and thought about what Ellie had said.

Turning 80 seems terribly significant! I think it's time to finish my process of redemption.

Then, for some reason, he opened a file drawer and took out a folder where he kept a few pictures and memorabilia. It had been a long time since he'd looked at its contents, but as always, it brought back lots of memories. He sorted through a stack of photos and studied one of the old farmhouse and then another one of him standing with his parents and his old dog Jake.

Those were good days, he thought. Then he browsed through more pictures from his and Emma's wedding. *That was really a happy time!*

He could have ended his nostalgia with Emma's picture in his hand, but he kept sorting through the stack and found one of Celine on the day she was born. She was wrapped in a soft blanket and cradled in Emma's arms.

And now she's Dr. Jackson, he mused and felt a nudge from his emotions.

He was about to put the pictures back into the file cabinet, when he picked up a packet of post cards from Las Vegas. It was one of those multiple card packets, which opens like an accordion with about eight cards folded together, and when he lifted the top flap, the cards tumbled onto his lap including a picture of Capricia, which he'd tucked inside and forgotten. When he picked it up, his hand trembled and he fought to hold back his tears. Ellie was busy in the kitchen, so she didn't know, but seeing Capricia's beautiful face brought back all his feelings from those years of loving her. She was his only light in the darkness of being with the mob.

"Capricia," he whispered. "Why?" Then he reached for a tissue to dry his eyes. It was hard to hold back the tears especially when he thought of his love for Ellie.

Does it really take this long to figure it out?

All of it was embedded in his life: his happy childhood, his rapid success, his love for Emma and Celine. It was a mosaic of memories. Then he remembered his conflicted feelings and the emptiness in his soul after Capricia was killed. He recalled his rage at his father and the sickening feeling when the gun fired and he fell at his feet. The memories were so vivid it could have happened just yesterday. Mostly, he recalled his confusion, while standing at Antonio's bedside and hearing him ask for forgiveness.

"This is the story I need to tell," he whispered aloud. "I need to fess up and close this chapter of my life, and maybe self-forgiveness is the only way I can honestly claim my father's gift of redemption."

He put the postcards back into the file feeling convinced of what he needed to do.

Before a beginning, there has to be an ending. Before I can completely reclaim my life, I have to close this episode and then celebrate the good things that have followed. I need to celebrate Ellie's love and the work we're doing with the foundation, but it needs to be identified as an exceptional part of my process of redemption.

It was one of those "Ah ha!" moments when light suddenly breaks through the darkness. Something had clicked into place, and now he had an answer to Ellie's question.

"Come have a sandwich," she called from the kitchen.

"I'll be there in a minute!"

She waited for him at the table, and when he walked into the kitchen, she noticed a little redness around his eyes but didn't say anything. He ate about half of his sandwich and then got up to pour their coffee.

"What were you working on in your office?"

He stared thoughtfully at his cup and then looked at her.

"I was reminiscing, and now I think I have an answer to your question," he said matter-of-factly.

"What question?"

"You'd asked why I feel the need to reveal my past sins."

"Oh, my, goodness! Are you still fussing over that?"

"I always take your questions seriously and here's my answer: I'm trying to make sense of how my past fits into my present."

"Good luck with that," she said with a smile. "Sometimes there's no sense to anything."

"Maybe," he agreed, "but in my case I think there's at least one thing that does make sense."

"And what's that?"

"It's what Antonio said to me before he died."

She arched her brow and waited expectantly for him to remind her.

"He told me to go home and reclaim my life, and then he died! I've been working on that for longer than we've been together."

"Well," Ellie concluded. "Maybe it takes a lifetime."

"Right! And that's exactly what I'm saying."

She looked slightly puzzled but tried to be accepting.

"I have no idea what you're talking about, Marco."

"What I mean is I need to say it out loud, and then it'll be settled."

"Say what?"

"I need to say this is who I am."

342

"What a strange kind of logic, Marco, but if that's what you need to do, I won't stand in your way."

Ellie stood to clear their plates from the table but took a moment to stand next to him. She lovingly stroked his hair and leaned forward to kiss his cheek.

"I was intending to make it a surprise," she whispered in his ear, "but we're going to have a blowout party for our combined birthdays. The last time we had a really good party was for our retirement, so it's time to have another one."

"I'd love to do that," he quickly agreed. "However, I must remind you it's actually better *not* to surprise me. At my age it could be fatal."

She laughed and swatted him on the arm.

"I'm setting it up right here in the Community Room, and I've already reserved a date and time. It'll be our time, so you can say whatever you need to say to all our wonderful friends. Just promise me you'll make it a celebration of our love."

TWENTY FIVE

A couple months before the big reveal, Marco was in his office at the foundation when his secretary stood at his door waving a message in her hand.

"*Time Magazine* is back on your trail, Mr. Jackson."

He looked up rather wide-eyed and waited for her to continue.

"A reporter called this morning to request an interview. She said they'd like to do a story about the foundation and tie it to your previous appearance in <u>Time Magazine</u>."

"And what did you tell this reporter, Rachel?"

"I told her you'd return her call."

Rachel handed him the message and went back to her desk, but Marco's mind suddenly made a sharp 180° degree turn.

What about my five-year stint with the mob?

He knew the publicity would be great for the foundation, but there seemed to be a major pitfall right in the middle of its potential. By the time he was ready to go home, he was in a quandary.

This is exactly what I tried to explain to Ellie. There's this dark side to my life that's unknown.

Later that evening, after dinner, he invited Ellie to have a glass of wine with him in front of their decorative fireplace, which they never used.

"I'll have Chardonnay," she requested, and he selected the same.

When they were settled, he nonchalantly mentioned the request.

"Oh, my, god," Ellie screamed. "That would be perfect! Just think of the publicity."

"You're right! Just think of the publicity! However, a couple of things have loomed up in my thinking. First of all, I would want the article to be about us. I may have started the foundation, but without you it would have never prospered." She smiled demurely. "But here's my concern; I think they will also want to include how I've lived my life since my previous appearance in *Time*."

"Oh, right," she admitted. "I keep forgetting you're a celebrity."

He rolled his eyes.

"If they do that, it will be a disaster for me personally, because my story runs directly through five years with the mob in Las Vegas."

Ellie arched her brow with an "Oh, well" expression

"I thought you told me you'd like people to know your whole story. Don't you remember?"

"Yes, that's true, but I wasn't thinking about making it a featured article in a national magazine."

Ellie shrugged.

"Nothing beats the truth, Luv. Maybe there's a confluence of forces in the universe helping you make your confession."

She waited for him to agree, but he silently stared at the cold fireplace.

"I'm conflicted," he confessed.

Ellie touched his shoulder reassuringly, finished her wine and then carried their glasses to the kitchen. Marco remained on the couch for a few moments, and then he abruptly went into the bedroom. By the time she came into the room, he was already under the covers.

"Don't wait for me," she chided and he smiled sheepishly.

"I'm still conflicted," he repeated. "I need you to comfort me."

She slipped in beside him and nestled in his arms.

"I'm always bold about what I want to do, but when I come face-to-face with it, I have turmoil in my gut."

She seemed to be listening, but within minutes he heard soft sounds from her sleeping.

~

The reporter confirmed his hunch about the connection to his previous appearance in _Time_.

"It's an exciting opportunity," she exclaimed. "People are very interested about what happens to successful people like you."

Marco felt a ripple of fear and paused noticeably.

He placed his hand over the receiver and turned to Ellie with an ashen wide-eyed look.

"She wants the whole story."

Ellie could see his concern; however, her strength had always been on the side of honesty, so that's what she suggested.

"Just tell the truth," she whispered and touched his arm reassuringly. "Tell her what happened and see what she says."

He took a deep breath and continued.

"I think I'd rather just have you write about the foundation and how my wife and I have worked so hard to make it successful."

"But there's a bigger story here, Marco, and that's what makes it so interesting."

"I know, but there's a part of that *bigger* story that's very dark, so I need to let you know about it and then you can decide."

"Tell me," she said expectantly.

Marco managed to give her an abbreviated summary and then waited for her reaction.

"It's absolutely fascinating," she said after a short pause, "and then you returned to San Jose, married Ellie, and together you've created this amazing foundation."

It was more a statement than a question, so he waited for her to continue.

"I'm blown away! What an amazing story, but how did you ever walk away from the mob? One of my friends did a story on the mafia and he said, 'No one ever walks away from the mob!' How did you manage to do that, Marco?"

He looked at Ellie, who was trying to listen and then took a deep breath.

"I had a redemptive moment at the bedside of my dying father," he explained. "He gave me a reprieve and told me to go home and reclaim my life."

"Oh, my, God," she said. "I'd love to write this story. Are you willing to go public?"

"Are you serious?"

"Absolutely! This is more than your average success story. It's about your rise, your fall and your redemption. My God! It will be sensational!"

Although he wasn't entirely persuaded, he agreed to do it if Ellie received equal billing, and then the call ended. When he hung up the phone, he looked at Ellie with pleading eyes.

"They want us to come to New York for an interview, and I said okay."

She smiled and touched his hand.

"It's okay, Hon. We can do this."

Then she wrapped her arms around him and he pulled her close.

"We can do this," she repeated. "Be brave!"

"It's ironic," he said, while shaking his head in disbelief. "They want the story featured the first week of September. When's the party?"

"It's the last weekend in August."

"Good Lord! The timing's incredible," he whispered. "The gods must be laughing."

~

True to her word, Ellie planned a blowout party for a grand celebration of their birthdays and to honor the transition they were planning for the foundation. She fudged a little on the date. His August 6 birthday would be on a Thursday and hers wasn't until September 10, so she planned it in between on a Saturday when their guests would be able to make it a part of their weekend plans. She reserved their condo's community room as a perfect setting for a growing number of invitees, including all of their long-time friends as well as the staff from the foundation. She was very pleased when Celine answered her RSVP and mentioned she'd also be bringing Quinn Douglas as her guest. As more responses arrived, she tried to keep Marco informed.

"Celine's coming and she's bringing Quinn Douglas as her guest."

"Did she say anything more? Who's Quinn Douglas?"

"Well, I imagine he's her boyfriend," Ellie said with a wink. "After all, she's over 50, so I'd say it's about time."

"I guess I'd kind of given up on ever having a son-in-law."

"Don't give up," Ellie instructed. "Things are different in this day and age. Remember, it took you over forty years to sort things out."

He rolled his eyes and wrinkled his expression.

"How many are coming?"

"There are 42, and the list is still growing."

"Wow! Are we going to have cake and balloons?"

"Go to your office and quit asking questions," she demanded. "I'm the party planner, and all you need to do is show up."

~

When Marco's real birthday arrived two days before the planned party, Ellie led him by the hand from the bedroom to the kitchen, where she'd prepared his favorite breakfast.

"Hum! I must be dreaming," he said with a sleepy smile. "Is this for my birthday?"

"Yes, it is! Happy birthday, Hon!"

He gladly sat down to enjoy his breakfast, and then she surprised him even more.

"In addition to this yummy breakfast, there are lots of good birthday things on the agenda."

"Such as?"

"For starters, KRON TV is sending a crew to the office at noon to film a segment about the foundation, so we'll need to look our professional best for the interview."

"Super! Did you set that up?"

"No! Rachel did!"

"Wow! That's great! What else is on the agenda?"

"After the TV session, the fun begins."

"Fun? I can't have fun at my age?"

She put her hand on his shoulder and smiled reassuringly.

"At three o'clock we're booked for a cruise on San Francisco Bay, which will be followed by a leisurely happy hour at the Comstock in North Beach. We'll linger there until you catch your breath, and then we'll be dining at 7:00 at your favorite Fior D'Italia, followed by a late night aperitif."

"Good Lord! All in one day?"

She smiled. "I also want to remind you that on September 10 I'll be expecting a similar extravaganza for my birthday." She leaned over to kiss him on the cheek and whispered, "I love you!"

He wished she'd given him advanced warning about the TV interview, but whatever questions they could ask about the Jackson Foundation, he had an arsenal of answers. He decided to dress casually and wear the new shirt Ellie had given him for his birthday.

They arrived at the office punctually, and the TV crew was ready when they made their grand entrance. Everything went really well, and when the interviewer mentioned his birthday, it caught him a bit off guard.

"Congratulations, Mr. Jackson! I understand today is also your birthday."

"It's number 80," he boasted. "Ellie and I have agreed it's time to step aside and let this amazing group of people carry on the work we've been doing."

"Well, the foundation is a compliment to your years. Both of you look strong and healthy . . . and someone on our film crew has already told me he'd die to have your hair."

Marco laughed. "It's not an option! My hair is my Italian inheritance from my father."

They handled the interview questions with ease and then stood proudly to the side as other members of their staff described a vision for the foundation's future. To end the interview, they all lined up in front of the office with their arms raised toward the sign above the entrance.

~

When they finally arrived home around 1:00 a.m., Marco was feeling a little weary but very happy.

"It's been the best birthday I've ever had," he said with a dreamy look of satisfaction. "It's unfortunate I had to wait eighty years to be treated so well."

Ellie laughed and swatted him on the arm.

"You're treated well every day, and you know it! In fact, Mr. Jackson, we're both living a very good life."

"I never thought I'd live so long," he lamented. "When I look back, I see a lot of things I'd like to change, but after a day like today, I think it's kind of amazing it turned out so well."

"I'm the reason," Ellie teased. "All that other stuff was just a dress rehearsal. Now come to bed!"

~

On Saturday they spent the whole morning decorating the Community Room and then took a brief nap before getting ready to greet their guests. The party was a noisy, happy affair, as they circulated among friends they hadn't seen for a long time. There were stacks of congratulatory cards accumulating in a basket by the door and quite a few bottles of wine, which people brought as gifts. Ellie had arranged for a limited open bar, so everyone could have his or her choice of libations.

He kept scanning the room for Celine, and nearly an hour after the party had started, he was feeling concerned; however, she suddenly appeared at the doorway with a strikingly beautiful woman at her side. Marco saw her and ran to greet her.

"Hi, Hon! You had me worried. We can't have this party without you."

She smiled and gave him a big hug.

"Daddy, this is Dr. Quinn Douglas! Quinn, this is my father, Marco."

Quinn smiled and leaned forward to extend a European greeting with a kiss on both cheeks, and Marco immediately sensed her sincerity.

"I feel like I already know you, Mr. Jackson," Quinn said with a devastating smile. "We should have met years ago, but Celine has always been hesitant."

"And you are . . ." he said looking directly at Celine.

"A couple, Daddy! Quinn and I have been together since med school."

At that moment, Ellie joined them and greeted Celine with a big hug. Then she took hold of Quinn's hand and smiled. "And you must be Quinn," she said graciously. "Somehow I just knew you'd be special."

Quinn leaned forward and gave Ellie the same European greeting. Then Ellie stepped back, while still holding her hands. She looked at Marco and smiled. "This makes it a very special day, Hon! Love is in the air." Then she led Celine and Quinn on a tour of the room introducing them to as many people as possible.

Marco watched and smiled.

"Well, I'll be damned," he whispered under his breath. *"Will wonders never cease?"*

~

*P*eople were having such a great time, Ellie hated to interrupt, but after tapping her spoon against her glass to gain attention, she motioned for everyone's attention.

"As you know, this is a combined celebration," she explained as the last conversations ended. "It's about birthdays and important transitions. My birthday is still a few weeks away, but Marco has already turned 80, so we wanted to make it a combined celebration because we're also stepping away from our duties at the foundation. However, since Marco has officially crossed over into his eighth decade just a few day ago, and since he's not accustomed to staying up too late, I think it's time for us to sing happy birthday."

She began the song, and then everyone joined in.

"Happy birthday to you! Happy birthday to you! Happy birthday dear Marco and Ellie! Happy birthday to you!"

Their song ended with an eruption of cheers, whistles and applause, as Marco and Ellie took a bow, which encouraged even more applause.

Then Celine intervened and told everyone to find a glass of something for a toast. It took a moment until everyone was ready, and then she raised her glass.

"Here's to a wonderful couple, who are beginning their eighth decade of life! Here's to you, Daddy, and to you Ellie! May you continue looking forward to many more days of promise and happiness!"

Everyone raised their glasses with shouts of, "Here, here," and "Way to go." Then to Ellie's surprise, Marco held up his hands to quiet the crowd and motioned for them to settle down.

He steadied himself by holding onto the edge of the table and noticed smiles and reassuring nods from his friends. Then he put his arm around Ellie and kissed her full on the lips, which caused an eruption of more hoots and whistles. He also put his arm around Celine, and motioned for Quinn to join them. People applauded and made more hoots and whistles.

"These are the women who bring love into my life," he said in a voice, which crackled with emotion. "Ellie's my anchor, and this is my daughter Celine and her partner Quinn. If I've ever needed a lesson on how to live, this is it!"

There was more applause, but this time in a more respectful way.

Marco choked up. He'd prepared his little speech but hadn't allowed for his unexpected emotion.

"It's okay Marco!" someone shouted. "We love you guys!"

Then everyone applauded again, and it helped him regain his composure.

"Okay, okay, listen up," he commanded. "I have something I need to say."

"Keep it brief," Frank called from the back of the room. "We all have short attention spans."

Their soft laughter reminded him of the trust he enjoyed with his friends, but there was more than humor on his mind.

"Anyway," he began and then cleared his throat to strengthen his voice. "Anyway, Ellie and I really appreciate you being here and for bringing plenty of wine. We were nearly out of wine, so your generosity is appreciated, but I have something I need to tell you that's mostly unknown."

He looked directly at Ellie and then glanced at his good friend Kevin.

"Most of you have known me for at least forty years, but there's another forty years of my life you don't know."

He had everyone's attention, and then he noticed Frank tapping his wristwatch.

"Just relax, Frank, I only need a couple of minutes."

Everyone laughed, and Frank wagged his head knowingly.

"I was born in rural Illinois . . ."

"Oh, god," Frank moaned. "He's going to tell his life's story."

"It's a synopsis, Frank! Mind your manners!"

There was a ripple of laughter; however, this time a hush fell over the crowd because they sensed he had something important to say.

"As I was saying," Marco continued. "When I was born in rural Illinois, I was adopted on my birthday, and my mother died while giving me life."

A hush fell over the crowd, and Celine looked at him with concern.

"My mother and father were Italian, so that's why I was named Marco, and when Hank and Aileen Jackson adopted me, they surrounded me with love and raised me with strong mid-western values." People nodded and waited for more. "I didn't learn about my adoption until I left home for graduate school at MIT, and then, years before Celine was born, I desperately searched to find my birth father. He was living in Chicago, and after meeting him, I discovered he was with the Chicago Mafia."

A murmur rippled through the crowd, and Marco noticed even Frank had a serious look of concern.

"I'll spare you the details," Marco continued, "but my father ran the mob's business in Las Vegas, and when he invited me to come work for him, I foolishly said yes and spent five years with the mob. It nearly cost me everything, and it turned out to be a very dark time in my life. I turned my back on my marriage and walked away from my beautiful daughter Celine. I also left a promising career at IBM and violated the love and values that had previously shaped my life."

The silence in the room was palatable, and Ellie tried to signal him by tugging on his hand, but he wanted them to know what had happened.

"Anyway, that's what darkness looks like, and that's what happened to me."

He took a deep breath and could almost hear people in the crowd exhaling for him.

"Anyway, here's the reason I'm telling you this; my father died from a gunshot wound, and while I stood at his bedside, he asked for my forgiveness. He felt he'd been responsible for leading me astray, so he asked me to forgive him, and then he told me to go home and reclaim my life."

He looked directly at Celine and saw her wiping her tears as Quinn embraced her.

"It seems like a sad story," he admitted, "but the birthday gift I need the most is to say the darkness has ended." He paused to take a sip of water and then continued. "That moment at the bedside of my dying father changed everything, and what I've been doing during the years you've known me is putting my life together again, and with Ellie I've rediscovered the power of love."

He glanced at Frank and saw him nod his approval.

"I know none of you expected this, but in order to be honest about this celebration today, it's something I needed to say."

Applause began softly and continued until everyone was standing to express appreciation.

Then Ellie took hold of Marco's hand.

"Tell them about the article," she whispered.

"Oh, right, Ellie and I also have an important announcement! Next week, _Time Magazine_ will publish an issue featuring the work we've been doing with the foundation. It will be a revealing article, and what I've just told you will be included, so if you want more details, you can look forward to reading about how darkness turns into light."

People were silently captivated and listening attentively as Celine moved to Marco's side and embraced her father.

"Thank you, Daddy," she whispered. "You're amazing."

He kissed her on the cheek and as people began applauding, he held up his hand signaling he had something more to say. The crowd quieted and waited expectantly.

"Maybe the most important thing I can say is how important all of you have been in my process of redemption, and believe me, that's exactly what it's been. You probably didn't know how you were helping me, but you have." Then he turned to Ellie and took hold of her hand. "Ellie, I think you came into my life to teach me how to love unconditionally." Then he reached to embrace Celine. "And Celine you've always been my treasure." Once again, he kissed her on the cheek. "You've taught me forgiveness, and you allowed me back into your life even when I really didn't deserve it. I'm sure you didn't know the gift you were giving me, but your love has been priceless." Then he reached for Quinn's hand. "And Quinn, even though we've just met, I'm already aware you'll be teaching me more about love. Thank you for loving Celine."

Quinn nodded and kissed Marco's cheek. Then the four of them embraced, and it was a powerful moment.

"Well, that was worth waiting for," called Frank, who stood near the back of the room and raised his glass in a gesture of friendship. Others followed his lead and raised their glasses as well.

"Thank you!" Marco said as he reached for his glass to respond in kind. "Sometimes you have to experience darkness in order to find the light."

AFTERWORD

Marco's Redemption is a very personal story, which resonates with the lives of many people, who have experienced forgiveness and redemption. We sometimes think of redemption as a religious experience, but I believe it happens frequently in ordinary life events, which occur when someone treats us compassionately and opens an emotional door for a new beginning. I found that writing this story brought me face to face with transformational moments in my life, so I began drawing on my personal experiences in order to tell Marco's story.

When talking with a friend about the title, he asked, "Does *redemption* mean Marco has a religious experience?" Actually, it's more than that. It's an experience, which comes into our lives with different meanings, but its common element is change. It's a change of direction, which transforms us and gives us a chance for a new beginning. At the end of the story, Marco says, "Sometimes you have to experience darkness in order to find the light." This may be true for most but not for all. The metaphor of light breaking into the darkness is only true if we choose to let it happen. Marco called it "redemption," because it allowed him a choice to reclaim his life. In other words, we must decide to be redeemed.

It's important to note the word *process*. It's easy to casually identify redemption as a single event implying transformation is instantaneous; however, it's more likely to be a process, which is triggered by an event followed by many choices and decisions. Marco's redemption was nurtured over more than forty years, and as he told his friends, it was the power of love and community that made it possible.

I hope you enjoyed my story and I invite you to remember its conclusion. "Sometimes you have to experience darkness in order to find the light." Wisdom allows this claim.

ABOUT THE AUTHOR

Curt Smith enjoys writing as a hobby. He has self-published a variety of books including seven novels, books of collected essays and a book of poetry. He's a member of the Pacific Northwest Writers Association and EPIC Group Writers. In addition to writing, he enjoys photography and volunteers as a literacy tutor at a local community college. Curt and his wife live in a small community north of Seattle, Washington.

Visit his blog at www.mochateaoh.wordpress.com/

Made in the USA
Lexington, KY
06 November 2019

56612588R10201